VOICES 2

ISSUES 7 - 13

1975 - 1977

VOICES 2

THE MANCHESTER BASED MAGAZINE

OF WORKING CLASS WRITING

ISSUES 7 – 13

1975 – 1977

PENNILESS PRESS PUBLICATIONS

Website www.pennilesspress.co.uk

Published in original format 1975-77

First collectd edition November 2008

This edition September 2019

ISBN **978-1-913144-08-1**

CONTENTS

.

INTRODUCTION

With issue 7 in 1975 Voices settled down to its A5 format and, perhaps intoxicated in that bright dawn like those French revolutionaries who reset the calendar to year 1, decided that issue 7 should be renamed issue 1. This continued for the next eight issues until issue 8 (new style) got labelled 15.

Ben was guardedly optimistic in his editorial to issue 8

"Voices" continues to progress, though its movement cannot be described as meteoric. We would welcome inquiries from bookshops, libraries, students' societies, as well as from trade unions, political organisations, co-operative societies, and individuals. Our chief advertisers are our dedicated readers. A growing number of Labour M.P.s have recently shown interest in "Voices". We see no urgent need to shake our begging bowl before readers' eyes. Our need is always there, and the response is so far modestly ample. We would give three resounding cheers for a leap forward in circulation.

"A London group was formed recently at a meeting held at Marx House to help "Voices" in various ways. People in Greater London area interested might contact Ian E. Reed."

In an editorial to issue 9 the magazine's place and purpose was defined:

"Voices" we believe has a function to play among the literary journals. It is not a vehicle for established writers. It is a means of dialogue between writer, of working class origin and/or of socialist tendency and the workers and socialists to whom they address themselves.

The begging bowl did come out in issue 12. Not bankruptcy though – just dizzy with success:

"The reason for this call for help was not because of decline and crisis, quite the contrary. Circulation is continually increasing. The men and women who write for us are a continually growing number. But we wish to expand. our circulation. still more. We need to make approaches to the Labour movement, to student societies, to bookshops, we generally need, more advertisement, And in a period of rising costs we want to maintain our price level. Hence our call for £250 to see us through the next 2 issues, or better still £350, which would enable us to complete our budget promotion to the end of 1977.

They got it too, most of it, and a subsidy from North West Arts. Rick Gwilt became joint editor by issue 13. Voices best years were just round the corner.

Ken Clay 2008

ISSUE 7

cover size 210 x 148 mm (A5)

CONTENTS

EDITORIAL

I recently reviewed "Crisis and Criticism" by Alick West (Lawrence and Wishart £4) for the "Labour Monthly". The Introduction, by Elizabeth West, quotes him as rejecting the slogan "Culture is a weapon in the fight for socialism", and quotes from his autobiography as follows:"I said that culture, as Caudwell had written of poetry in "Illusion and Reality" heightens our consciousness of the world we want to win and our energy to win it. In this sense it was true that culture is a weapon in the fight for socialism. But the truth depended on recognition of the greater truth that socialism is a weapon in the fight for culture. For our final aim was not the establishment of a political and economic structure, but the heightening of human life. Without this recognition, the slogan became a perversion of the truth, since it degraded culture into a means to a political end." "Voices takes this stand. Of course, culture is a weapon in the fight for socialism: but of course Socialism takes its justification from the necessity of creating the social conditions in which men can live free from want, free to live life more fully.

From this issue "Voices" will be quarterly, and its format will be stabilised in the shape and size of Voices 6 and 7. When we prepared the issue of Voices 7 we had material sufficient to have produced three or four such issues. We can never have too many contributors. The more people who write for us, the wider our range, the greater our appeal. We try to deal sympathetically with all contributors, but haven't the resources to do so as fully as circumstances demand. One 'thing we want to arrange as a regular feature, the meeting of writers and readers of "Voices" where writers will read their material and dialogue about it can follow.

With this issue we will be continuing our approach to Trade Unions and Labour Party Organizations, to student bodies and English staffs at Training Colleges. For the first time, we are beginning an experimental approach to a limited number of Left bookshops.

Finally the flow of generous donations continues, and we have every confidence that a growing number of friends will fight to keep "Voices" singing, arguing, shouting, whispering, in various ways adding their sounds to the fight for a better world.

Ben Ainley

THE BEARER OF CHAIRS
(translated by C. Cobham)

You may believe me or not believe me, but forgive me if I say that what you think about it is of no interest to me at all. It is enough for me that I have seen him and talked to him, standing face to face with him, and that I have seen the chair, and thought that I was witnessing a miracle. But what was more miraculous, and so awful, was that neither the man nor the chair nor the story made anyone stop, not one of the people passing in Opera Square at the time, nor anyone in the crowds going to and fro in Republic Street or anywhere in Cairo, perhaps not even one person in the whole world.

It was an extraordinary chair which looked as if it had descended from another world or been built for a festival, so huge that it was like a whole establishment in itself. Its broad seat, softly furnished with leopard skin and silk cushions, would have evoked in you, had you seen it, an over-whelming desire to sit down on it, even if only for a moment. It was a moving chair, which went forward slowly at the pace of a religious procession and seemed to move of its own volition: it would have aroused fear and wonder in you, and you might have prostrated yourself before it, and offered sacrifices to it, as if it had been an idol. But at the last minute I noticed, between the four massive legs with feet shaped like gold hooves, a fifth leg. This leg was small and thin, a strange sight in the midst of that monstrous luxury, and then I saw that it was no leg, but a slightly-built man upon whose body the sweat had formed ditches and canals and made the hair grow. into woods and forests. You must believe me for I swear by all that's holy that I'm not lying, not exaggerating, but just telling you what I saw, because I can't help it. I wondered how such a thin, fragile creature could carry a chair that weighed at least a ton and probably much more. It seemed like a conjuring trick, but prolonged scrutiny at close quarters revealed that no trickery was involved, and that the man was really carrying the chair, and moving along with it.

The thing that I found so amazing and so strange, and that really frightened me, was that not one of the passers-by in Opera Square or in Republic Street, or possibly anywhere in Cairo, showed the least surprise, or treated it as if it were anything out an ordinary event that they had ceased to question, as if the chair were as light and mobile as a butterfly carried by a young boy, who passed by them and was gone. I watched the people and the chair and the man, expecting to catch sight of a raised eyebrow or lips drawn in in wonder, or to hear someone uttering a cry of astonishment, but there was absolutely nothing.

Just when I had begun to feel that the whole situation was too incredible and complicated to think about any longer, the man with his burden came within a few inches of me, and for the first time I could see that he had a good face in spite of its many wrinkles, although it was impossible to tell his age. I noticed a much more striking fact about him: he was naked except for a girdle tied firmly round his waist, from which hung a piece of canvas covering him in front and behind. It was enough to make you pause and realise, as your mind gave back echoes like an empty room, that in these clothes the man was alien not only to Cairo but to the whole age, and that you had seen drawings of men like him in History books or among archaeological remains. So I was surprised when he gave a submissive smile, like the smiles beggars give, and then spoke:

"God have mercy on your father, my son. Have you seen the good Batah Ra?

(Batah Ra - an ancient Egyptian king, supposed to possess divine power.)

Was he speaking hieroglyphics in Arabic, or Arabic in hieroglyphics? Could the man be an ancient Egyptian? I turned upon him.

"Just a minute. You're not going to say that you're an ancient Egyptian?"

"There's no such thing as ancient Egyptians and modern Egyptians. I'm just an Egyptian."

"And what's that chair?"

"It's my load. But why do you think I'm going around looking for Batah Ra? So that he can give me the order to put it down, as he gave me the order to carry it about. I'm exhausted."

"Would you say you've been carrying it for long?"

"For a long, long time. I don't know how long."

"For a year?"

"What do you mean a year, my son? Tell anyone who asks you, a year plus a few thousand."

"A few thousand what?"

"Years."

"Since the time of the pyramids, you mean?"

"Before, since the time of the Nile."

"What do you mean, the time of the Nile?"

14

"From the days when they didn't call it the Nile, and they moved the capital from the mountain to the river bank. The good Batah Ra came to me and said:

'Carrier, carry.' I carried. And since then I have gone all over the place looking for him, so that he could say to me, 'Put it down', but from that day to this I have never found him."

All power and indeed all inclination to feel astonishment had quite left me. If he had been able to carry a chair of such great size and weight all that time, he could go on carrying it for thousands of years, without provoking astonishment or opposition, but only a question:

"Suppose you can't find the good Batah Ra, will you go on carrying it?"

"What else can I do? I'm a carrier, and I've been entrusted with it. I had an order to carry it, so how can I put it down without another order?" Perhaps out of anger.

"Put it down. Aren't you fed up? Aren't you tired? Throw it down. Break it. Burn it. Chairs are made to carry people not people to carry chairs."

"I can't. I've got used to carrying it. I carry it to earn my living."

"So what? Instead of wearing yourself out and breaking your back, why don't you throw it down. You should have done it a long time ago."

"That's what you think, because you're on the outside. You're not a carrier and it doesn't matter to you. I'm a carrier and I've been put in charge of it, so it's my responsibility."

when, for God's sake?"

"Until the command comes from Batah Ra."

"He's as dead as a doornail."

"From his successor or his deputy, from his great grandchildren, from any-one with a sign from him"

"All right. I'm ordering you to put it down."

"Your order will be obeyed. I'm much obliged to you. But have you seen him?"

"I haven't."

"Then I beg your pardon."

But I cried out to stop him, for he had begun to move away. I had noticed something like an announcement or a message fastened to the front of the chair. To be precise, it was a piece of gazelle hide with ancient writing on

15

it, that looked like the early script of the Holy Books. With some difficulty
I read:

O bearer of chairs
You have borne enough
And the time has come for the chair to bear you
This mighty chair
Like which there is no other
Is yours alone
Carry it
Take it to your house
 Put it in the centre of the house
 Sit upon it all your life
 And when you die
 It will belong to your sons.

This is Batah Ra's order,
Bearer of Chairs.

An order given clearly at the same time as he ordered you to carry the
chair, and sealed with his signature in his writing."

All this I said with great joy, excessive joy so that I felt almost strangled
with emotion. Since I had set eyes on the chair and learned its story, I had
felt as if I were carrying it, and had carried it down thousands of years, and
as if it were I whose back was being broken, and now it was as if the delight which had seized me was for the release which had finally come.

With bowed head the man listened. Not a tremor passed through him. He
just waited, still bowed, for me to finish, and as soon as I had done so he
raised his head. I had been waiting for some demonstration of joy, even an
explosion of delight, but none came.

"This order's written above your head there and it must have been written
ages ago."

"But I can't read."

"Haven't I just read it for you?"

"I'll only believe it if you give me a sign. Did you bring a sign?"

And when I didn't answer, he muttered angrily as he turned to go, "You've
just been wasting my time. All that for nothing. And the day's short enough
as it is."

I stood watching him. The chair had begun to go forward at its steady, dignified pace, as if it were moving by itself, and the man had become once more the thin fifth leg, strong enough to move it alone.

I stood watching him as he went away from me, panting and grunting, his sweat running freely. I stood bewildered, asking myself if I should follow him and kill him, to give vent to my frustration, if I should rush forward and push the chair off his shoulders forcing him to rest in spite of himself, or if I should content myself with feelings of annoyance and irritation towards him or calm down and merely bewail his condition?

Or perhaps, indeed, I should pour blame upon myself because I do not know the sign?

Usuf Idris

(Translated by Catherine Cobham from a collection of short stories by Usuf Idris called House of Flesh, published in Cairo in 1971. This story was first published individually in a Cairo magazine at the end of 1968).

WRITTEN IN GREAT HAPPINESS IN RETIREMENT

Years starved of beauty, cheated by drabness,
skies blocked by buildings;
And now almost too much splendour day after day.
My heart will burst, it cannot contain the beauty,
the riches of the scene
Colours, shapes, light, which fill the mind.
This is too good a life, too soft;
Cradled in the lap of greenness,
Tall trees, and ever changing sky,
The world's problems a myth;
War an unimaginable science fiction!
Never before such a spring
Every sense aware; colour, shape, light, shade, sound;
Above all the greening; the all embracing greening.
Behind this, humanity; the throb of the human race;
Some places atune, each growing, striving
For the good of all; in others the screaming discord
Of greed, sadism, lust,
Makes a mockery of the natural world.
And why this year has spring been so superb?
Because there will be only four more for me.

Isabel Baker

DECLARATION

Nightingale in a warm valley by the sea
and blackbird singing on a city steeple
you are to me;
no less that birds do not always sing
and there are winters when one despairs if ever spring will be
to bring the frivolous cocks and hens displaying
on every ledge and tree.
And you are Bach and Shakespeare and John Donne
and Picasso and clean woodcuts
of wild horses; none
easy or soft or compromising life;
you are high places and bleak seas where keen
winds hustle the incapable and screen
the sturdy and the obstinate and strong;

you are the fireside when the day is gone,
the hour of rest when, her assignment done,
this worker lounges to recover
energy for another.
You are the man
to my unconformable and restless woman.
We cannot sit,
until not only our own place is fit,
but must be fidgeting till all in common
have peace and prospect and enough to eat.
Come home,
smarting and savage from the daily rough
struggle with heart breaking labour,
bitter and gruff,
till being together gentles our irritation to that quiet
which is our inner therapy against the riot
of market place and shop floor, school and street,
where today's pressures of class interest meet.
So be old age when strength ebbs and we take
time off in the last days of our December
maintained through separation and heartbreak
our love our banner to its final ember.

Frances Moore

THE PLACE WHERE SUITCASES HAPPEN TO EXPLODE

If truth is what you want
the news is bad.

From this place where
suitcases happen to explode
where the last legal bomb waits
ready to retaliate in your defence.

And the last bad luck
enemy or friend
who waited for a letter
that now no-one will send
from the place where
suitcases happen to explode

screams through broken teeth.

Certain assurances
made in private
haven't been confirmed.
Certain witnesses
questioned in public
have remained evasive.

All the stained bedclothes
All the dirty linen
cannot be washed whiter.
Here comes our political correspondent
Here comes our economics correspondent
Here comes blurb and blab
Here comes your bleeping news.

If truth is what you want
The news is bad.

Here comes our parliamentary expert
Here comes our religious expert
Here comes gab and grab
Here comes your news views blues.

Legality is a knackers yard
where social systems tear apart
the maker from the thing he makes.

He that makes and that which mutilates,
in the marketplace where
suitcases happen to explode,
where dreams casually rip apart
and the last legal bomb
maintains the 'national interest'.

If truth is what you want
watch the bubbles bursting in the beer
and hear something ticking through the ring of the till.

Yes, the news is bad
in this land of the last legal bomb,
in the sad case of the place where

suitcases happen to explode.

Paul Lester

FREEWAY FLIER

Freeway Flier
leaping forward to attack,
then standing back
to laugh at the blood.
Cheek-bones gleam chrome
like motor-way direction signs
without direction.
Freeway Flier,
eyes like black holes
without soul,
sucking in light,
sucking in concrete and glass,
sucking in chrome and vinyl,
reflecting them all
in perfect mirror image,
like an autowrecker
regurgitating crippled steel.
Freeway Flier rapes to love
as he rapes to live, and keeps score. Freeway Flier read a poem once,
on the wall of an abandoned tenement.
Read a book once, but
he keeps that to himself.
Watches the sunset over
the flyover and pylons
like some crazy belisha beacon,
plays pinball with girls whose
names he remembers occasionally,
where midnight jukeboxes spin records at 49 r.p.m.
when the night is p.v.c.
subdivided by cones
of symmetrical light.
Watches the sun rise over the railway bridge through the conden-
sation
of his own breath framed by
arches of mildewed brick-work.
Freeway Flier feels pain,

but even feeling pain
is better than feeling nothing
at all.

A. Darlington

O MY BROTHERS

Every movement
must have its martyrs,
though high the price
they pay.

Take
The Shrewsbury Two,
put away
for something
they didn't do,
as a lesson
to the others.

O my brothers,
pity any comrade
taken alone,
but pity more
the movement
that fails to
cherish its own.

Bill Eburn

BUILDING SITE

Hurled up, stranded out, smoothed, shaped out and blazed;
the timbers rack-out livings, whip places
up. Brick, width, and span, flipped up, make buildings.
This hard way creates the places used, gazed
at that we Know, our ends, our traces,
shacked dreams and bedded nightmares, silly lights
and hopes. Plants upwrenched rootless, in bandings
taping-up existence, bulge with nails. Razed
earth provides the living shaking places,

the steps and seats and standpoints, life's bursting
seams of wood and rust. On the heaved up heights
of man able we scuttle and slither and
slap down the hard slates. Come evenings and nights
the wood is cold, sprized out. The structures stand.

Keith Lloyd Jones

SALT OF THE EARTH

We are the people
We
Scrabble in river beds when
They
Sweep away our farms
We know them well
-They come like snakes
From the pit over the horizon
To swallow our world
They button their sleek coats
With our Eyes
But we see them
Marching with night
Between their shoulders
As they plunge
To gouge gold
From our land
They run like wolves
When the cloud above us bursts
And we glow
In the ashes of our scorched dead
Every day is a new start
Our women scream
And spill our children
On the hungry earth
We listen as our ploughshares
Uproot our past
Which is cast in sand and clay
And written in the path of
Every star
In every twig is twisted
A death
Every flower trumpets freedom

In every blade of corn
Is the sudden power to
Cut through these bonds
Which fell on us which
Scar our soil
We have been waiting for centuries
We waste nothing
In every pebble a dream
We build the fires
From the mouths
Of our starving children
And the flames flying high
They singe the wings
Of the vulture
which dices with our lives
In his throat
We have luck
And our rice shines on the terrace
We turn the devils out
From our villages
They spit on us
As they burst from Hell
To spill our blood through the vineyards
But we build our fires higher
And sing from the flames
Their faces shake with sweat
As we burn from their bones
Their claws shiver
As we wrench
The sun
From their stomachs.

John Salway

LISTEN TO ME

Listen to me
The grains of the desert are in my hair,
on my damp forehead,
weighing down my eyelids.
The green moisture of the oasis is on my knees and elbows.
Disillusionment stares at you from the blood and grit in my fingernails.
I am weary from digging too long.

Listen to me for with this match I give you as my last gift
you may burn concrete:
You may mimic the lark with your mind
But you will never sing,
You will see the death of mountains and the birth of icebergs
But no eyes can ever follow the line of your pointing finger;
I have travelled long to tell you this
I have come from the land you wish to see
Come from the eyes of all who went before
Descending like a melancholy October mist upon the shores of your
expectancy
I have come to give you ashes
Come from the heart of anger
Come from the throat of perception
Come from the lips of bitterness
I am the voice of desolation
Listen to me and understand now
Or forever be haunted by my receding echo.

Alan Arnison

TIME HAS NO BEGINNING

Time has no beginning,
Time has no end.
A word with meaning and measure.
To Youth it stretches into eternity,
Golden with unfilled days, month, years.
To Age it echoes into the past,
Mirrored years, months, days, rushing by.
Time, given in work,
Time, lost in sleep,
Time spent in leisure,
Time, pass through, past, present and future,
Has no beginning, has no end.
Today I saw the cottage of my youth,
Dingy, broken, derelict and deserted.
Yesterday, I recall the cottage of boyhood days,
Cosy, solid, curtained, and warmly lighted.
One is real, the other was.
Who created the real? What killed the other?
Time, then moved slow.
Now, it races by in furious haste.

Time, then with so much to do.
Time, now, with all too little done.

Crispin

THE CHAPEL

The chapel is set back from the road
As if shy of passing traffic
Its doors are quietly open
Offering a bowl of roses in invitation
In the patchwork of a mining village
It alone is white painted

The Father strolls past the Club
The men have strayed there after Mass
He waves to self-conscious grins
And pats the heads of milling children

His Irish heart is glad of the fine morning
He had spoken fine words this morning
They had been stirred, he knew it
The chapel walls had echoed his lesson
God-granted stereo preaching for the needy
The children had sung so sweetly
Life is good where salvation may be had
For the price of a Hail Mary

Vivien Leslie

THE JOURNEY

He spat the raw November morning out
A small part of him abandoned among the dog shit.
His overalls firmly gripped by his stocking tops
Rides off to sell the rest at the shipyard
The load no lighter or the journey shorter for the parting

A deposit until tomorrow,
When the next payment will be met.

A.M. Horne

LOVE POEM

My love 's a river flowing relentlessly
It narrows and it widens nervously
It trickles and it surges,
Goes forward and diverges;
My love.

My love is a lake,
with a stream running into a river.
The river reaches the sea,
And with changing tides we both take;
we're both the giver.

But love is more than a metaphor;
it's a sledgehammer to break down doors.
It's an axe to free the chained.
Free each other, work for each other, love each other,
Enough to feel each other's pain.

Tony Harcup, of the Basement Writers

MIXTURE AS BEFORE

Society is sick, sick, sick,
Send for the Doctor quick, quick, quick.

The Doctor arrives with a box of pills
Guaranteed to cure all ills.
And prescribes, with some severity,
A generous dose of austerity.

Take it from me" says he,
That hard work and less to eat
Will soon put us on our feet."
Now this is very odd you see
For it was this same remedy .
That put us on our back,
And got us all the bleeding sack.

Bill Eburn

XMAS DAY

I walked out on Xmas Day, stale and glutted,
From the warm womb of the family,
From meaningless chatter,
From manufactured music,
From television culture,
From plastic tree
And met two tramps striding ahead of me.

One was silent with many coats, the other chattered
About the I.R.A.
About the police
About the world
And I walked quietly close and listened
Catching pieces, fragments of philosophical
conversation.

Later we walked together through the Xmas forest
Amongst the peaceful trees.
His words were wisdom
His talk idealistic music
His cherished hope - a workers' state
And I shook his hand and returned to my comfortable
mediocrity.

Peter Relph

LOVE SONG.

I'm red in a time of black, hot in bliss,
unharmonized wholes; in front of me slurred
persons glide. Life's burned at the dogs, retches
and binds, catches and grinds, things jolt and press.
But thou are time's bliss, colours' echoes heard
when points shade to one, sounds hang wingless, free.
Thou' art the X and apex, grip and latches
of my swinging soul freed, singing time's mass
and evensong. You are the Autumn's bird,
the colour of blood, the sweet in snatches
of time and living, all I wish to be
to sew or scan, with the song from my lip,
the red from my hands. With myself I thee

28

adore, with my body I thee worship.
Keith Lloyd Jones

EXILE

Ten years of exile had made him distrustful. He started work at six in the morning and for a month after they had met he refused to give her his keys.

She had to get up with him - she only started at nine and from six till nine she had to wait in a bistro drinking one coffee after the other. Curiously enough she did not mind. Only one thing worried her: at this time of the day she was the only one to drink coffee. A few customers were also drinking coffee but, it was always accompanied by a little glass of wine. From eight o'clock , though, she was not the only one to drink coffee.

And everything seemed normal...

They used to take the first metro. And from the way they were looked at people must have thought that there was something strange about them.

Maybe because they used two languages in their conversation. He used to speak Spanish to her and she answered in her language. sometimes when she was not tired she answered in Spanish. And when he wanted her to understand something that she had not understood in Spanish, he used her language.

When she met him he was paid 900 F a month as a cleaner and he paid 400 F for his sordid little room. Paris is full of such places. In his country he was not a cleaner but it is known that cleaners in France are preferably among the Arabs, Portuguese or Spaniards.

He was working ten hours a day ... after the real life started ... he had political commitments.

She arrived almost always before him. A 'charitable neighbour', used to stick her head out of her door as soon as she heard her steps, to tell her "He is out."

Every night she was there to tell her that "he was out". She then used to slam her door behind her with a contented smile on her face.

Between 8 and 11 she used to buy all the Spanish papers that she could find. He spent all his money on Spanish papers. She used to cut a few articles for him, or translate others.

He used to arrive at eleven and in the meantime the neighbour's husband had come back, and through the thin walls of the room they could hear the same arguments every night, over everything and nothing, money probably ... And it was the only entertainment they could afford. Usually it ended with a plate falling in pieces somewhere or they stopped suddenly without reason.

He never told her much about the time he had had spent in the carabancel prison.

"You and I we are the future" he answered to her numerous questions.

One day he received a sunny postcard from his country which made him angry. It was only from a well intentioned friend but he kept repeating, "He does not understand, he does not understand or he would not have sent this stupid card "His friend was not Spanish and this is what he could not stand. The roles were reversed.

Sometimes a few Spanish friends visited him and then his exile ended for a while. They opened a bottle of wine and he was happy. She had noticed that he laughed only when he could speak his language. He was never pessimistic or cynical about the future when he could speak Spanish. It was only when people did not know his language that he was sad or even arrogant.

This truce never lasted for long. One of them usually announced that such and such had been arrested. Another one had received a letter from Madrid ... It was the end of the illusion, the silence, again in the room.

The glasses remained on the table, half empty; After a year he had lost a lot of weight ...

One morning he received a letter from the French Police.

They wanted to see him. He did not feel like seeing them. Lately he had been talking more and more about going back to his country.

She never answered anything. What could she say?

One night she came back and waited for him all night. She had the key now.

She came back the next day. The neighbour was at her post.

"He is out", she said, "He is out ..." Out.

A few weeks later there was a wave of arrests in the town where he had come from. She wondered if he was one of them.

Dominique Hughes

SUSPENSE

Always when he goes out I am afraid.
Is not one's love always disaster's target?
The bricks that fall, the fool behind, his wheel,
bacteria of horrible diseases
-they lie in wait, they gang up on my love.

One learns to use a habit of stoicism
-such as we had to fadge up in the war
and never to admit one is afraid.

Surely, say Common Sense and Cynicism,
fashionably contemptuous of such folly,
Sure after all these years you cannot still
so freshly tremble!

Cannot I indeed?
(And let's rejoice that after all these years
I am so vulnerable - a sign of grace,
the green leaves of the living rose,
its very thorns symptom that it grows.

Frances Moore

WAITING FOR THE TRAIN

Puce of face, dark of suit, tongue in cheeked,
Bowler hatted, umbrella shod synchronised marionettes;

Look left
Look right
Straight ahead!

Glassy glances, awkward stances,
Ramrod stiff, bottomless, belly paunched,
Oiled, groomed, fed;

But dead
Or frozen
Or waiting for the train;

Thin girl on a platform seat
Underweight, undersized, underfed,
She moves, she sees and smiles;
Part of her is still asleep,

Not dead.

From her bag she takes a coin,
Insert here," says green machine,
As from its bowels
A groan pours out;
Followed by a plate
Of smash;
Two pink capsules,
A knife, a fork, a slip of paper,
Marked thanks customer
The smash is grey,
The fork is red,
The knife is cracked;

Two ruby lips entice
Capsulated meat
On smash enveloped
Tongue;

How strange;
An egg drops;
Silent waiting trains
See it fall and break:
See its yolk dribble
On the line;
Yet dare not move to hide it
From the public eye;
It's go-slow day,
Not one train shall move today;

A bomb explodes;

Where has the station gone?
Where to, the trains?
Where the automated men?

Are they
That row of bats in bowler hats?

Hanging from a telegraph wire
Open brollies upside down;

Quite dead.

Thin girl, white, still, flat,
Not dead;
Ill from her undigested pill.

J. McFarlane

TRY ON A HYPOTHESIS

(to the Women's Liberation Movement)

A blanket is too simple, too final,
We must be able to know what we see
I do not wish to die of asbestosis at thirty nine
I do not want the wages and hours of a farm worker
Being a teacher and barmaid to make ends meet
Is no ideal to wave angry placards for
Scurrying around with slack breasts and hysteria
I do want to buy my own Tampax
I want to write a novel
And my children sometimes irritate me
I am not disabled with pneumoconiosis
Nor have I been crushed on a building site
I do not want equality of opportunity
To be unemployed, exploited or poor
Cancers before pimples is what I say

Vivien Leslie

FAIRY TALE CHARTER

Once I slept for a hundred years. That was alright. It was waking again in the chill dawn - being woken, they said, by a kiss. That, certainly, was dis-enchanting. Now I go on happily ever after, which is almost sleepless and certainly endless and not at all of my own choice; and I'm not the only one. There's Cinderella, Snow-White, Rapunzel and other assorted beauties, princesses, goose-girls and kitchen maids who share this dilemma. We are left happily ever after with men who claim their privileges solely on account of elevated rank, who, having fitted on a shoe or cut down a few briars, do nothing ever after, and about whose conduct the history books are misleading - that story about the princess being bruised because she slept on a pea, for instance; so now we've started to organise and demand the following basic rights: The right to complain, be angry, be depressed. The right of divorce, spinsterhood or sexual deviation.

The right to revert to our original state or to write our own endings and to repeal sentences on various wicked step and godmothers who were merely protecting us from a worse fate.

Footnote: Rumplestiltskin deserves compensation. Please note: I have patented the spinning wheel with the lethal needle. Insomniacs may contact me Once Upon a Time. Proceeds to our campaign - the goose that lays the golden eggs isn't ours.

Sleeping Beauty, Organiser

Pat Sentinella

R.N.A.D. BEITH

To the honest folk surrounding Beith,
Our dying system did bequeath
Factory, bereft of wheel or lathe,
the Admiralty,
where waste and non-creation both exist in parity.

A branch of that great Woolwich store,
Where guns and shells are placed galore,
The whims to please, of yon hard core,
among politicians
Impetuous sponsors shout, 'Encore!'
in secret sessions.

With conscience clear they justify,
This great deterrent without which we'd die,
From some onslaught right out the sky,
like some doomsday.
Myself, I think it's all a lie,
I'm glad to say.

No grass will grow if this death rains,
No towns or cities that life sustains.
No people left to wash their brains,
so where's the reason?
Will the foe like cannibals, eat remains? that's out of season.

Our masses here with theirs compare.
Against them should we war prepare?
When the enemy we in common share,
within our prism.
This paper tiger in its lair,
Imperialism.

Our foes alleged I will concede
Are well endowed with arms they need.
So, if in the arms race, they speed
with undue haste

Not for profit, or for personal greed are they abased.
Can all our Arms-kings claim likewise?
As all their victims drop like flies
With every sample the Government buys,
up goes their profit,
Whilst humanity suffering, unheard cries, 'Will they come off it!'

Their counterparts in the Feudal age,
For similar gaining, war did stage,
But frequently, whilst battles rage,
did often lead.
Today's men count their grizzly wage, whilst others bleed.

They claim in unison (but acquiesce),
To keep the peace and war suppress.
If profits suffered, they couldn't care
less if mortals breathe,
Forgive, ere I too long digress,
and so to Beith.

The ground this depot did deface,
To better use the cows did place,
A benefit to the human race,
a cause worthwhile,
Not shells explode in human face, mankind defile.

Some say, 'Employment we've enjoyed,
In place of economic void,
Where hundreds would be unemployed,
with no prospects,'
What's left? When myth has been destroyed the bureau's
annexe.
No credit to mankind is known,
Our labours to the winds are blown,
As thoughtlessly the seeds we've sown,
of self destruction.
Posterity will blame when shown
our non-production.

Is this to be our valley's lot's'
Man's proud creative urge to rot,
To blame (whilst Keeping cold war hot)
the Iron Curtain.
For better things we were begot.
Of that, I'm certain.

Oh! would not these men happier be?
If fruits of labour they could see,
Blossoming forth, on life's great tree
of man's endeavour,
The tales to offspring tell with glee a joy forever.

There's time left yet to make amend,
This paradise of fools to end.
Great men of calibre we must send
down to Westminster,
All thoughts of self, they must transcend. like William
Gallacher.

They will when there, I'm certain sure,
The ills of this society cure.
And henceforth, we'll have memories fewer
of men like Heath,
And for nobler things, like Furniture, remember Beith.

Alexander Jamieson

THUNDER

Where is it? That thrashing force,
that rage, when heaven opens up its jaws
to devour the Earth. When the
black clouds pile moodily across
the gun metal grey of the sky, as if
to drop some load across the howling
countryside. Where is the terror of
the sea, churning and tearing
at the shores of this black Earth.

Where is it? That anger of the
might ridden deep of the abyss
of the sky. That ploughing wayward
gale, that carves at the trembling heavens,
tearing it into shreds, ripping and
pounding at the shuddering buildings of
this town, this city. That carving
relentless inferno of sheer power.
The released force of heaven's temper.

Where is it? Where the power and
the wrath, let it fall, like a prophecy,
let it blaze its sermon across the sky.
Let it rip up the sea
into fearful emotion, until it quakes
and trembles and howls, and pleads
to be released from its prison.
Tears at the bars of the shore
in sheer frustration and rage.

Enough of this tranquillity,
enough of this complacent peace, this
listless aimless meandering of those
insignificant specks of lazy white.
I look out of my window at
this scene of frozen peace, this
emotionless garbage heap of this too
early spring. Surely the Winter,
surely the Earth has more to say than this.
Ian E. Reed

SONG OF SOHO

Adam in me, in you Eve grieves to tread a world not moulded to the heart's
desire.
'Edgell Rickword 'Poet to Punk'

Do the songs of Soho sell good food and sex,
The easy habits men like when their thoughts race away into chaos?
Is this the Playland where we touch but cannot trust magic thrills?
Are these the sound made when an emptied head bangs on a hollow world?
And is it also the sparrow, whose song may be sung within?

Step inside gentlemen, leave your guilty minds;
Sit in the warm and worldly lap of your genesis.
The hounded brain obeys and kills the rhythm in the blood.

The photo doesn't show what tarted-up the shy Sicilian girl.
Green as young oranges when her family came awkwardly
To these streets, strange as her customs are narrow to us.
Something devious about the roses here made an earthquake
In the quiet childhood garden where she'd heard spring birds,
And when alone she sang her sad and fragrant songs
We threw her stares like hard flashing pennies;
Our suggestions, like neon, scarred the meaning of her tears.
Then she learnt the bitterness in our easy laughter; fancy

Flower that has forgotten home's provincial evergreen.
O what made it seem that she was not assaulted?
Perhaps she mistook the colour of ripeness for the sweet tang of life?
She is singing now in empty shaded groves, her mind
Out of the terrible sun of her solicitous night.
Step inside gentlemen, dull your guilty minds;
Sit in the warm and worldly lap of your genesis.
The hounded brain obeys and kills the rhythm in the blood.

What makes George believe that be can only sing in her secret holy
passage
when his song is for us all in a frank and generous sky?
After his hurried act he left the pain of the world unmoved,
Lingering in bright alleys with the well-respected fuck.
Does he mistake its vigour for his freedom? Is he too unsure
To chance it behind her eyes? Unsung. Love
The chains of freedom, jeered-at
By the winking eye of a cynical world. Trapped

The dirty-old-man is murdered by the sterile lust in these streets.

Step inside gentlemen, forget your guilty minds;
Sit in the warm and worldly lap of your genesis.
The hounded brain obeys and kills the rhythm in the blood.

Along exotic pavements a youth tramples his confused soul.
Can the music he finds there be welcoming the chaos of change?
To move but not to change, to sing but not to alter
The image of himself is his cool and desperate hope.
When he finds himself different, in a new light,
He gives this stranger a ticket to an anonymous side-show,
So that no-one will see him with strange love, and forgets
Where he has come from. Fearfully he pockets his soul.
By the slot-machines of the Crystal Room his leaping notes ring bells
And impressively turn lights on within reflecting walls.
Kept inside glass his songs are surrounded by the night;
His sun shut-in burns a hole in his heart.
Now he never stops trying to bed his genesis, being so holy with his
dreams.
Desperately he fucks the world-green sweetness out of himself.
O but he was born also from the midst of growing and ravaged forests,
The cold winds, rains and stones of rough-diamond Nature.

Will I and my world-joining hope of Communism be drowned in this lust-
ing ocean?
Never more the pained soul's angry leap to the loving edge
Of an inchoate and curiously generous world?
Between the difficult need and the easy solace there can be no
Communion.
I must fight against my lust, to yield a song of sweet struggle
In the arms of the universe I'll find the liberty of my becoming.*

Pierce-loving bells of Saint Martin's are tolling
Against the difficult cause of Man-bound History.
Perhaps if we could ring-out from within the frail
Unspoken substance of that to-be-died-for meaning
In our hearts, our songs would carry us to heaven.
I dearly hope when dead to spend eternity in Hell,
For when with comrades in these streets we do not sing the
Internationale
Our painful thoughts disturb the arguments of brotherhood therein.

Out of weeping shadows that the lurid lights have left the persistent
Drumming of bitter strangers from the downtrodden Orient mocks the
greyness
Through bloodless streets we hurry home, to bury our heads
Before the rosy raucous dawn of neglected brothers.

A rasping melody of charlady morning challenges our conscience.
One day her arid rain will scour Soho
And the man see himself out-up in its razor light.

Now that the hellish throbbings stopped
A drunk's daydreams break across unfamiliar streets,
And a songthrush wake his mournful love for Ireland.
Why can't he take his daily threnody with milk?
He observing the gentile flowers of Soho square through a haze of
insult,
Fallen with conforming hours, would find them stunningly funny,
But that their blooms are not worth bleeding for by their thorns.
This evil animated by his grin simplifies the stubborn world.
O once when the city's smirking stars are out he'll dig up this garden
And plant the soft wild Irish flowers that bloom on tears.
Now Candy is waking choked with our consuming narrow passion
And he must numb the throbbing void with Whisky.

Here we all become outcast; English with Chinese and Italian.
If we could form a choir, our one and many voices
Would pluck the heartstrings of London.
The suffering Cockney must make, with his tunes and whistles,
Tough worldly songs of bitterness and irony and hope.

see the essays of Christopher Caudwell "Studies in a Dying Culture"
David Kessel

THE LEFT WERE ALWAYS RIGHT

The old order lingers,
though changed in ways
undreamt of save by
those who could foresee
the young moon
in the old moon's arms,
the sun in splendour
set in a sullen sky.
Bill Eburn

MAN

Man; most noble being,
you, who with your hands
have re-shaped the Earth
you walk upon.
You who faced the mightiest
with bold heart
and overcame fear,
unravelling infinities secrets.
You who made known
the unknown,
the desert, a fertile plain.
You who have changed
the course of river and sea.
You, who when beaten,
killed, feared yet fearing
faced the mightiest of
destructions and by
struggle overcame them.
You stay eternal.

Man; You singer
of joyful songs,
you lover of the sunset
and the storm.
You, who have faced an
angry mob, bearing in your hand
the truth.
You; who have been
poisoned, persecuted and
massacred by tyranny
for glimpsing the future,
remain unbeaten.
You; who have built
and unbuilt legends,
along countless honest
crowded corridors,
bringing time,
to your heel.
What could defeat you?

Man; you thinker,
shedding your light

of understanding over fear.
You, whose eyes, ours
and other worlds
unfold before,
bringing science and beauty.
You seeker of truth,
a flame throughout
the universe you carry,
aloft and proud.
You, who have worked together,
loved together,
laughed together
and died together
yet grow stronger with each death.
You are unkillable.

Man; you lover,
you fighter of evil
you teacher
with your life.
You, bringer of music,
opener of hearts.
You; who carry humanities flame
beneath work worn sighs,
tired, confused and pining,
yet still trying.
You, brave soldier
of life, who carve
the way of the future
and reshape whole destinies
with one sweep of your hand
and with each step
unbloom another petal.
You are immortal.

Ian E. Reed

END OF THE LINE

Englefield sat at his favourite table in the deserted club, a whisky bottle and a smeared glass, both empty, before him. His mouth felt burned out by too many cigarettes, his head thick and heavy from all the alcohol he had put away within the past four days. Four days. Four days in which he had beaten a disorderly retreat from his responsibilities, finding his haven in whisky. Who'd have thought that I would have turned to whisky? Back in England, he had never touched it. When things got rough he had reminded himself that one day he would be going to South Africa and that life would be easier, and that had sustained him. But here, in the Republic, life was still damned hard, hence the whisky. Here in the Republic. The Republic Bar. Christ, I'm going daft.

He was in his early thirties, a heavy man, although his body had nothing about it which even suggested power; it was just heavy. His back was arched in defeat and his thick, hairy arms, as white as ever despite his year at the Cape, lay flat on the table, clumsy and awkward. Time no longer had any meaning, he had lost all track of it just sitting in this one position, afraid to move almost, as if he feared that something terrible would accompany even the slightest movement. His life was in crisis. I can't understand what's happening to me. If only I could understand, it wouldn't be quite so bad. I'm sure of it. All his life he had stumbled from one crisis to the next and now he was vaguely aware that all the time he had been on railway lines, that each crisis had been but one station on the way to this, the big one. But I don't know what it is!

Slowly, he lifted his head and gazed about the club, his club. Wonder what it would look like with proper lighting. Better not to know, maybe. Place stinks. The afternoon heat fell through the doorway, penetrating the walls, seeking out every mysterious odour. The smell reminded him of building jobs he had had in England, for it was like the smell of building sites, of the sand used to make cement. Urine. I'm sure those bastard seamen piss themselves down here.

"Englefield."

Someone was at his side. The odour of cheap perfume somehow broke through the building-site smell. Moving his head slightly to the right, he saw that it was Franky. My star fairy. He shuddered and for some reason hoped that Franky didn't notice.

"Leave me alone."

'You're nearly out of cola. You'll need some more for tonight." Franky's voice was light and sibilant, deliberately so.

Englefield sighed heavily and looked up. "Okay, I'll ... look, could you 'phone for some more?" He was repelled and yet fascinated by Franky's face. He continued to look up at him.

Franky smiled, showing a line of teeth which were yellow but goods The heavy coating of makeup seemed about to crack into tiny earthquakes whenever he smiled. "You want me to telephone?" He paused, considering the treatment he had received in the past few days. "You'll have me cooking for you next." He resumed his indignant silence for several seconds and then sighed, relenting. "Very well. Have you got any money? - They'll want cash after the trouble you've given them."

Englefield's haggard face went through the motions of wincing. Just like a wom... Bloody hell! 'There's enough in the box under the bar. Here," he took the key from his shirt pocket and threw it carelessly - "And if that lazy coon's about, tell him I want a steak. I've Lot to straighten out, beef up a bit."

The key had missed Franky and dropped to the floor. Franky retrieved it and straightened up, eyeing Englefield contemptuously. "Trusting me with money at last," he sniped.

Englefield tore his eyes away. "Yea , and that's all I trust you with, you queer bastard." He watched out of the corner of his eye as Franky walked away. There had been a time when he would have had to laugh at the sight of a man in high heels, but now he groaned inwardly and placed his face in his hands. Franky represented just one insane piece in the surrealistic jigsaw puzzle of his life.

According to the rules, his troubles should have ended as soon as his feet touched South African soil.

He had lost his job. The union had promised this and that, but what was the use of bringing more trouble down upon his head? Then Marion had started her damned nagging. What am I going to do for next week? What's the kid going to wear to school? .I don't even know that he's mine., he'd said, the messy little bast... She'd slapped him across the face right in front of the kid, saying that he might be able to jeopardise their security and get away with it, but he wasn't doing to use language like that in front of Bobby I jeopardised her security alright. After that slap it was down to the Shipping Federation the next morning and off to Southampton to join the ship a couple of days later.

He had jumped ship in Cape Town, gone to Johannesburg, where he had held indifferent jobs in two factories and then drifted back to the Cape. There, he had met up with a Rhodesian, a former mercenary in the Congo, and they had placed their meagre savings together to open the club. Looking back, Schuyler must have thought me a fool, all the things I told him. Sex things. He had told the Rhodesian of the highly masculine fantasies he had woven around his future in South Africa while on his way from Southampton, even back in England. Yes, I first thought of those things a long time ago. Without actually saying so, he had let Schuyler know that he was disappointed by the reality thus far - a few middle-aged women who went around the clubs and who did just the usual things were as far as he'd got. Not that I paid for them, of course. But no coon women. I bet you've had your share, he'd said to Schuyler, and Schuyler had laughed confidently, saying nothing. Hope he gets it shot off, wherever he is.

The two men had quarrelled the first week the club was open. After the first few nights, Englefield had noticed that some of the women in the place weren't women at all and, enraged, he had confronted his partner. Schuyler had looked at him in amazement and then shrugged. "Of course," he had said. "It's the same in most clubs like ours. But don't worry about it - it's good for business. A fairy gets hold of a seaman and encourages him to spend. Besides, they're always grateful of a place to drag up - do anything for you." It was good business, but Englefield was made uneasy by them, although he was quick to realise that he was able to wield a certain amount of power over them. When he barked an order, they obeyed. Some of them, for their part, suspected that he was afraid of them, but they also sensed that he might lash out at them at any moment, and so they handled him carefully. Except Franky.

Then, last week, Schuyler had nipped of f somewhere with the takings and since then things had been chaotic. But the majority of the bills were paid with Franky's help - he put off creditors and demanded something from all his friends who used the club - and now things were just beginning to quieten down again. Englefield realised that for the past four days he had been hiding behind the whisky while Franky and Daniel, the Cape Coloured who worked behind the bar and in the kitchen, had run the place. He vaguely remembered having warned Franky to keep away from the money. Christ, what a mess. I need a woman to put me straight.

Franky came out of the kitchen and crossed the floor to the toilets. Now Englefield almost smiled in spite of himself. Bloody fairy.

"Is that steak coming?' he called.

Franky halted, an eyebrow raised irritably. "Yes, the 'lazy coon' who's been helping me to save this place is getting it now." He turned and walked off.

Englefield was considering Franky's motives in helping him when Daniel arrived at his side and placed a well-filled tray before him. He looked down at the table and cleared his throat. "Tell me something, Daniel," he began nervously.

"Yes, Mister Englefield?" Daniel was puzzled by the man's manner. He was almost courteous.

"If a white man wanted a woman, where would he go?" His short, thick fingers played restlessly about his face.

Daniel smiled inwardly, his incomprehension dispelled. "Do you mean a coloured woman, Mister Englefield?" He was twisting the knife.

Oh god. "Yes." Englefield's voice was quiet.

"I wouldn't know, Mister Englefield. I'm an old man." He was no more than forty.

"Couldn't you fix him up?" Englefield became more embarrassed as the humiliating ordeal progressed. "He might make it worth your while."

Daniel's face was a mask, unreadable. "He would get into trouble, Mister Englefield. It's against the law. Besides I'm an old man, I don't know any women."

Englefield realised that he would get no further, that Daniel was laughing at him behind the mask and that his embarrassment had been for nothing. "Alright, get back to the kitchen," he snapped, reasserting his authority.

It was four in the morning before the last group of customers left. Englefield listened as they made their way out, the excited jabber of the young Japanese who flirted regularly with the fairies mingling with the drunken laughter of the seamen. Franky was with them, his arm around one of the Japanese. As they reached the door, he glanced over his shoulder at Englefield, his face full of mockery and defiance. He pulled the Japanese to him, kissing him on the lips.

Englefield groaned in disgust and walked to the bar. He sat for a moment, feeling the sudden stillness settle about him before he called for Daniel. The coloured man put an apprehensive head around the kitchen, door.

"Bring me the whisky and a few beers from the 'fridge'".

When the drinks arrived, he poured himself a whisky, downed it and followed, it swiftly with a mouthful of beer, straight from the bottle. He had slept for six hours and now he felt almost normal again. He poured another whisky and sipped it slowly, each sip followed by a large swallow of beer.

His mind floated back to sex. I need a woman so bloody badly. Look at me, teeth clenched. What a state to get in. He considered asking Daniel again but dismissed the idea immediately. It would be like begging, and anyone who'd beg from a coon shouldn't be in this country.

After his third whisky, he left the bar and walked slowly to the open door. His limbs were like lead. As he mounted the three steps leading up to the street, he almost fell and he realised that the three whiskies had acted as a fuse, igniting the alcohol still in his system. He was drunk again.

The chill breeze off the sea touched his chest and he fumbled unsuccessfully with the buttons of his open shirt. He cursed and let his hand fall limply to his side. The streets were silent except for the occasional sound of a taxi as it sped its drunken cargo to the docks or. to one of the more respectable sections of the city. Then he heard someone walking close by. As he caught sight of her, his heart began to pound. This was it. He forced his voice to work.

"Hey, coon. Want to know how a white man does it?" The words were barely coherent through his grating teeth.

The girl worked in a club nearby and was out walking in defiance of the regulations. She was slim, no more than twenty and attractive. With a glance up the street, she slid into the doorway, inches from him. She placed a hand on his arm, feeling him shake. She tossed back her head and looked into his face.

"I know how a white man does it. It'll cost you ten Rand."

"Pay for a coon!" Englefield spat the words out involuntarily. The girl's very calmness seemed insulting. Something told him that she should have been cowering before him, yet here she stood, loose-limbed and insouciant, her face turned up to his, unflinching. She's beautiful. No, dammit, how could she be! Coons Coon! Coon! Ugly, stupid bitch! He became angry, for he felt like a simpleton before her, confused and slow- witted, like the seamen when the fairies began playing around with them, making fools of them. He grasped the neck of her dress and pulled her to him, thrusting his mouth to hers. It went all wrong. She was biting his bottom lip and the next thing he knew he was doubled over as she brought her knee up into his groin. Tearing her teeth free, she let out a piercing scream which chilled and horrified him. It was the last thing he had expected.

A coloured night-watchman lumbered down the street, his heavy club swinging. Seeing the white man, he stopped in his tracks, frozen by the sight.

"What do you want me to do?" he hissed urgently to the girl. "Do you want a beating from the police, woman?"

"Get them! Get the police!" the girl shouted, combating Englefield's frantic efforts to subdue her.

A slight smile flickered across the watchman's face as he understood, then he shot Englefield a glance loaded with contempt and was gone, loping off the way he had come, shouting and waving his club in the air.

"I'll pay you! I'll do anything!" Englefield pleaded. It was too late, He pushed the girl from him and staggered down the street, his mind a confused blur. He had no idea where he was heading. For one insane moment it occurred to him that he might hide away on a ship, but where could he go now? Nowhere left to go. When it had become hard to breathe and his lungs felt as' if they were on fire, there was the sound of a car pulling up, of the tyres brushing the kerb, of several pairs of feet hitting the ground and running, this last sound echoing and resounding in his brain. Then he was in a dream state, pursued by a horde of people; by the foreman back in England; by Marion and Bobby; by the police; by Daniel; by everyone he had ever known. And it seemed, just before he felt the blow on his shoulder and dropped to the pavement, that Franky's face was there before him, blocking his way forward.

They released him at midday, his body bruised and racked with pain. How could men do these things to each other? White men, that is. Doing those things to me for messing with a little coon. He remembered having awoken to a sound which had seemed familiar and he had mistaken it for the flat sound of the policemen's feet on the pavement, but it had been the sound of his face being slapped. He shuddered as he walked onto the street, whimpering, afraid that the blows would begin to fall again.

He was let out onto a side street and the first person he saw was the girl. She was being helped along by an elderly man who might have been her father, and it was clear from the way she moved that her pain was much greater than his. Yet she smiled as she caught sight of him. She looked drained, exhausted, as if they had pumped the energy out of her, and yet she was victorious. He realised that it would be over for her as soon as the pain stopped. It will never be over for me. He stole a second glance at her, to try to gauge what she felt for him, whether she truly wished him dead, but there was none of this in her face. She doesn't wish me dead because I am dead. They killed everything in me, even my hate for her.

Franky was sitting alone in the club when he arrived back. Englefield could not look at him. He stumbled to his usual table and buried his face in his arms. A chair scraped as Franky got up and walked to his side. There was a long silence.

"I heard what happened." Franky said at last, sympathetically. "It's nothing to worry about, you know. You're not the first and you won't be the last."

Englefield tried to hold his tears back, to hang onto something, however small. "If you want this place, you can have it," he said through his folded arms. "I can't stay here now - in South Africa, I mean. It's what you wanted, isn't it?"

Franky was slightly taken aback. Then he smiled. "No, I never wanted that. I thought you knew." His voice softened. "Look at me."

Englefield looked up, into the face which had so often caused him to shudder. It was a nightmare face now, the hair stiff with lacquer over the heavily shadowed eyes, the powder as thick as ever. Yet he had always been fascinated by it.

Franky placed a hand on his shoulder. "You know I never wanted that. Besides, where would you go? You've nowhere to go now, have you?"

He remembered now how he had seen Franky's face the previous night. He let Franky kiss him gently, feeling his neck and hair being caressed. He broke off with a sob and crushed his face to Franky's chest. "I need you," he said. "I need you, Franky."

Daniel peered around the door and grimaced. He crept silently back into the kitchen and, with an adroitness which spoke of much practice, spat through the door into the yard.

Ken Fuller

CAPTAIN NED

I know a bloke called Captain Ned
Who spends his days lying in bed
Dreaming of his stocks and shares
For which he, like a lover, cares,
And holding forth with animation
About the causes of inflation.
Upon his face a look of pain
As he sips a fine champagne.
The fault lies with the common masses,
Militants, the layabouts, the working classes.
Who always seem to be on strike,
And this is something I don't like.
Get the Army ... make them work,
And never let the blighters shirt.
Tell them of our island glory -
And make the bastards all vote Tory".

Michael Ferns

MUTUAL AID

Whilst others are at their prayers
I to my counting house go,
to learn from the day's reckoning
whether to praise HIM, or no.

And should it appear
that my deserts are small,
I'll have to make it clear
that he'll get bugger all.

Bill Eburn

PACE T'EGG

Nooan t'th'ard-biled sooart ut's med bi us,
scallion-stained, eawr comrade gi'e us,
a pace-t'-egg fotcht o'er fro' Praha,
deft brush-wortcht i' shades of ochre,
warm yerthy yeller, rust an' breawn,

wi leavs an' blobs an' scrows a' reawnd:
a beauty neaw beawt no inklin'
o' t'th'addle-egg it wunet 'ad bin,
whited sepulcher of a thing,
fair shaped wi'eawt, feaw shit wi'in -till,
prickt an' blow'd an' swilkt an' tem'd
o' t peawsey clennin's, th'ur an end,
that spring, t'it innard hell:
Pravda vitezi" - truth mun tell!
This bonny brindl't britchel shell
neaw wur whul all of itsel',
be-ribbin'd throo, hung uppo t' wa'
i' pride o' place, a joy t'us a'.
While t' mornin' when we feawnd
t' red ribbin theer beawt nowt areawnd
bu' shameo' sumb'dy's clompin' clot-yed blame.
t' Pace-t-egg lay all i' bits alow,
wi t' white o' t' backs o' t' shards on show,
scruncht an' smasht to smithereyns.
Ther'd bin nobody in bu' frien's.

Jone o' .Broonlea

pace-t-egg ('paste'-egg/pace-egg), boiled and stained Easter egg;
scallion, onion; wortcht, worked; scrows, scrolls; feaw, foul;
swilkt, shaken (of liquids); tem' d, poured/emptied out; peawsey, rotton
(cap. of eatables); clennin's,stuff cleaned out (in husbandry, afterbirth);
britchel, fragile; whul, whole; while, until; clompin',heavyfooted, clumsy; clot-yed, 'thick-skulled'; alow, below; shards, fragments.

A WEEK IN THE LIFE OF IVAN IVANOVITCH

Sunday

Ivan Ivanovitch Candidov was standing in the road outside Heathrow Airport. "It's wonderful to breathe the fresh air of a free country, " he thought, gulping down great lungfuls of diesel fumes. He had been expecting to be met by a reporter from the Daily Gazette but that paper had all hands following a rumour that a member of the royal family was secretly engaged to an ice cream salesman.

Ivan wandered along the road until he came to a few shops; there was a cafe open with a man outside selling newspapers. Ivan consulted his phrase book (a wave of homesickness came over him as he was reminded of Maria Alexandrovna, his English teacher - "but I must forget her," he said to himself, sadly. "She accepted the system."). Then he approached the newspaper man and asked for the most popular paper, thinking that that would help him to attune himself to his new found freedom. It was beginning to rain, and Ivan decided to seek the shelter of the cafe, where he asked for a cup of coffee and sat down to study the News of the World. The first mouthful he took convinced him that his English needed a lot of improvement, for, whatever else it was, the drink certainly wasn't coffee. He found the paper hard-going, too, even with the help of an English-Russian dictionary. There was a man sweeping up the fag ends, toffee papers and empty bags of crisps which carpeted the floor, and he noticed the dictionary and the bewildered look on Ivan's face. Presently, he came over and said, "I wonder if I can help? in perfect Russian.

Ivan was amazed. "In Moscow, the cleaners do not understand English. You must have a wonderful educational system if people in such humble jobs speak foreign languages so well." The man with the broom bridled at this. "At any rate, it's a useful and honest occupation, which is more than you can say for those layabouts", he said, pointing to a photograph in the paper of top-hatted and fashionably dressed racegoers. "But the fact is, I teach Russian; I need this job as well to pay for the mortgage."

Ivan was curious to know more, but a group of young men at another table began fighting. The teacher-cum-cleaner hurried over and managed to persuade them to calm down and pursue their arguments more quietly. Ivan, assuming that this was a political or philosophical argument, strained his ears to try to catch what they were saying, but their conversation consisted mainly of four-letter words which Maria Alexandrovna had not taught him. "Too much Shakespeare and Dickens!" thought Ivan, "And not enough of the modern idiom." He had to wait until the teacher/cleaner (whose name was Martin) had finished clearing away the crockery on and around the young men's table, and was able to return to Ivan. "has it a political argument?" "Not exactly," said Martin. "They were arguing as to whether Osgood was offside when he scored the winning goal yesterday."

A group of somewhat older men who had been playing darts began another discussion, and Ivan again tried to catch the drift, but made no more headway with them than with the other group; again the incomprehensible four-letter words came thick and fast. Ivan got up to go - but where? He hadn't much money and, having missed his newspaper contact, he was beginning to feel uneasy; where was he to stay? "I must 'phone the paper," he thought, but wasn't confident that he could cope. Fortunately, when he'd explained the position, Martin came to the rescue and 'phoned the paper himself.

"No go today I'm afraid," he reported to Ivan. "Not only are they pursuing the ice cream salesman, but the word has gone round to play down the anti-Soviet line; the government is negotiating with Moscow to see if there's any chance of getting some oil. But if you're stuck. for somewhere to go, I could put you up for a night." It was, as it happened, a mutually advantageous arrangement, for Martin thought that Ivan would be able to help him understand the current Moscow scene. A much happier Ivan settled down to wait - Martin said he would be free in half an hour.

The darts players were still talking and laughing noisily, and Ivan was still unable to understand what they were talking about. Once more, Ivan, eagerly looking for evidence of the free exchange of ideas in this great western democracy, begged Martin to explain. "They're choosing Miss World," said Martin, "and the criterion is bedworthiness." Ivan returned to his News of the World and sought in its pages for material to satisfy his enthusiasm. The reports of court cases were certainly a change from Pravda editorials, but he still felt that he was missing out on the uplift to his spirit that he'd come to expect.

Martin took Ivan to the nearest bus stop; there was no shelter, and the rain was teeming down. After half an hour, Ivan ventured to ask how frequently the buses ran. "Every ten minutes," said Martin. Ivan was still trying to make this out five minutes later when three buses came along together; two didn't stop, and the third took two people from the queue in front of them. However, fortune smiled upon them immediately after; a car stopped and the driver called out to Martin. "It's Joe and his wife, Mary," Martin explained to Ivan. "She's my wife's sister, and they're lunching with us today." Martin introduced Ivan as a refugee with nowhere to go.

Over lunch, Joe and Mary, who'd been house-hunting, told them the story of their morning. "We thought we'd found it at last," said Mary, "our dream house. There it was. a triumph of the jerry-builder's art, a terraced house sixty years old, opposite the gas works, fifty yards from a motorway, used car lot at the bottom of the garden, broken down fence round a garden of weeds, paint and paper peeling off everywhere ..."

"... and dirt cheap," broke in Joe, "only forty times what it cost when new, though it's impossible to believe that it ever was new. We'd paid our deposit - we were walking on air (there were a lot of floorboards missing) when - Gazump! - another couple arrived and upped our offer by £500. So that was that."

Ivan was puzzled. "Your paper over there," he said, "has lots of very nice houses for sale." "Yes," said Mary, "and at very nice prices. Only the rich can afford them." Ivan was even more puzzled. "surely the rich have houses already?" he said. "Yes," put in Joan, Martin's wife, "but maybe the wife is tired of the wallpaper, or they're slumming it with only two bathrooms, or they want three houses in the country instead of two."

By the end of the evening, Ivan's head was reeling with the new impressions he'd taken in; Martin had just about pumped him dry of all he knew of new literature in Moscow; it wasn't at all what he'd expected to happen, and his new friends had shattered some of his illusions. "But to-morrow is another day, and maybe I'll..." but he was asleep.

Monday

In the morning, Ivan, acutely embarrassed by the hospitality he had received and by the knowledge that he was quite unable to return it, thanked Jean and Martin as well as his English would allow, and set off for Fleet Street. his English money was nearly exhausted, and he had been led to believe that the Daily Gazette would help him to find some kind of employment and a roof over his head.

Oliver Baldich, described by the Daily Gazette as "our fearless reporter, who has uncovered the facts behind a dozen scandals which have been exposed in this paper, and which have made the Gazette the envy of Fleet Street" (most of the exposures were in fact of bosoms and bottoms, which had given the paper a circulation which was indeed the envy of the rest of Fleet Street), was in a foul temper. He had spent most of the previous day pleading unsuccessfully with the Soviet trade delegation for an interview on the oil supply situation; he'd left his name and address in the faint hope that an interview could be arranged on Monday. but he was not hopeful, and had a strong suspicion that he was going to be sent off in search of the ice cream salesman. Known by his contemporaries as O.B. and by the irreverent younger staff as Obi ("old, bald and irritable"), he was living up to his reputation.

His phone rang. "There's a Russian here asking for you, Obi." "Show him up, then, for the love of Pete - don't keep him waiting." When Ivan was shown in, Obi greeted him effusively. "Come in, come in -how nice of you to come - have a glass of sherry -have a cigar - is that chair comfortable - not too stuffy in here, is it?" Ivan beamed at him - here was more wonderful hospitality, and he was gladder than ever that he'd come to England.

"Now then," Obi went on, "this oil business. By the way, what's your speciality?"

"I'm an architect," began Ivan, rather puzzled by the reference to oil.

"Derricks and so forth, I suppose?" said Obi. "What's the prospect of your great country supplying us with a few million barrels?"

"I know nothing about oil," said Ivan, "and, as you know, I'm completely disillusioned with the Soviet Union."

"What did you say your name was?" mumbled Obi, his world collapsing around him, but he didn't need to ask for he had just remembered about Ivan. how the hell could he get rid of him?

"Excuse me a moment," he said, and picked up the phone. "If there's one of those starry-eyed reporters about, send him up here, will you? I've an interesting job for him.

The only young reporter available - the demands of the ice cream salesman story and a 'flu epidemic accounted for the rest - appeared presently in the doorway. "Oh, it's you," said Obi, his usual ill temper now fully restored. Ivan here has just come over to us from the Soviet Union; take him and show him something of London

- then let's have a story for Wednesday's paper (though there isn't a snowball's chance in hell of it getting into print, thought Obi). Get some petty cash from old Fred; £100 (no - £150 should do you."

Marilyn Smith was not exactly starry-eyed. At the age of two she had told her mother that she did not believe in Father Christmas or in the Christmas story, and she had never looked back. Now she didn't believe in anything at all, not even that the sun would rise in the east. However, she thought that this sounded a more interesting job than oil or ice cream, and Ivan was a very goodlooking young man. So she took him in tow and went straight to Fred. "£150 Obi said," she reported unblushingly, to the elderly guardian of the petty cash. "There would you like to go, Ivan?" she asked, having managed to attract a taxi - she was an attractive girl, and that helps, even with taxi drivers, especially when they see a large bunch of £5 notes.

"The House of Commons," suggested Ivan. "Not till this afternoon," she said. "They're not awake yet nor will be then, for that matter." Ivan then proposed one of the railway termini, as he had been involved in the design of one of the post-war Soviet stations. Marilyn directed the taxi driver to take them to London Bridge ("somebody else can show him Waterloo or Euston," she thought to herself). On arrival, she conducted him through the tunnels, over the footbridges, and through the holes in the walls that do duty there instead of the imposing entrances enjoyed by more favoured termini. On emerging finally from the Brighton side station, Ivan observed an arrow pointing straight up into the air and the legend - "Southwark Cathedral"; looking up he saw a towering building which looked more like a block of offices. "So it is," agreed Marilyn. "Completed about six years ago, and empty ever since. It takes gallons and gallons of oil to heat it; they say it would deteriorate if it weren't kept warm, and of course it wouldn't do for it to fall down before it was ever used. Must have cost about a million pounds to build, and the man who owns it has three or four other empty buildings like it. Six years ago he was reckoned to be worth about £25 million, and now –"

"Bankrupt, I suppose, poor man," said Ivan.

"Well, not quite," said Marilyn. "He's worth about £270 million now. There's another block finished more recently, a few yards away."

"And what's going up here?" said Ivan, looking at a building site in front of the station.

"You've guessed it," said Marilyn. "A block of offices. The cathedral's behind the first block if you're interested," but he wasn't.

Michael Balchin

(This is the introductory chapter only. Readers may recognise the parody of a "best-seller" written in the days of Krushchev, forerunner of some of the most slanderous anti-Soviet, anti-Socialist books by a Russian writer).

WARNING TO THE POET

When you look sad
I know that you are writing a marvellous poem
in your mind.
When I look sad
You comfort me with fingers, lips
And your thoughtful eyes
Eyes that watch my tears slide onto the page,
My frowns shape to your curved letters
As you catch my pain in a word.

When people talk in corners
You watch and smile absently.

56

As they talk, you absorb the expression in their eyes
And the lines on their faces become your lines.
They think you are fascinated,
Though you never listen to a word.

When I tell you
How very much there is to do
You look troubled.
When I tell you
We have no need of epitaphs
And that the slogans have all been written;
That lines have creased the paper
And my tears blur every phrase
You look away.

Blindly tapping,
You think you have life at your fingertips.

Pat Sentinella

THRUSH AT LONG KESH

Thrush at Long Kesh,
Perched on cruel barbed wire
Coiled above mesh
Of which we tire;
And heartfully the bird sings,
Greeting each day
with a song bold and gay;
Echoing among posts and tin
Prisoners hear the song -
Pause in their thoughts
And gratefully look at the bird -
The sky its world, the earth its port,
And its nest a fort
For the survival of its kind -
Prisoners strolling dejectedly
Always feel their heart lift,
As each note leaps to the sky -
And thank nature for this gift,
For here there is no humanity,
Every word of nature is opposed -
But they can't deprive this bird of its wings

Its rights cannot be bulldozed -
We are only human beings here,
No wings have we, nor can we sing a cheerful note
So dear thrush, while happiness you bring'
My heart you smote
with thoughts of the freedom you own
And the freedom I lost.

Thrush at Long Kesh,
You are one of the things I'll remember
When far from here and free -I'll remember ye.

Peter J. Monaghan
Cage 21, Maze Prison, Long Kesh, Lisburn, Co. Antrim,
N. Ireland.

LOST LEADER

We worshipped you once
but no more.
Sold down rivers
our bodies carry the scars
of rapids
our minds the darkness
of the murky depths
buffeted on currents
leaderless
it was not always so.

We worshipped you once
but no more.
Our backs
pyramided
were your ladder,
young hearts accepted
your promises
visions seized
our purpose
exploding
our minds;
lives, limbs
devotion
showered you.

Our feet were
never cold,
we understood
transition, the
inevitability of gradualness
the tightened belt.
You ratted on us
whilst our blood
was hot
our vision
clear
New Jerusalem
within grasp.

We meet still
dwindling numbers
singing freedom
songs
looking for signs
but we're older now
wiser? well,
but the scars and
the nightmares
frighten us.

We worshipped you once
but no more.
After the State
funeral
and the gunned
salute
after the citation
when the flowers
have withered
on your tomb
we shall come
and bring you
homage
stare and
remember.

Vincent P. Richardson

THOUGHTS ON DEATH AND DYING

Despicable deception of life!
Fifty, sixty years of storing up knowledge,
Learning wisdom, ability to analyse, connect, and see the way ahead,
Enlarging capacity of appreciation of all forms of beauty.
Then in a flash, a crack - gone all of it; the mind dead - the body just a frame.
That utter waste! What clown's conception this!
There would have been worlds to conquer;
Centuries of untold beauty to absorb.

I would die to the strains of the International, in Red Square, on May Day!
The thunder of marching feet in every city in the world.
Such a May Day it'll be! Such a May Day! With news of world wide victories!
And although it may be my last day, I won't mind:
For it'll be the last fight too for mankind!
Isabel Baker

BIRDSONG

Fly away bird.
Fly on the wind of the hopeless word
And the meaningless verbal ploy;
Fly on the breath of the fatuous sigh
That crawls from the girl like a cruel white thigh

To jab at the heart of a boy.
Fly away thrush.
Fly to the mouth in the living bush
And the breasts in the chiffon mists;
Fly on your wings to the planet that sings
Of the staleness prolonged captivity brings,
That changes the hands into fists.

Fly away rook.
Fly to the flesh of the lawyer's book
And peck out its printed heart;
Fly and let fall a splash of white sludge
Into the hair of that righteous judge,

60

And tear his icy limbs apart.

C.James Mac Veigh

AMERICA

A touch of magic in the night wind's eyes?
America dances over the burning graves
laughing,
America -
Atonement is long overdue.

Land of the brave, and
(did I hear a word about fortresses floating unassailable
over the shattered land?)
Land of the free,
(who said that about chains of hatred
locked around the ghettoes?)
Atonement is long overdue.

We of the world scream -
We are drowning under America.
America!
Point your sewage somewhere else.

David Tatford

AGITPROLETPOEM

For every penny on the pay,
for every minute off the day,
for every inch of the way,
we have fought.

Caked in muck we have stood:
we have poured out our blood.
every crumb of our food
we have bought.

With hammer and with spade,
with tools of every trade

look round you now!- all that's made we have wrought.

Bob Dixon

APPROACH TO WORK

1
What these people do with it is not my way.
Mine is nearer to the stove and washtub
than their desk methods - not a white collar
but rolled up sleeves and a shabby apron.
Snatched from multifarious
exacting and ever demanding duties
food and fire and eternal washing,
marking of endless exercises,
committees,
agitation and demonstrations,
the needs of my children and grandchildren,
of my elderly relations, of neighbours.
Caught from sheer weariness of mind and body.
Composed in Assembly or waiting for buses,
set down on backs of envelopes,
paper bags, kitchen paper.
Not neatly, not leisurely, not composedly
can I await and invite the Muses;
must be Muse to myself; must be rigorous
exacting precision of thought and wording,
insisting on cut, not drapery swirling;
stripped and athletic in joyous activity
striding upon the bedrock of reality.

2
Not for me your trance states or
phoenix or Muse or doublefaced deity!
Not for me myths wisdom no more
takes for truth literally,
reach me downs millenniums old
cut down to modern tatterdemalion
savers of face and fenders from cold
for poets afraid of naked reality.

3

Slush there is, filth, phosphorescence
stinking and rotten and trash underfoot,
the sewage and unhealthy putrescence
of a way of life passing away from man's use.
But dreams will not keep you from soiling your boot,
nor phantoms shift it, nor theories of art
transform it to blossoms that gladden the heart.
Bull dozers, muck shifters, lorries and shovels
can transform a desert of rubbish and slush
to arterial road or blocks of new houses
with gardens and bushes and roses and such.
But all their machinery's not up to much
till the skilled hand comes and lets in the clutch.

4

Metaphor and simile
hammer and cold chisel be,
tools to set the meaning free.
Arabesque and curlicue
take more labour time to do
wasteful of material too.
Modern taste is for a line
sparing both of stuff and time
grain of wood and clean design.
Let my words in every breath
clarion man's war on death.

5

And to whom am I to speak
but those I live with,
labour with,
the movers of messes, shifters of rubbish,
makers of machines, movers of mountains,
wielders of spanners, builders and miners,
moulders and furnace feeders, tanners and weavers,
drivers and hauliers, porters and cleaners -
hands indispensable
to make man comfortable;
honourable.
Unsophisticated
in all this complicated
intellect created
froth upon activity;

63

this parody of creativity
which mocks true intellect
and makes all art suspect
to those in direct contact with reality.

6
To such men and women I
try to speak of real life
as they and I know it.
Not only the waste and the strife,
the shoddiness and the lie,
but somehow to show it
movable as the muck on the building site;
for when they grasp at last what they can do
they will set all right.

Frances Moore

SUBSISTENCE LEVEL

The mundane consumes us
drabness blights our vision
with cataracts.

Years eaten up with locusts
spell it
routine
respectability
dutiful parent
kind to grannie and the cat.

We live sifting greys.

Brilliant sunshine avoiding
the cavity of our commune;
darkness kept at bay
by the light engendered
in our struggle for bread.
Just sifting greys
-we exist

Vincent P.Richardson

ON SEEING A FILM OF STALINGRAD

No words remain.
Such pain and anguish
Cannot be contained within the human frame.
It should have torn the world in two;
Mountains be burst asunder,
Primeval fire from innermost earth
Spouted through the cracks.

And when all the piled up agony of the years
That runs through history like a fiery vein,
Wars after wars, torture and persecution of
the common man

Mounts up to heaven,
The very universe should scream,
Galaxies dissolve and new stars be born.

Isabel Baker

VOICES 2

ISSUE 8

cover size 210 x 148 mm (A5)

CONTENTS

EDITORIAL

We receive an increasing flow of letters about "Voices", both critical and laudatory, and would like to print some of them. The tussle is between cramming in as much attractive prose and verse of a creative kind, on the one hand, from a growing body of contributors, and widening the scope of "Voices" to include criticism of this kind, book reviews, etc., on the other. We would welcome opinions on this issue.

"Voices" continues to progress, though its movement cannot be described as meteoric. We would welcome inquiries from bookshops, libraries, students' societies, as well as from trade unions, political organisations, co-operative societies, and individuals. Our chief advertisers are our dedicated readers. A growing number of Labour M.P.s have recently shown interest in "Voices". We see no urgent need to shake our begging bowl before readers' eyes. Our need is always there, and the response is so far modestly ample. We would give three resounding cheers for a leap forward in circulation.

A London group was formed recently at a meeting held at Marx House to help "Voices" in various ways. People in Greater London area interested might contact Ian E. Reed, 58 Lenham Road, Sutton, Surrey SM1 4BG for details.

Ben Ainley

OLD BILL

It was raining. Old Bill Arnold stamped his feet as he walked into the warehouse, relieved to be finally in the shelter and warmth of this tightly packed shed, after two miles of fighting the downpour on his bicycle. Still thinking of the weather he clocked in, bent down, pulled out the cycle clips from his soggy trousers and shuffled down between the well-stocked racks to his cubby hole, without consciously thinking, his tired blue eyes peered out from gaunt sockets and glanced with experience up and down the racks and along the cracked concrete floor as he walked. All was in order. Not one box, not one packet had been moved. All was just as he left it.

Having completed his subconscious appraisal of his domain, he arrived at his cubby hole, a small hollow underneath the stairs that led up to the office. Inside, on the end of a shelf, hung two coat hooks; opposite on the wall was pasted a picture of a vintage car, cut out of the "Observer" magazine and a photo of the 1962 'Hartfield's' Christmas dinner. On the shelf was an untidy pile of old-type packing notes and a collection of 'Daily Mirrors'.

Bill took off his blue plastic raincoat and carefully hung it up, pulling out the sleeves and removing from his pocket the 'Daily Mirror' and his sandwiches, which he stowed upon the shelf. This routine completed, he proceeded to load up his pipe, slowly turning round to face the rows of neatly stacked shelves. For the past fifteen years since that extension had been built, he had shuffled, each morning up between the racks, along the gangway that led from the clocking-in machine to his cubby hole, in the same manner, always casting his eyes up and down the racks and along the concrete floor, always turning his back on that world to hang up his coat and unload the pockets, and finally, with the air of an experienced golfer approaching his tee, turning and facing the warehouse.

Thirty years ago this warehouse did not exist. The two Hartfield Brothers had started up their business then, with Bill as their only employee, they had worked in the small cramped shed that now served as a garage, fitting together the parts of coffee machines and sending them out to various customers, with Bill helping to assemble and deliver the machines in an old beaten down Ford. Those days had been hard. Many times Bill had stayed up half the night helping the brothers complete an order, and arrived early in the morning to load and deliver them. Bill chuckled to himself when he remembered how his wife had moaned at the time, but he had stuck it and watched the firm grow: first the old recording studio next door with half a dozen employees; next, the building of this warehouse and fifty employees. Bill had then become a full time driver, driving one of the five vans and would have been for a lot longer if it had not been for his illness resulting in five months in hospital. But Bill's earlier efforts had not remained unnoticed and Ron Hartfield agreed to let Bill continue to work for him after his release from hospital. He was no longer allowed to drive but Ron gave him a job in the warehouse, loading and unloading the many components from lorries, stacking them in the shelves and making sure that the girls had all the parts they needed for assembly, plus emptying dust-bins and other odd jobs. Of course he got less money, but he looked upon the job as having more responsibility.

Bill took a few more puffs at his pipe and wandered off to empty out the rubbish and make sure that the girls had enough parts to get on with when they came in. He always came in earlier than the rest. If the dustbins were empty, it would give Mellors the foreman no excuse to shout at him. Mellors was an unpleasant person at the best of times, a lot younger than Bill, only ten years with the firm and already a foreman, and big-headed with it. If the dustbins were not empty when Mellors came in, he would stand over Bill as he struggled with one of them down the stairs from the office. "Come on Bill, pull your finger out, they should be empty by now!" Bill grimaced to himself as he moved through the racks, he had complained many times to Ron Hartfield about him but Ron had been too busy to listen. Of course Bill realized that Ron was busy now, so he did not usually complain, mainly just ignoring Mellors and getting on with his job. "If it was just Mellors" he muttered, "I would have left this job long ago." But it wasn't Mellors, it was the firm that counted, he would be childish to leave on account of Mellors after having been with the firm so long. He had been with it from the start and helped it grow, he had helped build it into what it was and it would be stupid to let Mellors drive him out now.

Bill opened the side door and walked across the yard. It was Wednesday and every Wednesday Bill would sweep out the older Hartfield Brother's garage. He unlocked the padlock on the door and swung it slowly open. It was still raining and large puddles had formed in the uneven drive from the gate to the manager's garage. Bill walked in to the empty space that was usually filled with Ron Hartfield's green Bentley. "Blooming good car, a Bentley," Bill thought to himself as he swept off the cobwebs from the ceiling. "Not like most cars, it has real craftsmanship built into it. Most things today are just thrown together. Nowadays, people have no pride." Bill began to think of the new labourer who would be arriving on Monday. "He won't last long," Bill muttered. It seemed a bit silly that Ron lately had been saying that Bill needed help with his job. Mind you, it would make it easier, but still, he could manage alone. He would do his best and show the lad the ropes. It would be difficult, most youngsters didn't seem to have the staying power somehow. Apart from Mellors and a few of the women it was a pretty good firm. Ron has always been fair. That was the trouble with most youngsters today, they didn't realise what was good for them.

Bill swept round the floor, sweeping out into the yard the rust-coloured autumn leaves that during the week had blown into the garage, occasionally straightening his back to ease his rheumatism, or just to peer across the rain swept yard towards the gate. eventually, having completed his weekly task he pushed shut the door and made his way across the yard back into the warehouse.

This was the most pleasant part of the day. Bill had the whole place to himself. As he painfully made his way past the empty benches where the women worked, he thought back along the endless parade of women that had worked there through the years. Very few of them lasted, but in time the firm had built up a hard core of regular women. Doris was the chargehand over the women, having had thirteen years service behind her. She was okay but sometimes she got a bit uppity. Her mate Silvia was a two-faced old cow. She would be very friendly with a "Hallo Bill", and "How's your back today Bill?" The next thing she would go running to Mellors moaning behind your back.

Bill had very little to say to any of the other employees. He had learnt through experience to keep himself to himself. "That way," he would say, you kept out of trouble." He would pass the time of day with the others, little else. He paid his weekly dues for the football syndicate run by the blokes in the packing shop, chip in a few bob for anyone who retired, or the boss's Christmas present, otherwise he just came in, did his job and went home. Nobody asked his opinion about anything and he never offered it. Life just went on and that was the way Bill liked it.

His last labourer had been quite an exception. He hadn't stayed long though, but while he had worked there, he had had plenty to say for himself. He was one of those people who thought he could put the world right. Bill had met people like him back in the thirties. They thought they had the answers for everything: unemployment, homelessness and what have you. At first Bill had tried to be patient with him and explain that it couldn't be changed, that things had always been the same and always would be. "You see," Bill told him, "You have to face it. There have always been bosses and there always will be, there are always those that can make it, and those who can't. It's just a matter of if you are prepared to work hard enough, you can make it." He explained that Ron Hartfield had worked hard to build the firm. Now he could afford to have his big car and all the other luxuries. But the youngster just didn't want to learn, he seemed to have a really strange idea of life, but he would grow up and face facts one day, the trouble is that he could get himself in trouble talking the way he did. He got stupid once when Doris had said that Ron was buying a villa in Bermuda. He started talking about Ron being a "parasite" and the girls got upset with what he said. Bill had to tell him to keep his opinions to himself. "I mean it's a free country, but you can't go round talking like that."

Next thing the chaps in the packing shop started complaining about him, apparently he was trying to get them into a Union. Of course they would have nothing to do with a Union. It was not long after that when he left. The trouble with people like that was that they weren't prepared to work. He refused to do overtime, then started moaning about how much money the boss was making. That had been a very busy week. He could have earned himself some overtime. That was the week that everybody else had been working flat out and doing overtime to complete a South African order in a rush, all this because Ron had heard a rumour that the dockers were going to " black" all ships going to South Africa. Ron wanted to get this order off before this happened. So he had no excuse, he could have got the overtime. It made Bill a bit annoyed to think of it. That week he took two days off and got the sack. "You see," Bill philosophised. "You can't change human nature."

It was the same with the women. They moaned at him when he hadn't brought in enough stuff for them, or they moaned saying that he had brought in too much.

"Bill!" they would shriek out. "Oh where is he, the senile fool. Hey Bill, come on, take some of these boxes away. You've blocked up our gangway." Bill would then move them. Very soon he would see Mellors staring at them and pulling at his moustache. "You don't think you are going to leave them there all day, do you? You better move them. But first I want you to unload that lorry, and don't take all day about it like yesterday." Bill would just look at him. It wasn't worth speaking to anyone like Mellors. He would proceed to unload, dragging the heavy boxes off and stacking them inside the warehouse with Mellors watching and still pulling at his moustache.

Bill was past retiring age but he believed in working as long as he could, at least he was able to and he considered himself lucky to be able to earn the extra money. Besides, after thirty years in that firm he didn't really like to think of life without it, it had been a way of life, a way of life that kept him going. It was all he knew and all he could know. Somehow he felt a part of it all, it was somewhere he could do something and feel useful. He fitted in. Those wooden racks piled high with glasses and components were like old friends. He knew every inch of them. He knew where everything was and where everything should be. It was a world so familiar to him after all these years, reassuring and solid. Outside the world thundered on, all too fast for Bill to conceive. Man raced to the moon, man dropped bombs, had revolutions, talked of pollution and nuclear war, things and ideas changed and moved and Bill couldn't move with them, it was all too strange, but inside time stood still, goods came in, got sorted, shelved, assembled and then left in cardboard boxes, the "Junior" coffee machine, the "Senior", the "4 square" model, yes models sometimes changed, names came and went, people came and went, but the racks stayed the same, sometimes empty, sometimes full, it was a world Bill knew well.

When the others come in the day will pass as usual; Bill will shuffle along between the racks pushing a small trolley with components on, he will stack them up beside the women, he will replenish the racks when it was needed. At tea break he will sit on his own on a chair by his cubby hole, eat his sandwiches, pull at his pipe and read the paper. Then back to the racks stooping slightly, aching from rheumatism and coughing. To the others Bill was as much a part of the firm as the benches they worked at, he was hardly noticed as he wove between them stacking up the parts, just some shadow moving between the racks, some means of replenishing their stock, no one knew how he thought and nobody wondered, after all, it was only old Bill.

After the day was done and everybody had left, Bill would silently pull on his coat and bicycle clips and walk slowly between the racks on his way out. His hand would rest on the last rack, turning he would silently gaze through his blue eyes along the racks before leaving. Everything would be in order.

Ian E Reed

Pete Carter

WHY CARRY BRICKS?

'Why carry bricks?" said the labourer,
"Why carry bricks if you don't intend to build anything?"

"But I do" answered Fraud,
"I intend to build false idols
on swallowing clay, I intend
to build houses of crumbling sand
and urge my Brother along
the road to a dry desert wall.
I intend to build a morality
that serves as a blindfold,
and by doing so, convince people
that night is day and that the storm they
feel around them is only the senses
of some exotic experience."

"Why carry bricks?" said the labourer,
"Why carry bricks if you have nothing to build?"

"But I have" answered hypocrisy.
"I have to build sentiment over
the death of murderers,
patriotism with every spurt of blood
from the oppressed I have killed.
I have to build sweet words
that overturn the power of a dying child,
turning eyes in other directions
to feast upon my gentle loving whispers.
I have to build gilded domes across
the imprisoned and convince them that
the chains I have forged upon them, are human nature."

"Why carry bricks?" said the labourer,
"If you hate the idea of building?"

"But I don't" said the bigot,
"I have to build chains of silence
across the mouths of those who would speak.
I have to re-build the past
so nobody notices the changing weather.
I have to build a wall, so tall
that it will blot every drop of sunlight

that could possibly fall upon my world.
And construct moralities out of hatred
distrust and ignorance, make realities
out of all the slime I can find.
and build shadows over my children's lives."

"But these bricks are heavy" said the labourer,
"We know" answered Fraud, Hypocrisy and Bigotry,
"And we intend to knock them down." said the labourer,
"Oh" answered, Fraud, Hypocrisy and Bigotry.

Ian Ernest Reed

DETERRENT

when our astronauts landed
on the ashes of Earth,
no cause could they find
for sudden death;

save for a signal sent
from a bunker far below
which being unscrambled read
"If we go, you go too."

Bill Eburn

THE FUGITIVE

Entering Reading General Station, holdall in hand, Terry began to feel the nervous flutter stir in his stomach. It seems kind of adult, going to see your girlfriend in Bristol for the weekend. Terry was seventeen.

He wondered if he looked very much like David Jannsen in The Fugitive.

On the platform, the three buttons of his Co-op bought sports jacket done up, he took out a cigarette and lit it all with one band, the other hanging, with deceptive looseness, onto the holdall in case he was forced to make a run for it. Whenever the eyes of other travellers came to rest upon him, he would shift his own nervously and sometimes cover one side of his face with his hand as he drew on the cigarette. Then, as they passed by, he would sneak a closer look to see if they had one arm - it was the one-armed man who had killed the Fugitive's wife and put the blame on him.

77

There was a nasty moment when a local hard man strode over and confronted him with; "What you starin' at? You wanna smash inna face?"

Deciding not to draw attention to himself by giving the lout a karate chop to the throat, Terry drew his lip back over his teeth in a half-smile and replied "Sorry, mate - honest."

He kept up the fantasy for a while on the train, sitting erect and alert, ready to hurl himself through the window and down the embankment should he be forced to, and giving the woman seated opposite a sad, world-weary smile as she answered the questions of her children, as if this scene produced an unbearable ache within him as he realised that such things were forever beyond his reach, that, until the one-armed man was brought to justice, he must spend his life on the run.

Finally, he relaxed and allowed his thoughts drift to Wendy, the girl he was going to see.

They had met two weekends previously. Along with a friend, he had planned to hitch-hike to Weymouth, but, as the first car which stopped for them along the Bath Road had been going to Bristol, they had made a quick change of plan. Five hours later, sitting in a village pub eight miles or so the other side of Bristol they had spotted two girls reading a travel brochure on Boston, Massachusetts.

Ralph, Terry's companion and his senior by eighteen months, thought himself to be strikingly handsome and was a serious student of James Bond films, having seen each of the three which had at that time been released several times in order to study the action and technique of his hero down to the smallest detail; he baffled barmen in the working-class pubs they frequented in Reading by ordering outlandish concoctions and, whenever he'd put in a fair amount of overtime at the bakery where they both worked, he would buy Egyptian and obscure European brands of cigarettes from a tobacconist's in Friar Street. On this occasion, Terry persuaded him to drop the Bond act and to assume an identity more likely to snare these particular girls.

They bought the girls a round of drinks and moved across to their table.

"You girls thinking of visiting the States?" Terry asked when they were seated.

"No - my sister's just gone out to Boston as a nurse," said the more attractive girl.

"Oh, you're American!" exclaimed the other, a short, small-breasted girl who was, Terry gauged, in the region of a decade older than Ralph.

"That's right, ladies, straight from the U.S. of A"

"What are you doing over here - on holiday?"

"No, we're training to be recording engineers.. We're with RCA in Nashville, Tennessee, and they sent us to London to study techniques in the largest British studios. We'll be over here for six months or so."

"Why, that's fascinating!"

"I suppose you meet all kinds of famous people."

"Well, just last week we sat in on one of Billy Fury's sessions and another with ... what was her name, Ralph?"

"Lemme think, now. There was Lulu and Kathy Kirby, or was it Lulu the week before last?'

"How come you're both wearing the same sort of sandals?"

"No, they're moccasins, ma'am."

"That's right. Last year we spent some time in the South-West. We bought these moccasins from a group of Navajos we came across in the Mojave Desert. Bought a whole heapa blankets too, didn't we Ralph?"

It turned out, against all expectations, that Terry paired up with the younger, more attractive girl while Ralph had to make do with her friend -at first, anyway, because Ralph soon reverted back to James Bond, taking Terry's girl to one side and putting himself forward as a much more attractive proposition for a girl.. of her undoubted taste and sensitivity. He also threatened to ruin everything as he now and then dropped his Tennessee accent to adopt Sean Connery's brogue.

The last laugh, however, was to be Terry's, as it so happened that the girl pirated from him hated Americans and James Bond, and when they were invited back to the plain girl's house, Terry was introduced to her younger sister Wendy. As Terry and Ralph were about to leave the house and book into a hotel for the night, Wendy's widowed mother returned from an evening out just in time to make the acquaintance of the girls' two American friends, and she expressed the hope that she would be seeing more of them.

She did. They returned the next weekend, Terry to see Wendy and Ralph just for the ride. It rained lightly and they went to Weston-super-mare, Terry and Wendy walking along the front hand in hand with Ralph following somewhat disconsolately a few paces behind. It was the one weekend in Ralph's life when he knew the taste of humility and Terry was secretly' glad, avenged.

As soon as they arrived that weekend, Terry had told Wendy that they were neither American nor trainee recording engineers, that their moccasins had been purchased in Freeman, Hardy and Willis's in Broad Street, Reading and that the nearest that he, personally, had been to anyone famous was when he had asked for Duane Eddy's autograph at the stage door of a theatre in Slough.

Ralph had looked the other way and said "It was his idea, anyway."

When they rode on the dodgems at Weston, the record being played was Elvis's Devil in Disguise, arid Terry was glad because a girl down the Witch's Cauldron, a dancehall in Reading, had once told him that he looked like Elvis. Placing his arm around Wendy's shoulders and steering with one hand, he pretended for a moment that she was Ann-Margaret.

Wendy was tall and slim, small-breasted like her sister and, when she pressed against Terry to kiss him, she excited him very much, and Terry wondered how he would ever survive the five days and one hundred-and-something miles which would soon lie between them and their next weekend together.

Now, in a couple of hours, he would be seeing her again, as she met him at Temple Mead station. He was the Fugitive no longer and, as he thought back to the ridiculous pretences which he and Ralph had put on, he decided that he was better off being himself. After all, Wendy seemed to like him perfectly well as an apprentice baker and confectioner, so what else mattered? Now that his relationship with Wendy appeared to be becoming firmer, he began to wonder why he had ever bothered to pretend to be anything or anyone other than what and whom he really was.

But why do millions of people all over the country, all over the world, I suppose, switch on to the Fugitive every week? It must be because he's so unlike them, is so far removed from their experience, because they're not satisfied with being what they are.

If that's the case, though, why don't the people who control television and so on put out programmes which make ordinariness out to be the most important, desirable thing on earth, programmes which show that people who work in bakeries, like me, are more important than people who run about the world killing people, sleeping with everyone under the sun and drinking things which are shaken, not stirred? That way, everybody would sooner or later stop chasing after things which they can't have and they might even be happy.

But it seems as if no one wants to do things that way. Someone's trying to mess everyone up and there doesn't seem to be any way to stop him or her or them.

Wendy was wearing a powder-blue raincoat and no makeup except for a little darkness around her eyes which punctuated her features, as she was fair and plain in the prettiest, kindest meaning of the word.

As he caught sight of her face, she seemed different from what he had expected, but it had been the same last weekend - ten minutes later, she would seem to snap back into her old, familiar self. With no photograph of her, it was sometimes difficult, during the week, for Terry to remember exactly what she looked like. By the time they reached Wendy's house, a long bus ride, she was her old self and they both felt comfortable and at ease with each other.

After tea, the conversation turned to work.

"What's the first thing you do when you start work in the morning, Terry?" Wendy's mother asked.

"Well, I usually put the first batch of sponges on the machine, lay out the flan cases, then weigh the sponges off and take them down to the oven man. While they're in the oven, I put the second batch on and put the fruit in the flan cases. By the time the second lot of sponges are out of the oven, it's usually time for breakfast."

"I beg your pardon."

"I said I usually put the first batch of sponges on, lay out the .."

"Yes! yes, I heard you. But I thought you were a recording engineer."

Bloody hell.

He threw Wendy a panic-stricken glance and it was clear from her all too-innocent expression that she had not told her mother the unexciting truth and that she was quite unprepared to help him out now.

"Well, I thought Wendy would have ... I mean, I told her last week that"

Sponges. Flans. Baker.

That evening, Wendy talked a great deal about a boy she had known a few months ago, an exciting daredevil who had been killed on his motorbike. In his thoughts, Terry showed no respect for the dead. As she talked on and on, explaining just how much the boy had meant to' .her, Terry was tempted to tell her that he sounded like a brainless yob, a perfect pain in the arse; but, although he saw by now what had happened, was happening, he said nothing, still hoping that things might work out the way he had planned, that he might still win her respect and, finally, her.

The lines of communication between them seemed, for the rest of that weekend, to have been abruptly and, for Terry, painfully severed. Nothing he said seemed to register with her - it was like trying to speak to someone through a soundproof wall. Wendy seemed to be deliberately and quite cold-bloodedly constructing a barrier between them, a barrier which became more effective as the weekend wore on. You'd almost think she was afraid of catching dermatitis from me or something. And it was all the more agonising because she didn't actually say anything about not wanting to see him again - it was all done by her attitude, making him feel that there were plenty of things she would rather be doing than walking about the place with him. And all because I'm not a bloody recording engineer from Nashville, Tennessee.

On the Sunday afternoon, they went to see Taras Bulba in Bristol and afterwards, as they walked to the station, Wendy gave him her eager and detailed evaluation of Tony Curtis's charms. As he boarded the train, Terry remembered the look which Wendy had given him the week before and, still hopeful that there was a chance for him, said "I've been thinking that it might be a good idea for me to move to Bristol - our firm's got quite a large bakery here."

The message in Wendy's eyes was quite clear: don't bother.

Later, as the train reached top speed, the wheels seemed to say: Ah'm goin' down t'Florida... t'get some sayund iyun mah shoes ... Or maybe Californie ... An get some sayund in mah shoes ...

A girl of his own age walked along the corridor, giving him a brief smile as she passed. Hey, lady! We soon be crossin' that ole Mason- Dixon line where any woman knows bettern to mess with a man like me!

He rubbed a pearl of moisture from his eye and swore.

Ken Fuller

WAR

Shot-up bodies hanging around,
Lying silently on the ground,
I hide them away for no one to see
Only their eyes are fixed on me.

Tanks, trucks all around,
Scattered about, making no sound
I hide them away from the world to see
Only one knows they are there, that is me.

I am fighting a war, a war of my own,
Of shame and evil, all my life I have known
I am hiding away for no one to see,
Perhaps they will even forget about me.

Christine Gibson

THE GREAT WIND
a sermon for today

"... and there was a sound of a mighty rushing wind"

The phenomenon, they say, started gathering
momentum along the Ho Chi Minh trail,
it wafted a cooling balm
to napalm burnt peasants.

Soon it gathered force sweeping the trail
U.S. Army helicopters Mark IV
were tossed off course,
out of control they fluttered
about the sky -
birds of eagle proportions;
urgent messages were despatched by radio
to the Pentagon,
top brass were soon planning
anti wind missiles.

It roared on through South East Asian
paddy fields across the Indian ocean
up the Arabian Gulf
scattering in all directions
Sheiks and their cadillacs.

As news reached Africa
tribal fires were lit, they danced
calling it the freedom wind
-there was much rejoicing.

In the east six hundred million flicked
through the little red book
seeking Mao's guidance;
in the west special prayers

were offered in the churches,
the Pope sent out a lengthy
encyclical, the Jews fasted
and beat the wailing wall.

The newspapers were full,
banner headlines read –
WIND STRIKES AGAIN
GONE WITH THE WIND
THE WORLD'S GOT THE WIND UP,
reporters hastily put together
hearsay stories of happenings –
how the great wind had
started up all the cottage
spinning wheels in India
now all working at umpteen
revs a minute, their economy
was booming - and
would soon outpace the west,
how it had blown open prison gates
in several countries releasing
political prisoners.

Some reports - although little
credence at first was given to them
-via satellite
told of the resurrection power
of the wind, that Gandhi was
back in India and Prince Litullu
the new premier of South Africa.

Consternation filled western capitals,
thousands filed past Lenin's tomb in Moscow,
the Common Market met in Brussels
and in France prayers were offered
for the return of General Charles De Gaulle
from his village grave.

The Prime Minister had urgent talks
with the 14th Earl at Chequers,
the President of the U.S.A.
visited the Lincoln Memorial
and re-read the constitution,
when asked to comment on the wind

he said "it's worse than Watergate".

Rumour by now was rife
and even gossip columnists
were on to it, one dared
report that the wind
had attacked a royal garden
party at the palace and the
Queen's dress was blown over her head
a certain member of the royal family
was heard to curse for not
having his camera with him
later the report was denied - officially.

On the Stock Exchange
the brokers were collapsing like dominoes
some had fatal heart attacks
the shares went up and down like yoyos
as one account said -
"it was like 'bulls' and 'bears' in a china shop"

In the southern states of America - where
they heard from their African brothers
that it was a freedom wind
the black community paraded the streets
shouting "Luther King Lives"
and the Governor of Alabama
hastily took off to rehearse in a
Black and White Minstrel show.

An extra-ordinary Special meeting of the
United Nations was called.
All the world's leaders gathered
in solemnity and decorum.
Speakers declared ... 'balance of power'
'sovereignty of nation states'
'collective security'
the platitudes dripped on and on,
finally the great powers were in accord
the status quo must be upheld.

The atmosphere at UNO
was summed up as
'frightened cordiality

85

against a common foe'
It suddenly became cold,
ice fell from the mouths
of several speakers,
delegates shivered in their seats
a great noise was heard.
The President announced –
'the WIND'

At this moment in time
the wind lessened in intensity
soon only a whirlwind at the rostrum
slowly personified as a child –
mongrel featured.
A hush descended as the child spake
"this is the wind of change –
the meek shall NOW inherit the earth"

At once peace broke out
and delegates dancing in the Assembly Hall
were seen exchanging presents
and H bombs, polaris and ballistic
missiles were given and received
for the museums in their respective capitals.
and a little child shall lead them"
Amen.

Vincent P Richardson

FIRE AND BRIMSTONE

The flood is away, I'm coming,
Only an hour downstream.
Strong, primitive, taut thuds
Urging me forward.

Screams echo distantly,
Birth cries, not death cries.
Bubbles of gas and air froth past
Panting hard.

All ready, breathe deeply
Force open the lock gates.

Breath again, pant, push again,
It is sure, I'm knocking.

It is certain I am here,
This time heave with the tide;
But the waters are boiling, on fire -.
Wait for the next wave and I'm through.

Fire, brimstone, tighter, stretching, fire -
Like a salmon into the cool sea ...
I lie washed up on the beach
Opening blue new eyes, shouting in air.

Gillian Oxford

TRIBUTE TO A UNION MAN

For all the times we worked with you,
We seldom dared to wonder what would happen
If ever the Big Man were to fall.
I often thought that to the Laings and Wimpeys
You must be like Captain Hurricane to the Japanese,
Always larger than life,
While some of our officials barely show signs of it
And then only when someone kicks them.

An agent once asked you if you were an official.
"Official? Do you know who you're talking to?
There's no-one bigger than me in this Union!"
Small consolation to a deflated agent
When he found out it was true.

It's not easy being the Big Man.
I remember one Saturday in the Co-op Hall.
Inside the air was close,
Men's concentration slackening,
Mentally playing draughts on the chequered ceiling.
You were determined to build an army
To free the Shrewsbury lads,
While they - the little trendies of the left –
Were bickering about what should be the rallying cry.

Long ago, in a child's picture-book,
I remember Gulliver as the Lilliputians tried
To hold him down.
And when I heard the news
How you finally buckled under the weight,
I thought, "God protect us from our friends!"

But you never were one to waste time complaining
Except about the acoustics.
Just told us to replenish our glasses
So as we could fight the next round.

Some men of energy keep climbing, alone –
To take the foreman's job or emigrate to South Africa,
Looking always straight ahead
Towards some half-remembered goal,
They turn aside for neither man nor beast,

But the tracks of your life are like a sheepdog's
Forever turning back on itself,
Guiding in the furthermost strays.
Crossing from flank to flank of the sheep's vision,
Returning for more of the endless flock.

Some say a Big Man should be like a spider,
Drawing after him the strands of his work,
So that if the man is lost
The web remains.

Perhaps it is true we lack this web.
We stand as on the edge of a great void,
Stunned and staring at the hole you have left.
And yet something unseen has held us together,
Perhaps a web in the darkness
As we work on and wait
For daylight to return.

Rick Gwilt

NOVEMBER POEMS -1

a complex surgeon
cut a caesarean section
in swollen reality
extracting a half-formed truth
(being prone to clutching at straws)
he pinned the jiggling nerves
to a broken tree.
the crucified foetus
spat upon by hordes of fans and admirers
screamed into the desolation
till, finally, mocked by echoes
it hung torn, bleeding, limp.

Brian Herdman

PROPHECY OF REVOLUTION

While realists and wise men talk only death and doom,
We who are working men look from the workbench gloom
And with keen eyes see dawn's golden needle light
Pierce the black factory to banish hungry night.
The ray thaws icy brains, promising us the earth.
The heart sings without pains, aflame with hope of birth.

Working men and women shall break the iron lords,
Throw down bane-lipped statesmen and holy maggots' frauds.
We shall tear asunder the fabric of today,
Shall roar vengeful thunder with lightnings fire the way,
Arid we shall plant the seed in ashes of despair
Of a world that sates need where Man shall have no care.

Though now we are not free, and the morning sun's low,
We know these things shall be, for we shall make them so.

M.S. Handley

THE CHALLENGE

"Seamen won the battle of Trafalgar not Bloody Angels"
With such words Able Seaman Todd had so often proclaimed his scepticism. He asked no favours of providence but an even chance to meet the challenge of this relentless monster where he stood. "On the brink of eternity."

Able seaman Todd stood at the entrance of H.M.S. Tallons after-flat, a scowl clouding his weather-beaten face,, as through a curtain of falling snow, his eyes measured the rise and fall of the destroyer's stern. Their first day out on patrol and they were running into heavy weather.

Eight bells had just struck. Time to change the watches. His relief should be here by now. It was practice to turn over the watches a few minutes before the hour. Todd was anxious to get forard to the messdeck before the weather deteriorated further and while there was still time to eat a meal in reasonable comfort.

"Come on Dodger". He almost groaned his relief's nickname. The thought of the discomfort ahead. The long hours, perhaps days, battened down. The foul air and monotonous swish of water across the mess-deck added fuel to his impatience.

He walked around the lee-side of the after super-structure and looked forward, but there was no sign of his relief.

He returned to take up his former position at the entrance to the after-flat. The stern was dropping more steeply he observed with growing anxiety.

"Where was that fat slob?" he muttered ungenerously as he blew some warmth into his mittened hands. "It was alright for Mr. Bloody Long, he'd eaten and drunk his rum ration ... and someone else's he'd wager?"

The thought of an extra tot of rum slipping down Able seaman Long's receptive gullet, while he waited to be relieved was too much! He kicked out at the ammunition hoist in front of him to relieve his feelings. Caught for a moment off balance the roll of the ship threw him heavily against the after-flat door. He winced with pain as the sharp comin bit into his shoulder. You B...!" The air was blue as he regained his balance.

A new concern now gripped his mind. "What if Dodger had one too many." He'd be stuck aft until the weather worsened and the order came from the bridge to abandon after-positions. lie was in communication with the bridge and could report the failure of his relief to show up. A practice laid down. Not without sound reason. A man could be washed overboard unnoticed and minutes wasted could seal his fate. But even such a possibil-

90

ity he could not weigh seriously against the betrayal that the action of reporting a shipmate to that bastion of authority represented in the eyes of the lower-deck. To argue the alternative risk involved would carry no weight with his mess-mates. The interests of the class struggle was served even in the King's Navy.

A pair of gloved hands appeared around the edge of the after-superstructure followed by a wet face with balaclava swept back from the forehead. Todd breathed a sigh of relief. Then fixing the cause of his anxiety with a stony look he said sarcastically, "So you have come! hardly before time."

Able seaman Long anticipating what was to follow decided to get a word in before relationships between them became too strained for calmer explanation. He waved his hand in a gesture of impatience as he mustered his breath to speak. He was edgy himself. It had been a struggle to get aft and he was in no mood for argument. "You're damned lucky I'm here at all" he said. "It's blowing up fast and as treacherous as hell. I near went over reaching you!" Having gained Todd's attention, he continued. "You'll have to watch it going forard." Then, almost as an afterthought he added, "Digger's looking after your tot."

Faced with this concern for his welfare Todd found it difficult to preserve an unfriendly attitude, and there was something in Dodger's tubby figure, emphasised by an oilskin too small to allow the centre to button across that he found disarming. And although he would not admit it even himself, he had been seriously tempted to communicate with the bridge. A strong feeling of apprehension with regard to Dodger's safety had created a conflict in his mind that Dodger's appearance had resolved. A smile flickered at the corner of his mouth as he said, "You look like a drowned rat. There is a towel inside." He pointed into the after-flat. "Better dry yourself, I'll be on my way." He looked with apprehension seaward, it was getting rough. He'd be glad to be for'ard out of it.

He waited for the ship to come onto an even keel then gripping the handrail, which ran the length of the superstructure, started, hand over hand, to work his way for'ard. The ship was now heeling over to starboard. He took the weight of his body on his arms as he watched the sea coming up towards him. It swirled above the gunwale and around his feet. If he let go now he could slip under the guard rail into the sea. Although conscious of the danger he was strangely exhilarated by it, experiencing much the same pleasure he got, when as a lad, he had hung out from the roundabout at the fair. But there was no time for such comparison. The ship was coming back. He felt the strain go from his arms and his feet more secure on the deck. As she levelled off he went forward again, hand over hand, until he reached the end of the screen. Here the handrail terminated. He was at the beginning of the Waste. The deck widened here and a long four-inch rope hawser life-line was rigged its full length. He traced it with his eyes to the break of the for'castle. There was his objective ... the entrance to the canteen flat and the messdeck. It seemed a long way measured by the slow progress he was making - though in actual distance it was some yards. He remembered pacing it out one day for a bet.

He waited impatiently for the ship to right herself again so that he could safely transfer his hands to the lifeline while she was on an even keel. The lifeline was too slack, he observed with apprehension, his critical faculties sharpened by the awareness of danger. He'd have something to say about that when he got for'ard. No wonder Dodger nearly went over the side. It wasn't good enough. He felt angry, as a man would feel in the face of an injustice. "Shipmates they called themselves. A man's life could depend on how taut a lifeline was rigged."

The ship was coming back; he had no time for further moralising. With one hand still holding the rail he reached out with the other and grasped the lifeline, then with a quick swinging movement he transferred his other hand.

The ship again passed the even mark and started to heel over. This time he knew, due to the slackness of the lifeline, he would be swung close to the ship's side. He was in for a soaking. The sea, he gauged, would come above his knees and may well force him off his feet. He pulled himself forward a few paces before taking the strain again on his arms. The sea crept above the gunwale covered his feet and then raced to his knees. He felt it pushing his feet from under him, but managed to hold against the pressure until it subsided. Each time the degree of roll was increasing. He would go deeper next time and the pressure would increase.

Back on an even keel, he went forward again quickly. He must make the under-side of the gun platform before the next roll to starboard, so that he could hold onto her supporting angle irons against the increase of pressure he anticipated.

Her roll to port now forced him against the starboard screen and pinned his hands painfully between the lifeline and this wall of steel. The ship was coming back. His eyes were smarting with the salt spray. He forced them open to gaze seaward. As he did so a chill of fear gripped his heart. From off the quarter a great mountain of water had built up and was bearing down on the ship. Todd knew only too well what this meant. In a matter of seconds it would hit them and sweep aft carrying everything before it. He had seen such waves flatten guard-rails, one after the other, like so many skittles and leave seaboats smashed like matchwood in their wake.

God! What chance did he stand? For a moment, stark terror took charge of him and he half turned to run back to the shelter of the after-flat. How far he thought he would get he did not consider. He just felt impelled for one mad moment to attempt the impossible. Then the hard logic of his position forced itself upon him. He knew that his only chance was to fight this relentless monster where he stood. On the brink of Eternity. But there was no prayer on Todd's lips as it hit him. He asked no favours of Providence, only an even chance.

Life had not been generous to Able seaman Todd, but on balance, it had not been unkind either. An orphan, he had graduated from Dr. Barnardo's Homes into the Royal Navy at the age of fifteen and a half years. Following the pattern of so many before him, with no great enthusiasm other than the desire to keep with his mates. Todd was blessed with great physical strength - a legacy from his father, a docker who had met an untimely end under a crate of machinery that had slipped out of its strop. His mother, her resistance lowered by the shock, had died not long after with pneumonia, leaving Todd, a strong bouncing baby mercifully oblivious of the fate that had befallen him.

In spite of the kindness of the staff of the orphanage, Todd was not unconscious of his lack f family bonds and had often felt his aloneness in the world, which had developed in him more than his measure of self-reliance. A strong spirit of independence, coupled with his great strength, made him a man to be reckoned with. A natural leader. These qualities he combined with a com- passion for the underdog whose cause he had championed, not only with his great fists when the occasion demanded, but with an inquiring mind that had never accepted, without question, a status quo.

He was not favourite with authority and had often aroused jealousy from officers not so naturally endowed. But he was a very capable seaman and a good man to have around in an emergency. They therefore put up with what they termed for want of a better word Todd's idiosyncrasies. The war had found him still an able seaman after two demotions from Leading seaman and the loss of his only good conduct badge, for drunkeness insubordination, and absence over leave respectively.

Todd had not taken the peacetime navy very seriously, although enjoying the travel. Taking an intelligent interest in all he had seen, but particularly after the Spanish Civil War, he had serious reservations as to its Imperialist role, which his contact with those who had joined the Navy from the ranks of the unemployed - with whom he found he had a particular affinity - further strengthened. Though he did not accept their generally held left-wing opinions without serious questioning. He was too much of an individualist.

The war came as something of a relief for Todd, a resolving of doubts. He knew now where he stood. Britain had come down on the side of right as far as he was concerned and he began to feel for the first time that he was doing a job worth while, although his change of heart did not bring him any recognition. He had stayed an Able seaman, he suspected because promotion would bring draft to another ship. And there was a tendency for Captains to keep experienced men.

Like a kite before a gust of wind, he felt his body lifted horizontal with the lifeline and his arms being wrenched from their sockets. Only his hands surging along the rope saved them from dislocation. He was being pushed back along it like a curtain along a rail. His great strength had so far served him well. Although momentarily stunned by the impact of this tremendous volume of water he held on. He would not be thrown over the side like so much garbage. F... the bloody sea! His mind spelt out the obscenity that became the symbol of his defiance thrown into the jaws of Death itself. His arms were weakening and he knew that he could not hold out much longer. Then his feet touched the deck. The pressure was off. The Great Wave had passed ... but not the danger.

The ship was heeling over to starboard. Forced by the weight of water, it ploughed deeper below the surface. Todd, with a superhuman effort, forced the lifeline down to rest in the crook of his arm, gripping his wrist he forced his head and shoulders above the surface. The pain in his arms was excruciating and only his perilous situation gave him the strength to resist the almost overpowering desire to relax his grip. It was a moment when the strength of the will to live was balanced evenly against the physical and mental power to do so. Only a change of circumstances could alter the balance on the side of life. But Todd's luck held. He felt an arm grip him around his shoulders and a voice, heard almost as a whisper above the howl of the wind. "Hold on mate, Dodger's got you. As the ship levelled off, a feeling of relief, such as he had never experienced in his life before, surged through his exhausted body. Then he saw Dodger's other hand was holding the after-superstructure rail. He was back again where he had started.

Able seaman Long in the shelter of the after-flat had felt the impact of the wave like a shell exploding against the bulkhead. He had been thrown from one side of the flat to the other and sat for a moment where he had fallen, stunned more by the unexpected than the impact of the wave itself. Then his thoughts turned to Todd. "My God! He couldn't have survived that one." he gasped. He picked himself up quickly and rushed for the door, tripping over the comin in his haste. He cursed but did not feel any pain, so agitated was his mind with fear for Todd's safety. "My God!" he kept muttering. "My God!"

He turned the corner of the after-superstructure to look for'ard, gripping the handrail to prevent himself being thrown towards the ship's side, for the ship was now heeling steeply to starboard. As he did so he became aware of Todd's huge frame just ahead. It hung on the lifeline, half submerged in the sea. Something in the almost grotesque position of the body told him there was no time to lose. He pulled himself to the end of the rail, then leaned out and gripped Todd's shoulders. He said something that he could never recall afterwards.

How he got Todd into the after-flat he counted as one of the miracles of his life. He had never experienced such dead weight before. He pulled and tugged at Todd's great, inert frame. Racing against time, for he knew that unless he could get him around the corner of the superstructure and into the shelter of the after-flat before the ship rolled again all his efforts would have been in vain. He could never hold him against such pressure. He doubted whether he would be able to save himself.

But he had managed it and now, aching in every fibre of his small round frame, he stood looking down at Todd, who lay semi-conscious at his feet, his jaw still set in a grim line of defiance. "You tough old bastard", he mumbled. But there was a look of great affection, combined with admiration in his warm brown eyes as he knelt to loosen Todd's clothing. "The Devil looks after his own."

Raymond Sims

EPITAPH FOR MAGGIE

'Twere an archway o'mops when our Maggie passed on
Ay'n it rained pure sops on t'day she were done
'n Hand-me-down shuen 'N' cast-off clout
Did a dance macabre to speed 'er out.

("I could sleep for a week")
Now she'll sleep forever.
Cross the dishpan hands
C' real cracked leather.

T'clubman's been 'n he's paid us out
She rode like a queen on t' last bus route
They said the words and all were over
For once, in her death, our Maggie's in clover.

Now when the wind's through the trees
With a Hoover's wheeze

'n' snow as it shakes
Is best soap flakes
Our Maggie don't care
She's no longer a slave
Away from it all
She's found peace in t' grave.

Rose Friedman

EUTHANASIA

She lies still
Cradled in a cocoon of blankets
Shrivelled with the years and sorrows that visited her
Her transparent skin lies in folds
Over the bright blue of her veins
The pulse shows in each vein
Slowing down

Each strained breath draws a sob from her
She is past pretence and bravery
Her death sits on the bedposts counting out the unspent hours
On the abacus of her sobs

I hold the bottle
The precipitator - the key
I turn the top and see her nod gratefully
Then I turn away in the knowledge that it is my suffering I seek to
end
And not hers
She must look for a greater love than mine
To open the door

Vivien Leslie

START

Not knowing whether I have prepared myself sufficiently, no
longer caring, concerned only,
as the wave of my fortieth

96

year breaks over me, that I try -

what I am not sure, but the thing
that I have dreamt of, and dreaming,
long longed to bring forth, tumbling
in its harness, voluminous
in its rude grace, and sufficient,

that that energy, neither mine
nor yours, but ours, abide with us,
presumptuous and insistent,
the deliberate gaiety
of the nail driven, and driving, home.

Roger Mitchell

SOLDIERS

When they kill a man
Do they unfold his flesh
Do they open him like a book?

Do they choose the exact spot
Where the bullet will sing
Like a bird?

Before they napalm
A woman and her child
Do they go up to her
Do they kiss her fluttering eyes
Do they tell her
What a moment
Of Ecstasy
Death is?

After they have decimated a city
After the fires have licked their lips
After the inferno has curled up to sleep
Who puts up the easel
In the rubble
And paints a tired Phoenix
Once more...?
John Salway

HIGHGATE CEMETERY

Marx's ideas gain
fresh adherents
every day;

his opponents
must be content
to topple his effigy.

Bill Eburn

DOUBLE MEANING

It is not uncommon in our society for those in positions of power to determine the form and content of our everyday lives. Put simply, such people will seek to determine the nature of our reality, i.e. the way in which we confront and comprehend our existence. In pursuit of this goal their weapons are varied and numerous. Perhaps their most formidable instrument of control is the use of language. As a means of communication the usefulness of language is based upon a precise double coincidence of meaning, i.e. that the word used to describe a particular aspect of reality has a shared common meaning between two people. However, those whose function it is to control others for the purposes of preserving the present relations of production have denied this basic use of language.

To many of our leading politicians, industrialists, journalists and broadcasters the function of words has become to construct and maintain an elaborate illusion, to weave a complex web of half truths and superficialities. The purposeful ambiguity of language is deliberately sought after to create a false reality, a mere appearance of life which is profoundly ideological and deeply committed to the preservation of an elitist culture and society. Perhaps a common tale of working-class life may serve to illustrate this principle.

And thus it was that Jack, a short, thick-set young man of twenty made his way to work. Out and into the miserable narrow streets which were only dimly lit in the early morning. He walked quickly, clasping his black jacket around his throat to ward off the chill. Approaching the bus-stop Jack's eyes confronted the unkempt waste land which once supported the meagre, but proud homes of a people now long since banished to the bland anonymity of the city's outskirts. The area was now the temporary habitat of the advertiser. He had set up residence in the form of five rather large wooden hoardings. One such hoarding periodically provoked concern in

Jack's not too nimble mind. The vision of a sedate, rather benign looking woman interested Jack immensely. She contrasted so vividly (and so mean-ingfully) with her surroundings. The accompanying slogan also perturbed Jack, he could decipher a number of words as he quickly passed by - 'Britain', 'Affluent', 'Freedom', 'Fairness', yet his understanding of them appeared inadequate in the face of his immediate surroundings. He hurried on to the bus stop.

Standing in the bus queue Jack had time for a moment's reflection. He found it difficult to reconcile the assurance of affluence afforded by the poster and his own perceptions of life around him. He concluded that the comfortable looking lady of the hoarding was either blissfully unaware or deliberately ignorant of the mean streets of his squalid town. Certainly these grim terraces could not accept any labels of affluence or prosperity. Simultaneously many thousands joined Jack on smoke- filled double deck-er buses making their way to the factories and mines of the area.

Gradually, and despite the bronchial coughs and depressing shroud of his fellow travellers, Jack became aware of the newspapers and magazines around him. As if. attempting to deliberately shun each other, the passen-gers on Jack's bus were intent on absorbing the puerile delights of the daily press. Jack, without a newspaper of his own, tried to steal a glimpse of his neighbour's. Immediately he became aware of the promise and prospect which the future held for him. The newspaper was running a special feature 'Habitat 75'. This was certainly the world for Jack, sleek, modern furniture in a luxurious home - this was what he thought of as 'real' living. Jack dreamt of the future, of finishing his apprenticeship, of marrying and inher-iting the fabricated delights of the 'ad-men'. Yet he thought again of the trouble at the factory, of rumour of redundancies, of troublesome shop-stewards making the situation worse by their irksome one-day 'token' strikes in protest. He wasn't going to let the unions spoil his future. Jack had watched the television news, he had read the 'papers. They had estab-lished beyond doubt the existence of a 'crisis'. What's more, Jack had be-come convinced of 'right' and 'wrongs in the issue, he knew the 'unions' were at the root cause of the problem, they were causing trouble.

Jack soon had these views confirmed when his mind wandered to the con-dition of his own factory. Mr. Peacock had explained that it was only fair to expect some 're-organisation' if the firm was not selling what it had pro-duced. Certainly the words the personnel manager had used had sounded as he had put it himself, 'reasonable' and 'fair'. Besides, Jack was soon to be-come a skilled man, he would always be needed, and anyway the manage-ment had talked of something called 'rationalisation' not 'redundancies

By now, Jack's bus had reached the factory gates. Simultaneously other buses arrived, and cars too, their passengers pouring out and' into the wait-

99

ing factory. The multitude of men and women made their way past huge, throbbing machinery, over rusting pipe-work through the entire labyrinth of metal and steam to their respective places of work.

Jack followed the others towards the fittingshop. As he approached, he saw and heard the rising murmur of a group of men standing before the notice board. Jack joined them and read the printed sheet:

'IN THE INTERESTS OF RATIONALISATION AND
EFFICIENCY THE COMPANY HAS HAD TO ENGAGE
IN A SERIOUS RE-DEPLOYMENT OF LABOUR. THE
FOLLOWING ARE THEREFORE INVITED TO
ACCEPT THE TERMS OF REDUNDANCY AS
NEGOTIATED'.

Jack remained for some minutes staring vaguely at the notice and the list of names underneath. He could not believe what his eyes perceived. Jack would no longer be required once his apprenticeship was completed in six weeks. He was receiving nothing after being promised so much.

Where were they all now? Where were all those fine words that sounded so well only ten minutes before? 'Affluence', 'Prosperity', 'Fairness'. Of course they had melted away, they had ceased to exist1 they have no meaning save their opposite. Jack had been their victim, deceived by those who had used such words to sustain their own private good. Jack wouldn't be taken in again. He went back to his bench, picked up his jacket and left.

Ray Hartley

THE MOTH

Nursing a scorched wing
The moth returns to the flame.

Poor dumb creature,
too dumb to curse the creator
that taught it to fly into the light,
into the endless night.

Bill Eburn

SPLINTERING

If all the holy one man bands
That splinter off the
Progressive-parties-in-opposition
Or are exorcised from
The Moderate-parties-in-power,
Were somehow to fuse into one mass,
They would form a solid block of teak
So large and heavy
That it could stopper up the sepulchre
Of the common man for ever.

But no, they are mutually retro-pulsive.
They wander through the world like troubadours;
Colourful marauders, pinching an idea here,
A policy there,
And somebody else's girl.
They sting like wasps, and flutter like butterflies
About our dusty heads and earthbound feet.
They are sawdust motes in a light beam,
The tang and scrunch of new shavings,
And the tinder that sets other men ablaze.

Connie M. Ford

THE COLD WAR

How did we escape in the fifties and sixties?
A hair's breadth from destruction, nuclear annihilation.
We did not see how near the scimitar was swinging
Now, looking back, we shield our eyes and shudder.

What tipped the balance? What but the people of
the world, above all, almost alone at times The people of the U.S.S.R.
Their policy, their self denial, in order to build
the new order in Europe, Cuba, Africa,
Help them with their science, knowledge;
They had taken such blows, they could take more, stand more;
No one else could have saved the day and us.

Isabel Baker

FOR MY DAUGHTER - SOME RECOLLECTIONS OF HER GRANDFATHER

My father bought me two volumes of Jane Austen when I was thirteen. At that age he had left school, top in mathematics and geography, and no one bothered any more about his mind until he lost it forty years later. Literally, it was lost. The surgeons were able to pass air bubbles through the cavities in his brain, so they told me. They didn't understand why this was so but seemed glad to have done it. Meanwhile, my father smoked a hundred cigarettes a day until he died of lung cancer five years later. Mindlessness, sadly, is no reason for dying.

When my father bought Jane Austen for his only daughter, elder child, he knew nothing of literature; merely that the stories had been serialised on the radio - some sign of status -but more that I had listened with absorbed delight. This delight he had noticed. It has taken me twenty years to be aware of this loving observation. He had so few loving words or gestures and it is for this that the child in us awaits, even in memory, even from the dead.

He also bought a book-case to enshrine the books he so respected, the encyclopaedias, his school prize, Barnaby Rudge. and a dictionary I once bought him as a birthday present and which over the years became more worn than any other book in the house. The rest of the space he left for me to fill which I quickly did for a while, until I took my books and myself from behind glass and left home, so I thought forever, at the age of twenty. We never quarrelled again after I left home, my father and I, but then we rarely spoke after I left home until shortly before his mind disappeared, when he discharged his memories at me without pause, urgently, as if seeking some other place to keep them when he no longer could. So I have his memories and never really got away after all.

My father read his encyclopaedias; sometimes he read them to me. He was able to help me with homework until I was fourteen, when the rows of figures became too complicated for him, too. This sounds as if we got on well, my father and I, and perhaps it was really better than I remember. I recall being at Brighton with him, sitting on a wall and watching the sea for what seemed hours. Precious seeds to sow on this dead, waste soil; precious threads to bind and join that long black rift that the war made and he was away. Separation, I have since learned, is part of the texture of life, its warp perhaps. Young as I was then, I mistook it for the whole fabric and now I pluck at the past in search of disconnected, connecting strands.

He planted and grew flowers and fruit in what we called the back-yard; roses and runner beans; blackberries entangled with everything, regardless. Later we had a garden and with endless patience in a hasty, restless man he again planted and grew beans and roses, white phlox in the borders; asters and sweet peas particularly he loved. There grass grew too. The roses and grass still grow. In his days of vacancy, my father used to wander and stand in the middle of the garden, as if bewildered by its growth.

I feel that my growth, too, must have bewildered him, and the shape it took; my constant waywardness as I opposed his every arbitrary command. Truly his daughter, I too would stand my own ground. If I could not have the sort of father invented by the story books he encouraged me to love, neither would I have things his way. His were not fatherly ways, which for many years made me think myself fatherless. A man who had headaches and often shouted inhabited my home, lived on in my memory long after he had no more reason to accuse us.

In these last days he would stand at the door waiting for me as I paid my occasional, fleeting visits, having the instincts of an animal for my arrival, welcome recognition in his foolish smile. "Patricia", he always called me when he called me anything at all. There was this formality between us always.

Formality and strangeness made up our relationship, with shy gifts of books and sharing of knowledge. All intimacy we angrily denied.

Now, according to his unwritten will, I call myself working-class still, despite my accent and the uninformed denials of my friends. And I love his London ardently. Out of this fatherless wilderness I am trying to clear a space for some-thing else to grow, something planted long ago. The gift of mind to mind.

Pat Sentinella

TO DAME MARGOT FONTEYN
'Dancing, not politics, is my business'

Dame Margot - every turn and pirouette
Of your performance there that night
Was so superb - and yet -
You'll never now be quite exempt
From Chile's working men's contempt:
How their cause was so abused,
Arid you yourself were so well used
To lend respect to Pinochet.

Anonymous

NOAH'S ARK

One day God were looking down

From his home atop the C.I.S.
And as he looked down at Ardwick he started to frown;
"Oo; look what they're doing: they can't be: they're not: they are, Oh bloody hell, yes;
We can't have this sort of thing."
So sent out St. Peter to have a look.
He flew out over Ardwick upon angelic wing,
Writing it all down in a book.
In Ardwick Green, they were having nude frolics,
Drinking and singing; it weren't at all right;
There were unclothed gentlemen revealing their knees,
And old age pensioners playing strip monopoly all night.
St. Peter were getting it all down on paper
As they drank evil intoxicant liquors;
He saw Gladys Murgatroyd incite a busguard to raper
Then choke him to death with her niquors.
There were leather-clad lollipopmen getting their oats:
He could sell all this to the Sun:

Then he spotted old Noah Ackroyd playing ludo and reading a book about
boats;
He were a miserable bugger and didn't like fun.
St. Peter went back to God and told him all this.
God said he'd turn the world to a watery ball.
He told Noah to get a boat for him and his missis,
And they could take a few animals an' all.
So Noah went out to Belle Vue Zoo
Though it certainly seemed at bit odd
To take all the animals out two by two;
Still, he could send the bill to God.
There they were in a line on Hyde Road,
Camel and Antelope, Elephant and Chimpanzee,
Hippopotamus, Crocodile, Rhinoceros and Toad,
Sea Lion and Platypus all waiting for a fifty three.
Well, the fifty three's service ran like it usually
does.
After two hours they sat down at the bus stop for lunch.
At about half past two they all saw a bus
Followed by thirty nine more in a bunch.
The bus driver were upset and looked in vain through all his regulations
For a rule about pythons or bears,
But it said nothing about them or pigs or dalmations,
So noah took them all for a smoke upstairs.
At Wilmslow Road they disembarked
(Except for the Unicorns who went to Old Trafford by mistake);
It were time all the animals were Noah's-arked
So they went to the hut by the lake.
Noah slipped the parky a thirteen pound note
And made it understood
That he wanted to hire a rowing boat
Three hundred cubits long, made of gopher wood.
"Right," said the parky, "I'll just gopher wood,
I'll be back again in a tick."
They got the animals aboard just in time for the flood,
All hung over the side being sick.
The storm-lashed fury of Platt Fields Lake was bad for both man and beast;
The spirit of mutiny had them all in its grip
As they sailed North-east-south-west along Moss Lane East
And both kangaroos tried to jump ship.
Noah ended this marsupial unrest
As for days they floated round town.
There was a cry of "Avast Behind" from the crow's nest
But it was just Noah's wife bending down.

One day they saw the parky on tiptoe, underwater save
For his head sticking up like a mine;
And he said his last words as he seemed to sink to a watery grave
"Your time's up; come in number nine",
Eventually it stopped raining; there was sun everywhere
And the water level started to fall,
So Noah dropped anchor in Albert Square
And tied up alongside the Town Hall,
As the water level gradually fell, oh
They saw a wet policeman appear,
With a salmon in his hand, he said "'ello, 'ello, 'ello;
You can't park your ark around here."
Noah tried to escape: the policeman looked pained:
He blew on his whistle and cried " 'alt";
But God sent down one of his great balls of fire and all that remained
Was a helmet and a pillar of salt.
It seemed about time to go home;
Morale was fast sinking lower
The Elephants hadn't taken to life on the foam
And kept being sick over Noah.
At Platt Fields they met the parky in snorkel and flippers
Stood impatient at the park Late.
He slapped Noah in the face with a handful of kippers
And said "That'll be two and six more, 'cos you're late."

Les Barker

106

BISCUITS

All day long she packed cream-centred slimming biscuits into white card boxes. The biscuits approached her along a shuddering chute that wound its way past the metal sculpture of wheels and rollers to her right before it ran straight and level past her towards the next stage. She couldn't see where they came from and didn't know what happened to them before she saw them. All she knew was that they arrived in nudging groups of twelve between clicks and jerks of the chute all through the day. They were square biscuits with a trellis-work imprint on their out sides and a thin lemon coloured splat of filling between them. She was allowed to pick out the broken ones, but when she did she had to make up the missing one from the subsequent sets of twelve and this disturbed her working rhythm, so mostly she let them go unless they were undersized, when a weight check further along the line tipped its rejects onto a desk where her output was docked according to their number. Once she'd asked if she might have a box of spare biscuits to make up shortages but they'd said it wasn't part of the system, it would mean extra paperwork adjusting the job specification and what was it to her anyway? So she fiddled it on her own. She bought a packet of each flavour from the supermarket and used them. It cost her but it allowed the job to fade into the part of her mind that kept her fingers' memory and after that, the only ripple in her routine was the twice weekly flavour shift. Lemon to chocolate, mint to vanilla, a fortnightly cycle that rolled invariably around and carried her with it in a haze of warm biscuit smell and small mechanical noises.

The screen showed a coffee cup being filled, the picture slid away from the cup and onto a plate where two familiar biscuits were being caressed by a female finger. The man's voice was confiding.

"Jennie thought that after ten years' marriage she would be shapeless and her husband would have lost interest. So she decided to include "Trimmicles" in her calorie-controlled diet. They've been married for fourteen years now and this is what her husband thinks...."

The screen showed a couple in a body-touching kiss, then the man's hand drew away and dropped a curtain over them and the blank picture bore the overprint. " "Trimmicles" keeps the inches where they count" and some muted music played the commercial out.

She upended the iron and nudged the man in the chair. She pointed at the screen.

"That's them, that's my biscuits' she said. "They put that silver paper on and the fancy wrapping round the box where Lilly works, but I put them in the boxes."

Her face was bright with interest. It was the first time that the television had seemed real to her even though the biscuits looked different sitting on the fancy plate and the young couple were far removed from the impatient monotony of the factory. Just the same, it excited her to see something she was a part of important enough to be on the television. It made her feel important. The man shrugged.

"Well, you should try eating the ruddy things instead of packing them. You're getting fat."

Her face collapsed and quick angry tears trembled on the full curve of her cheek before they pitched and ran over them. She was suddenly aware of the overall stretched in circles between the buttons down to where her thighs made double hips under her skirt. The fingers on the iron looked rough and podgy and she knew her legs were fatter since the children.

"I can't afford them. They're dear, you know. Dearer than ordinary biscuits and they taste dry..." she stopped before the tears were in her voice and he sighed and said no more, only diving into the newspaper that laid on his lap until she would recover herself. A little later he said, "Are you getting tea... ?"

It hadn't really hurt her but she couldn't get it out of her mind the next day at work Each time the biscuits were at her hand she thought of the thin china plate and the couple kissing, and then looked at her own wide lap and her knees that seemed like large anvils to her. On impulse she took a pencil up and wrote across a slip of paper. IT'S ALL A LIE. She tucked the paper carefully between two biscuits in the packet in front of her, being childishly fussy over wedging the biscuits together again over the folded paper. She knew the weight check would miss it and it would be sheer bad luck if that packet were the one out of a hundred that was picked for a final check. The packet was well out of sight before she remembered her blind oversight. The biscuits had to be wrapped.

Perhaps Lilly would get it. There were only two wrappers. Half a chance then, for Lilly would surely bring it back, have a laugh about it, maybe at her, but she'd bring it back. She didn't know the other girl at all. Yet she was strangely unworried about it, as if it had nothing to do with her at all. At heart she felt it had not been such a foolish thing to do and the feeling stayed with her all through her nervous afternoon. By the end of the day she was expecting a foreman at least for the biscuits must have been packed, wrapped and dispatched by now, but the hooter sounded and nothing extraordinary happened and she went home with the incident puzzling her. Lilly was her usual self on the bus, and Lilly would have said something, she was like that, but Lilly did talk about the day's work, about getting cellophane wrappers too small for the packet, about the heat- seal not working but she said nothing about the paper slip.

Lying in bed that night she thought about it carefully. The slip couldn't have fallen out and since each biscuit was wrapped individually, it must have been seen when it was wrapped. She was left with a warming conviction that the other wrapper had received it and for some reason had chosen not to mention it, either to Lilly or to herself. She might even have let it be. She might have actually sent it on for dispatch with the paper slip still there. She was surprised at her own desire to believe her speculation but with the morning, she was surer than ever that the possibility existed and more, she wanted to find out.

She went early and waited in the wrapping area. There was no-one about and she looked through the refuse bin under the chute quickly but there was no slip there. Then the other wrapper arrived. She nodded to her and felt suddenly uncomfortable. What was she to say? There was no way to explain its importance to the other girl who was setting her bench up for work to begin.

"Do you like it here?" she asked on impulse.

The girl looked up and smiled. "It's all right. Same as anywhere else. Nice company. You're a friend of Lilly's aren't you?"

'Yes, we knew each other at school. Er What do you think of the biscuits...?" she blurted it out, one eye on the approaching Lilly who would want to know why she hadn't been on the usual bus and the other trying to keep the girl's face in focus. The girl laughed.

"I've wrapped aspirins, biscuits, sweets, batteries, Durex and oh, I don't know what else in my time. It's all the same. A bit of pretty paper and a fancy box, I got so I never thought about it. It's just a game, isn't it? A way to earn money. The biscuits are just biscuits, it's this stuff that's important," she said running a finger over a pile of cellophane sheets. Then Lilly was upon them and there was nothing more to say between them. She made quick excuses to Lilly and went to her place. Almost immediately the chute shook into motion and the first set of biscuits appeared in front of her. She dropped them right into the waiting box and smiled to herself. All day she wondered who would receive the "Trimmicles' with her message, and wondered if they would be angry, puzzled, surprised or merely indifferent as they munched their way towards love with the aid of the dry expensive biscuits. She felt a suffusing warmth towards the girl who had sent her packet on its way without betraying her foolishness and she did not regret her action, impulsive as it had been; she felt as if she had done something honest, something in defiance of the mocking television. The biscuits jerked towards her, the first of the chocolate batch and automatically she reached for the deeper boxes, for the chocolate ones were packed differently.

The woman emptied the packet into a plastic tub. She threw the packet, wrapping and the paper slip into the waste-bin and took two of the biscuits from the tub and placed them crosswise on a thin china plate. She poured coffee, lifted her diet card down and checked off the calories she was about to consume. Her reflection in the glass door was dark enough to be part silhouette. She patted her stomach while holding her breath and smiled at the reflection. Her teeth clamped over the dry biscuit and shut. Perhaps he would kiss her tonight

Vivien Leslie

POLLUTION

You children playing in the dusty; street,
or running, not unwillingly, to school,
or turning homewards on light stepping feet,
each moment lived and savoured to the full.
You cannot guess that you may be the last
of all man's generations come and gone,
through all the fervent seasons of the past;
the sap of life in torrents flowing on
till now - in your fine veins the blood
may thicken with the toxins of the age
and dam forever the once endless flood
of glorious life. None will survive to rage.
You are not doomed by God. We are your fate
and if we saw, it might not be too late.

Vera Leff

BOURGEOISIE

My flaming eyes still burn to hate you;
you and your fenced-in little world.
My jaded hands just ache to stab you,
to push in deep the blade of truth.

And in your trimmed back-garden land
I see the hungry picking worms,
and in your smart, fat children's faces
the flattened colonies of ages.

Yet when I raise a blood-drop from you
your daughter's slender hand persuades me
that I can't bear to see you bleeding
nor to feel you breathing.

Keith Armstrong

NO. WE DON'T LIKE TO BE BESIDE THE SEASIDE

the slapstick cream trickles
down the red face of another fool
parted from money
blackpools funny that way
ducky
mucky jokes poke fun
like fingers in a fat man's belly
jelly babies cock lack
a slapped back and laffs in the lav
ring like mad bells
for the desperate near dead
newly wed fed up wrinkled uncles in deck chairs
chew chips
lunch
time to crunch another sand sandwich
to watch waves the colour of flat beer
beat the pier legs
kids cram spam
into mouths made to suck rock
the floral frocks of sunnier swish
in a gale force wolf whistle
and the promenades promise of pleasure
threatens loud the leisure of a lazy day
girls and boys burst into easy tears
in the glaring light of parental leers
"I won't tell you again'
"when do they open then"
the men leave for liquor
"language lads - ladies present - don't fancy yours

kiss her quick - i should cocoa - call me duggie
beer for bugger all - laugh a minute innit
no we dont like to be beside the seaside
as drunks like driftwood on the time gentlemen tide
pour like puke from the overfull inside out
to shout shoot shit and mess about
pick narks about nowt
we mustn't go down to the sea again
the kids cant constantly be bought
with lyons maid bucket and spade sport
no its naples next year
the sugar pink false teeth of time
take mouthfulls of magic
from a golden mile of cheap chipped gilt
the tower shrinks and sinks
in the silt of a forced laugh
the lack lustre lingers like a bad cough
as blackpool lights are
officially
switched off
John Cooper Clarke

TO PEACE

Oh Peace, Thou precious hope of all mankind.
Can'st Thou not suage and calm the troubled mind,
Let dove and olive branch and healing palm,
Rid fear of bursting bomb and war's alarm?

To distant realms in life's too short a span,
The poor bemused soul can scarcely scan
Who is the faithful friend or ruthless foe?
Who builds for peace or strives eternal woe?

From pilgrim's suppliant knee, devout and meek,
Rise up with vision clear your purpose seek.
Peace is no Goddess from Olympian Heights
To succour all the weak and helpless wights.

Seek out and keep the truth, man's own estate,
Nor gain nor servile press turn you to hate,
The will of each and all to banish war,
Is more than all the gods enthroned afar.
C. Hargreaves

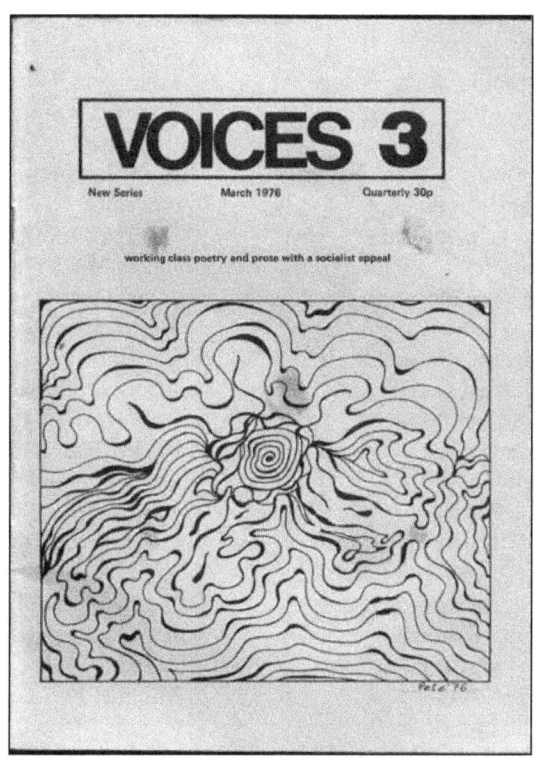

cover size 210 x 148 mm (A5)

CONTENTS

EDITORIAL

"Voices now has an Editorial Board of six members: ALAN ARNISON, FRANK PARKER, JOHN COOPER CLARK, TED MORRISON, LES BARKER and BEN AINLEY. A decision is pending about a woman coming on the Board. All those named are contributors to "Voices

We welcome the activities of the S.E. group which operates in the London area: people in South East England who want to make personal contact should write to Ian E. Reed, 58 Lenham Rd., Sutton, Surrey SM1 4BG, or meet the group on March 19th (see below).

In a recent review of "Voices" in the "Morning Star" Rick Gwilt suggests that this would be a suitable moment "to start including an edited selection and summary of the increasing volume of criticism that is being fed back" to us. We agree, and if the response warrants it propose to print in the June issue comments favourable and unfavourable to our publication. "Critical", of course, does not necessarily mean derogatory or niggling: it simply implies some judgment of what we are doing and where we are going. Please take this as an invitation to take part in this "critical feedback".

"Voices" we believe has a function to play among the literary journals. It is not a vehicle for established writers. It is a means of dialogue between writer, of working class origin and/or of socialist tendency and the workers and socialists to whom they address themselves.

The London Group of "Voices" which calls itself "Voices" (S.E. Group) is holding its quarterly meeting at the Metropolitan Tavern (corner of Farringdon Road and Clerkenwell Road) on Thursday March 19th at 7.30 p.m. (Tube Farringdon).

Ben Ainley

JOHN WILLIAM HOSEY (SEAN) Arrested 28th October, 48 hours after arriving in South Africa from London. Kept in solitary confinement and brutally treated. Charged with five others - four black, one white citizen of Australia. They became known as the Pretoria Six.

A charge of conspiracy and distribution of anti-state leaflets was dropped.

Sean eventually charged with possession of two passes with intent to give same to guerillas. The judge (Boshoff) declared that prosecution had not proved his case but likewise that Sean had not proved his innocence, that is to say, had not proved that he brought the passes to give to a trade unionist.

He was sentenced to five years.

John (Sean's father) attended the trial, and wrote this poem.

> You smiled quietly as you mounted the steps
> From the cells below. I couldn't hear
> As your lips moved, but I knew you said
> Hello dad.
>
> Your cheeks are pale
> The flesh is taut
> I will bring you some food tomorrow
> Some apples and pears and oranges too
> Am I staring too hard?
> Have they broken you
> With obscenity and cruelty
> Joe Boshoff, surrounded
> By a dozen Mein Kampfs
> A court of jackboots
> Make you tremble
>
> I will watch your hands
> To see if they shake
> In submission
> Perhaps tis not submission
> But wrath
> I am no good at guessing
> Nor am I psychic
> I will wait till I hear
> If you condemn or condone.
>
> My brain is afire

I cannot sleep
I pace the room
Accusations, accusations, accusations
That you
Hosey, Moumbaris, Cholo, Mthembu, Sejaka, Mpanza

Did
Conspire
Conspiracies, conspiracies, conspiracies
Did
By leaflet, disturb the minds
Of peaceful people
Leaflets, leaflets, leaflets.
But did you succumb
Tomorrow I will know.

I don't like this V.I.P. box
I would sit with Cholo's mother
And hold her brave black hand
But I cannot hear so far away
And I must hear
To tell the world
The Actor man beside me
Makes me sick
He shouldn't be here
In this land of Apartheid

Regaling the 'Boss-man'
With his actor talents
Then acting still, remarks
They are all very brave
Hypocrite!

You looked at me
As you walked to the stand
And smiled in that delightful way
My heart was bursting
My son, my son
What would it be
Defeat or victory
And then I heard you
Loud and clear
'I'd do it all over again'
I clapped my hands in rapturous

117

Delight.

John Hosey

FRIDAY NIGHT IS MUSIC NIGHT

Public bar paddies
amid farts and darts
burp and slurp
Watneys Red,
slewed eyes glued
on three in a bed.

Saloon bar smoothies
spurn the spitoons
endlessly discuss dope
that they've scored
and how they are
so terribly bored.

Cocktail bar snobs and slobs
perched on their stools
prattle pretentiously
about their dreary careers

In the snooker halls
everyone's full of booze
fighting like fury
with billiard cues.

Streaking down the street
chop suey bill dodgers
chased by cheerless Chinamen
itching to chastise them
with knives and choppers.

Slumped and slobbering
behind the bus shelter
drunken randy couples
belch and squelch
obliviously to orgasm.

Outside the fish shop

chips, chewed and spewed,
sodden and trodden
into the gutter.
Mike Pentelow

IT PASSED ON BY

Trekking eastwards towards Toronto one cold October day
Upon another travelling guy it was my fate to stray
Just a few miles beyond Osaquam along the Canada Way
As he sat there on a boulder by the shoulder of the road
To rest a while a wore out frame the burden of its load.
He looked so sad that lonely lad so weary downtrodden and blue
That I tried to be cheery came up with a smile
And greeted him with a "Waddayasaytheremanwhatsnew".
He answered me back with a shivery shrug
Said "By god man this just ain't bin my day
For it's sure bin quite it'll soon be night
And it looks like that frost's here to stay."
He was just about beat through sheer lack of heat
Clad in clothes that were threadbare and old
And he looked so sad that lonely lad
Sitting there all alone in the cold.
Such a woebegone sight I forgot my own plight
Yes, forgot my own hunger and cold
But I sure heard a sigh somewhere deep inside
Saying "Oh for a world without hunger and cold.
Vehicles on the highway had been very few that day
And the blue skies above were turning grey
Things were anything but bright we must have looked a woeful
sight
When suddenly from out the west a green van came into view
And it was heading eastwards almost like a dream come true
For scrolled across the bonnet just below the windscreen

This great big slogan: BE HUMANE! could be seen.
Now if what them "sky pilots" say is true and there are
angels up on high
It could be they heard our laughter when that RSPCA van sped
right on by
For no sooner had it past us than the sky began to cry.

Robert Moore

THE LONER

For him the birds
no longer sing,
he'll never know
the joys of Spring;
seated alone,
on a park bench
far from home,
he gazes with
jaundiced eye
at those happy
passers-by
who have found
something to do
than listen
to Radio Two

Bill Eburn

HELLO YOU WALRUS FACED BASTARD

THE SHREWSBURY PICKETS

What crime did they commit,
but stand up for their rights.
The right to strike the right to picket;
for that they were sent to prison,
to be punished like common criminals;
is this the fate that awaits all good
trades unionists?

THE FLYING PICKET

500 they did come on that sunny day in Shrewsbury,
and nearly as many building sites they did stop.
The cancer disappeared that day - the lump!
And remember not one arrest was made,
that clean up day in Shrewsbury.

THE VICTORY

On that date of 15th September 1975, it was over,
the strike had lasted for three months.
Not all the demands had been won,
but it was the biggest wages increase
the building workers had ever won.
Tories were screaming for blood;
the employers were crying out, 'We've been robbed!'
The capitalist press were writing vicious lies.
It must have been because the strike had been
a tremendous success.
And then - six months after came the arrest of the 24.

THE CONSPIRACY

On the 2nd October 1973, the first trial began.
At that political trial at Shrewsbury,
between state, police and court,
those pickets didn't stand a chance.
read the pickets' speeches from the dock
On corruption and distortion.
And then the judge pronounced sentence,
with all the might of bourgeois' law.
Six trade unionists were sent to jail.
At those political trials at Shrewsbury.

POSTSCRIPT

Did the trade union movement forget
the courage of the Shrewsbury pickets?
Who went to jail for their beliefs.
John Hamblett

CHANGE OF COUNTENANCE

"You can read me like a book" she said,
but there was that in her visage
which caused him after one look
hastily to turn the page.
Bill Eburn

THE LIONS OF LONGLEAT

i have seen the lions of longleat eat
their toothless gums sucking meat
as milk from others tender teat
i have seen the lions of longleat sleep
tossed on horns that honk and beep
through matted manes ive seen them peep
i have seen the vultures of longleat
loom
amid the promises of doom
cloaked in clouds of smoke black plumes
gliding on the petrol fumes
above the marabars half consumed
melting into afternoon
i have seen the baboons
too
wearily wanking with nothing to do
escape, scraper but where to?
a less humane zoo
with cages and bars
and no cars to break
no crisps and cake
no tooth decay or belly ache
i have seen the lions of longleat
greet
grannies in their passenger seats
through the british summer sleet
i have seen the lions of longleat
creep
over broken bottles on fagburnt feet
marvelled at how fast and fleet
they hunt the flying sweet
i have seen the lions of longleat
in viscount weymouth's careful keep
who rides his zebra painted jeep
who sells bits of africa cheap
who loses not a minute of sleep
as the gods of the congo watch and weep

John Cooper Clarke

MANIFESTO

In rich men's cars and city bars
And alleys flanking shabby clubs
She lives a life of tarnished stars
And yellow breath, and furtive rubs
From men who grope at young girls' breasts,
From vicious porno-loving males
Who quickly jerk to feeble crests
And soil her legs with rotting snails.

They lick her mouth with boozy tongues
And drag her through the oral noose.
They buy her heart, her pride, her lungs,
Her blood - and pickle them in filthy juice.
They grovel for religious wives
Who live in worlds of polished chintz,
They snigger through disgusting lives
Depraving girls with tawdry hints.

They'll never peer behind her mask
Or watch her playing with a child –
They'll never stroll and bathe and bask
In love with her when sex goes wild
As I have done on sugar days.
They'll never feel her fingers turn
Like dancers in a loving haze,
Or see her when she wants to learn.

They wash their cars and now their lawns
And moralise about the Pill,
With plastic teeth and painful corns
Alert for any worthless thrill.
Their daughters go to Grammar Schools
(Their panties clean, their minds sincere)
And spend their lives obeying rules
And never seeing Daddy leer.

I'd teach those men to sneer and grin
By throwing acid in their eyes.
I'd boot their flimsy faces in
And laugh to hear their squeaky cries.
But subtler methods might derail
Their law-wheel more effectively:

I'll send them hymens through the mail
And give their daughters LSD!

James MacVeigh

NIETZSCHE'S BIRTHDAY

Ferny sat in a cloud of ozone practising fillet welds behind Henderson's screens. The process fascinated him; the crackle of the current, the pool of bright metal moving in total blackness. He lifted his rod when he felt Barrow's hand on his shoulder; the lilac light went out.

'Where is the skiving get?' said Barrow.

Ferny shoved up his eyeshield. Under its crust of slag the weld cooled into a perfect herringbone pattern.

'Henderson? Trap three.'

Getting down on his knees in the toilets Barrow could see, under the bog door, Henderson's boots which still bore their distinctive traces of red lead. One day, when he had fallen asleep in the dinner hour, Wogga had painted them and tied the laces together. Then he'd dropped a bin full of scrap iron right behind Henderson's head. Henderson invited such assaults; he was a bit naive, a bit too serious, although everyone agreed he was one of the lads.

'Now then 'Enderson!' Barrow affected an army sergeant's bellow. 'The shareholders aren't paying you sixteen quid a week to abuse yourself over pictures of naked women in company time! Just get yourself out here lad or I'll kick you up the 'ole so 'ard you'll be shittin' out the top of your head!'

The silence was broken only by the sound of a turning page. Barrow ran the tap. Henderson listened apprehensively. Water started showering over the bog door. Henderson plunged out.

'Ey! What the fuck! A bloke can't even improve his mind in this place without somebody interferin'!'

'You dirty bastard!' Barrow pulled the magazine out of Henderson's overalls, flipped through it and stuck it back. 'How you fixed for a booze up next Friday?'

'What's it in aid of?'

'Not in aid of owt. You don't need an excuse do you?'

'I'll have to tell Brenda something.' Old Gobby walked in, attracted by all the shouting. As the amenities attendant he was justified in considering the hardware his responsibility. They called him Gobby because he had no teeth; he wore them only for weddings and funerals.

'Boof up?' said Gobby.

'My mate from Crosfields was telling me about this new club what's opened in Manchester - the New Luxor Club its called.'

'New Lukfor Club?' said Gobby.

'A real good night it is. They've got strippers on.'

'Ftripperf!' said Gobby.

'Strippers!' said Henderson.

'You can booze until two o'clock in the morning.'

'Two o'clock!?' said Gobby.

'It's only a dollar for membership and two bob for a supper ticket.'

'What about transport?' said Henderson.

'A dollar?' said Gobby.

'I can get a minibus for thirty bob. What do you reckon?'

'Aye! Strippers eh? I'll have to tell Brenda something though.'

'I'll put you down then.'

Barrow put Henderson down on the back of an engineering drawing.

'And what about you Gobby? Do you a bit of good mate. I bet you've not had a hard on since VE night.'

'I'd like to Barrow but itf me bowlf night.'

'Bowls?' said Barrow.

'Aye, we've got floodlightf now.'

'Floodlights?'

'We're fecond int league. I couldn't let ladf down.'

'Second?' said Barrow.

'Ey Barrow?' said Gobby, 'are you takin' t'piff?'

'All right then Gobby luv. You'll just have to get Henderson to tell you all about it when he comes back. All we need now is another eleven to fill the bus.'

'Ferny'll go' said Henderson, 'and don't forget Sikorski.' Barrow grinned:

'Aye! Sikorski!'

Sikorski was a queer hawk: he was Polish for a start. That wasn't his real name but at least it did begin with the same letter as his real name which was generally considered unpronounceable. Even the foreman called him Sikorski. His Christian name was unpronounceable too. He wore a pair of pince nez which he reckoned had been with him all through the labour camps of Kazakhstan and the Second World War, which he got into by walking to Palestine to join the RAF. Nobody knew just how much of Sikorski's stories to believe. He was never caught out bullshitting in areas where he could be checked, but, on the other hand, he never seemed to take anything seriously. He had a trick of saying something apparently very profound, pausing to let it sink in, then opening his big mouth, full of oversized horsy teeth, and laughing his head off. He was articulate to the point of eccentricity, probably the result of being married to a schoolteacher and having a passion for Victorian novels.

Barrow found Sikorski and Fleet the student apprentice in a corner of the Instrument Workshop. Fleet was spending some time in each department; he'd already done six months with Barrow in the Fitting Shop. Sikorski was sitting on a tool box eating meat paste butties and drinking coffee out of a pint cup emblazoned with roses. Fleet sat on a bench reading a book. It was baggin time.

'Fuck me! Don't you lot ever do any work?'

'Greetings Barrow' Sikorski looked up. 'The increased mental strain of our profession necessitates, shall we say, a concomitantly longer period of recuperation.'

'What's this rubbish he's filling your head with?' He looked at Fleet's book.

'Nietzsche.' said Fleet.

'Bless you' said Barrow.

'What?'

'I thought you sneezed?'

'That's the bloke's name you ignorant puddin.'

'Ignorant puddin?' Barrow put on a tone of deep hurt. 'Is that the way to speak about the man who taught you all there is to know about the Salt Plant centrifuge gearbox? Here, give us a butchers.' He took the book and read: *'Nietzsche was born in Rocken, in the Prussian province of Saxony, on October 15 1844. His father, Ludwig Nietzsche, a Lutheran minister and the son of a minister, was thirty one...'*

'You read that very well Barrow, but I saw your lips move.'

'I've not got time to hang about here muggin up on old Kraut headcases. On to the real reason for my visit. It just so happens we're having a do, and you two gentlemen, on account of your superior breeding, have been fortunate enough to get on my short list.'

He described the attractions of the New Luxor.

'What's it in aid of?' asked Fleet.

'Neechy's birthday' said Barrow. 'It's next Friday, October 15. Your mate Neechy would have been 118 if he'd lived. He is dead in't he?'

'Course.'

'Well that's worth celebrating then in't it?'

'A festival of Dionysus!' said Sikorski in ironical wonderment.

'That too!' said Barrow. 'Better bring a spare pair of binks Sikorski. What you're going to see will probably melt them crappy Polish bottle ends!'

He put them both down and left. That Sikorski! thought Barrow, he's unbelievable! He could talk for half an hour without anyone knowing what the fuck he was on about, yet any workshop get-together and he was there straight away: bowls, darts, cricket matches, booze-ups! And a bloody good sport he was as well. Get him and Stanier together and we won't need any comedians!

Ignoring the bell and its notice *'Please ring for attention'* Barrow slipped under the counter and into the gloomy body of the stores. At the centre of this maze of racks was the office, or rather the cubicle, of Ernie Hardman. Sikorski called it the Temple of Aphrodite. From floor to ceiling, on all three sides, were sellotaped pictures of women. Hardman obviously had a preference, not to say fetish, for big tits. Even the most grossly inflated five gallon dugs with areolas the size of dustbin lids failed to jar his aesthetic sense. His pursuit of size knew no limit. In the bottom drawer of the filing cabinet, always kept locked, was his collection of hard-core. Ernie, reading, didn't notice Barrow creeping up on him. Barrow got close enough to make out the print over his shoulder. Together

127

they silently, synchronously read: '*His hand moved feverishly over the smooth silky border of her stocking tops and on to the soft resilience of her magnificent thighs ...*' Taking a breath as silently as possible Barrow bellowed out the next sentence as though he were addressing a large audience.

'*His hot throbbing member forced itself urgently against her...!*'

'Wha!? Ey!?..Bloodyell!!' Ernie jumped violently, spilling tea over a pile of requisitions.

'Barrow! You dozy bugger! What's the bloody game sneakin in like that!? Jeezus I nearly had a flamin heart attack!'

'Sneakin Ernie? I could have loaded half the stores onto a ten ton truck and you wouldn't have heard.'

'Spilt me piggin tea now an all!'

'I don't know how you get away with it Ernie, honest I don't.'

'Get away with it?! I'll tell you how I get away with it. Who the hell d'you think'd do this job for eight quid a week? Cooped up in here all day, no winders to look out of, no-one to talk to. Can't go out for a walk round like you whenever I feel like it! Get away with it he says!'

'Very homely though in't it Ernie? Family photos on the walls. This IS the missis here in't it? This blonde piece with the big knockers?'

'Well how would you like to be starin at steel bulkheads all day?'

'Say no more Ernie. I've come to offer you something better than all this paper rubbish. I've come to offer you...' He leaned close, staring hard into Ernie's wide open eyes. '...the real thing!'

Jud Stanier's face took on a look of concern as the pitch of his mechanical saw altered from a low, rasping grunt to a higher, skidding squeak. Barrow offered an observation:

'You could do with more skilly on that Jud.'

'Gerrout! I don't want that stuff splashin all over t'place!'

'They say it gives you cancer of the scrotum.'

'Scrotum?'

'Balls Jud.'

'Aye. It sounds a right load of balls.'

'Can't imagine a company of this size exposing its workers to such a risk though can you Jud?'

Jud grinned but refused to take the bait. He switched off the saw and took a new blade from a nearby locker. Inside the locker door was pinned a photo of V.I.Lenin. Next to it was an unfaded patch about the same size where J.V.Stalin had been. Stalin had been taken down following the criticism of the Cult of the Personality at the Twentieth Congress of the Soviet Communist Party. As his body had been transferred from the Mausoleum to the Kremlin Wall so Jud's photo had migrated from the locker door to his tool box. Some reckoned Sikorski had talked him into it; others thought Jud had moved it just to have Sikorski on. Lenin looked up inquisitively with a gaze of penetrating comprehension; it was one of the 1917 photographs. He seemed to be saying: *'It's that 316 stainless Jud, wears blades out in ragtime.'* Jud turned off the coolant valve and looked closely at the six inch diameter bar in the machine.

'It's this bloody 316 stainless' he said, 'wears blades out in ragtime. This is the third I've had in today.'

'I'll have the old one off you mate, they make good scrapers.' Barrow crouched down by the machine and put the new blade in. He knew Jud was a sick man, ever since he had been gassed ten years ago on the Phosgene. He had difficulty breathing. His face was a mass of broken purple veins.

It wasn't long before Barrow got him to go over the incident again. It intrigued Barrow. He was constantly on the lookout for stories of industrial atrocities or incidents which illustrated the cruel, inhuman side of capitalism. Jud's case seemed to be all those things and more. His treatment, it appeared, verged on the criminal. In fact Barrow was almost ready to agree that they'd tried to do Jud in.

"I was working on the Thionyl Chloride then; used to be down the bottom end, it's closed down now. Let me fill you in on the background." Jud was always keen on the background: it must have been his Marxist training.

"Remember Barrow in them days, we're talking now about 1952, just after your lot lost its nerve and let that bastard Churchill in, in them days this place was completely unorganised. This wasn't the Liverpool Docks you know, just a piddling little Warrington Chemical works. Half the labour was trained up bog Irish, not that I've got owt against the Irish, it's just that, historically they've always represented a pool of docile, cheap labour for British Capitalism to draw on..." Barrow saw the danger. If he didn't head him off it could be eyes down for a lecture on Cromwell's wars, Wood's Halfpenny and the Potato Famine.

129

"But you sorted that out, eh Jud?"

"I did my bit towards raising consciousness. Before long I had the whole yard in the old Chemical Workers Union; this was before it merged into the T and G you realise. Next thing you know we're on strike. I was Steward of course. The first bloody strike this company had had since it started forty years ago! What an eye-opener that was Barrow! That toffee-nosed get Saunders wouldn't even speak to us! He was works manager. Wouldn't even speak to us! Anyone would think we'd shit on his desk. He thought we'd fold before the end of the week. They got the bosses trying to run the plants. What a laugh! The maintenance men told us about it. Dashing about like blue-arsed flies they were. This was before the days of big, fancy control rooms Barrow. We weren't sat on chairs pressing buttons like they do now mate. Anyroad, three weeks later the whole works is flat on its arse. Saunders talked to us then all right. Tried to come the hard-nosed stuff at first; offered us half of what we'd asked for, but the lads weren't having any. Solid as a bloody rock! And some of these buggers hadn't even been in a Union a year ago! Never underestimate the proletariat Barrow! All we were doing in the union was just channeling the discontent that'd been building up for years. You can shit on the working class for only so long Barrow. What was it Engels said?.."

Barrow considered quotations an even more dangerous distraction. Jud had an unnerving habit of digging out books from his locker and rummaging through them for underlined passages.

"Then when you came back off your summer holidays?"

"Then when I comes back I'm on the night-shift; leading hand I was. Patterson had left a note in the book; he was the Plant Manager. 'Increase main feed flows to the reactor to four point five and twenty eight metres cubed an hour'. Well you'd have to use the auxiliary lines on those rates, anyone new that. And it wasn't unusual to run the plant flat out at night because of all the shit it pushed out. Jeeesus! If the locals could have seen us they'd have had the law on us!"

"Same as the power station; they just don't bother controlling smoke density at night."

"Course not Barrow. It's maximisation of profit int it? You don't think big business cares about stinking out a few local slums do you? It wasn't dropping on Saunders' house now was it? He was living in bloody Lymm, damn near twelve miles away!"

"But that auxiliary line had gone duff the week before hadn't it?"

"Gone duff!? There was an expansion piece there with a crack in it you could get your hand in. It was down in the book as a maintenance request but they were too pulled out to get to it: the usual thing. Didn't even have a bloke spare to spade it off. Anyroad it would have meant a shut down and this twat Patterson was trying to make a name for himself by breaking all production records. So about eleven o clock I goes down and opens the valve. Now there's another thing; that valve was as stiff as arseholes. I reckon some bastard had tightened up the gland on it. Next thing I know I'm in the middle of a bloody great cloud of phosgene. Five minutes in that stuff Barrow and you're dead! Its a bloody killer! My first reaction is to run like hell. But somebody's got to shut this off, its coming straight out of A forty ton liquid stock tank. So I'm wrestling with the flaming valve trying to shut it down again. How the hell I got to that phone I'll never know! I was in the Borough for forty eight hours on pure oxygen; that's all they can do. It was touch and go. Then I was off for three months. When I comes back in they gives me this bloody job on the saw. I'm not much good at running up and down stairs anymore."

"You reckon he'd set it all up though, Patterson?"

"Well what can you think? It's impossible to know for sure. I thought it was just one of those things till Harry got talking to me. See, they used to leak test those lines with a nitrogen purge before we went onto the high rates, especially if we'd not been using them for a while. They'd done this while I'd been on holiday and found the crack. I thought I'd got them then, but the only real evidence is in the Maintenance Book. Comes to look for it and its bloody well lost int it? Bloody well lost see? And even if Patterson's in the dock and has to agree he knew that line was in a dangerous condition he'd probably say those rates could have been met without using the auxiliary lines. How's a bleedin halfwit magistrate going to know any different?"

"Christ Jud it makes you think!"

"I'm not saying he was trying to do me Barrow, but he got what he wanted in the end. After I came in here that arsehole creeper Gibson gets the Steward's job. It all adds up mate."

He restarted the saw and turned on the coolant valve.

"Its fishy about that book I reckon Jud. He must have felt guilty to get rid of it."

"Them Maintenance books did get lost sometimes Barrow, but that bugger vanished the next day according to Harry."

"And Patterson? What happened to him?"

131

"He disappeared too, about a month later. They say he got a kick up the hole for the accident but look where he is now?"

"Aye, works manager at St. Helen's in charge of a place four times the size of this."

"They think I'm a bit cracked in here Barrow, you know. Not about this; I don't go blabbing it to everyone, I've got more oil in my can. I know it's a serious matter and I know I can trust your discretion as a fellow trade unionist. But some of these young uns! Harold McMillan's told them they've never had it so good and they're running around in cars, up to the eyeballs in HP. They're getting as much as eighteen quid a week on bonus and they think the sun shines out of Hodgkin's arse. They don't want to listen to me, but it'll change Barrow. They're living now on the fruits of our struggle. They haven't had to go through it like we have, but their turn'll come! That's the only real teacher Barrow: struggle, confrontation! Its a dialectical necessity. They won't read Marxism but they can't avoid living it! Their turn'll come!"

What was going on inside Fleet's head? That day, as usual during the dinner hour, he sat on a flaking length of creosoted pine and read Nietzsche down by the canal. But why Nietzsche, that lonely, loony prophet of the Superman? Sikorski had something to do with it but it wasn't that simple. At first he'd fed Fleet his own passions: Jane Austen, George Eliot and Trollope. Revulsion was all Fleet felt. The delicate ironies of Miss Austen couldn't enliven a subject of mind-numbing narrowness; the inflated turgidities of old Horseface bored him rigid; and the superficial narratorese of tripy Trollope reminded him of the soulless, middle-class stories of Somerset Maugham he'd had to slog through a school.

Then Sikorski brought in Joyce; volume one of the two volumed Hamburg Odyssey Press edition of *Ulysses*. At the end of the week he was asking for volume two. The poetry, the fierce, concentrated individualism, the apparent omniscience, the dazzling melange of styles: he was bewitched. He went out and bought it: it was the first book he'd ever owned. Almost immediately followed *A Portrait of the Artist, Dubliners, Stephen Hero, Exiles* and even *Finnegans Wake*. The tone of proud separateness was exactly in tune with his own adolescent sense of isolation. Sikorski was stunned. He'd never been able to read Joyce, and what he had struggled through confirmed his impression that Lawrence had been right in calling it 'old fag-ends and cabbage stumps.'

He decided to test his prodigy further. Nietzsche was the natural progenitor of Joyce; the quintessential philosophic base of that post-Yeatsian elitism.

Besides there was an arrogance in Fleet that needed tempering. What better to subdue this proto proletarian polymath than the dense, allusive ironies of Nietzsche. Writing of such compact rapidity that even Freud found it bewildering. Fleet struggled with the text. The meaning came and went like the sound of a distant brass band on a windy day, but what he did understand intoxicated him. As with Joyce, in which there must have been a hundred words which weren't even in his dictionary, he was gripped spasmodically by the transfixing sensation of a great mind setting up reverberations in his own. Nietzsche's manic tone illuminated his grey, factory existence like sheet lightning.

It was as much an emotional response as an intellectual one; a response which Sikorski hadn't reckoned with. He observed Fleet's reaction with alarm, admiration and amusement. Sometimes he felt like a hedgesparrow watching a cuckoo bursting its nest. He tried to flatten Fleet by probing his comprehension of such Nietzschean mysteries as the theory of Eternal Recurrence but he remained uncrushed like a religious zealot in contact with the source of some life giving truth:

"Only an idiot demands total understanding" he said with an eerie poise, "I've reached a point where I recognise that anything I can understand straight away isn't worth reading."

It was a remark worthy of Sikorski himself; he laughed out loud.

"Perhaps Stanier could lend you Das Kapital, such a passion for Teutonic mysticism should be indulged to the full."

"I've had some stuff off him but it doesn't touch me here." Fleet put a hand to his heart melodramatically.

"I imagine" said Sikorski, "that Vladimir Ilyich was aiming for a higher organ."

"Besides" said Fleet, "the print on those pamphlets reminds me of the Watchtower".

They both laughed.

As for Sikorski, well, Fleet had come to the conclusion that he was either a genius or a phoney; if such divergent options can be called a conclusion. Perhaps the thing he admired most about Sikorski wasn't his knowledge, or the erudition, and certainly not the taste which he so often disagreed with, but the style. The elegant ironies of his latest mentor contrasted sharply with the honest, dogmatic simplicity of Stanier whom he had spent so much time talking to in the Fitting Shop. But was there ever an adolescent who preferred the ethical to the aesthetic mode of life?

Stanier saw the familiar signs; the cynicism, the self-absorption, the single minded passion for judging social events by an abstract moral code without reference to their historical context. And, following on from that, a profound ignorance of European history itself. Fleet had a keen mind and an argumentative eloquence but he was, Jud reckoned, on the way to a lower middle-class job, probably in the drawing office. Some of Stanier's points had left Fleet dumbfounded but his as yet unrecognised interest in preserving the status quo placed him beyond recovery; a lost soul, a hopeless case. Especially now he was doing six months with that bugger Sikorski!

Barrow needed one more to fill the bus. He knew just the bloke and planned to detour on his way back from a job on the Glauber Salt plant. As soon as he walked into the Carbon Electrode Machining Shop with his labourer Owen and his apprentice Trellie, he heard Screawn shout above the noise of his lathe:

'Hey Barrow! Here a minute!'

Because it was next to the Chlorine Production Unit the average temperature in the shop was eighty degrees. Screawn was an extraordinary sight: carbonized, purple and glossy, hair stood on end, with sweat tracks down the side of his face, he looked like something off the cover of a science fiction magazine. They reckoned he wore nothing under his overalls. He liked to grip Barrow about the new starters in the Bagging Plant.

'Got a fag?' said Screawn.

'What's that behind your ear?' said Owen.

'A brain. What's behind yours?'

'Fuckinell! You got out the wrong side this morning!'

'To me the outside is the wrong side.'

'Every one a gem' Barrow offered him an Embassy tipped.

'You don't want them coupons do you Barrow luv?'

'What are you saving up for? A mechanical cunt?'

Screawn's activities were well known: he was the works' ram.

'I've already got one; it's fixed between the wife's legs. Fuck me! I tried it this morning! No kidding, it was like sticking it between two house bricks! Talking of cunt though...'

'Subject normal' said Owen drily.

134

'Have you seen that one on the stitching machine with Big Irma?'

'No.'

'Real horny Barrow luv. Just left school, fifteen or sixteen. Should see her skirts! What a leg!'

'Stretches right up to her arse does it?'

'S only flesh though in't it Scraggy' said Owen, 'Think of all the mither you'd have to go through to get your end away. Is it worth it for a few hours' pleasure?'

'Anyroad if she's only that old she's not going to be interested in a dirty old get like you' said Barrow. 'Sounds to me like she's more in our Trellie's line.'

Trellie looked uncomfortable. He glanced at the big clock at the end of the shop hoping to flush Barrow into an early retreat.

'I'm not greedy' said Screawn spreading his hand palm downward in a gesture of altruism. 'I'll let Trellie here break her in. After all its a big jump from candles to a hampton like mine.'

'Spoken like a gentleman' said Owen

'What do you say Trellie? Shall we get Scraggy to send her round Satur- day night?'

'Oh aye. I think I can fit her in.' Trellie tried to play along. it was the only way.

'Can she fit you in though!' cackled Screawn. 'That's the question.'

'See to it then Scraggy. I've been getting a bit worried about Trellie late- ly. He's wanking so much he can't hold a chisel steady these days. What he needs is a good, steady supply of young, fresh, succulent, virgin hole.'

'Don't Barrow!' moaned Screawn lifting his leg off the floor, 'I'll get a hard on!'

'That reminds me. Next Friday we're going to a strip club in Manchester; I suppose I can put you down?'

As they left Screawn held up a polished black thumb. Suddenly, as if it had just occurred to him, he shouted:

'You're not taking Trellie as well are you?'

'He can't make it' said Barrow, 'He sees his married piece on Friday nights.'

Owen, behind him, flexed his arm and winked with his whole face. Screawn started to laugh, stopped, and then raised his eyebrows.

'Perhaps he is an' all!' he bellowed, projecting his own obsessions onto innocent young Trellie.

At the end of the afternoon, as Barrow was getting his moped out of the bike sheds he saw Henderson crackling bluely on the Caustic Shed roof.

'Doing some overtime then you grabbing get?' he shouted.

'No, just practising my fillets' said Henderson.

'Hey! The strip club trip - tell Brenda it's in aid of Neechy's birthday'

'Neechy?' shouted Henderson.

'Bloody Neechy'. Barrow bumped over the wet rails and headed for the time office. Henderson turned to Ferny who was squatting on the vent fan casing holding a bunch of number eight rods.

'Must be that new starter on the horizontal borer'.

Peering through his violet, slag-spattered eyeshield he struck the arc again.

Ken Clay

POEM

Age long, life long juice of my body
flow to the sea
and run down to the deep ocean buried silt,
Let my bones welcome the plow,
kiss the sweet earth
and hobnob with the ground worms.
My flesh ignite with the air,
take it, and be taken
in a whirlpool of flesh and air.

A.R. Whitfield

IN MEMORIUM

In a lonely field in Flanders
There's a stick of rhubarb standing;
It standers
As a monumole

136

To Captain Richard Prongs.
It commemoroles his landing
In Flanding
By parachute
In his officer's suit
(Dashing
Richard, devil-may-care
don't-give-a-hoot)
From a very tall horse.
This tall equine brute
(Whose name one should know
Was Walter)
Didn't want to go
To war and called a halter
At a field in Flanders
Where rhubarb now standers
As a monumole to his rider
Who floated down like a deflating prider
Lions pricked by a thorn
Or worn
Down by five years in the trenches
Sat astride a horse;
There's nothing worse
Than riding up to your fetlocks in British and Frenches
In the muck and bullets trenches
And nothing to show but menches
In despatches
With mud on your stirrups
And blood on your spats:
And that's
Mere infantry blood
And not very good
For your boots
Not that the nobility gives many hoots
Especially when they're dead.
And let it be said,
Solitary, noble, deceasted Captain Richard Prongs
Lies all alone with his wrongs,
Aloof from the masses
The bleeding classes
Who never
Ever
Understand.
The late

Great
Captain Richard Prongs
Lies remembered
By a solitary stick of rhubarb
That is forever
England.

Les Barker

NATIONAL DRIED AND ALL BRAN

when i was young and in my jeans
and shirt all empire made
i played the national slot machine
and i was never paid
the U.S. kids they rocked and rolled
over here the kids just rolled
on the crest of a brylcreem wave
while jets and sharks went shootin pool
with names like larry and buzz
it was weetabix and off to school
for post war prefab us
suez and conscription
bromide in the tea
the age of non description
rationed by the B.B.C.
woodbines work and wireless
playing mantovani's strings
they'd service with a smile us
robbery with violins
the gaffer was a bastard
who fought the war with quids
he thought he had us mastered
and i suppose he did
"up yer arse wi yer fuckin job"
said a cinema full of teds
bill haley opened up his gob
and they ripped the place to shreds
for about 2 years they had their fling
and then like any square
they married - did the proper thing
for the slippers and the easy chair
the party political pantomime
its wondrous ways to work

138

says wedlocked slavery can be mine
i demand the right to smerk
here's to the Youth Of Britain
YOB let' say for short
is your future to be a ballpoint pen
on the ration book of thought

John Cooper Clarke

SATURDAY'S SAVINGS

There was never enough money for the following week after everything had been paid out on a Saturday.

Richard stood leaning against the mantle watching his mother pushing a penny in one pile and a threepenny bit into another. She rested her head on her arm and sighed.

"Jawch" she shook her head, "I'll have to owe Davies the shop another fourpence for last week That will be three and six I owe him altogether. He won't like it."

"Cut the milk down by a pint main, we will have to go without in our tea," said Richard.

She looked at him and tried to smile. "Good for us the milk is see ... can't afford to cut down on it ... where will you and your father get your strength from...

"We'll manage main, don't worry."

She looked again at her figures and moved two pence from one pile to another. Then quietly she said, "P'haps I will tell George to leave one pint less. I owe him two bob, too." She blinked back a tear and then went upstairs.

Richard turned and looked at the fire. He felt the bitterness twist and burn his stomach. His mother worrying about tradesmen and food. The worry making her grey years too soon; making those once bright blue eyes dull and shallow. She was a small woman, but strong and good willed. It hurt her to owe money to anyone - but it seemed the only way for her to keep her family fed and clothed. Pennypinching and scraping was the birthright of our family - for we had always been in coal: and consequently had always been arranged and pushed aside by the colliery owners like animals more than human beings.

Yes, he was bitter: angry at watching his mother tormenting herself about who should have the extra penny or ha'penny. And he, too, didn't help by being a shift short last week and his father two shifts short. Not that it was his own fault -he had gone to the pit only to be told there was no work ... come again tomorrow ... there might be work tomorrow. Colliery owners didn't care about feeding hungry mouths ... Children could die and old people could die, it did not concern them. All they worried about was coal and keeping the worker begging.

"Damn them?" he cursed and spat into the fire.

It was still early evening and the sun was about a foot from dropping behind the Drumma mountain. He went outside and took his last but one Woodbine from the packet that held five. He looked at the wall that hid the garden from Dudly Street. It was not a well kept garden; his father and he were not attached to flowers and the like. As a result the weeds grow happily and everywhere. The fence between them and Mrs. Williams was broken and what was standing was rotten. All the gardens on Rectory Road were the same; some a little better, of course, but in the main the menfolk were not lovers of gardening.

His mind was full of ideas as he looked from the wall to the lavatory, then to the rear of the house to the broken fence. The tap next to the back door was always dripping.

"Dic, hello Dic."

Richard turned and faced little Wally from next door. "Hello bach. Out late aren't you? When I was your age I was abed hours since."

Wally smiled. "Ah, but I'm getting a big boy now. My Uncle Donald said so when he gave me a penny."

"A whole penny!" said Richard.

Wally nodded proudly. "Dic?" he asked slowly.

"What?"

"Do you dream at all?"

Richard looked at him with amusement. "Dream, Wally? Yes, sometimes."

"Oh good. 'Cos I do too."

Richard lit his last Woodbine and drew hard on the blue smoke with enjoyment.

"Tell me about your dreams, Dic."

Richard was silent for a moment as he considered this unusual request. "Well, Wally, bach ... dreaming is a wonderful pastime; so easy, so cheap, so effortless ... It can be done at day or at the night time ... more often at night though..."

"Yes, it is at night that I do it best," said Wally.

"You can climb mountains, win races, drive cars, ride on trains, have a good, regular job with good money, you can travel on trips to the seaside in a train instead of walking to Jersy Marine like we've got to ... there is nothing one can't do in a dream. I dream about having money to spare. If I had money to spare I would be able to buy my main a nice, big house with a fancy garden and a gardener to tend it ... I would buy her a car and a chauffeur to drive it ... I would buy a headstone for my poor brother's grave ..."

"Which brother is that?" asked Wally.

"Bert. He died in the colliery before you were born. A good lad he was too. But there it is killed trying to scrape a living from those grasping bosses!"

"My dreams are about horses mostly, Dic. I don't know why, but I'm riding them very fast and there is a lot of shouting and everything. But I am up there with them ... I am one of the best."

Richard laughed kindly. "P'haps we've got a jockey 'ere, is it. Walter Williams rides the favourite! Walter Williams wins the Derby! Dreams are wonderful, Wally, bach. You keep on dreaming and from time to time we will have a chat and swop them. It should be very interesting."

And with that the lad's mother was shouting, "Wally!"

The lad made no move to go indoors.

"Wally Wall-y!"

"I had better go in, Dic," he said.

Richard nodded. "Ay, we don't want her in a mad temper, do we?"

"No," he said and left Richard to his thoughts.

Richard waited for a few minutes in the silence of the early evening before going indoors, He thought about various things: last Saturday's match at the Knoll, his walk with Brenda Bando up past the Ivy Tower on Sunday night, the leg-pulling at work the following day about that walk. And did he worry as Terry Samuel began to talk in his loud echoing voice, telling everybody within a hundred yards radius and his father due out of the canteen any second. He had sweated then for his father was strict about such things. Heavy with the Welsh baptists was Joseph James. This religious trait could be traced back along the family line to his grandfather whose roots were firmly imbedded in the rich soil of Kidwelly, Camarthenshire, Wales.

Robert King

SANTIAGO SUNSHINE

How black the sea rolls
against this solid shore,
but how it leaves a slime of blood fresh from the ocean's floor.
how the high specked seagull climbs,
its lonely voice like a death knell chimes
lost in the ocean's roar.

Now the winter drags its cloak across this passing year,
but how like fast approaching night
it shrinks the Earth with fear.
What gangling marionette of death
has played its song and breathed its breath,
what nation paid so dear.

What superstructured might
has stabbed the day and breathed the night,
and thrown its shape against the light
that poured across from Chile.
For what deadly masquerade
was this bloodshed chess game played,
that needed all that many slayed
that drank the sun, in Chile.

The tank and gun and fascist boot
made human life its legal loot,
it's torn the flower from the rest
and ripped the soul of Chile.

All this to satisfy the wealth
of some faceless fiends who used their stealth,
to finally destroy the health
of youth and love, in Chile.

The wind it howls and pleads and screams
throughout this deadly night,
passing on such stenchfilled scenes

ever present in our dreams and never far from sight.

Let our fury like stormclouds swell
in all determined might,
let this thunder be the knell
of those purveyors and their hell,
those butchers of the light.

Let those ghoulish souls be weighed
in all of mankind's sight
and reckoned up with all they slayed.
Against their grisly masquerade
all humankind must fight.

Santiago sunshine,
blackened by the night
Santiago sunshine
soon it will be light,
soon it will be light.

I.E.Reed

OLD ALBERT

He had scraped through the years with empty pockets
But had never known the poverty of intellect
That beggared his neighbours
When they poured their growing wages down their throats

lie only joined them after a page or two
Even than the drinking was behind the talk
Which he steered with strategic facts
What passed in him for drunken aggression
Was tolerance at a low ebb
When drunk, his isolation closed in and alienated him
From the family who walled him out with ignorance
And sent him scurrying to his bed and books

When I caught him like this I would corner him
And spike his socialist guns with laughter
I loved the passion in his face as he argued
Circling fists in emphatic motion too

143

Long into the nights we performed
While his petrified wife sat straining
waiting for the angry word or blow
Expecting an explosion that never came

Father and daughter we might have been
Two shades of a hue we were, flame and spark
Better than drink or books it was
Socialist garbles in a pit kitchen

Vivien Leslie

STRANGE GRAFFITI

The past is a fast, and far receding wall
where strange graffiti have been near-erased,
blurred by so many winters' sodden fall.
Those savage words whose fury's gone to waste
are echoed now by new, old anguished cries
torn from the living flesh, and dripping blood
upon cold stones.
Each child that dies
maimed in a world of plenty, swells the flood
of guilt sweeping us all along, whether or not we care.
We know it in our bones. The dead past knew
and left unheeded records of despair.
And we can only cry - what can we do?

We can try love - for hate will drown us all.
That, is the writing on the wall.

Vera Leff

AFTER AN ULTIMATUM

I have been here before –
in this waste of littered slag-heaps, derelict huts,
wrecked cars.

I have already smelt
this stink of dumped rubbish
ashes, rotting cabbage, rusty tins.

Too often my root have squelched
ice-wet across this weed-choked sludge
mined with broken bottles.

I had hoped
never to shudder again in this February wind,
trudging towards a grey horizon
humped only with more slag-heaps.

Pat Arrowsmith

REMEMBER

remember

when we walked through vendelpark together
with all those hippies sprawling on the grass around us

keep to the path you said

yes i said

all the way to Vietnam

Keith Armstrong

ENCOUNTER AT LONDON BRIDGE

I was just enjoying a quiet drink in the refreshment room at London Bridge Station when a perfect stranger came up and said - "I see you're a member of the Society for Planetary Travel."

I opened my mouth to explain that the badge I was wearing was for members of the Stoke Pages Temperance Society, but it wasn't tea I was drinking and explanations can be difficult sometimes. Anyway, it seemed a promising opening to a conversation, and it isn't often that a pretty girl seeks my company. I said she was a perfect stranger and 'perfect' is just the right word to describe her looks.

"You're a member then?" I asked.

"In a way I am," she said. "I'm from Venus."

145

I wondered if I'd heard aright. She was just like any other girl - except that she had four eyes; no, she hadn't. I get a bit of trouble with double vision now and again. I tried to guess her age; she looked to be about twenty, but what did that mean on Venus? The year on Venus is two hundred and twenty five over three hundred and sixty five and a quarter comes to ... but I can't do sums like that in my head and I wasn't sure that it shouldn't be twenty multiplied by three hundred and sixty five and a quarter over two hundred and twenty five.

"From Venus!" I said. "Where's your saucer?"

She stared at me. "I haven't a cup yet," she said, "so - oh! I see what you mean. You surely don't believe that nonsense?"

I took the hint and fetched her a cup of tea. "Then how?"

"Simple," she said. "Just a matter of telebiotransitation."

"Of course, of course," I said. "I can't imagine why I didn't think of it myself. Any special reason for coming here?

She explained that they'd been listening to our radio broadcasts for the past fifty years; previously they'd been quite unaware of our existence. Because of the very thick clouds around Venus, they can never see any stars or even the sun. So when they managed to understand our broadcasts it was the talks on astronomy which really excited them, especially when TV began - Patrick Moore is a household name on Venus too. The broadcasts stimulated them to think of space travel, and, as their scientific development is far in advance of ours, they soon managed it. Of course, they learnt a great many things from our broadcasts - not all on the credit side.

The trouble was that the more impressionable Venusians had been adopting some of the customs they saw here. This was a matter of great concern to the authorities, and it was decided to send investigators here to discover the reasons for the curious practices which were leading their people astray. One of the investigators went to the Soviet Union and came back an absolute mine of information about the production of pig iron in Omsk (or was it Tomak?). Another went to China and returned humming "The East is Red" and reciting the thoughts of Chairman Mao. A third went to America and became an expert on Watergate - he was very nearly appointed Attorney General -but not on anything useful. And now she had come to England, hoping for better success.

"What have you found so far?" I asked. "Well, I had an interview with a parliamentary under secretary, I think he was, but all I got from him was a lot of waffle about a blue print for a new society; wind of change; in this day and age; at this moment in time; etc., etc.

Then I tried people in the street, but that was no good either. It was 'Sorry, I've a train to catch' or 'The wife's expecting me' or 'You'd better ask my husband' or 'Not today, thank you'." I ought to mention that she said that she'd made an intensive study of English before she came; certainly she had an astonishing fluency.

"But you'll help me, won't you'" she pleaded, giving me a lovely smile that made me wish I was fifty years younger.

"Of course," I said. "What do you want to know?"

She plunged straight into the deep end. "All these religions - Christianity, Buddhism, Bingo; however did you come by them?"

I knew the answer to that one. My next door neighbour is a rabid atheist, and when one of these earnest folk spreading the Gospel comes to his door old Sam lets fly so that all the street can hear.

"Religion," I said, "is based on fear and ignorance -" but I got no further. A bunch of football fans came in, arguing loudly about a game. I hoped that Venus's vocabulary didn't extend to the language some of them were using, but it did. She frowned.

"That's another thing," she said, interrupting me. "Half our young men now spend hours charging round a muddy field with a ball. At first they didn't understand the game - they thought they had to kick the ball into the net - but now they've got the message and they're kicking and tripping each other, swearing at the referee, spitting and pulling their shorts down; real First Division stuff. And the girls are now better," she went on, looking at a pair of platform shoes hobbling past. "Our girls are going around on stilts; those that aren't nursing broken ankles. And you can well imagine that neither minis nor maxis, which are all the rage, are entirely suitable for girls on stilts.

Somebody turned on Radio 2 at full volume but fortunately only for a moment. "And of course," said Venus, "we've got groups mushrooming all over the place, each dressing more outrageously than the next, and waving their - what do you call them -guitars, isn't it? Some people thought they were musical instruments but as they were seen to be used like weapons it was soon realised that, like the painted faces, they were relics of some ancient barbaric rites. And each group has a horde of demented girls after them, screaming so that the group itself is, mercifully, inaudible. Mind you, our teenagers wouldn't fall for an elderly baldhead sucking a lollipop; no, no, - the current heart throb on Venus is a toothless ancient perpetually stoned on moths. But there are worse things than pop groups - LSD for example."

147

"Ah! You're out of date there," I said. "We changed over from £sd to decimal currency some years ago - I forget when exactly."

"15th February, 1971," she said impatiently. "I'm talking about lysurgic acid."

"Sorry I can't help you there," I said. "I didn't do any chemistry at school. If you've finished your tea, shall we go? It's a bit stuffy here."

Outside, she looked up at the huge office building which stood empty for several years. "We're building them, too," she said. "Just the outside walls, of course; if they're not going to be used, what's the point of putting in floors and stairs? But it's still a terrible waste of money, isn't it?"

"I can't agree with you," I said. "Spend three or four million pounds putting up one of these buildings; keep it empty for ten years and its worth fifty million. Good business, I call it."

Venus didn't bother to reply. "Look at these cars," she said, pointing to a line of them parked at the side of the street. "This one's Japanese, then German, French, Swedish, Japanese again and -why what's this? It's a British car! Why import all these foreign cars if you can make them yourselves?"

"But how could we sell them our cars, if we didn't buy theirs?" I was beginning to think there wasn't much brain behind her pretty face.

"It's worse on Venus," she said. "Anything you can do, we can do better. When we heard of your lorries from France coming over the Channel to Dover, going round a roundabout and then straight back across the Channel without unloading, we really took off. The thing now is to buy only those products - whether food or furniture - which have been sent round the planet and back again. I had the finger of scorn pointed at me because I was caught eating an apple straight off a tree in my garden. And my sister scarcely dares go out since she incautiously let it be known that she was breast-feeding her baby instead of adopting somebody else's baby and feeding it on powdered milk from another continent. 'Just like an animal,' the neighbours said, and their wretched little boys moo at her."

The mention of food prompted me to ask if she would like a little something, and we went to a cafe nearby. It was rather crowded but we did find room at a table where two men were intently engaged on completing a pools coupon. They left after a few minutes, and Venus, who had been observing them with curiosity, begged for enlightenment. "We heard many references to the pools on your radio and television," she said, "but couldn't quite fathom it."

"This is even more ridiculous than we'd imagined," she said, after I'd explained the pools system to her. 'You say that only about a third of the money paid in by the punters is returned by way of dividends? It's absolutely crazy."

"Crazy?" I echoed. "Not a bit of it. It's better than a gold mine for the promoters - they can't lose. You don't seem to appreciate good business."

Venus looked exasperated, but didn't pursue the subject. "We've done some work on the origins of some of your customs. Cricket, for instance, this is clearly based on the stoning of the early Christian martyrs. The Miss World contests are a reminder of some barbarous custom of ravishing virgins captured in war. Boxing and all-in wrestling are obviously in a direct line from the gladiatorial contests of ancient Rome, and the Grand National no doubt has its origin in the Charge of the Light Brigade."

I lit a cigarette to steady myself after that farrago of nonsense; she declined one, rather acidly. "It's a good thing that the tobacco plant is unknown on Venus," she remarked. "But I believe they're experimenting with a plastic substitute." I felt I could safely assure her that there wouldn't be any future for plastic tobacco.

"But why the craving for lung cancer?" she wanted to know.

"I couldn't answer immediately - I had a sudden fit of coughing. "I've been smoking for fifty years," I gasped, eventually, "so I don't think I need to worry."

"Well, I can assure you that we do worry," she said, rather heatedly. "We shan't be satisfied with a warning on a cigarette packet."

I was getting a bit annoyed myself. "Venus," I said. "You seem to think we're stupid because we let people smoke if they want to. It's a free country. But if they drink too much, we don't let them drive."

"Big deal!" said Venus. "Hundreds of people are killed on your roads every year. You don't let blind people or babies drive, either, do you? You'll be patting yourselves on the back next because you don't let monkeys drive."

If I hadn't suffered another fit of coughing at this point I think I should have said something I regretted. However, Venus must have realised that she'd gone too far; suddenly she smiled, leant across to me and kissed me on the forehead. "Do forgive me," she said. "I've been abominably rude to you and you've been so kind and helpful to me. And there's a great deal to admire about your way of life. What I like best of all is -"

I was all agog to know what it might be that did meet with her approval but she suddenly broke off, looked at her watch, and said she would have to be going. She suited the action to the word, jumped up and nearly upset the table as she did so. I concluded that she had to get back to her own planet and, of course, the time of departure would have to be timed to the second.

"Good-bye," I said, and she gave me a smile and a hasty "Good-bye" as she hurried out into the street, nearly colliding at the door with someone I recognised as a matron from Guy's Hospital, which is very close to the station. She gave Venus a frosty glare and said something to her which I couldn't hear.

By the time I'd paid the bill and reached the street, Venus was nowhere to be seen, but there, low down in the sky was the planet itself, shining brilliantly. It looked very red but as I watched it changed, oddly enough, to green; then a passing train blotted it from my sight. Perhaps the change of colour was a signal to her to return.

I bought an evening paper and went to catch my train. I tried to absorb the news of the day but my thoughts were still of Venus and the headlines didn't register. There was more violence in Northern Ireland; a threatened strike in the Midlands; fighting between the Arabs and Israelis; and, because it was a London paper, an item about a stupid rag by students at a London teaching hospital. "Students at a London Hospital," I read "undertook an unofficial experiment to test the gullibility of the public." It seemed to me to be quite irresponsible for young men - and women too, I suppose - to behave so childishly. I couldn't help wondering what Venus would have thought of them.

Michael Balchin

THE MAGIC MEDICINE

Once there were three men. There is nothing surprising in a world so full to the brim with men of every colour, creed, and shape, that a story should contain three men. But, said the signpost, "Beware", these men are different; even though they look exactly like any you would find in an industrialised town.

The men were of varying heights, one of them being tall and spare, who seemed to live habitually in faded blue denim overalls; he also wore rimless round glasses. Another was of medium height, and build; he wore brown overalls, and hob-nailed boots. The third was quite a short man who was rather well protected by fat, especially round the stomach and behind; his clothes consisted of an odd jacket and trousers, with a loud checked shirt. Each, on week-days, wore a cloth cap, and a muffler to protect his

150

neck from the wind, rain and snow. Two carried little bags slung on their shoulders by a strap, which had in them their sandwiches; the third disliked little bags, and preferred to put his sandwiches in his always bulging pockets.

So far there is nothing to distinguish them from millions of other men. However as we look at their eyes (of which two had blue, one brown) we are aware that the eyes of all seem to have been deprived of the sight of too much green. We feel at once that here are six eyes whose only glimpses of green have been confined to a patch of grass in their back gardens, or for they all possess cars, seen reflected in the windows of these cars as they zipped along the motor-ways, in quick dashes to the country with their families at week-ends.

There is another feature of the eyes, which is noted after a time; they always look straight ahead, not upwards or downwards, neither to the left nor the right.

These three men were never late for work, never off sick, were always ready to do overtime, were kind to their wives, and children. Pocket money was never forgotten, nor was their regular Friday date at the Black Bull.

Yet in view of all this seeming normality, everyone of these men began to be attacked by nagging doubts concerning the state of their health. The urge to work was absolutely overpowering, which usually got worse at Christmas.

Their families were in the habit of thinking of them as lodgers, they worked until late in the evenings, on Fridays too, as well as at week-ends, so of course there were no visits to the Black Bull, nor dashes to the country.

One day when it had seemed that their eyes had been more than usually riveted into one position, they noticed on coming back to their work bench, after the dinner break, that not only had they failed to examine their sandwiches before eating, to see what was between the bread, but that they were singularly apathetic in their conversation, and did not once discuss either racing, politics, religion or football. This caused them much surprise, they decided there and then to visit a doctor.'

It so happened they were all on the panel of the same doctor, and decided to visit him together, without telling their wives.

As each man entered the surgery, the doctor ,busy writing out prescriptions, had scarcely lifted his head, but merely barked "Yes?" in an interrogative tone of voice. He heard each of their complaints over the strong desire for work, the voices they had in their ears the whole day, insisting the more they did, the more presents they could buy their children, the fatter the turkey they could buy for Christmas dinner; in fact they feared for their sanity, for the voice even haunted their dreams. The doctor had only said that he didn't see that there was much wrong, but they had better be off with their shirts and down with their trousers. After a quick examination, he told them it was just as he thought, there was nothing wrong with them, that they should go back to work thankful they were lucky to be so fit, when he had so many poor creatures come to him, asking for medicine to help them keep working, the men had thanked him and returned, to work harder than ever, taking home an extra large pay packet.

Their wives were delighted with the extra money, and very good humoured. In consequence, the men felt it was time to take the wives into their confidence about the visit to the doctor, and the reason for it. The wives however thought it was a huge joke, and didn't take the matter seriously at all.

That night one of the men dreamed he was being followed by a red light. It upset his sleep so much he was almost late for work. He told his two friends of his dream, who seemed to think the doctor chap could have been wrong, as they thought such a dream was an omen, and decided to call on the doctor once more.

They did not however mention this to their wives in view of their amusement over it. They went together as before. On stepping inside the surgery again, the doctor possibly remembered them. In any event he was rude. They were determined though this time not to come away without a prescription for medicine, The doctor, being as usual busy, wrote one out. It was easier anyhow-all their talk about having no time to do the things they wanted to do because of this strong work urge - he simply let go in through one ear and out through the other.

Two weeks went by, until the day three women visited him. As each one walked into the surgery, he felt vaguely that he ought to know them. The first one interrupted his dawning recognition by saying that her husband had died yesterday. She blamed the medicine, and of course he couldn't tell her it was little more than coloured water. He only said that her husband must have been working too hard.

The second woman astonished him even more, for she grumbled that since having the medicine, her husband had acted very strangely. He took days off from work. He had bought a fiddle with the money intended for a big turkey. In fact there had been great difficulty in consoling the woman, until she asked 'for some of the same medicine' in order that she too could spend her time fiddling like her husband.

152

By the time the third woman came through the door, the doctor was prepared for anything, though he hardly expected her thanks, as she said that her husband - since taking the doctor's medicine -was a changed man, who was happy to stay at home, look after the children, cook and clean, besides finding time to paint beautiful pictures with green fields and trees in them. While she, who had always wanted to do a man's job and have the same money and opportunities, had been given her husband's job.

When she had left, and the morning's surgery was over, the doctor sank into his chair. And if anyone had been close enough to hear, they might have heard him say, "Now I shall take some of my own medicine."

Jean Pooley

WOMAN'S QUESTION
Not, comrade, as a woman
I ask for liberty,
but demand equality
as the right of a human.

It is but quibbling
to call us different
by the mere incident
of animal functioning.

Neither of us alone
can mould another life;
without the womb of wife
the shed seeds are unsown.

Neither of us alone
can mould environment
but jointly we have bent
the cosmos to our own.

Who should be integrate,
my slavery's your disgrace,
I demand my place
shoulder to shoulder, mate.

Frances Moore

POOR ALBERT

He used to do the brake and clutch assembly
and he was never absent or ever late,
yet he was slowly dying from the slavery
which began, as he came through the gate.

As he changed his clothes poor Albert worried
about the long, hard day, which lay ahead,
and as downstairs to work he once more hurried,
thought, sadly, that he'd be better dead.

He had five kids and a sharp, nagging wife,
a mortgage, and many debts to pay,
but he faced up like a champion to a sorry life
of slavery, every minute of the day.

He struggled on, did Albert, like a hero in the war,
in and out of cars. IN OUT IN OUT IN OUT
doing brake and clutch assembly on every shining car,
up an down. In and Out. Up. Down. In. Out. Lout. Lout.

His back and legs were screaming with the pain;
bitter sweat was streaming down his face,
and an awful worry paralysed his brain,
that he couldn't - couldn't stand the killing pace.

He thought about the kids, the mortgage and the bills,
and about his worried, nagging wife.
He felt weary of the struggle, climbing all these hills
With a pain in his heart, like a knife

Poor Albert: as he reached to seize another door,
he gave a cry and staggered back.
And as he slowly fell upon the cold, grey floor,
thought, that surely he would get the sack.

"Stop the Line", someone cried, "Poor Albert's on the floor.
let's help the poor old bugger up, he looks bad he won't do any
more,
and for a moment, they looked at Albert on the floor.

"Don't Stop the Line", the foreman fiercely cried,
"You know that the line must never stop,

even if old Albert's gone and bloody died;
Well, that's it ... we work until we drop."

Poor Albert lay there dying, shivering with the cold,
and the foreman looked down at his blue face.
"You stayed too long, Albert, and grew too bloody old.
Ah, well, I'll. get a youngster in your place."

Upon that floor, the cold, cold floor, Albert simply died;
He closed his eyes upon the scene and drew a gentle breath.
And in that place of greed and spite no one cried for Albert,
as he lay cold and still in death.

The hooter went ... the banshee voice shrieked out again
and held the greedy line at bay.
In their thousands men rushed out to catch cars and train;
all but one ... for poor Albert died to-day.

Michael Ferns

MEDITATION IN A FOLK CLUB

He sang "The Peat Bog Soldiers"*
For him it was old enough to be cherished as 'Folk'
For me the courage and yearning stitched into that tune

Prodded old scars, still sensitive.
I was his age
When the concentration camps were an ugly rumour
Which the Left believed and the Right suavely denied,
While the Liberals kept their ever-open mind.

They hardly bother denying things today -
Just mop up the blood and carry on with football.
You say the Stadium stinks? How petty minded!
We sang "The Peat Bog Soldiers" in memory of friends.
I must learn to sing the songs of Santiago.

*Song composed and sung in Nazi concentration camps, World War II.

Connie M Ford.

155

DERELICT

derelict, and dressed in yesterday's headlines
the down and out stretches in the morning light;
lies on a city shore,
lolls like seaweed, washed up in the night -

and all that drifts around him;
the dancing office girls,
the dry, drab businessmen,
the plastic spoons,
spins in a cold, cold sea;
spins and swims and skims his ashen face -

not that he cares,
he knows he's sinking,
he knows they're all sinking.

so, pulling the bottle back up to his lips,
one eye on the clock,
he wraps the headlines tightly around himself,
and nods off through another crisis,

using dusty words for bed-clothes;
for arm rests -

dried-up slogans.

Keith Armstrong

ISSUE 10

cover size 210 x 148 mm (A5)

CONTENTS

EDITORIAL

Do we date the advent of Capitalism from the 14th century when wage relations began to replace feudal forms of service? Or from the growing tendency of a later century for sheeprearing for a woollen industry to oust subsistence crop growing agriculture? Or from the transfer of monastic lands in the sixteenth century into a new landowning class's hands? Do we date the political arrival of capitalist power from the civil war of 1640 or from the glorious revolution of 1688 or from the culmination in 1832 of political changes triggered off by the astonishing industrial and agricultural development of the eighteenth century?

These are debating points to be argued out by historians, and will have answers determined by the content given to the term Capitalism itself. But all will agree that Capitalism did not spring from its feudal matrix as Pallas Athene fullarmed from the head of Zeus, but rather that like the equally immortal Topsy she growed.

These somewhat profound thoughts of mine are occasioned by the discussion of the issue of Proletarian Literature which a respected friend of mine has been recently examining. A proletarian literature, he deduces, can only arise after the proletarian revolution, and the citations, especially from Marx, about the changes in the superstructure following changes in the economic base of society, are very weighty. But now, the questions posed in my first paragraph may seem to be important and not merely rhetorical questions.

If the phases of capitalism's rise, maturity and decline cover a period of six centuries, will it surprise anyone that from Wat Tyler, More, Winstanley, Blake, Shelley, the Chartist writers of the 19th century, the anti-war poets of world war I, and the major poetic influences of the thirties, Auden, Day, Lewis, Spender, the dominant bourgeois voices should have been accompanied, sometimes invaded, by a growing army of writers challenging the current dominant ruling class values?

To imagine that the chicken will emerge out of the egg without carrying with it some of the egg's contents on which it was nurtured, to imagine a proletarian literature cut off from all associations with the past is to misunderstand what literature is as well as what the proletariat is. A socialist culture will necessarily carry with it, embody into itself all that culture bequeathed it by previous societies.

In the very prisonhouse of capitalism itself, socialist culture will arise necessarily using the forms history has put into its hands. The break between capitalist culture and proletarian culture is seen in a revaluation of the human content, in the outlook, the ethos, of a new class, a class proceeding over one epoch to take its historical place as the controller of its destiny, and then proceeding to fashion a society without classes.

Proletarian culture won't suddenly begin after the revolution, though it will then much more rapidly grow. It is in every beginning made in the course of the conflict of classes within capitalism that proletarian writing plays its part in creating the conditions for the victory of socialism.

The useful thing to say at this moment to workers seeking to express themselves, to middle class and bourgeois writers aware of and anxious to take the proletarian side in the conflicts of the day in the fields of literature and drama, and other arts is not: "it can't be done, you are backing a loser, wait till the revolution" - but "feel confident, pick up your half brick, and throw it," confident that as millions are being drawn into struggle, you too can play a useful role now. Historians and Doctors of Philosophy in years to come will estimate your contribution, objectively. it is important you can see a place for yourself in the demo now.

Ben Ainley

A MATTER OF TEMPERATURE

I once was told how cold it is out there,
how freezing the temperature,
you'll need iron fingered gloves
abrasive boots, a mask to wear they said,
you'll need your fags and gum,
a cool stare of indifference
against frozen principles.

It's not just hard that world of theirs
in which we all must race,
it's lonely sterile, filled with fear
of speeds, tearing in pithy silence
down the passages of ears.

It's too long since we ran barefoot
made our castles out of sand
sang carols on the pavement
wore only woollen gloves against the cold,
try to understand, the mood is gone now
and we like you are here to share
life's last cold altitude.

Jean Pooley

LONELINESS

Loneliness, is when a
man walks alone among an
army of philosophies
which seek to destroy him.
Loneliness is having
something to say
and no-one to say it to.
Loneliness, is the dusk
that brings with it, silence
and decay.
Loneliness is the night
without morning.
Loneliness, is being alive
in a metropolis of death
and somehow knowing that
part of you is dead.
Loneliness, is the
figure in the sunset
that seems
forever waiting
and watching.
Loneliness, is the tick
of the clock and
distant hollow
laughter.
That' s loneliness.

Ian E Reed

TOMORROW'S NOTEBOOK

Tomorrow: waits,
what is tomorrow but some dream,
some hope not always wise
nor satisfied
some goddess in disguise in whose hand reposes
signed document or pact,
answers to future plans disclosed
exposed and verified?

Like a champagne bubble
she sits within my glass. I court her favours
but dare not reject her offerings.
I was there when they brought him in
drowned effigy of dignity
more like newborn kitten than a man.

They gave him the kiss of life
put him between white sheets,
"he may come round tomorrow," someone said,
when I saw him again they had covered up his head.

Jean Pooley

THE HEADACHE

Arnold Bottomore realised, and accepted the fact, that he was awake and
with wakefulness there was again possessing his brain or head or mind an
ache, progressing stridently into shattered pain, which had originated the
previous day, manifested itself in dreams full of actions and drama, and
now had him once more, with consciousness, in its grasp.

He would have to leave the house surreptitiously if he was not to psycho-
logically maul the children and box his wife.

Was it migraine? he asked himself, he would not succumb. Let others faint
away in darkened rooms; he would brave the elements, be strong, shake off
the vice-like grip clamped over the back of his head, down his neck and
across his shoulders. It was all in the mind.

Eyestrain - that was the explanation. Time to make an appointment with
the optician. Dare not mention it to Marjory.

He had in his memory store the tape of her "solicitous" whine.

Had he been eating too much cheese? Was it sinus trouble?

His teeth were clenched together, top and bottom. His eyes felt yellow and black.

He moved eventually because a day at work was a preferable prospect to that of a day at home with Marjory and the kids on school holidays.

Jesus. He could hardly stand up. Vertigo? If he blew his nose might that do the trick? He felt as if his head was getting bigger and smaller, bigger and smaller.

As he dressed he felt himself restraining himself from vomiting. It was like the worst sort of hangover. Hadn't had a drink since Christmas.

Bending to tie his shoes he almost blacked out. Pass out. He could have passed out and if he'd never come round again he wouldn't have cared.

All the symptoms of concussion? What had hit him?

If he lay down again, fully-clothed a) he'd have to take his shoes off; and b)... He sat on the chair in the bedroom with his head in his hands. He could have cried.

"Marjory!" he bellowed coarsely.

She'd never hear down in the kitchen, radio on, kids yapping.

Maybe there were asprins in the cupboard in the bathroom.

He raised himself and in pain walked like Frankenstein's monster across the landing.

There they were on the windowsill and there was a clean tumbler close to them into the bargain. They were the soluble kind. He waited for them to dissolve, sitting on the lavatory, with its candlewick cover in yellowy-green. Every blow he'd ever taken in a fight, every kick or collision in a football match, every time he'd ever hurt himself by accident - the trace of the pain was now illuminated. His body was wracked.

He stood up and felt bricks crashing around him. It was as if he had pushed his way through a brick wall.

"You're imagining things ..." he thought desperately and remembered it was one of the old masters at his old school who had put the idea into his head when he'd said: "If your work doesn't improve, Bottomly, I shall be down on you like a ton of bricks.

"Bottomore, sir."

"Is that understood?"

"Yes sir."

"Understood, understood, understood" -what the fuck could geezers like that old burk understand? Never done a day's work in their lives.

"Are you coming down?" said Marjory through the bathroom door.

"I've a terrible headache."

"Don't go then."

"No-I have to go."

"Suit yourself." She closed the bedroom door.

"I don't want any breakfast."

"D'you want some coffee?"

"Are the kids making noise?"

There was a pause.

"They're not monsters, Arn..."After he'd left they asked their mother if he was in a bad mood. No, she replied, he just had a bit of a headache. The Janice girl at work was probably giving it to him, with her short skirts and tight jeans and skinny, clinging sweaters over a pair of big boobs. And she was as cheeky as hell. What was the point of hoisting yourself up by your bootstraps out of the shop-floor class of people just to have some sexy bint giving you lip day in day out all day long? Exerting his authority, that was the difficult part. That was what being a manager was all about. He'd made it; made it into a trainee managership with full credit to Marjory for her help and hints and support and encouragement. Now he was on the receiving end of the hostile facial expressions which in his younger days he himself had unconsciously doled out so generously. He was the man in the grey suit among the girls in turquoise and navy overalls in the machine-room. Okay, so he hadn't had the education or the cushy upbringing which flash Joe MacIntyre exhibited so nonchalantly. He was learning, though, he was learning. Learning to be tough. Learning to be hard. Fair enough, so you felt sympathy when someone had to get the push; but if a woman couldn't do the job she had to go.

Do the job, do the job. Sales figures. He had to work on them today. Stir it up in the travellers' section. Get them at each others' throats.

"Flip the lid ..." that was an expression Janice was always using. It used to be that whenever he walked into the general office she'd been "entertaining" the other two clerks who'd be sitting leaning on their machines. So he'd had her moved into his office. Keep an eye on her. He usually worked late doing dictation so there was plenty for her to do first thing in the morning. Little bitch.

Some release was the day a week at College. Advancing himself. Getting qualified. City & Guild. Tailoring and Design.

"Roumania and Czechoslovakia you say?" the old fogey lecturer had asked kindly with reference to competition in the clothing industry. They didn't have labour troubles over there. It was alright for them. No unions.

"Ah well of course there are unions in these Eastern European countries," he rambled on, "but they do operate on a very different basis, in a very different manner, or fashion."

"How d'you mean?" asked the Irish fellow.

Arnold stared at the almost life-size illustrations on the wall of the muscle structure of the human body. And there was the skeleton which hadn't moved in all the four years he'd been sitting in this classroom week after week after week.

"That is the question of our times," the teacher was saying, in his corduroy suit. Bloody cheek, really, turning up to lecture Textile Design students wearing a perishing pair of Levis. Useless load of crap he came out with anyway. What was the point of going through all that business about Lebanon and Cyprus and Angola and Northern Ireland?

"People there are working eleven hours a day and their equipment's all out of date ..." Arnold had to say something to have a go at the flabby socialism which pissed him off so much. where had this geezer's smart ideas got him? Boring people to death in a Tech. What experience did he have of the real world?

Making people work.

Janice was wearing a fluffy pink sweater. Arnold's chest tightened at the sight of her backview.

"Oh, sorry Mr. Bottomore, I didn't know you were in." She put into her handbag the bits and pieces of equipment she had been using to paint her face. "Actually, I was having a bit of difficulty following your dictation. It's not very good."

She despised him.

She despised his big-headedness, the way he was getting too big for his boots. It was pathetic the way he arselicked to Joe MacIntyre just because Joe was the son of the Chairman of the Board of Directors. And who was Arnold Bottomore? A creep who'd wheedled his way into the trainee manager's office after five years as an aggressive salesman. Cleverdick. Janice knew for a fact that when he'd started at Prosser and Clark's it had been a toss-up whether he'd go into the warehouse or be sent out doing a bit of selling. Now look at him. Putting on a stern face to try and intimidate her. Thick idiot. She picked a piece of imaginary fluff from the bust of her pullover.

"Could you listen to it for me please.."

It was hell; it was hell - Arnold knew it was hell. If he died, however, Marjory and the kids would be well-provided for. The monthly cheque, the security, being on the other side of the line. That's what counted; that's what was important. He was proud to put in the effort to live within his means. It just needled him to think of all those car workers earning £90 a week.

"Here you are Mr. Bottomore ..." she said, her crutch at his face level as he knelt getting ledgers from the bottom drawer of the filing cabinet and she placed his tea on top of it.

"Chocolate biscuits today ... for some people

He knew he could trip her up. He knew he could bring her down. He would, one of these days, union or no bloody union.

Mr MacIntyre Senior had made it quite clear to the management side that loyalty to the firm was the key thing in these days of economic recession. Inevitably Prosser and Clark's had had to give way to union demands to some extent (within the £6 limit, of course - the Social Contract must be adhered to), but the trainees appreciated that a responsible position had to be adopted by people in authority

In Leytonstone Marjory was counting her losses. An upbringing in army quarters in Aden, training as a domestic science teacher and now the battle to maintain suburban standards in a street "infested" with coloureds and Pakistanis.

It was a very long time since Arnold had "had a wank" but there was no way round it. Either that or he would strangle the girl.

"Everything under control?" quipped Joe MacIntyre blandly as he pissed and Arnold was washing his hands. Surely he couldn't have guessed that Arnold had been more than having a crap?

"Motoring along ... motoring along," Arnold forced a grin.

"I'm stoned out of my head I must admit..." MacIntyre zipped his fly.

"A bit early in the day isn't it...?"

"Yeah ..." drawled the heir to all he surveyed. "Yeah ... I'd better start looking like I'm in charge"

Arnold held open the door for him. He'd spend an hour now in the Managing Director's Office "reading" the Financial Times. Janice looked up at Arnold beseechingly as he re-entered the Office."Oh Mr. Bottomore, I've done all the tapes you left for me and I'm sorry to bother you but I was wondering if I could go home after lunch I've got these terrible stomach cramps. You know ..."

"It happens a bit often doesn't it?"

"I can't help it Mr. Bottomore ..."

"Oh, very well ..."

She turned away from him.

"But I shall make a note of this occasion and a record is going to be kept of all these odd afternoons off. It's going to have to stop. We are considering that any time off in future, even just part of a morning, or afternoon, is going to have to come out of an annual leave

"Oh ... Mr. Bottomore ..." she said, coyly. Going through her mind, however, was the thought, "You just try it mate, and we'll be down on you

Alone in his office that afternoon, picking his uncomfortable way through the individual sales records, Arnold was overcome by several sneezes. So - it was flu after all. Marjory would be able to tuck him up in bed with a hot lemon drink and honey. He might even be able to get her to buy some whiskey. That'd be nice. Marjory, that afternoon, was glancing at the copy of the Times which had been delivered by mistake instead of the Daily Mail which was the Bottomore 's paper. She was leaving it on the side for Arnold to take back to the shop and complain. She wouldn't have minded doing it herself but she thought Arnold would prefer it if she let him do it. One thing that puzzled her was an advertisement in the small ads. for "Philippine servants. Experienced. All arrangements made." It was surprising that people still had servants. Marjory had been led to believe that all that had gone out with "Upstairs-Downstairs". She decided to make a lemon meringue pie for tea while the children were watching "Jackanory".

Fran Hazelton

SUCCESS STORY

"Turn it up" I said
to the kid
with the transistor,
and he did.

Bill Eburn

RACIAL PREJUDICE DAY

It makes you proud, yes
to be of this company.

We're not a thinking people,
admit it. Or a feeling
people: we take things
as they come. Perhaps you'll say,
we're dead. That's a mistake
of intellect. You see
We've got this great asset
(and it's truly national:
the Polls agree) of recognizing
the foreigner. The skin,
you know, helps. We don't like
him: what to do, what to do?
We can say the contrary
and hope to be disbelieved.
But there's a thing of honour,
our word. To keep our word
then, and be true to instinct
we must raise the argument
into metaphysics. Takes the mind
off Economic gloom and old
farts drowning in their tepid
morals pool. Yes, we've carved
an evolutionary handle
out of this race thing.

Paul St Vincent

THE MAN WHO MOVED MOUNTAINS

The man was much admired. He moved mountains. He could lift them up and throw them. Many miles they travelled and landed in the sea. Flattening fish and causing waves that flooded fields.

The other man who also admired him would try to drain the flooded fields to give air to the choking flowers.

And the first man could run very fast. While the other man planted seeds and potatoes and told stories to frightened children at night so they could go to sleep, he would be training to keep fit and improve his time.

And at night time he would explain, I have to relax. As he grew stronger the second man grew weaker but hid his pain behind a smile and carried on.

But the time came when the second man couldn't get out of bed. Everyone grumbled. No one made breakfast. The fire in the kitchen was unlit. The fields untended.

The first man lifted him up with one hand and set him on his feet. But he couldn't stand up.

Reluctantly he put him back in bed and sat down and cried.

Frank Parker

QUEBRADA

Some 50 miles north-east of Oporto, in the baked, rugged lands of Tras-os-Montes, lies the small village of Quebrada.

A carpet of soft grey cloud lay low over the valley that morning. The rain in the night had left a sweet, sticky wetness clinging to much of the valley, and its floor shimmered, like green taffeta, in the stiff morning breeze. The air was chilling but succulently fresh. From behind the long, peaked line of mountains several miles eastward the sun was now climbing. Already its watery glow half-filled the now starless sky suspended as a vast inverted sea of gold above the waking countryside. Here and there, where the cloud-cover was pierced or where the clouds drifted apart, shafts of cool milky light fell like immense spotlights onto the vines decking the shelving west slope. Serried in faultless symmetry, these vines stood as unobtrusive shrines to the toil of their cultivators.

Far across the valley, about three-quarters of the way up the steeper east slope, stood Quebrada, a tight cluster of sixty or more squat, old-world houses, nestling comfortably on the gentler part of the gradient and hemmed in on one side by a small, circular grove of sun-gnarled olive trees that thinned out in pear-shape towards the ridge, and on the other side by a smooth, sharply rising rocky outcrop, almost overhanging the villa of the local latifundisto or landlord, for whom the peasants laboured.

The houses themselves were splashes of dirty-yellow, pale and sickly, though noticeably fresher and less soiled around the village perimeter, where the newly married sons and daughters had gone to live. Without exception all had the same rooftops of faded red tile, slowly bleached by an often broiling sun. All wore the same shrivelled wooden shutters on their sallow, haggard facades; now open with the sun at their back but always closed by noon.

Within these dimly lit dwellings the women, when they were not needed on the land, would pass their colourless remaining hours. Such time would be spent in looking after the children and in the kitchen, usually preparing the main meal of the day: often a scanty dish of potatoes and favas, the popular large beans, or a greasy stew laden with much vegetable and little meat. Now and again the women would boil up some chourico, those small spiced sausages, cooked in blackened cauldrons over an open hearth. These would be ravenously eaten at the end of day by their menfolk, who would complain afterward that there had not been enough and would ask, though they well knew the reason, why they did not have this more often. The peasants' thirst was slaked usually with milk or the cheap coffee their latifundisto, da Silva sold to them - at a profit. Only very occasionally did they get to taste the vinho branco, the grapes for which they themselves grew and picked.

Outside on the land the men and often the women too would labour, sometimes from dawn to dusk, just as their forefathers had done. Like beasts of burden under a burning sky, the men with flesh like toughened hides and the women, exhausted with work and childbearing would carefully tend the vines and gently pick the grapes at harvest-time. They would labour usually in silence. There was little to be said. It was almost eternal.

And above the village and the land on the rocky ridge, watchful and solid, was the village church of Sao Miguel. It stood out with importance. Its towering steeple was fawn and dusty, holding the bell that tolled the angelus three times daily, with a monotonous regularity that had not failed in centuries. The bell was sacred. Just as its commanding peal marked with dignity the rites of day: the dawn when the peasants sleepily rose to work, the noon when they rested to eat their small meal, and the eventide when they left the fields for home to eat, make love and sleep, so its peal marked the rites of life: birth, copulation and death. The village bell presided over a simple, unchanging beauty and hid the secret conflicts and oppressions of village life with its pure metallic thunder.

It was a little after eight o'clock when the cloud broke. As the long purplish shadow it cast peeled slowly back, the length of the valley was for the first time aflame with sunlight. The solemn unveiling should have revealed the scores of peasants enacting their daily ritual: labouring in the vineyards, or busying themselves about the dozen or so outhouses surrounding the low, elegant villa of their landlord, Senhor Amilcar Agostinho da Silva. For there was always much work to be done, and Senhor da Silva, a strict and firm landlord, ensured that it was done. He was the law in these parts and few chose to cross him.

Yet, strangely, no such scene opened up that morning. Not a peasant - man, woman or child - was to be seen, either among the vines or on the valley-floor. The sole activity, anywhere, seemed to be that of a couple of young hogs fighting ravenously over the scraps of swill in an almost empty trough outside the villa courtyard.

Senhor da Silva and his portly, respectable wife, Maria da Silva, the youngest daughter of a former Portuguese Ambassador to Spain, and their three sons were breakfasting leisurely on the verandah. Cereals or grapefruit to begin, a copious main course of fried sausages, eggs and bacon, some grilled tomatoes, and toast and marmalade to follow. Breakfast would end with fresh orange juice for the sons and a strong Brazilian coffee for the sophisticated palates of the Senhor and his wife. Yes, the da Silvas did eat well and they did live well. They enjoyed eating and living well. They ate and lived well because of the wealth the estate brought thorn, wealth from the vines daily tended, slowly nurtured by the work-hardened hands of the peasants of Quebrada. Yet the peasants saw none of this wealth and good living for themselves; they knew only the squalor and misery in which they lived in their hillside hovels, and the handful of escu-dos that da Silva gave them out of the sale of the produce, after their work, deadening, back-breaking work, on the land.

Yet on this morning no peasant broke his back or wet his brow with sweat from working. Da Silva was confused because he could see no one in the yard attending to the usual tasks. It was already hot and da Silva was sweating as he gluttonously swallowed his English breakfast. His wife ate more fastidiously, and the sons ate in an orderly, serious fashion. Da Silva was troubled by the fact that no one was working in the yard, and was de-termined to find out the cause of this 'peasant idleness' as soon as he had finished eating. He was angry but at the same time afraid. Ever since Cae-tano's overthrow and exile, da Silva had been bewildered and frightened by all the political changes that were happening in the big towns and in many of the villages in the South. Workers and peasants were evicting their em-ployers and masters from their property and running their own factories and farms. For da Silva this was outrageous and criminal. Often he would speak to his obedient and attentive wife of all this and dismiss it as so much nonsense, and on other occasions he would talk of the danger of Communism and of Russia. Having eaten, da Silva got up from the table, irritated and afraid.

It was on the eastern slope outside the village that the peasants had congre-gated in an almost festive mood. Here, almost since dawn, they had been discussing the events in Oporto and in Lisbon and the changes on neigh-bouring farms, in particular on a large estate several miles to the west. News had been slow to filter through after the revolution against fascism, and the peasants had remained unmoved by and uncomprehending of the strange talk of liberty, equality, of an end to fascism and exploitation and the building of socialism, which they sometimes heard.

The arrival the day before of two young labourers from Sao Pedro, where the latifundisto had been thrown out and his land seized by the whole community, had inspired many of the young and middle-aged villagers in Quebrada who, though they hated da Silva for his meaness, his greed and severity, had sullenly tolerated him, feeling powerless to resist him and rarely considering life without him. These two young men, brothers and the sons of a peasant family in Sao Pedro, had been workers in Oporto at the time of the revolution, but had returned home, full of new ideas, to help with the grape-harvest.

One of the brothers was now speaking: "In Sao Pedro we used to have a bloke - a manager - appointed by some Senhor Moneybags in Lisbon. Manager! All he did, was organise us so as his boss in Lisbon could screw us for more profit. Yes, we all used to accept that set-up. The Government and the Church, and our old parents too all told us this was the proper way to live and things couldn't be otherwise."

"Yes," an elderly peasant, who had worked for the da Silva family for over forty years, said, "But if we get rid of da Silva, who is going to run the farm?"

"Look what does your da Silva do? We kicked our manager out and made sure no sponger in Lisbon wasn't going to live off our labour. Now we run things ourselves -democratically." The final word was pronounced clearly and precisely.

A younger man spoke, "Yes, we all of us here, who have been working the farm all our lives, shall run the farm."

"That's it," the other brother from Lao Pedro replied, "for the Government will help you, like they helped us. They'll give you a tractor and fertilisers. They'll guarantee you a fair price for your grapes, your wine and other produce. Pa Silva won't take any rake-off. All that your labour produces will be for you to sell and for you to enjoy."

There was much cheering and the whole mass of peasants seemed to be possessed by a new spirit, a spirit of justice and hope.

"Well, what are we going to do?" the brother asked when the cheering had subsided. "Shall we kick out da Silva and take the land that he owns but on which you work? Are you going to work for yourselves in the future, or be exploited by da Silva, who grows fat while you sweat and toil?"

The decision was rapidly made, but there was an uncertain shuffling of feet and nervous mumblings of conversation amongst some of the peasants. Then one man cried out and pointed down to the villa, a symbol of da Silva's robbery of the peasants. The peasants began to move, at first with slowish and irresolute paces, but soon with more confident, measured strides. Some now began to shout, while others started to sing. Even the elderly peasants felt they had stood for the parasitic da Silva too long and things ought to be different and more justly arranged. And now they were surging forward with the same unity of purpose and elemental force as the waves of the ocean rolling to break against a rocky shore. They poured down the dusty track to the white villa, where da Silva now stood about to tour his land.

The peasants flowed into the forecourt of the villa. Da Silva was sweating in his summer suit. He mopped his brow, but though afraid, was determined to face this mob of peasants. his pose in itself demanded that the peasants explain their indiscipline. The peasants wavered visibly at the sight of da Silva, who was holding a shot-gun. Da Silva was alone, but his presence imposed on the peasants a silence of momentary diffidence.

"Well, what do you want?" da Silva roared. "You know this laziness will cost you part of your pay. Well, who's leading you in this stupidity? Come on. I won't have my time wasted".

Da Silva' s sense of authority remained with him. So far the sea of men which threatened to drown him, had not panicked him. Would the peasants disperse? There was murmuring in the crowd which seemed intimidated. Would they disperse? It was then one of the brothers from Sao Pedro stepped forward.

"We want what is ours. We want what is the work of our toil. We want the earth we till, the vines we grow, the grapes we tend and pick. We want this land."

Da Silva was bewildered and was like a man hearing a language he could not understand.

"You want my land, the land that was my father's and his father's?" da Silva stammered incredulously. "My land! You thieving, lazy scum." Da Silva's face was flushed with exploding rage.

The peasants were growing impatient, their purpose now defined and affirmed. More murmuring shook the whole mass of them like the first tremors of a violent earthquake. Da Silva was beginning to feel pathetic, for he could do nothing. He could kill a few peasants with his shot-gun, but there were more than two hundred of them and they were determined. It was hopeless. He felt like a child, powerless and insignificant. Yesterday he had owned unquestioned all this land with complete certitude. Today these peasants whom he had allowed to earn a living from his land, were demanding what had been his family's for centuries. But now all certainties had vanished like a mist.

"All right. You can take the farm and the land for now. I am going. But I will return and take back what is mine by law. You thieves. I will go to the Authorities and they will drive you from my land. You shall never work for me again," da Silva uttered barely articulately, unconscious of the truth of his last sentence.

"What law? What authorities? The law is made for the people now, not for exploiters and oppressors," one of the brothers shouted in reply.

174

Already some of the peasants were wandering around the farmbuildings and taking care of the live-stock. Da Silva was beginning to feel redundant. What if the law would not help him? His doubts grew. He spoke again to reassure himself.

"The law will avenge me. Damn' you all. Justice will be done, and you'll suffer for this."

His empty words served only to increase his impotent fury. In a spasm of rage he waved his gun in the air. The gun went off. For a moment there was silence. The peasants and da Silva were equally astounded. Then the mass of peasants moved forward, pushing by da Silva. Someone grabbed the gun and da Silva was lost in the torrent of men, a flood of spinning images and chaos.

While the da Silvas packed their bags, the peasants began to get themselves organised to run the farm and the lands that their work had cultivated for centuries, not for another man's benefit, but for themselves. In a spirit of exuberance da Silva's villa was declared the new village meeting house. While the peasants prepared a new way of life, da Silva, his wife and sons crept away in their estate car.

Epilogue:

The Armed Forces Movement gave the peasants of Quebrada a tractor and fertilisers in order to help them modernise their farm and land. The peasants, with government advice, started to form a wine-producing co-operative with neighbouring estates that had also thrown their landlords out. Da Silva himself fled eastwards into Spain, swearing that he would return and reclaim his land. The peasants of Quebrada, however, have a surprise waiting for da Silva should he ever return - an armed guard

Martyn Handley

AFTER HEARING A RADIO PROGRAMME ON THE GERMAN SAILORS' REVOLT IN 1918 AT KIEL AND WILHEMSHAVEN

Salute to you, the unknown, nameless comrades of the past,
Who, not knowing if victory would be yours,
Took the great step over the precipice,
In mutinies and revolts;
Risking all in one courageous action.

When all is won, and we stand at last
Facing a future of peace and limitless advance;
Monuments should be built, sky high, pyramids of rock,
In memory of ordinary men; not statesmen,
not even political leaders;
But you who risked your lives, and often lost.
Let's make anew our list of saints;
Rename our maps to honour them:
And stand in solemn silence awhile
In memory of such.

So, the generations will not slip, care not sink back;
But, inspired by these, go forward without stop to reach the stars.

Isabel Baker

IF

If…
If I could awake
To see you waking; make
Your world a wonder;
To see the sun's rays falling
On gold-orbed banners, heavy with golden thread and brocaded silks
That wave high above the heads of your Imperial Cavalry;
calling,
Proclaiming, my love.
And you would ride a sable stallion decked
In turquoise; half hidden in the long white folds
Of your robe, trimmed in ocean blue and autumn gold
You would ride proud before
Your banner-bearers,
Sword bearers

176

Infantry in scarlet and blue,
High officials on she-mules too:
And cymbal-beating negroes from the Sudan.
You would hold court, be entertained
By snake-charmers and acrobats;
Give audience to little deputations
Of country jews and jewesses in tight white collars;
And groups of grey-dressed scholars.
We could eat spiced chicken,
Hot turkey, steaming;
Couscous, whole roast sheep and kebabs;
Almond pastries and sweet mint tea,
Sat around a fire of crackling juniper in the cold night; warmly
you and me
And all around, glowworm glowing lanternlight through
coloured glass;

And the soft murmur of a singer in the stillness.
There would be
Gifts from all the world;
Musical stuffed parakeets and kookaburras;
Bulldogs with false teeth
Immense cases of corsets from Kenya hidden underneath
Grand pianos; crates of champagne,
Barrel organs and hansom cabs
Macaw parrots and the claws of a million crabs.
You would converse with portrait painters,
Puppet Sultans, memsahibs of Malayan rubber men,
Conjurers,
A German lion tamer, a French soda-water manufacturer, a man
who thinks
He's Mickey Mouse,
A fireworks expert, Consuls of Great Powers; ambassadors
Of every Great European House
And a stout Spanish lady of Uncertain Age.
A Scottish piper alonely on your evening battlements;
A ring of zebras, emus, wapiti, hindu cattle;
Stags with their antlers locked in battle;
Antelope and llamas in the garden
With a curvature of flamingo..
And the pick of a Bird of Paradise shop;
And a tall, night-time stork on your chimney top.
If
If not, I'll see you on the bus sometimes.

I don't think they'd let all the others on.
Especially the emus,
Bus conductors get a bit stroppy about emus.

Les Barker

FOR DESMOND TROTTER

Will the Queen be hanging Desmond Trotter
Knight the freedom fighter?
We English it is well known are very fair,
Even on holiday we'll see justice done.
Horizon-drunk, ocean sat-upon, native-girl plucked:
Tyranny ripening in our minds like fruit.

Strung between the royal past and the plebeian future, a youth,
All black between the sea and sun.

Back home bitter we contemplate our rotting state;
Then to dreams silent as snow, sick with sweetness.
The moaning world outside like a great flowing tide
Staked-round with guns and secrecy, briars and blindness.
Death leaps from Dominica to Hackney keen as daylight;

I stumble out into my back-garden, where snowdrops swing
Black as the earth-trapped spring.

David Kessel

Desmond Trotter has since been reprieved due to a successful campaign.

SELF VIEW

This person seems effective:
controlled , articulate, unruffled;
able to pause and think, consider,
look pensive, give unhurried answers,
smile at times, even appear light-hearted
reply to every question in a reasoned manner.

I quite like her, quite approve –
we'd probably get on quite well together,
find a fair amount in common, have discussions,

178

respect each other, share a joke.

But surely we have met already?

There's something faintly, puzzlingly familiar
about her hair-style, general cast of features.
This person cannot be a complete stranger.

On second thoughts, she is - she just resembles
someone I once saw or met or knew,
noticed in a shop or on the underground.
And yet

"That went well, flowed smoothly, was provocative;
must have stimulated audience reaction.
Thank you very much indeed for coming.
It really was a lively, gripping interview..."

So that was it - was why I felt I'd met her:
that fluent, relaxed woman whose words I'd hung on,
wondering how she'd deal with every question,
impossibly, incredibly was me.

But I never realised that my cheeks were moulded
in that way when my mouth was talking;
that my forehead crinkled in that fashion
when I cogitated for a suitable or honest answer;
that my laugh was quite so clipped, abrupt
when I decided to appear amused.

She couldn't have been me, this woman
compact with firm ideas, collected thoughts;
frank, self-assured, high principled,
humorous, never at a loss for words.

For my thoughts are a knotty stretch of knitting,
loose, uneven, punctured with dropped stitches;
my face constructed of cracked cardboard;
my inside just a heavy vacuum.

I am all tangled and in bits, unfinished off.
At night the low wind menacing through my hollows
stirs a debris of rag shreds, torn paper,
bone sticks, flutter of dried leaves.

No, I was not that solid person on the screen.

Pat Arrowsmith

SOMEONE'S WORN THIS THING BEFORE

Someone's worn this thing before
It's been places I've never been,
maybe next to me, eaten things
I'd never eat, fallen,
gotten up and moved on, whistling.

The paperclip in your pocket,
bugbite in the morning,
the stain on your clean pants,
hair on the mirror,
the life you find yourself living.

And here it is, a smile on its face,
waiting. Not long, but waiting.
It stands at the back door, hands
in its pockets, watching the sky.
Hurry, it says. Hurry.

Out of the dark, children.
Out of the night, day.
I won't be back for a long time,
but I will be.
Out of I don't know what, something.

I'll leave it in Nebraska, maybe.
If I ever pass through.
If I don't, look there anyway.
By the clump of grass, by the road, by the bright sky.
Folded, dusty and torn.

Roger Mitchell

THE PARTING

Kathy and Jenny had been together from their first awesome day at school when Kathy had wet herself and Jenny had been the only one who hadn't sniggered but quietly handed Kathy her clean white hanky to dry her stinging legs with. Kathy had responded by sharing her apple with Jenny at dinner time; their first secret, hidden behind the janitor's coal bunker they had taken turns to leave crimp-chiselled wedges in the white fruit and Jenny had been allowed the last bite. Their friendship lasted all through their school years. Jenny had always been brighter than Kathy but she was also more gentle and used her brightness not as a stick to beat with but as a rod for Kathy to catch hold of while Jenny pulled her up towards herself. On countless nights Jenny copied out her homework twice, the second time in a well practised and near perfect imitation of Kathy's writing style, reversing b and d every third time and crossing the Te with an overwide stroke slanting from left to right. If anyone noticed they hadn't cared and on the day they both left school, Kathy with a certificate to say she had completed a secretarial course satisfactorily and Jenny with a large envelope containing the details of her three O levels, they were hardly less close than they had been at the end of their first day at school.

Three weeks later they gawped at the factory together, eyes blinking in spontaneous rhythm with the thud of the presses, ears trying to cope with a conglomerate sound that did not repeat itself but hissed and banged into their ears in irregular vibrating strokes, a thin high wail hard to pinpoint wove a tin thread through the heavier sounds and every now and then, in a random lull in the main body of the noise, the sound of human voices reached them and turned their heads towards their speakers too late to catch what was said before the thick din reasserted itself and made mutes of them all. Kathy mimed to Jenny that the noise was unbearable and Jenny pulled a sympathetic face. The instructress with them intercepted the exchange and yelled over the noise, "You won't notice it after an hour or two", and grinned at them. The girls shrugged. They toured the factory floor in the wake of the instructress, looking where she pointed, touching the components she handed them, watching in awe as they observed an assembly bench where a row of girls sat working, passing metal plates that bristled like grey porcupines with yellow and red lead for spines, up the row so evenly that they took on the appearance of a strange group-being, a technical animal with automated limbs each immersed in its own function and aware of its relation to the whole so that no waver in a hand failed to be compensated for by all the waiting hands ahead. The girls were fascinated and suddenly nervous of the intricacies of what they were watching. Their fingers felt enormous, clumsy and stiff as they watched the girl nearest to them twist, loop, prod and thread a silver wire through a hole they could scarcely see, doing the job with one hand while the other reached for the next plate. The instructress touched Kathy's shoulder and had to yell again, it looks difficult, but you'll pick it up sooner than you think." Kathy looked doubtful.

They passed on to an area where the sound of the presses and solder baths was eclipsed by series of short teeth-grinding electronic whoops and howls that rose and drooped in arcs of sound , one falling low as another reached its hysterical peak, and the girls could see the twisting wrists of the operators here as they coaxed the sounds through their acrobatics by watching their progress on glimmering green screens at eye-level, the physical curve matching the audial one before the operators slapped the jig-release and tossed the units they were testing onto the conveyor belt at their side. Jenny wanted to linger behind the screens. The flashing images made to move and cross over themselves, sometimes collapsing into fluorescent worms at the bottom of the screen (when, she noted the offending plate would be discarded) excited her into curiosity. She asked the instructress what was happening. "Alignment," the instructress said pulling her away and onto another assembly bench, but Jenny's eyes stayed behind for the rest of the tour, resting on the green fuzz around the alignment benches.

Back in the training room the girls spent their first week learning to solder, sort, inspect and code a nest of tiny components and leads. Jenny was slow and careful and Kathy found herself able to hold and handle the small components with ease. In no time, Kathy was whipping through whole boxes of' simple assembly work, unafraid of the smouldering iron as she pressed its red tip onto the eyelets before melting the solder wire into a sizzling drop of liquid over the eyelet and lead and snipping the trailing end from the solid joint. Jenny envied her friend her confidence and found herself constantly doubting the strength of her own bubbled joints so much that she tested them too much and often snapped the lead off before she was satisfied, and then had to begin again. All this was noted by the instructress who had also noted the girls' closeness and was human enough to seek work for them together. Remembering Jenny's interest in the alignment benches, she rigged up a practice board in the training room and then it was Jenny who fell to work with enthusiasm, relishing the many dials and switches at her fingertips and learning their uses quickly. She found herself understanding the strange sounds her equipment let forth so instinctively that before her first day was out, she had learnt to detect the faltering, however slight, in sound or visual curve that meant the unit was not working properly and without the prickling doubts that had dogged her mechanical efforts. Kathy wouldn't look at the equipment, far less touch it. She said the noise made her wince and she was terrified of getting a shock from the humming machine. They laughed together, happy about their happiness with the unfamiliar work and when the instructress arrived and told them they were to work on the same assembly line) they hugged each other with pleasure.

They were separated by three operations on the line, something that did not displease either of them because Kathy had hoped for an assembly job and Jenny had wanted most of all to work on the electrical side which was what happened. They made friends with the other girls and immersed themselves in the easy society of the line and in their work, but breaks always found them together, exchanging proud knowledge with one another and each admiring the other's new skill. They hardly noticed that the rest of the line split into strictly segregated groups at teatimes, the mechanical workers huddling at the front of the line and the electrical workers at the rear, and there was no reason why the split should be noticed for it was not a hostile separation but it was complete. Kathy and Jenny went their own way and the small frustration of not being able to compare appraisals of the quality of their work bothered them little at first. They merely kept a tactical silence when the frequent discussions about the relative merits of their kinds of work came up. The electrical girls made sneering remarks about the "thickies" at the assembly stages, laughing at their greasy overalls and calloused thumbs, and the mechanical girls affected to despise the "fine ladies" who, as far as they could see, sat on their ample behinds all day fiddling with buttons and not much else.

Things became more threatening when there was trouble on the belt and targets were hard to meet. Jenny could not stop herself from secretly agreeing that the number of reject units had a lot to do with sloppy soldering and could do no more than keep silent when Kathy boasted of a new higher target met with only that morning, and say to herself that she knew what price was being paid for Kathy's success. As the piles of rejects grew, the assembly workers began to grumble that the alignment girls were being over-fussy - must be looking for promotion - they had murmured in bad temper and Kathy had found herself annoyed at her friend whose own pile of rejects was brimming over. At tea time, Kathy prodded the jumbled units and said, "That won't help them keep their leads in, you know, keeping them tossed about like that. No wonder they don't work when you get them." Jenny had smarted under the remark but only murmured that she'd nowhere else to stack them and there were rather a lot of them. Kathy had laughed and gone back to her bench where she began furiously slotting, prodding and soldering her work together, trying to throw off the feeling that Jenny's remark had been against herself but there were only two of them doing the assembly work that day and the other girl was an old hand at the work and just didn't make mistakes often. Her ill temper stayed with her for for the first time she spent her next break with the other mechanical girls, feeling guilty as she saw Jenny looking for her and eventually eating her tea along, but she knew if she went to her she would say something nasty and, she felt down to the tips of her clever fingers, true.

The bad spell lasted for a week, not long as bad spells on assembly lines go, but enough to snap the bond between the two girls completely. The unmet targets at the electrical end of the belt had generated anger. Though the electrical boards hummed and hissed through piles of units, the numbers going on up the belt as passed units and the only ones to be counted, got fewer and fewer and as the numbers fell and the pay with it, the girls started to twist and fidget with frustration at the dead blanks on their screens. Jenny suffered it longer than the rest of them and calmed them out of stopping work altogether until something was done, but after the fourth unit in a row had refused to squeak into life under her fingers, she joined the mobbing girls at the supervisor's desk and demanded with them that the units be made properly or they would walk out. The supervisor, well-seasoned in line arguments, made a gallant attempt to approach the assembly girls tactfully, giving them a cheerful pep-talk mingled with outrageously exaggerated praise before she asked, almost absently, if they would please solder just a little bit more carefully. It backfired.

The girls surrounded her like mobbing crows, diving in with sharp jibes and complaints against the electrical girls who, they said, always blamed them for their own mistakes. Flattened thumbs were shoved under her nose to show the hardness of the work, one girl proffered a blistered finger, another a scorched hole in her overall, while another dragged a box of assembled units and dropped it at her feet, asking her to check with her that the leads were soldered and the joints sound. The supervisor fell back before them, walking backwards with hands held flat before her as if to ward their anger off and it was only the group of electrical girls standing firm at the other end of the belt that halted her retreat.

"Well?" they said, as if they hadn't heard everything, their faces grim in the quiet before another storm. "I'll get the foreman", the supervisor fled for a saviour and left the two gangs facing each other. They began to exchange remarks among themselves but in overloud voices so that their insults flew home to their objects as intended. The normal job-jibes gave way to more personal ones very soon afterwards, and Jenny was astounded to find herself in a sudden cool moment in the heat of her temper, accusing Kathy of being a dimwit while Kathy taunted her as a teacher's pet, Kathy's face livid and filled with what must have been years of resentment which Jenny felt equalled in her own mind, the weight of Kathy's demands on her. She was appalled at her own words. "Kathy, Kathy" she said. "We shouldn't talk like this, it's only work. Come on, I'm sorry."

But Kathy was still high on her release and pushed her away, and Jenny could feel in the rigid arms something of the depth of the resentment that

Kathy was feeling. Kathy sneered, "Oh, just you get back to your machine, it's all you're fit for."

Jenny walked away and sat at her board, looking at the dials and knobs and switches that seemed to be responsible for Kathy's anger. They were mute, lifeless, inanimate until she, Jenny, should manipulate them, coax them and tease them into performing their work. They pleased her, the little black buttons all in a row and the pulsing line on the screen. Really, she thought, Kathy should have more sense. It was a pity she didn't understand how important the work was, far more important than her mechanical job, anyone could do that, even a monkey could do it in time, but this called for judgement, appraisal, a little intellect and well, Kathy had never been strong on that now, had she? Jenny flicked a switch and began the series of checks over a fresh unit. The speaker crackled into life, blipped, howled and then soared into a rising squeal. Jenny patted the side of the machine affectionately.

REPORT ON LINE STOPPAGE BELT 546 MONDAY 3 PM – 3.30 PM.

IT WAS FOUND THAT A BATCH OF LEAD
675 87 654 B4 HAD HAIRLINE BREAKS
INSIDE THE PLASTIC SLEEVING -
LEADING TO BREAKAGE WITH MINIMAL
HANDLING - THREE BATCHES SENT BACK
TO MAKERS FOR CREDIT - NEW ISSUE
RELEASED 3.30 PM. WORK RESTARTED
DITTO. FOREMAN REPORTS TROUBLE
OVER.

SIGNED E. GORDON (SUPERVISOR)

Vivien Leslie

THE DAY THE TORY LIGHTS WENT OUT

ted heath groping in the dark
his shaking hand
reaching for an exit from his self-sprung trap
the shaft - is blocked

'so this is what it's like to chivvy in the dark,
so this is what it's like to breathe in black silt

ted heath groping in the dark

185

his clammy hand
reaching for the door
reaching for walls
feeling only the chiselled-stone faces of miners
cats' eyes stabbing at him from the night

there is no daylight between these vaulted faces
their solid ranks are closed

ted heath groping in the dark
your only way out is to crawl

through tunnels
and potholes
and mines

vomiting your last false promise as you go

Keith Armstrong

DIC

Dic Penderyn (Richard Lewis) was hanged in Cardiff in 1831 for his part in the Merthyr Riots of that year. His crime was "That he wounded a soldier of the King" - he denied this with his last breath. About 50 years later in America there was a Welsh speaking Welshman on his death-bed crying for a minister who could speak his tongue.

He told the minister that it had been he who had wounded the soldier and not Dic Penderyn.

Dic had indeed been murdered by the State.

When they cut Dic down from the scaffold his body was laid on a cart and they went through Cardiff and the villages west looking for a church who would accept his body for burial. No church would take him until they had travelled some thirty miles and arrived at the town of Aberavon where the vicar of St. Mary's accepted Dic.

A POEM FROM NEATH ABBEY

Merthyr Mountain burned
A satanic fire through the night
Marking out the points for the men
To meet, to organise a fight against
Crayshaw!

Crayshaw's cry must be turned from
"Men must work for me for nought or die."
- to men must live and love their lives.

Dic laughed
And was hated and watched with the eye of
A trout watching as he walked about
The town.
Crayshaw scowled; the troops marshalled;
Dic refused to obey their command ... the
Command from King!
In Welsh he spoke of injustice and children's
Hunger ... Is the King without food ... No, nor
will we be.
Fight!!

As a tower will not bend to the wind, Dic said,
it will crash with the weight of angry men
Storms rage and the still time lingers with
blood of the men who wanted food but were told
by the King's guns to lie still.

Dic Penderyn cried.

Dic said his hour would come when the men
Who filled those iron cuts would too be
Filled with bread.

Arrested!

King's command, see!

A trial he was given - mockery they
said and J.T. Price from Neath Abbey
Fought to save his life.

"Teach those men a lesson ... hand Penderyn
And they'll see that we won't stand for
This nonsense ... then work they will with no sound.

Cardiff, a sultry morning. Thunder in the
Air. People openly crying as they hanged
Dic who had started singing.

Towns shunned the man who had started the
workers' cause but onward went his friends
"til Aberavon said "They will."

Now under the lilt of the church, St. Mary's,
Aberavon, Wales, sits a small cross with
the words: Dic.

Dic !
Dic Penderyn
Aged 23
Hanged at Cardiff ... murdered!

The first Welsh working class martyr.

Robert King

POET AT WORK

He sits frowning
pen in hand,
and from a distance
sees himself lean forward
trying to record
the message clearly received,
but only dimly understood.

Bill Eburn

DURCH DEN KAMIN

"We nivver knew nowt o' no gooins-on",
Ferswoor t'brant sackless grouwn-ups o' Dacko;
Bu' t' breath frac 'is lips hissed th'Horst Wessel song,
As dad tanned 'is brat's aree wi some whack-o:
"T's a lie dost' yer, ut aw'r a Jew-baiter!"
Bu' t' childer'd a' known what they'r on abeawt
When these browtins-up o' Struwwelpeter
'ad warned they'd else stoke 'em up t'chimbley speawt.

brant, erect, upright.

Jone o' Broonlea

188

THE IRRECONCILABLES

Men can manage
without masters,
but masters
must have men,

so in the long run,
we must win.

Bill Eburn

A SHEFFIELD WOMAN LOOKS AT HUGH McDIARMID

Bonny bragging babbling bard
over apt to talk too hard,
in amongst the straw and chaff
corn falls out that pays the draff.

Garrulity's so much the mode
let's be thankful yours is good;
but, lumme lad, tha's o'er brash
wi' a' this swaggering male man trash.

Well I may, as poet, mock
this sort of little woman talk,
who as a woman knows the chore
that keeps such fellow on the floor
(while feeding, servicing my man
producing poetry where I can).

Frances Moore

RAINBOW

Witshud, stood i' t' rindlin' loane
Gawpin' yond'ly on mi own...

Wi t' lat' sunleet silin' low,

189

t' Wa'-stooans catch it gowden glow

Neaw t' rain's teemin's checkt it spate
t' Fell sheyns green 'gin t' welkin's slate

Reet aboon loups breet-hue merth:
t' Rainbow straddles ower t' yearth

- an' hid theer at it foot i' yon teawn eawt o' t' sect
ligs t' kipper heart o' gowd aw claspt to mine las' neet.

witshud, in leaky footwear ("wet-shod"); rindlin', flowing like a stream;
loane, lane; gawpin', gazing vacantly; y'ond(er)ly, abstractedly;
silin', streaming; welkin, sky; aboon, above; loups, leaps;
merth, abundance; kipper, loving amorous.

Jon O' Broonlea

IN DEFENCE OF T.S. ELIOT.

Tony Whitfield had some hard things to say about TS. Eliot (Voices 6), and as these found an echo at one of our meetings held in London to discuss Voices, I would like to say something in reply.

(a) *Eliot can only be appreciated by someone with as good an education.* True and false. Read say "The Love Song of J. Alfred Prufrock" to a dozen people and ask them if it is poetry. Most of them will say it is. Ask them what it means and they will look blank. However, read "Khubla Khan" and you are likely to get the same response. Coleridge would doubtless agree with the verdict for he believed that poetry gives most pleasure when it is only generally and not perfectly understood. Yet few would deny that he was one of the greats.

(b) *Eliot's poetry has so many references that it can become like a Times Crossword Puzzle - interesting, taxing but pointless.* True again, but not wholly true. If I begin a poem "From the troubles of the world! I turn to sex", some will recognize that I am parodying "From the troubles of the world/I turn to ducks", and this awareness adds a further dimension to the poem. But it is not essential. Anyone who has enjoyed a foreign film without benefit of translation will know what I mean.

(c) *Poetry has been preserved like a Ming Vase for all eternity - daring imitation or improvement* Technically at any rate this is not true. There have always been rebels against artificiality. Wordsworth and Coleridge attempted to use the language of common speech, but were bound by the existing conventions (regular number of metrical feet per line etc). Following Whitman and the Imagists Eliot established an oral poetry closely allied to speech in rhythm and in language. For good or ill his influence has probably been more widespread than any other poet in this century.

d) *Art is of its time - do we need this over indulgence in past expression - expressing what has gone is dead?* None of us writes poetry, or anything else for that matter, entirely out of his own head. Each of us stands at the end of a long tradition. Reference has been made to Whitman and the Imagists, but to trace the source it would be necessary to return to Beowulf.

Tony seems to recognise this when he says "reality has to be re-examined in the light of our *total* experience which differs from generation to generation." (My emphasis).

Eliot expressed this very clearly:

'And he (the poet) is not likely to know what is to be done unless he lives in what is not merely the present, but the present moment of the past, unless he is conscious, not of what is dead, but of what is already living."

(Or as his friend Ezra Pound put it even more succinctly, "Nothing exists which isn't in rapport with the past and the future.").

But as Alec West observed Eliot lacked a true historic sense. "He dissociated tradition from the struggle of the men who make it, and this was the cause of his limitation and his decay as a critic and a poet."

2. There is so much in Tony Whitfield's article I agree with. A self-styled "classicist in literature, a royalist in politics, and an Anglo-Catholic in religion", Eliot's poetry is not our poetry. But he could write. Like Coleridge he believed that poetry can communicate before it is understood; that a poet convinces not by the words he uses, but by the music he sets these words to. And in his literary criticism' he was prepared to take us into his confidence and show how it was done.

3. As Tony says, Eliot was a poet who wrote for poets. As poets we can learn from him. Not to attempt to do so is to throw the baby away with the bath water.

Bill Eburn

"Selected Prose of T.S. Eliot" Faber paperback £1.95, or any library.

PICTURES OF THE THIRTIES

a poem by Arthur Clegg (Reality Press, 16 Portree Street, London E.14).
15p.
This always beautiful, always interesting and sometimes deeply moving
poem carries the atmosphere of Cardiff's Tiger Bay in the '30s. We have
asked A.D. Clegg for permission to quote extensively from this poem in
September's Voices.
Ben Ainley

THE ROAD TO BARACOA

In this small town
We were bred born and reared,
Here we wed strove and died,
For there was no road out of it.
The sea lapped and slapped at our feet
And the hills walled us in behind.
Foreigners came and went in their ships,
But for us there was no way out.

They all said there ought to be a road.
Some said there would soon be a road.
Batista raised a tax specially for this road
But still the hills held no way out for us.

Then Fidel Castro came.
They said he was different,
But how should we know?
Once he'd survived his battles
He might have been like all the others,
But he too said there ought to be a road.

Then, suddenly, it was being built.
Magnificently agile
It strode round the hills towards us,
And our young men climbed up to meet it.
There was noise and dust and machinery,
And strangers from Havana,
And slowly it wound its way down
Right into the town.

Now the buses come and go along it.
We leave and return at will.
There are teachers and doctors,
Musicians and politicians,
Coming and going just for us.
Women go to hospital on it
And bring back strong babies.
Youth goes to college on it
And brings back new ways.
O the wealth that flows
In and out like the tides,
As we give and take with all Cuba
Our fruit, our coffee, and our labour
For shoes, concrete, and guitars.
There is no end to the blessings of traffic
To and fro on our road.

So now we know that Fidel and his comrade. are different,
For they built our road.

Connie M. Ford

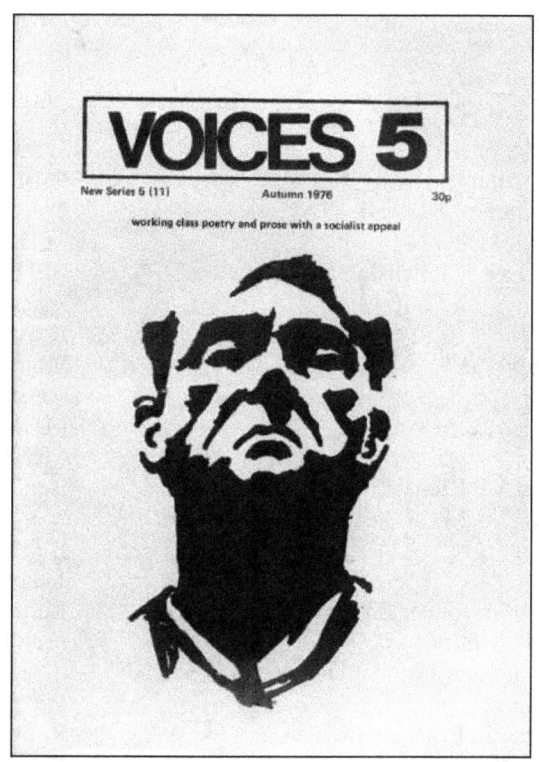

cover size 210 x 148 mm (A5)

CONTENTS

EDITORIAL

This is the eleventh issue of "Voices" Our total output has covered more than 650 pages, and over 250 contributions have been printed from more than a hundred writers. The flow of material coming in gets wider and more varied with each issue. Any comparison of the first and second issues with later ones will recognise what the achievement is.

In the first editorial, I wrote apropos the title "Voices": - "We felt at this stage we had not achieved a single purpose; our writing was not yet a manifesto, or a call to action, but a series of individual utterances. Later perhaps a more unified and challenging character may emerge in future collections." That was in 1972. In the second issue, the editorial asked for notice in Union journals and the progressive press. "Is a publication like "Voices" worth keeping alive?" we asked.

The third editorial, written by Ted Morrison, said, " "Voices" exists because its publishers, 'Manchester Unity of Arts Society" recognise that there is a need for magazines in which the literary potential of working people can flourish unhindered by traditions unrelated to their way of life, or by literary fads or fashions or commercial considerations."

In No. 4 we addressed our readers in this way: "If you think there is room for a committed publication which thinks of writing as a weapon in the hands of the Labour and Socialist and Communist movement, help us.

In No. 5, we wrote: "We think that the political stand of "Voices" is crystallising: we still want to make it as broad and catholic a publication as the labour movement wants and required: confident, critical, and reflecting the growing struggle for socialism. We are primarily a literary publication: the ideas, the activities, the spirit of working class activity, pugnacious, unapologetic, but committed to inspiring people, not sending them to sleep ..."

From No. 6 onwards through the new series we have had the low-profile streamer across the front cover: "Working class poetry and prose with a socialist appeal." No.3 of the new series contained a significant sentence in its editorial:

"it ("Voices") is not a vehicle for established writers. It is a means of dialogue between writers of working class origin and/or socialist tendency and the workers and socialists to whom they address themselves."

The editorial in No. 4 was a contribution to the discussion on Proletarian literature which made the point that within the culture of capitalism a culture of people in struggle against capitalism emerges as a part, and as an expression of The general struggle for socialism.

It is possible now to see that "Voices" takes its place alongside "Fireweed", "Ostrich', and I am certain scores of such publications, each with their own writers, and that their role is best understood by an examination of their contents than by any explicit credo.

Ben Ainley

HEARTS OF STONE

The great old city of Manchester
O how you lived and grew;
Now a true Manchester story
I thought I'd tell to you.
It's only a little something
Not a right old town to-do;
I know it happened for I was there
So I ought to know it's true.

You'll find our City fathers
When old Queen Victoria died
At great expense to the city no doubt
Proclaimed their civic pride
A mass of stone was chiselled fine
Great work of hand and brain -
And on her throne she sat and stared
In sunlight and much rain.

High on a plinth of stone steps
Too hard and cold to sit on,
The Queen has decently sat and gazed -
At the panoramic vision.
No marching mobs, no religious wakes,
No police cars, brass bands, none,
Have altered her stony visage, as
World wars have come and gone.

And thus she has sat and gazed for years
Upon the passing throng,
From the galloping horses till the day
When motor cars came along.
The pigeons squawk and squeal in flight
As they flutter round her face
They know and squeal "It isn't real,"

As she stares through endless space.

One fine workday went passing by
In Nineteen Thirty Nine
Off to the Labour Exchange to sign
On the dole's dotted line
Quick from the passing crowd I saw
A. couple with child and pram
Ran from the pram, up the high stone steps
And there they uptipped the pram.

It wasn't a babe in the pram that day
They tipped before the throne
But chains of iron jangled down
And clattered on the stone.
The woman gone, the man with speed
Chained the pram round the Monument's base;
A wink at the queen, then he ran from the scene
A smile lit the Queen's stone face.

Busy Mancunians hurrying by
Stopped, or just turned around;
A crowd soon gathered upon the steps,
To their surprise they found
A banner painted in words blood-red
Was tied to pram and chain
Fluttering bravely in the wind
This message to proclaim.

"THREE MILLION SIX HUNDRED THOUSAND
UNEMPLOYED WORKERS' CHILDREN STARVING"
The message was clear, it raised a cheer
Some people said "Disgusting!"
With dole queues big, dole payments small
Yates's soup kitchens were crowded;
But this was lost in a greater grief
Dread War our country clouded.

Policemen came to cut the chain
No time was lost removing:
The banner bright was folded from sight -
The Press men came with questions.
I mentioned the queen and what I had seen
Folk said I was dreaming surely

But papers next day had the story (front page)
With pictures of pram tied securely.

Take it from me the story is true
Why did the Queen smile so?
I know it is stone without organs or bone
What did her sly smile show?
In thoughtful mood, I can now see through
Why the man with the pram protested
With ten babes of her own - he couldn't go wrong,
Victoria was interested.

On a visit to Manchester last year
On a summer's day last year
I saw many changes, but I saw
The old monument still was there;
I found warnings and cries, and scares
And I thought of the pram and chain -
What would Victoria think of us now?
Would she ever smile again?

J. Kay

THE TWO JOHNS

His wife called him Jan because he was a Pole, and he told me a little of his adventures in Germany in war time.

As a boy of twelve years of age he was taken from his family by the Germans and sent to Germany as a slave worker. He had many different jobs. One was in a brewery which was bombed at the time of his working shift. After being discharged from hospital he was sent to work on a farm where there were many other Polish and Russian slave workers. Here the work was heavy and the food was light and they lived as best they could in the barns and outbuildings of the farms. They went to the farmhouse once a day and drew their rations. He was dressed mainly in rags and one time a rumour went through his little group that if he were able to find an old pair of trousers and get them to a Polish tailor in a village about seven miles distance; they could be altered and made presentable for him. When he did acquire some clothing he decided to visit this tailor. In order to make the journey from his place of work to the tailor and back without being missed by the farmer; he decided to go without his evening meal. As he did not

200

turn up for the meal at the farmer's house the farmer reported the matter to the police.

When Jan returned to the farm the policeman took hold of him; threw him into a barn and beat him unmercifully. He lay in the barn three days recovering from the beating. His fellow workers were too fearful to visit him to offer him help. He recovered and went back to work.

Little by little the Germans were feeling the results of the defeats in the battles in Soviet Russia, and living became harder and harder; not only for the slave workers but even for the Germans themselves.

The policeman who had beaten Jan, being of military age, was removed from his village post and an elderly policeman took over the district. This new policeman had the habit of working in his cottage garden in full uniform except for his helmet. He was a very keen gardener and every minute off duty he seemed to use in the garden.

Jan told me that once again he was reported by the farmer to the police for some misdemeanour and once again he was thrust into the shed, presumably to be beaten. The elderly policeman closed the shed doors, ruffled Jan's hair, yanked his shirt out of his trousers waist band and commenced with his stick to beat the walls crying loudly in German at the same time. Those outside undoubtedly thought, poor Jan, he is getting another terrible beating but the policeman was only going through the motions, probably in order to cover himself.

By this time the Russian army was racing towards Berlin, and the Americans had made a landing in the West.

The village doctor, who probably had something on her conscience, one day committed suicide by throwing herself from a window of her house. Shortly after this some American troops were seen travelling near the outskirts of the village and as they grew near they could probably see the policeman working in his garden. A German policeman's tunic is quite like that of an 'SS man' and possibly the Americans thought that they had one of the members of Hitler's Elite in this sights. They arrested the policeman, took him to the woods, shots were heard and Jan never saw that policeman again.

John number two was a London boy. When he was Jan's age his mother died and left brothers and sisters and his father to live on. Someone approached the father and told him not to worry about the children because they would report his case and the Church Army would give him assistance and relieve him from all worry and responsibility for the future of his children.

Through the officers of the Church Army John was sent to Wales where he worked for a farmer for four years. During these four years he never once was in the farm house but, like Jan, went to the farm house to collect his food. He slept in the outhouses and barns and the farmer, when he thought fit, would bring home from market a pair of trousers or some shoes.

The farmer and his wife always spoke in the Welsh language and, unless some gypsies passed down the lane, John never heard English spoken for all those years. When John was about sixteen, the farmer's wife fell ill and the farmer brought in a woman helper from the nearest town, which was seven miles distant. This townswoman became very interested in John and asked him all about himself; his family and his life. When she heard from John that he had never been away from the farm for one single day since his arrival and that he had never been paid any wages; she became more interested. She advised John that he must go and face the farmer and tell him that he wished to return to London and that he wanted some money for having worked for four years.

The farmer did release John and when John arrived in Paddington station from Wales he had in his possession thirty-two shillings; the rest of the money that the farmer had given him he had expended on a single railway ticket.

Some would say that John had been treated nearly as badly as Jan. Others might say that he had only been robbed of wages and freedom. But when John's full story is known the full extent of his loss is shown to be great indeed.

Where was his father, his brothers and his sisters? No one knew. John applied to the Church Army and they said that they could not give him any information whatsoever and when I left John in 1960 he was still searching for the family which had been robbed from him.

F. Mcgee

NO BALL GAMES ALLOWED

Breaking bottles on old bomb sites,
chucking rocks into the Thames mud;
well, it was something to do.

Making castles on the greasy beach,
playing football 'till late at night;
ruining trousers and shoes.

Riding our bikes in the jungle
deep darkest underground car park;
and lighting bottled bangers.

Sneaking rides in City office lifts,
always where we shouldn't have been;
because there was nowhere else

And now I look around me,
and see kids doing just the same;
because there is nowhere else.

Except that the bomb sites
are now building sites –
soon to be empty office blocks,
with windows just made for kids' games.

Tony Harcup
Basement Writers

Pete Carter

PRODUCTIVITY DEAL

A. short story in verse

The screwdrivers lay on the bench, heavy and gleaming,
fine-made tools, from the paint on their wooden handles,
and the shiny cylinders holding the springs and ratchets
and the oily shafts with their grooves in crossing spirals
and the roughened grips for the fingers that guided them home
to the blades where energy whirled the tempered steel
each of them nearly as long as a grown man's arm..

Outside, the frost was hard on slippery pavements
and factory blocks stood rigid against the dawn.

Charlie turned from the sky, took off his coat,
perched on a stool with a paper in front of his face,
and started to read this English as far from his
as the frost from the hot Jamaican sky of his childhood.

But this morning his mind wouldn't stick to the print or the pictures:
the gale of thoughts that had swept through his head in the night
made everything else as unreal as the door he'd closed
when he'd slipped from the crowded house, and the shadowy figures
that he'd passed on his way to the bus-stop, hunched in the wind,
or the garish lights that had come and gone in the darkness
as he'd stared from the top of the bus through the dirty window.

Fixed in his chair by the bench, Tadziu was smoking,
knowing he'd pay for his Sunday drinking soon,
but cheering himself with the thought of the money he'd won
at cards from his Polish friends as they swilled the vodka.

The claxon wailed; they were up on their feet in a second,
and bent to their work: Charlie was stacking cartons,
and Tadziu fetching a rack of electric meters,
wheeling it round and unloading it onto the bench.
Then dropping the screws in their holes, they lifted the screwdrivers
and pumped the handles, driving the cylinders down
on the whirling shafts, so they danced on the shiny screws
and spun them fast in the meters. Rising and falling,
their accurate arms moved over the bench like machines.
Round them, the factory spluttered and whirred and whined
as meter on meter was trundled along the line

205

till ranged on the racks for Charlie and Tadziu to pack them.
Tadziu mumbled and moaned when he came to one
with some fault that inspection had missed, and fiddled and tinkered.
Charlie groaned with impatience and urged him on:
'Come on, man, it isn't our business." He let it go.
Back to the noise of screwdrivers beating down,
then the bump of cartons loaded onto the pallet.
But with bodies in gear, their minds could escape, they were free

Charlie could see his girl as she danced at the party,
her big eyes shining, her body flaming in rhythm
with the frenzied guitars, the release in the shout of the singers.
But afterwards fell the shock on his drugged excitement
as he kissed her outside the house in the dimlit street.
She had covered his mouth with her hand – her bangled wrist
was cold on his cheek. She pushed him away from her breast.
"Hold off, loverboy," she whispered, "You got to get on,
if you want me to stay. I'm not going spend my life
squeezed in a house that's bursting with all your family.
We need more money to buy a place of our own."

"We will, girl," Charlie kept urging, "Just wait. You'll see."
"When?" she asked. "We got to be saving now, and you'll never earn
enough in a hundred years."
He bluffed and sulked, but coolly she went inside.
He felt the frosty air on his sweating cheek
as he pounded along the bench, still raking his mind
for escape from that terrace-house with its rooms divided
by curtains strung on ropes from one wall to the other
to a semi-detached, its woodwork glossy with paint,
bright curtains and carpets; whisky and rum in the cupboard;
a washing-machine in the kitchen; and parked out side
a new-bought car as flashy and fast as the foreman' s.

Tadziu was feeling the strain, now. His body was sluggish,
though he drove it hard. He thought of the bitter years
of exile in Kazakhstan, where the Russians had sent him,
a boy, with his father and mother: his elder brothers,
more dangerous stuff, had vanished in camps in the North.
Bawled-at, bullied and starved by a foreman-jailor,
their huddle of exiles had worked a collective farm
that survived the piled-up desert of winter snow
with some grain and cattle fed on the feeble grass
of the summer's heat. The plain had no trees, no thing

206

to break its endless level but cheerless scrub
crouching beside the riverbed. Little to eat
but a measured portion of flour to be mixed with water
and baked to biscuit on stones by a smoking dungfire.
Here, at least when the evening claxon hooted,
he was free to choose to go home or stop in a pub,
with money for food and beer and occasional vodka,
and rent for his tiny bedsitter, with telly and gasring,
and, a couple of evenings a week, a bet on the greyhounds.
He plodded doggedly on at the line of meters.

The foreman appeared round a corner; his smart white coat
stood out from their dusty grey. With his shoulders bent,
he turned his anxious eyes to the dirty floor.
"Bonus down last week," he moaned to the ground,
"I don't know why," and hurried away to his desk.
Had they been working too slow?

"The bastards," said Charlie.
"If we gain on them one week, they count us behind in the next."
"Last week too much," said Tadziu.
"Don't be so stupid,"
said Charlie," the press shop boys get three times as much.
If I work here alone I do better than stuck with you."
"I go fast enough," said Tadziu," and I not greedy.
You it was asked for us first start work on bonus,
and when they come measure the job, you work double quick,
so we slaves on timework. Before, we working in peace

"Don't be so dense. It's the only way to make money,"
yelled Charlie.

No more from Tadziu, not even a grunt.
Charlie lit up and puffed at his fag as he worked.
Tadziu was right: it was Charlie asked for the system:
it was gradually creeping through every part of the works.
Unions and management both applauded its progress -
it meant money for all, in the new productivity deal.
So two workstudy men came round in leisurely suits,
carrying clipboards and pens and stopwatch and tape.
One of them leaned on the wall, cool and relaxed,
and noted neatly each action of sweaty arms or back,
or legs, as they laboured over the meters.
The other one hopped around them in fussy circles,

207

using his tape and watch to measure their motions
in tenths of inches and seconds. Sometimes they paused
to chat for a while about holidays, houses or gardens
to the floor-supervisor, whenever he passed, or the foreman.
Then they withdrew on their own, to plan in their office
a perfect system with measured times for each movement -
no bend of the body, no turn of the head to be wasted,
the whole of the muscle-machine meshed into production.
So on Thursday afternoons, when Charlie and Tadziu
opened the envelopes handed them, sealed, by the chargehand,
the notes and coins that they slid out onto the bench
hung on the race to work in the times allotted.
He stubbed out his fag as he thought how the workstudy men
were rewarded for planning their 'Time and Motion' method.

How different it all 'had been at home in his boyhood!
(Deftly he spun each screw down fast in its hole).
The sun had measured the day as it rose up high
over the farmhouse roof, to ripen the rows
of green, then yellow, then red tomato-clusters,
or dropped below the banana-trees at the limit
of his grandfather's land, or at night the swollen moon
had shone on the lapping seawater where they waded,
holding their breath, searching for lobsters in rockpools -
in its light they could see the resisting claws where they groped,
and grip from behind. His feet had moved on the soil
running shoeless between the tended rows,
or shuffling along as he bent his back to the hoe,
or striding with baskets of fruit to the storage shed.
But the portion of fertile soil that was left for the family
was too mean a living for all. They embarked for Britain.

The day he arrived, a teenage boy, at the works,
the bland Personnel-Office clerk who took him round
from office to shop, asked "What did you do before?"
"Farming," he said.
"Ah well, then, you'll like this job"
-as they entered the bakelite shop - a concrete shed -
no windows except for a few glass squares in the roof
-grimy and grey with the ash of bakelite dust,
shaking with heavy machines that chugged and clanked
where they rose to the ceiling, hot with their chemical breath
as they pressed and melted the powder to shiny plastic.
He stayed there a year, then fought for a move to packing,

which he'd stuck six more. So now was he broken in?
He rammed the screwdriver down on the little screws.

Tadziu'd forgotten their quarrel. His thoughts had wandered
through childhood in Poland, the farm, the trees in the orchard,
the carp-pond where they had bred the sleek fat fish,
the cavernous kitchen where sausages hung from the ceiling,
to the years of manhood that taught him to bend to the wind.

He had left his parents to die in their desolate exile
when Stalin had formed an army of Polish prisoners,
and he found himself in Persia, nourished and trained,
fattened for killing. Soon, the Italian fields stank with the Polish dead.
But Tadziu survived. Then the currents of war had cast him aground in Britain,
where peacetime came, and he courted and lost a girl.
He had overstrained his back on a building site,
was burnt in a factory once with industrial acid,
then landed here, where he'd rooted in ten long years.

He was like a fragment of rock that was wrenched from its bed
by the gelignite-charge in a quarry, hacked and sawn,
built in a wall to be marked by the dirt of time
till shellfire buried it under a heap of rubble,
then bulldozed aside, half hidden in an earth embankment
where turf grew round it and on it, and one or two weeds
flowered alone. So he nestled in quiet routine.
He noted a hundred meters down in his book,
wheeled out the empty rack, and returned with a full one.
Charlie looked at the clock as Tadziu passed him.

The scent of a sweet tobacco came on the draught
that blew round the door - Kelford the supervisor.
Plump and relaxed in tweeds, puffing his pipe,
he arrived with a suited cluster of management types,
discussing some changes planned in the shops in his charge.
Charlie and Tadziu, pounding the screws in the meters,
could hear through their bangs, and the buzz of machines next door
(Assembly and Testing) some bits of their leisurely chat.
"Beautiful job - drove down to Brighton on Sunday -
very smooth ride."
"Be different driving in Europe
-those cobbled roads."
"Costa Brava at Christmas."

"Well, shall we move these packers across to the landing?
They don't need much."
"The test racks are more important."
They lounged there a while, gossiping, joking, discussing,
then drifted away, as remote and cut off from the packers
as though they were shut in a luxury plane that flies
serene over crowded streets.

Still the machine
of Charlie's body was working, but under the beat
of screwdriver down on the screws was another note
shrilling high in his head at the well-paid loungers
who altered jobs that they only half-understood,
treating the hands that worked and the ears that heard
and the brains that thought like contraptions of lifeless metal
- just dumb equipment, moving packing-machines.
How could he fight them? Shopstewards wouldn't support him
except on conditions or money. The foreman? His answers
were "Ask me tomorrow", "Remind me on Wednesday," "I'll see",
so that all roads petered out on a rubbish-dump
littered with rotting ideas, forgotten complaints.

Tadziu had heard their chat with a like contempt,
but he kept his temper untouched. Enough, to survive.
Staidly he laid more meters out on the bench.

Now Charlie was finishing packing the previous row.
He looked through the glass partition behind the bench.
Threading her way through machines and testing-racks,
the foreman's clerk was coming towards their corner clutching a work-
sheet.
Guessing her business, he scowled.
As he piled up the cartons and started putting the screws
in the new row of meters, she checked some numbers with Tadziu,
scribbled a note, and fussily hurried away:
he'd made a mistake in the book that would cut their bonus.

Charlie stood back from the bench and glowered at Tadziu.
"You stupid bastard," he said, "why I work till I'm weak?
Sweat through the day to cover the muddle you leave?"
"I make a mistake," said Tadziu. "Now it all right."
If nobody seen it," roared Charlie, "we been short on our money."
"You crazy about your pay," said Tadziu,

210

"you want I cheat in the book, so you fill your pocket."
"You can't even count, you're too lazy for that," bawled Charlie,
"you stubborn Polish."
"You thieving black" yelled Tadziu.

Like machines gone out of control, the sound of their shouting
grew louder and louder. Charlie lifted the screwdriver
over his head, and aimed it at Tadziu' s skull.
Tadziu drew to one side as it fell; the blade
drew blood from his scalp, but glanced off, missing the bone.
Charlie bellowed with rage that rang through the shop.
Hands stopped work on the line as they heard it echo.
Talking ceased, and the buzz of the air-powered tools.

Two who were working nearest the packers' corner
moved in quickly. When they came round the partition,
behind the piled-up cartons, they found them clinched
together, the screwdriver poised in Charlie's hand,
and Tadziu's clamped on his wrist. They drew them apart,
easing the tight-clenched fingers that clung to the weapon.

In the office-block the affair was quickly resolved.
Tadziu was taken to hospital, dazed and bleeding.
Charlie, rigid and silent, was sacked on the spot.

The next day, other hands took their place in the line,
Michael D. Butler

ADAM & EVE & PINCH ME

Not a word was spoken
but we both knew
that I was being punished
for something I had said,
or left unsaid,
or done, or failed to do.

Two can play at that game;
it was fine for a start,
but later we began to wonder
what it was all about.

Bill Eburn

211

PSYCHE

We don't talk.
Inhabiting different worlds
Our inner selves,
Revolving around an inner core of life.

Mood is sensed,
Balance maintained,
Like animals sniffing the wind
We avert danger
Of speaking, using man magic
To clarify, qualify: behaviour.

There are maps to show
The promontories of land
Geological disparities - Fissures,
Sea depths, and watery mountains.
Usefully could the makers
Map the populations varied
consciousness,
Of self, of depths of depravation.
Of lacks, of needs,
Of usefulness and uselessness
Of one man to another.
Language and languages
Are dull, and useless weapons
Fighting an ignorance of awareness,
In the so-word-blind many
Attempting to see reality

Through the facade
Of simulated truth
Consciously erected by the
(professional blinders.

Love is life
And truth is loving one another.
A lie is that that baulks the attempt.
Any act that deteriorates the forward road,
Makes booby traps in the
great highways: Painfully, slowly trod.

But we? A microcosm of this
Many headed host, which way for us?
Which way in our headlong fling into the grave,
now gathering momentum?
Shall we break the silence?
Shatter that wall, that opaque edifice
the psyche erects, maintains,
and constantly strengthens?
Or shall we stop peering
Questioningly through?
Depart our separate ways?

Frank Parker

(horns and child)

GIORGIO TAVERNITI

Born S. Italy. Studied Rome and Paris. 1st main
exhibition Mexico City, 1967. Brief stay United
States,then to England. Meeting with Barbara Hepworth
influenced extension of work to sculpture. Exhibited
Venice Biennale 1970, Redfern Gallery, London 1970/71/
72. Still lives in London, with frequent stays in
Middle East.

THIS

this
used to be countryside
shapely acres of land and now it's
ground for genocide
the sheep jostle with exploding tanks

townsfolk
use our land to plan in
clean out their minds and
leave us

all their rubbish
tins and tanks

listen
to the weekend artists stumbling mumbling in their cottage country haunts running free
between the gunbursts

tins and taunts and
towns and tanks

yes this used to be countryside
shapely acres of land and
now it's
ground for genocide
the sheep drift in city waste

artists amongst tanks

Keith Armstrong

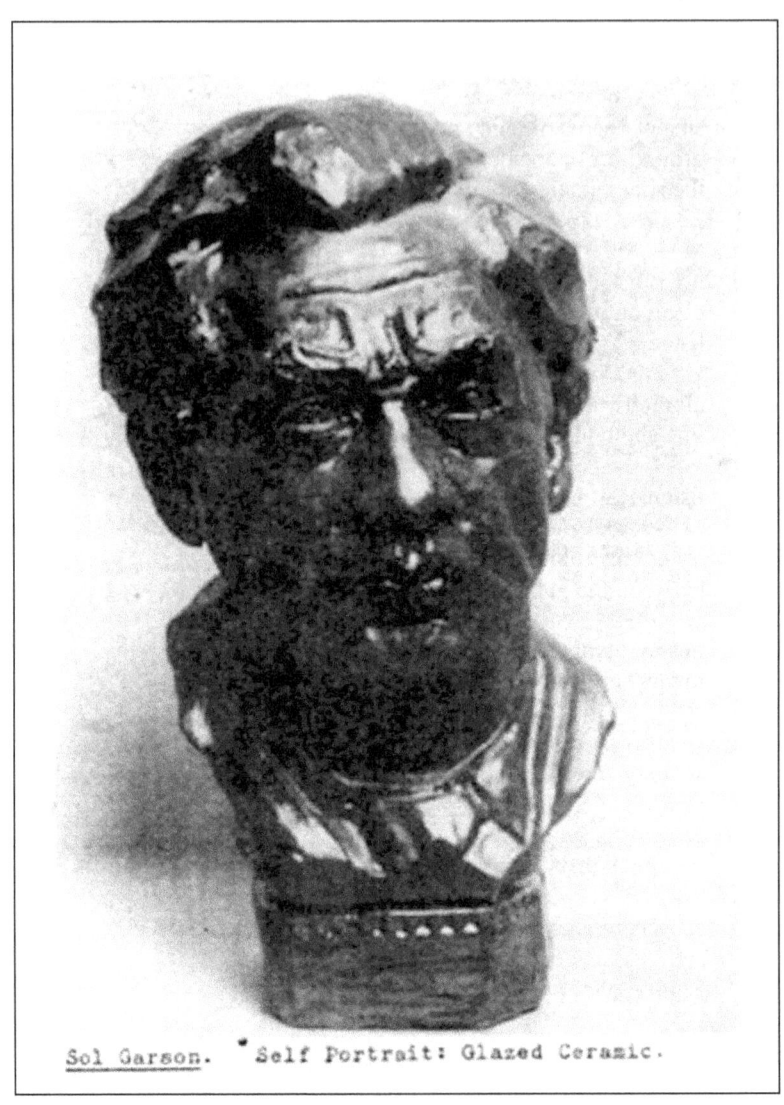

Sol Garson.   Self Portrait: Glazed Ceramic.

Sol Garson. Starving Mother & Child: Concrete.

FLOOR SHOW

All we have and are
negatived by this
below the mongrel bitch
covered in back street.

profaning the clean beast,,
the gaiety of flesh,
with showers of epsom salt
for lavatory sex.

foreign to the gay
interpenetration
of character and flesh
in endless permutation
when individuals play

when individuals play,
mates by every meaning,
all they have and are
dancing in love's teaming.

Frances Moore

HERITAGE

It had taken her over an hour on the bus to get to Camden. She turned into the street and stood on the corner for a few minutes to get her bearings. The noise of the traffic confused her. You had. to cross so many roads just to get somewhere you could see opposite.

She walked slowly, keeping an eye out for cracked and broken paving stones. The pavement was as bad as it had been when she'd lived here nearly forty years ago ... She remembered there was a little graveyard right next to the pub, she'd go in there and get he; breath back .a bit before finding where her shop used to be ... Yes, still there, the boneyard, 'as they'd called it. A scruffy, narrow little strip of ground, a path and a couple of benches. The bottles around showed the winos hadn't moved anyway. It's funny no one in the street had known, anyone buried hero. They were mostly foreign names on the stones. Some names looked a bit Jewish, she remembered having heard that some were French names Well, it looked much the same, smaller, but that was probably because of the tall buildings that' had been built around the back of it.

'She sat, enjoying a late bit of Autumn sun. Looking through the gateway of the graveyard over to the other side of the street she saw that now there were only six or seven of the terraced houses that had been all along that side. Further up the street she could see the tops of tall blocks of flats. It was like the street had been cut in half. It looked small and shabby with those tall blocks on two sides of it. She suddenly thought, "Was Kit's house still there?" Yes, by standing up she could see it, number 48, nearly opposite the shop. She was in no hurry to get to the shop. She knew it was there, she had seen that that block was still standing. Besides she knew more or less what she would find, she was just curious to know how she would feel about it now ... "Curiosity killed the cat", she'd always said that to the kids when they'd wanted to know about things that weren't their business.

It was getting chilly sitting here. She could do with a drink. The pub should be open now and she could go in and have a Guinness like she used to do. She used to leave the shop with her daughter for half an hour at twelve o'clock and meet Kit and Doll for a drink. She remembered the last time they'd met there, before the Blitz and they'd all said, "See you after the war then," but Kit had stayed on in Canvey Island and she never found out what had happened to Doll. Perhaps Doll had come back after the war, the way she'd come back that one day, and seen the foreigners everywhere. She hadn't known who they were at first, only later she was told they were Greek Cypriots. Everywhere they were. Some had already taken over the shops and they walked around the place as if they owned it. She'd gone back to her sisters. Tom had died during the war so there had been nothing to come back here for.

Still, she was here now, she wasn't sure why. She was seventy eight and she'd lived for forty of those years here so perhaps that explained it.

She gathered her coat about her and went to the pub, 'The Raven'. The door she used to go in wasn't there anymore so she walked around the pub until she found one ... Well, she might have known the pub would be different. They were changing all the pubs, they all looked the bloody same. There was only one bar where there had been three and it was bare and clean. On a shelf above the bar was a television and around the bar were a group of middle aged men, in their overcoats, silently drinking and watching the television ... some lunchtime programme, a bit like 'Crossroads'. ,I bet they scoff at their wives for watching rubbish like that," she thought. She went to the counter and then sat down at a corner table by the bar with her drink. She was facing the line of men who all had their eyes glued to the screen. She searched the smooth, emulsioned walls with her eyes, trying to make out where the old walls had been. Then one of the men moved and walked past where she was sitting, into the Gents. From where she was sitting she could hear him piddling ... "Well I must be more or less where we used to sit", she thought smiling to herself. "We always used to have a chuckle at that." Then grimly she thought, "Is that all there is to remind me of forty years in this street?" They'd hardly ever gone on holiday. A couple of years they'd gone on charabanc outings to Broadstairs and once or twice for a week to Margate. But otherwise it was this street year in and year out. The shop taking all your time. We were open day and night. Five-thirty in the morning to get the papers ready and to get the kids up delivering them before school, then open last thing at night to sell Woodbines or tobacco and fag papers to the people coming out of the pub who needed their smoke for the morning ...

Open all hours and yet never made enough money to shut up for a fortnight a year and go on a proper holiday. Too many people with too much on the bloody slate, that was the trouble. But what could you do when the kids came in, white faced and snotty nosed, with only half the money they needed for the few groceries. They'd say, "Mum says, could she settle with you at the end of the week?" You knew if you didn't give it to them it meant no tea for them that evening ... Ah well, that's past. People seem to have a lot more money since the war.

She got up and put her empty glass and bottle on the top. The woman couldn't have heard her say goodbye. She stepped into the street and the wind whipped round her, making her shiver. She walked a few yards on and there it was, Number 29. Now a cooked meat shop, Greek of course. She crossed the road to. look up at the rooms above the shop. The curtains were all drawn tight; gaudy, chintzy bloody things! "Christ knows what those rooms must look like now", she thought. She crossed back and looked in at the window. She didn't know what they were selling, looked mostly like sausages. She realised she'd been standing there for a few minutes because she saw one of the men inside watching her. She moved away embarrassed and angry. "Bloody cheek", she thought. "Who does he think he's looking at?" She walked on without really looking where she was going, walked in a kind of cold fury which at the same time wasn't that far from tears. She hadn't come expecting anyone in the street to know her nor had she particularly expected to recognize anything much, but when she stood outside the shop she'd lived in for forty years and was looked at as though she'd no right to be there ... If they'd been English she could have gone in and told them or not even said anything at all, just bought something. What could she have bought in there though, nothing.

She slowed down, she was a few yards into where the flats were, a kind of housing estate. Well she might as well look around it. Draughty hole. There didn't seem to be anyone around. Did they all go out to work? It looked cold and dead. There was one woman, over on the other side, head down, bag of shopping in each hand, she disappeared into one of the entrances. The grass by the path was all scuffed and kicked and there was litter blowing around. She came up to the entrance the woman had gone into. The glass in the door was smashed and kids had written all over the walls. It looked dreadful. She was frightened to walk any further into the estate in case she got lost. She turned around and went back to the part of the street she knew. The wind was in her face, making her eyes stream and her head ache. She felt tired and a bit wobbly. "I'll have to sit down and have a cup of tea before I fall over and make myself a laughing stock", she thought. Then she realised the only cafe left was run by a Creek. What could she do. She had to sit down and get a cup of tea before she could face crossing those roads and finding the bus stop.

A slight giddy feeling made her decide She opened the door. The net curtain tacked to the back of the glass in the door was grey. One table lay uncleared, on one plate the remains of a white porridgy looking stuff. She nearly went out again but the cold, biting wind from the street made her step inside and close the door after her. There was no one in the cafe. She gathered herself together, pushed back some hair which had escaped from under her hat and went to the counter. There was someone moving at the end of the passage leading off from the shop but she didn't want to call. On the counter was a colour photograph of a man in his late forties, sitting by the window of the cafe. The net curtain looked clean in the photograph and the sun was streaming through the window. He looked pleased. "So he bloody should", she thought, "Coming over here and taking over the street." She had been staring angrily at the photograph when she heard a

221

noise, someone coming up the passage. For a moment she felt frightened, almost sick, but before she could turn and leave he was standing at the counter in front of her. "A cup of tea", she said, and without locking at him again she turned and sat at a table, her back to the counter.

He didn't look anything like his photograph. Sixty if he's a day and that great head of hair was false - a toupee. She hated vanity in a man, worrying about being bald at his age, bloody daft.

He was a long time bringing that tea. She wished now she'd sat facing the counter so she could see what he was up to. He might slip something into her tea. She shifted nervously and took her purse from her handbag and pushed it into the pocket of her cardigan, underneath her coat.

(What was he doing? He'd put on some music, twang, twang, what a racket. Then that stopped, a few moments' silence and then 'Green grass of Home'. "Well that's better", she thought, "At least you can understand what he's singing."

At last he came with the tea. He put it down along with a paper serviette. She stared at the table in front of her, both hands gripping the edge. She could see from the corner of her eye 'that he hadn't moved. She jerked a look up at him. "English music", he said, pointing to the place the music was coming from. She didn't say anything. Then he said, "Something to eat?" "Oh, no, no I'm not hungry, no nothing to eat", she said, almost fearing that he would not understand and bring her some of that awful food. He probably didn't wash his hands after using the lavatory and Christ knows what went into those sausage things she'd seen on the other side of the counter.

He'd gone back now and she felt for her handkerchief and nervously wiped round the rim of the cup. The tea was good, hot, strong and fresh. He'd gone back along the passage. She put her handbag down on the chair beside her, painfully stretched her legs out in front of her and drank the tea.

Sun must have broken through a cloud outside because a white stream of light shone through the net curtain at the window onto the lino tiles on the floor showing them streaked with the marks of a floor mop. Opposite were the same terrace of houses that had been there forty years ago. She could see the top windows clearly through the glass above the curtain. Then she remembered clearly something that had happened, seeing those windows reminded her.

It was 1932, a terrible time, no one had any money, very few had any work. It had been in the summer when a car with a megaphone had come down the street and stopped. Naturally everyone came out to look. A car like that didn't come down the street everyday. There was a young man at the wheel looking self-conscious and two ladies in the back. One stood up and said, "I am here particularly to talk to the women", but the men and boys didn't move. There wasn't much in the way of entertainment around. She cleared her throat and t then went on to talk about the importance of keeping clean and to say how we weren't feeding our children properly. She said she'd suffered seeing little mites with rickets and all sorts of diseases that really were not necessary. 'Good, nourishing meals can be made with very little", she said. She then went on to tell us how to prepare cods' heads. We listened but then at the end Kit Adams, who lived opposite, called down from her top window, "Who had the cod then?" ... we roared.

She picked up the tea cup still smiling a bit to herself. The cup was empty, she must have finished it. The old Greek boyo was back again, nodding and smiling. "Another cup of tea, lady", he said. "Yes, alright", she said.

He hummed as he made it. He came back and with the tea he brought a small plate with one square of pink, sugar-dusted Turkish delight with a small wooden fork stuck into the top. "My anniversary", he said by way of explanation. "I came to this street, to this shop ten years ago.

He stood by the table, pleased and friendly. She didn't know what to say. Happily the door opened, a man came in, greeted the owner and sat down. The owner bustled away to get whatever it was he wanted. He must regularly eat the same thing because he hadn't ordered anything. The man was sitting two tables away, opposite her. A grey, thin, lined man wearing a dusty black jacket. He wasn't English though, he was Greek and the newspaper he pulled out of his pocket was Greek. Now all she could see of him was the paper and the rough hands, streaked with cement or plaster, the nails grimy and bitten down. She remembered Tom coming in for his dinner with hands like that and she'd always nagged at him to go and wash them before he ate.

She sat for about five minutes, slowly drinking the second cup of tea. It was as good as the first. She realised, with surprise that she'd relaxed and had been daydreaming. Well she must catch that bus and get home. She got up and left the money for the tea on the table. The old Greek was busy cooking, out at the back somewhere.

She walked to the door, past the man with the newspaper, who looked up and nodded. She stood for a moment outside the cafe and thought, "Well, I'll leave you to it. I don't suppose I'll come back again".

Anne F. Johnson

1976

Last Christmas Eve I walked the streets
frustrated and forlorn.
Had no toys to leave that night
Wished my kid had not been born.

Like a tramp I trudged the highways
That cold December night.
Christmas trees and lighted displays
With tears I dimmed their light.

Though things are better for me now
I'll not forget that night.
Nor you who call "Work for all
Be they black or white".

You who call for work for all
Call for a "Human Right"
And a child that has no Christmas
Shows a wrong that we should fight.

M. Doyle

SIMON

Without you there is no melody –
No you - life is too long.
There is no song.
The boys and girls who were your friends are growing tall;

With hair unkempt and beard uncut they saunter by:
They pipe their ballads - mouth their songs
With voices harsh and garish noise and sweet guitar.
The parents wail, "We have been cheated -gave our all –
These are our seed - oh what went wrong?"
Wierdos, inheritors of the earth,
Shrug, calmly say, "We want not birth
Or sex - or bomb - or drug - or you -"
The dawn in gentle roseate stirs
And where are you?
Health-giving sun flattens like lead my head:
Dusk whispers, but I cannot hear
For you are dead.
There is no song for me, no strange discordant melody
Plucked from taut strings, affirming you - and thereby me.
I listen to the inner truth of coming generations;
Envy demented parents soul-searching complications.
Without you there is no song.
Some breathless nights I wake
To echo of a long-lost note -

And you are surely there -
Remote - but so remote -No touching distance in your sphere
No flesh no time no hope no joy -
Safe with your melody.
And I am here,
My boy.

Marjorie Dearle

RETREAT TO APATHY -
VINCENT P. RICHARDSON PHAETHON PRESS

In spite of a title which suggests discouragement, the poems collected here from a number of publications, including "Voices" indicate satire, irony, compassion. There is room to quote briefly, the poem entitled Unemployed.

> We are the outriders
> the discontinued lines
> the statistician's graph
> diaboloes tossed
> by politicians
> - the bishop's prayer.

Anger here, not apathy. The last poem in this little booklet which gives its title to the collection seems to suggest that disillusion with the violence through which "angry young man/ degenerates/ to urban gorilla/ Blake's ideal/ to a bloody sword" is responsible for the apathy. You can get this booklet of interesting verse from the author, at "Brocket Willows" Daw Lane, Appleton Roebuck, Nr. York Y05 7BL.

Ben Ainley

CARELESS SILENCE COSTS LIVES

> The Greeks for instance:
> I saw your program on 'Greece: the Seven Black Years'.
> I suppose it's safe now - now it's all over;
> the 'dictatorship',
> the 'filthy' tortures,
> the killing,
> the arrests
> and the silence.
>
> And it's silence I want to talk about
> because I didn't hear overmuch from you
> while it was all going on
> and I wonder what your silence cost, in lives.
>
> And even now you didn't tell me
> what I most wanted to know:
> just how the colonels got there.
> I want to know who paid the piper

and called the silence
and who was puppet-master.
how
Very instructive to hear about democracy
gave way to dictatorship
Fly away Peter,
come back Paul
which suddenly collapsed
Fly away Paul,
.come back Peter
- for no apparent reason.

Tell me the single-edged truth.
Two little dicky-birds
sitting on a wall,
one named Peter,
one named Paul.
Fly away Peter,
fly away Paul,
come back Peter
- is this all?
Very noble of you to put on your program
the experiences of the 'ordinary people'
but the silence at either end
was battering my ear-drums.
How much did it all cost?

The voices of the dead clamour in the winds;
they shrill in the wires around the earth;
they twitter like distant radio stations at night
when the B.B.C. has gone to bed.

One day, they will find your frequency
all the dead Greeks.
Twittering among the wave-bands
when you are asleep:
they will tell us the truth –
all the dead Greeks.

Bob Dixon

GREY DAY

9 a.m. The last of the world travellers had just fled through the back door, leaving behind a trail of pyjamas, soggy cornflakes and rejected crusts. A forgotten sports bag sat forlornly on the kitchen floor.

It was a dull grey day - inside and out.

From my near horizontal position in the armchair, it was possible to see a thin film of grey dust between the T.V. and the radiogram which supported it. I sat up straight to protect my sensitive eyes from this distasteful sight. The carpet shrieking for attention spat grey dog hairs round the edge of my dressing gown.

I was surrounded with all shades of grey. My lucky colours - silver and grey.

"You mightn't even like the colours associated with your particular zodiac sign, but wear it, bring it into your home, it will bring you luck," Leon Petulengro had said.

"If you believe that crap, you'll believe in fairies and witches next," my down to earth husband had remarked to me.

Ah witches! Soon, with wings on my feet, and a bewitching twiddle of my nose, with Samantha-like efficiency, my unlovely grey house will be shining silver bright. That's how it's done - didn't you know.

You can even do it standing on your head, or, with one hand tied behind your back. All in ten minutes too, so - not just yet.

I reached for the 'Morning Star', and flicked grey ash from my cigarette on to the grey, grey fire.

Jean Sutton

THE SOLUTION

(translated by RICK GWILT)

After the rising of 17th July
The Secretary of the Writers' Union
Had leaflets given out in the Stalinallee
Saying that the people
Had lost the Government's trust
And could only regain it
By working twice as hard.

228

Wouldn't it have been simpler
For the Government to dissolve the people
And elect another one?

Bertolt Brecht

A STATE OF AFFAIRS

"Look at that bloody pile of washing!" he said, glowering at it in an aggressive pose. He should have been an actor or a singer. He'd never had the training. The soiled clothes, all textures and colours, were like a small psychedelic mountain cascading over the bedroom armchair and down on to the floor. Next to the chair were two cardboard boxes also overflowing with clothes. The wardrobe, small in dark brown wood with a front mirror faulted so it gave a double image, was empty where clothes should have been hanging although its floor was loaded with soiled garments.

"That the fuck am I supposed to wear?"

She was slowly waking up.

"I nearly broke a window yesterday", he continued more placidly. "I could have easily gone to the Launderette in the morning and 4 o'clock seemed a reasonable time -only to discover all of a sudden they've changed the closing-time to 5.30 on a Saturday so they can get all their bleedin' service washes done. It's only 'cos they make more on them."

"Well what d'you expect...?" He was bulling again; best thing was just to let him rant. "What about tomorrow?" she moved.

"What about it?" he snapped as if it was her fault.

"I thought you said there was a late opening tomorrow night... ?"

"Yeah. "

"Well that means you've only got to wear smelly clothes tonight, today and tomorrow and we can do a double wash tomorrow night okay?"

"But I spent the Launderette money when they wouldn't let me do it yesterday. I bought some chocolates and ate them all myself.

"You would."

Money: money: money: silver they called it in France. Greenbacks; dollars; cheques; bankers' cards; capital; finance. It wasn't as simple as that.

"All the different things people do for pleasure, amazing isn't it?" he volunteered as they were reading the Sunday papers. "Nearly all sinful things."

229

"That's not true," she said.

"No?"

"No - of course not; people breed dogs; and pigeons; go motor-car racing; scrambling; swimming; smoke hash; read books; do gardening et cetera et cetera ..."

"Yeah: but most people are only interested in sex and smoking and drinking: how many people belong to these societies? Those clubs? How many people go walking in the countryside? Play sports? They can't afford to. There's nowhere to do them."

"Want another cup of tea?"

"Yeah, okay

"You have to work, don't you? And when you work you're too tired to get it together to do any of those healthy things. Remember when we were in our early twenties how we could try anything, do anything: then you get a bit of sense - reality knocks you on the head a few times and you just have to conform."

"Yeah - but what is this 'reality' knocking you on the head - it does feel like that doesn't

"You have to earn your living..."

"Yeah" .

"You have to have money..."

"Yeah."

"To get money you have to have a job..."

"You don't have to ..."

"But most people do: anyway, you can't get away without working for very long. You lose your self-respect if you're on the dole."

"It's funny, isn't it, the way everybody goes through a stage of thinking they can escape?"

"Not everybody does - you might have but I didn't ..."

"Oh come off it..."

"I didn't. I had no illusions. I knew from when I was about 11 I was going to have to work all my life. I thought it was great. Free from school. I hated school. You know what they say - your schooldays are the happiest days of your life? I reckon it's true, however bad they seem at the time. The teachers make it rotten for you, though, because they don't really want you to get educated. Some people - most people, have to stay ignorant to do the shitty jobs, don't they? The sooner you get used to that idea, when you're a kid, the sooner you learn to be content..."

"You're not content ..."

"Well - that's me. That's 'cos I wanted to be a ballet-dancer..."

"You did that go-go stuff.."

"That's different - just throwing your tits around"

There was a pause.

"I told you you wouldn't like it."

"Okay - you were right and I was wrong but still all my life I'm gonna be miserable because I wanted to be a ballet-dancer and I couldn't be. There's a ballet-dancer inside me aching to get out and she's gonna be trapped inside me all her life, all life."

"You want a kid that's all that's wrong with you."

"I don't."

"Yes you do. You want a kid you can send to dancing classes"

"That's different. What I'm saying is I wasn't born to be a bus-conductress. I hate being a bus-conductress..""You love it ..."

"I only let on I love it.."

"You're completely different when you're working. I've seen you: putting on a big act..."

"Ah fuck off."

"It's true..." he was laughing.

She was deadly serious. "It's a bloody miracle my mind's still my own and still working..." It was a miracle. One of the modern miracles which had nothing to do with Jesus Christ or God or Holy Spirits. Just some people were lucky to bump into other people who helped them along. Her husband was a hospital technician and had never been through the "humiliation process" she had had to go through. She'd survived because she was a strong character, because she was at heart a ballet-dancer.

"If I was meant to have been a bloody conductor I'd have been born with a bag strapped round me and all the stages in my head. D'you think there's anything enjoyable about taking money off people all day, feeling your varicose veins getting worse and worse and wondering all the time what bloody use you are? What bloody use is a bus-conductress, tell me that?"

She was becoming tearful. He knew it hurt her. He knew she really only wanted to read and study. He knew the situation was totally unsatisfactory. But they needed the money. She'd had an abortion. They were still paying back the money they'd borrowed. They'd been out of work - they were in debt from that time. Now they were just about breaking through, out of debt, and breaking even. But unpaid bills were no longer the brave joke they had been when they had been younger.

"It seems like everybody's my enemy ..."

"We all get like that sometimes..."

"Why? Why? Why?"

"I think life is just one big con."

She began to cry. Their clothes were filthy - she was a useless housewife. The kitchen was filthy. There was rubbish all over the place. She had no energy. She tried and tried. And all the time she felt like killing herself. She was killing herself. Killing off all the bits which cried out to be satisfied but could not be. Killed off all the bits which were not herself in her uniform working her way through endless shifts. He put his arm around her.

"Jack it in Barbie if you hate it that much."

"I can't, I can't ... you know I can't." She began to sob. Most of the time she was 'alright'. "You've ... you've got to have buses," she said eventually, breaking bravely away from his comfort.

"Yeah . .

"Somebody's got to do it..."

"Yeah ... nobody said anything different...

"It's important ..."

"Of course it's important."

She got up and went into the adjoining kitchen with the cups. She picked up the large kettle they used to get hot water from the bathroom. The geyser was broken. They were waiting for the landlord to come and fix it, send somebody around to fix it.

"Everybody's in the same boat; everybody's in the same boat..." the thought kept running through her mind. Every time she picked up the kettle she wanted to throw it on the floor and scream, "It's not good enough! It's not good enough!" Everything was so small, so cramped. If she had a big house in the country she would be so beautiful. Money was like a chain around her neck. Who was holding the other end of the chain? She remembered seeing an Escapologist in Leicester Square once all tied up in chains and a sack - it had been very exciting, the crowd had gathered around and watched him being chained in by somebody from the audience and then, just when you thought he couldn't possibly get out he wriggled about a bit and the chains fell off him and he got out.

"Let's go out for a walk..." she said when she'd cleaned up in the kitchen and Gregg had swept the front room and the bedroom.

It was cold but sunny. They decided to go to Hyde Park. They got off the Tube at Knightsbridge and walked past Harrods.

"We'll go window-shopping", said Barbie.

There was a room like the room she would like to have. How different from the scruffiness of their furnished accommodation. She'd done her best to make it 'nice' but it was a home and not a home. One whole day's work a week was not for herself but for the landlady, the Company who collected from them every week. The suite of furniture she looked at now - luscious velvet - why it wouldn't even fit into their front room with any room at all to move around.

They passed a grand hotel. There were big houses everywhere. A girl came out of a turning on a horse. Making her way to Rotten Row. She had a beautiful figure. The horse was sleek and rippling with power, brown and shiny. The girl was high, high above them.

"How's your gee?" Gregg yelled at her.

Barbie, on his arm, angrily told him to "Shush..."

The girl on the horse was completely oblivious to them. Insults from envious hoi-poloi were an annoyance of the same order as splashing rainwater from passing cars.

It was beginning to get very cold and Barbie had no coat on her, only a cardigan. It was her rest day the following day. She would do all the Launderette, she had a spare pound, and they would have a fresh start.

That there should be these 'class differences seemed as natural as the air they breathed. The girl on the horse was only a symbol. The important thing was who had what. Who had money. It was like a game of monopoly: the more you had, the more you got. It was a game of skill, of course. Skill not hard work. If you just worked hard you didn't necessarily get anywhere. You just kept going. No - you had to have brains and 'know how'

233

to really get on. 'Know-how', however, was really a matter of 'know-who': the girl on the horse was no different from Barbie in her flesh and blood. The only differences were superficial ones - the way she talked, the way she walked: and, above all, the money she had in her pocket or, if she didn't have any money, who she knew who would give her credit. And the credit she could get was quite different from the credit Barbie could get when she was a kid going to the shop on the corner to buy things 'on the book' for her mum. How did it work? That's what Barbie wanted to know? How did it work? It depended who your mum and dad were! she knew that much. If your dad was a lord you were a lady and did all genteel things. If your dad was a factory worker you were likely to be a factory worker too, or a typist or a bus-conductress. Gregg had saved Barbie, she knew that. He loved her and treated her with respect. But although half of her wanted to think of the two of them, snug and cosy in their little home, the other half, or another part of her rebelled all the time. She was popular in the garage. Chances were she might get chosen for shop-steward one of these days. They all liked her. Even people on the route liked her. She was a good laugh and she did the job well. It was just that Barbie found it hard. Acting, acting all the time: maybe she had forty years to live -what could she do in that time? Have children? But what for? What good was that if they were only going to end up with crummy jobs. She felt the shame coming on again. Why should she be ashamed? There was nothing to be ashamed of about being a busconductress. It was her life. She wasn't a ballet-dancer. Fair enough. She never would be - she just had to accept that. What sin had she committed? What had she done wrong? Blame herself - blame herself always she was doing that. A psychiatrist might have described Barbie as a hysteric. She would not accept her lot. She was not satisfied with her life. She could not be happy or content. She could sleep but she could not rest.

"Is there something funny about me? Or wrong with me?" she would sometimes ask Gregg. "I'm never the same. Sometimes I get sick asking people for fares when I know they can't afford them. Other times I get sick with them for getting on the buses all the time and making work for me and I feel like charging them double for the fare, just out of badness."

"Calm down Barbie," was Gregg's usual response. "You get too het up. You can't change the world in one go. Overnight. We have to do it gradually."

"There's some things you can't do gradually," she had once answered him. "Like like, well, like turning a pillow-case inside out: you can do it slowly, but you can't do it gradually: well, you can, but it's really all of a sudden everything's completely different. You know, like in the Olympics when you see the relay race: one minute one bloke's got the stick and the next minute somebody else has got it. Or when milk boils over. Everything is upside-down; or inside out; or back to front. Like me riding the horse and that girl clocking in at half past six."

She slept soundly. She had her dreams alright. Her dreams that one day everybody would be happy and healthy and wealthy and wise. There were two types of people, she thought: those who felt for others, who took others into consideration; and those who only thought about themselves. But somehow it happened, in the whole of life, that everything was geared to benefit the bastards, the greedy, nasty people. It didn't matter how smart they looked. Just because somebody was goodlooking on a horse and had lovely mariners didn't mean to say they weren't a greedy, selfish pig. It was like a big, moving pile of people - the ones at the bottom did all the work and loving and running around and suffering, and the ones at the top got all the benefits.

When she was a little girl Barbie used to dream the pixies would come and do all the tidying up while they were asleep. She even planned with her sister to get up in the middle of the night to do it as a surprise for their mum. But they slept soundly through the night and when they woke up the room was just as messy as when they'd gone to sleep. Making the country better would be a million times harder - but there were a million times as many people to do it.

The night before she was starting back on a shift a couple of weeks later, Barbie was watching 'Upstairs-Downstairs': things had come on a bit since then. Barbie wished that when she wanted to shout and scream and shake herself out from top to bottom everybody else would as well and when they calmed down there would be no more aggravation and competition. Everybody should be able to 'get high' together, holding hands in co-operation - instead of 'climbing' in society over other people's heads. She was agitated, agitated, agitated.

"Hold very tight please!" She called out automatically. She rang the bell twice and the bus moved off. A young child stared at her and marvelled at her power.

Fran Hazelton

Further comments on 'In Defence of T.S. Eliot'

After reading "In defence of T.S. Eliot" I turned to the introduction to John Beecher's "Hear the Wind Blow". What a good description of Eliot and his clique.

"His cautious articles on criticism did not impress me, nor did his erudition, scholarship or his lack of a sense of either life or literature. His mouldy poetry struck me as the perfect expression of a clerkly and liverish man's apprehension of life.

Here is a quotation from John Beecher.

"If you're looking for him here you might as well give up
I doubt if he'll be back.
That sermon on our Christian duty to pay tax for bombs
was more than even he could take.
Maybe he's gone to Tennessee.
You've heard of how those negroes registered to vote
and how their landlords threw them off their farms
and how the negroes pitched a camp and called it "Freedom City".
That's the kind of place you're apt to find him.
Jailed maybe for bringing food and blankets in
Like that preacher McCrackin all the elders and high priests are out to get
Might even be he ran the block to Cuba
Can't stop him once he makes up his mind to see things for himself.
Could be he's building them a school
or housing for the folks of the bohios
That wouldn't be a trade he'd need to learn."

Unless the poet takes up the struggle against exploitation and poverty and can reveal glimpses of the new dawn I cannot be bothered to read his effusions.

Clifford Hargreaves

A SLOW DEVELOPER

53 paces down the street
(53 you're doing fine). STOP:
On the right, one floor off
the ground, is your brother's
room - and yours. Why

are you bleeding? The house
cannot be climbed, is not
your coconut tree. Use the key
man, use the key. The key
will not fit the door today.

The sign, unlike the blow
means it's bad but not that bad.
You're doing well, my friend,

236

you're doing fine, You've got
the number right, but the street

LOOK AT THE NAME OF THE STREET!

Paul St Vincent

PRACTITIONER IN EMANCIPATION

For today's lesson he draws graphs
Points out analogies, compiles theories
To prove the absolute
He has renounced speculation for science

And by now he has completely
Broken with the great deviationists
- the "zoo" is good for neither
Man nor beast

Emotionally vulnerable
His adrenaline count rises
With each act of aggression
and indignity
Imposed upon it's "inmates"
Urgently he seeks to dissipate
The possessor's smokescreen
Obscuring the beacon's light

Merchant of the long-fixed
Chromosomal number,
Second hand memories of
Exquisitely shared experiences
Spur him on

Within his present cup
The bitter tang of temporary defeats
Is laced with the sweet nectar
Of exhilarating visions
Of future freedoms

Even though his cross is made
The target of the slings and arrows
Of ridicule and derision,

He will continue to cry out
Until his last breath is drawn

Tomorrow will be best
He promises, if only
They would listen today.

Rose Friedman

FUNNY WEATHER

Through the evening fog
a young girl's face
imprisoned at a window.

A kitten
in the gutter
mangled.

A face
at the window of an empty house
like the soul of a zombie
flickering.

Through the Autumn rain
her paleness
bears a strangled smile.

Ray Baker

ISSUE 12

cover size 210 x 148 mm (A5)

CONTENTS

"VOICES" Financial Appeal

We circulated our appeal in the last weeks of October, less than 4 weeks before "Voices" 6 went to the printers. The reason for this call for help was not because of decline and crisis, quite the contrary. Circulation is continually increasing. The men and women who write for us are a continually growing number.

But we wish to expand. our circulation. still more. We need to make approaches to the Labour movement, to student societies, to bookshops; we generally need, more advertisement, And in a period of rising costs we want to maintain our price level. Hence our call for £250 to see us through the next 2 issues, or better still £350, which would enable us to complete our budget promotion to the end of 1977.

We hope never again to shake a begging bowl before our readers, and are very grateful for the response so far (Nov. 12). Total £164.23.

LIST OF CONTRIBUTIONS

Sol Garson £10,
Martyn Handley £1,
Anon (Watford) £5,
Ben Ainley £5,
Bill Eburn £2,
H. Burgess £1,
Joyce Stebbens £5,
M. Orbach, M.P., £1.50,
Roy Melven £5,
C.S Bescoby £1,
J. Wolmark £3,
Mike Pentelow £5,
Mrs.E. Sheldon,£1,
C. Morris, M.P., £2,
M. Balchin £2.40, -
Brian Simon £5,
Rose Friedman £5,
H.G. Klaus £2,
V.P. Richardson £1,
S.M & K. Karim £2,
Bernard Barry £2.50,
Fran Hazelton £5,

F. McGill £10,
J.M. Hawthorn £3,
Sarah Windlebank £4,
Julia Murphy £2,
Anon (M/c) £2,
R. Howard £2,
Sam Watts £1,
H. Morgan £1,
C. Hargreaves £2,
F. Seyd, £2,
W. Hodgart £1,
N. Wylie £5
A.D. Clegg £5,
M. Butler £5,
B. Hodkinson £2,
C.W. Page £5,
Alf Morris, M.P. £5,
Connie M. Ford £9.93,
R. Hartman £2,
G.Restie £1,
P.G. Gallop 40p,
J. Hanby £2,

E. Jessup £2.50,
M. Sedgley £5,
N.L. (Hale) £5,
Craigavon Gp C.P.I. £3',
John Pinkerton, £2.

ON A LOWRY PICTURE

From these drab streets, these too much clouded skies,
who shall condemn a painter if he flies
to where the sun some brilliance supplies?

Though those that tread French pavements, Spanish dust,
barefoot for poverty not pleasure, must
like us unsatisfied and hungry rust.

For rain is not responsible for slums
nor smoke nor industry alone benumb
people into the shadows they become.

These who are lords of molten metal, kings
of locomotives, makers of fine things,
should walk with dignity, nay, swaggering.

But since they hardly earn a living pay
which well may vanish on a rainy day,
how can they walk unbowed, much less be gay,
but in the hopes we blaze abroad each May?

Frances Moore

TO A NAMELESS JOE

like a nightclub in the morning
you are the bitter end like a freshly harpic' d bathroom
you're clean round the bend
you give me the horrors
you put me in the poo
all of my tomorrows
are black because of you

like a death at a birthday party
you ruin all the fun
like a sucked and spat out smartie
your usefulness is done
like the shadow of the gallows
bad noose as I would say
bad blood marks the sidewalk
as you go your wicked way

you put the shat in spatter
you put the pain in spain
you're mad as a bleedin' 'atter
you're so lethargic you're lame
your very presence in my view
is an outrage on the eye
a motion picture reminds me of you
each dawn I die

You went to a progressive psychiatrist
who recommended suicide
before scratching your bad name off his list
and pointing the way outside

the day god spat you on the stack
was the last day of laughter
you crawled you walked you jumped on backs
lived apathy ever after

John Cooper Clarke

CREDIBILITY GAP

The parson mouthing
his theological jargon.

the writer's pen
dripping empty cliches.

the politician open-gobbed
showing his rotten teeth.

the lunanaut in orbit
deciding to travel by bus.

me - pretending.

any mirrors around?

Vincent P. Richardson

REAL PEOPLE

There will come a day
When nobody will think
Of looking for a reason
For living, they'll just
Be living and that'll
Be reason enough
For doing, jumping,
Running, singing,
Laughing, working.
Nobody'll stop wanting
To do things, the way
They do now, because
Most things you want
To do you'll be able
To do. Nobody'll be
Shy of doing things well,
Of having dreams
Too big, too grand,
Too loving, too
Magnificent. Nobody 'll
Nip their plans in
The bud because
Plans are frowned upon,
The way they are here
And now. Nobody will
Cower and be humble
In the presence of
Trash. Nobody'll be
Embarrassed or ashamed
Of the ambitions they
Have for themselves
And their children.
Nobody will conceive
Of tolerating anything
Less than the best
Available. Nobody
Will accept a
Restricted area of
Understanding, a playpen
In the explorable world.
Nobody will ever have
The thought cross,

Their mind that they
Don't matter. Nobody
Will imagine that
They matter more
Than anybody else.
Nobody will despair.
Nobody will triumph
Except over their own
Limitations. Nobody
Will grow and grow
Old like a calf
In a veal-house;
Nobody will walk
Like a horse fixed
To a milk-cart;
Nobody will be
Like a fat
Splayed cat or
A clapped-out old
Dodgem-car. I
Can't say what
People will be
Like when they've
Made a leap
As great as the
Leap into language -
But I hope I
Can discern what
Our social silence
Is doing to us
Now.

Fran Hazelton

MONEY ON THE BRAIN

(Number of unemployed in Britain on 20 July 1976, 1,463,456).

Money on the brain
Money on the brain of all classes
So no one profits

Men and women exchanged for their use

in making things that make money
involving a surplus they never see
In a word: exploitation
What kind of value is this?

Do the ruling class and the clerks of the state
know that the quality of the unemployed
increases with the number of the unemployed?
Including: old workers soaked with rage
mothers and wives upset in their guts
black and asian youth coping in their stride
- up to a point
white working class youth putting their
literacy to use at last filling in their
first B1 forms
ex-students and their varieties of contempts
All realize their potential for a higher value in
being so
devalued

The top cat politicians break for tea
And air their sweaty backsides at the expense of working
people
and the unemployed, whose daily life is to be scuttled further

on behalf of the money on the brain syndrome

Think: as the T.V. eye of U.S. space technology extends to Mars
(is there life on Mars?
is the class struggle on Mars?)
as the spurious Olympic vision is made a mock of
- if not or. British T.V.
(how is the class struggle on T.V.?)
as the T.V. spells out the latest
unemployment figures
as if matter of fact
(how is unemployment a consequence of
class struggle?)

Everywhere there is money on the brain
money on the brain of all classes
so no one profits

Alec Gordon

PORTUGAL 1974

Can you hear, Brain, on Robben Island? Can you hear in Chile?
Are the trade winds whispering tonight the news, of Portugal-?
Mozambique, Angola, Guinea-Bissau?
The tide of people's power is surging up the
black rocks of fascism:
they'll be engulfed.

One should live for a hundred years to see the future;
No longer just co-existence;
But a new Socialist World, A Fourth Dimensional World
With Fourth Dimensional Man!

Will he go to the other galaxies?
Will the universe yield us the secret of eternal life?
An answer to our population problem?
To our inborn longing for everlasting life;
And life then no longer mockery;
a clown's act, finished in a puff of wind,
But last forever in the skies!

Isabel Baker

THE GOOD CHRISTIAN

It is a hot, dry morning, and the veld burns beneath a fierce, hellish sun. The air is still and all is silent save for the song of cicadas strident in the scorched grass. The compound 'seems empty, for the black labourers have long since left to continue the harvest of the maize. But one man remains half hidden in the shade waiting. Why does he wait? The foreman told him to report to the boss first thing in the morning. Then there was nothing ominous in his words. But the black man knows that the man for whom he is now waiting is harsh and' just, and that he hates thieves even when they steal to feed a malnourished family. He is afraid, but resigned to his fear and punishment. His Life has given him a servile and sheepish appearance. Perhaps he hopes the man for whom he waits, whenever he troubles to think of him. Why does he work under such bad conditions for such long hours for him? He neither knows nor asks. Perhaps it is because the others all do so. Perhaps none of them yet knows how to ask the question why. Perhaps they are waiting for something that is now as distant as the sun at midnight, but which shall come as certainly as the dawn. Why does he not flee from the dusty yard of certain punishment? But where? They must all flee together. Why does he not arm himself to kill him for whom he waits? But how? They must all strike together. He stands with dignity, but not in the sun. He does not want to be seen. His body is of bone and muscle: on the rich and white can have fat. Perhaps there are vestiges in his bearing of his Zulu ancestry, or are they the signs of a future whose birth is inevitable? How long must he and his people wait? Now he stands immobile in the quiet of the morning, a quietness that only the white man breaks.

Christian Bloemfeld is the owner of a maize farm in Northern Natal. He is the proud descendant of a line of Dutch settlers who rode in ox-drawn waggons into the heart of South Africa to seize the virgin lands from the native tribesmen whom they either killed or enslaved. His grandfather fought as a young, enthusiastic guerrilla against the British in the Boer War, but although the' British won and the miners gained the freedom to exploit the country's vast mineral wealth, his grandfather kept his lands and kaffirs along with the other settlers. The farm is appropriately called 'Kruger'. Bloemfeld himself is a hard, tough man, 'brutalized through an inheritance of endurance, determination and tenacity and through a Calvinist faith that sanctifies ownership and wealth as signs of divine favour. Bloemfeld sees the world as something to be ordered and used to his own advantage. The soil, the grasses, the seed, the timber, the rains and the sunlight, the animals and the birds, and the black men are to be' dominated and controlled through incessant effort. 'In the sweat of thy brow shalt thou labour to eat thy bread'. This formula is engraved on his spirit. Bloemfeld believes in hard work, running the farm with efficiency. His days are spent in giving orders backed by the threat of the whip, ensuring that the maize is planted properly and harvested, buying and servicing implements, and then selling the maize at a good price. He is moderate in what he consumes compared to his relatives in Johannesburg and Kaapstad, and has the reputation in the local community of being a generous man, his donations to the Dutch Reformed Church being not inconsiderable and evidence of his piety. He is much like his ancestors whom he deeply respects. They were conquerors, so branded by natural adversity, and he feels he is of that selfsame stock, identifying closely with their traditions.

Bloemfeld now nonchalantly enters the compound. He does not strut, but his air of self-confidence. He is a tall man, a little fat with hair cut short. His face is heavily tanned, since he spends his days out in the fields. He wears shorts and leather shoes. His shirt is unbuttoned to reveal a firm, stone-like chest covered with dense hair. He strides powerfully over to where he has noticed from the corner of his eye the black man standing coweringly in the shadow of the storehouse. In his right hand he clutches the ivory handle of the bull-hide whip. The black man seems to shrink. He wishes to merge with the whitewashed wall, but it is impossible. Bloemfeld now looks at him piercingly straight. The black man's head is bent to look at his naked feet, whitened by the dust. The ground softly crunches under Bloemfeld's feet: the only sound.

"You been stealing grain?" Bloemfeld addresses him. The words are merely part of the' role - the role of being master. The black man is dumb. There are no words to be spoken, for they speak different languages of work and communication. The black man is old, though only forty, for the work ages so inexorably fast. He has ancestors, but they are unrecorded in history. His timorous eyes are caught by the hands of Bloemfeld who almost sensually grips the handle of the whip. He has seen other black men who have stolen or been too tired to work with ugly weals on their backs. This man has worked hard and obediently to avoid- Bloemfeld's anger until now. But had his family to starve?

Bloemfeld is relaxed, legs apart and his eyes now locked on the whip. Both men's eyes are fastened to the whip. It is the medium through which they see one another, the bond which joins them in an inhuman relationship. They never look at one another face to face as men. They cannot, for one fears and the other despises. When does one man's fear become the hate that can one day kill and when does one man's contempt dissolve into fear? The black man continues to wait. He wishes to run - to be with his family and friends. He remains in silent paralysis. Yet though afraid, he does not 'tremble or plead, to surrender his last possession, his dignity.

"You stole grain. The foreman has told me." Bloemfeld has spoken the accusation in a language only he understands. He interprets the black man's silence as stupidity in the face of an irrefutable charge. The black man is detached from the shouting. He is tired, and only an amorphous foreboding about the severity of the punishment floats through his mind. Perhaps he sees Bloemfeld as a puppet. "You know thieves must be punished. 'Thou shalt not steal.' You know the commandment." Bloemfeld who feels he is the intermediary between God and this man, thinks he has said enough. He is a laconic man who frowns upon conversation as 'wasteful. He knows that it is his duty to protect this man from evil and to enforce God's will, as his grandfather and father did and as they taught him to do.

Now Bloemfeld raises the whip and begins to beat the black man, cursing a little as he strains to bring the lash down forcefully upon the naked black body. The black man is forced down almost at once to the dusty, white ground. His body is contorted with the impact of each cutting stroke and blood begins to stream staining red the whiteness of 'the earth. 'He brings his knees tip to cover his agonized face and tightly clasps his feet as an embryo. Bloemfeld labours in this rhythmic motion breathing heavily and oozing sweat'. He is enjoying the destruction of a human being. His pleasure is a grim ecstasy. His consciousness is absorbed into the single, repetitive action: the whip" is raised and it falls to be raised again. The black man becomes a symbol of what is still to be conquered. He is a part of nature untamed, evil and dirt. He must be beaten, for he is a threat 'that' can engulf Bloemfeld's whole' life: his 'religion, his livelihood, 'his family, his race. lie is" all what 'Bloemfeld hates and fears. Bloemfeld clenches his teeth. His ears are sealed to the pitiable cries. He hears' only the dry crack of the whip or. the yielding flesh. His, facial muscles constrict into an appalling mask. He strikes until exhaustion overcomes him. The black man is silent, semi-conscious.

Bloemfeld walks slowly back to his home, a spacious bungalow several hundred yards from the farm buildings. He is pleased to see the minister's car parked in the driveway. Bloemfeld casually climbs the steps and enters the hall where he ignores a young black maid who takes his whip before meekly vanishing. Bloemfeld politely enters the lounge where, as he anticipated, his wife and the minister are talking amicably over coffee: the atmosphere is civilized. They greet Bloemfeld with obvious pleasure. The minister, a somewhat gaunt, grey-faced man with a scrawny neck and faint voice, dressed in the usual black, rises to shake hands with the master of the house. His smile is candid and unexaggerated, as he explains that he can now accomplish the main purpose of his visit, namely to express his deepest gratitude to Bloemfeld for his recent 5,000 rand contribution to the Church. "There was never such an honest, generous and god-fearing man as you in my chapel, Mr. Bloemfeld." He says this sincerely, clasping the farmer's still sweating tight hand. "I need not hope to see you at church next Sunday, Mr. Bloemfeld, since you're sure to be there in the front pew as usual." He smiles ecstatically over his little joke about Bloemfeld's piety, and leaves after an exchange of farewells, wishing he had more parishioners like the Bloemfelds.

As the minister is driving away from the Bloemfeld's residence, he notices a black man hobbling painfully outside the farm compound. He is bleeding and seems to be drunk. The minister who is upset by the sight of physical suffering, feels slightly sick and presses his foot down on the accelerator. The black man who recognizes the car watches it disappear in a whirl of dust with hateful eyes.

Martyn Handley

VILLANELLE

The World, as yet, allows the C.I.A.
Subversive, patterns on its secret jigs.
A day will come when they have had their day!

As hidden dancers in the U.S. pay,
They turn up here or there in different wigs;
The World, as yet, allows the C.I.A.

Cuba! The Yanks, uneasy, turn away!
Who tried a fast one at the Bay of Pigs?
A day will come when they have had their day.

Chile! This time they act without delay.
Allende might be offered Russian MIGS!
The World, as yet, allows the C.I.A.

Vietnam! Angola! Mozambiquel Ole!
They laugh, though, who control the oil rigs!
A day will come when they have had their day.

Time's running out for those the prop and stay
of Capitalism and its whirligigs.
The World, as yet, allows the C.I.A.
A day will come when they have had their day!

Fred Seyd

TALKING POINTS

The garden scene is quiet here
It is the essence of stillness
And of Winter waiting
Almost like a suspension of time
On a damp dank breath.

The tidy lawns have been laid to rest
For the drab duration
And inside the red topped chalet
Under dust sheets gathering dust
The Summer trappings hold a multitude of memories.

But for those inside the house
A kind of living is ticking on
The man brings home the rich cheeses
And fine game for the pot
To a wife with painted oval nails.

And soft hand-lotioned fingers
That can shuffle a pack of cards
For Bridge with a slick dexterity
Like nobody's business
And Christian charity is oblong-shaped.

Neatly tailored to fit closely
Into the narrow limits of the fat cheque
That is thrust into the outstretched
Malnutritioned hand of a brown-skinned
Pot-bellied child with a patterned rib-cage.

Whose image stares out with vacant pop-eyes
From the columns of a national newspaper
(He committed the unpardonable indiscretion of.
being born)

As a talking point he soon loses out to
"Gas-oil-off Peak" - "we'll make it a world cruise."

However before long (Before one can say
Scotch and Soda in fact) the seasonal wheel
Will have turned full cycle
And the jolly merry-go-round

of outdoor living will, re-start.

Then on one particular hot
And quite unmemorable Summer day
In a bright gay world of striped umbrellas
And still lemonades calculating fingers will
Reach out and make an impromptu fan out of a national newspaper.

And the image of a brown-skinned boy
(Perhaps mercifully dead by then)
Will sway crazily to and fro, to and fro
To the stimulating rhythm
Of the town's latest gossip.

Rose Friedman

ALAN

No moon - no sun - no stars
No morning - no evening - no light
No trees - no flowers - no spring
No birds - no song - no rainbow
No seas - no sky - no streams
No smiles - no joy - no laughter
No music - no warmth - no love
No tenderness - no beauty - no
feeling - no tomorrow
No Alan.
Sam Watts

FROM "PALESTINIAN RESISTANCE' No.4 April 1976

Your hand lying over mine,
Your being flowing through my veins,
The green of your orchard!
The smell of newly ploughed earth!
Children
Fearless
Climbing almond trees
Splashing in the streams the reflection of
our faces.
Now that you are no more,

The seed that fell is growing.
As time sweeps your images from my mind
I can only nourish that sprout
Our struggle.
Astronomers can foretell the appearance of a comet
Its age, its course.
Who will listen, to the night rain,
Stand proudly to the sun?.
You told me, that ants have a mill-stone
under their nest,
Make flour, music.
Now that they cover your forehead
Do they know of your clear mind?

Giorgio Taverniti

CRANTOCK BEACH

There he stands, in the shallowest wavelets
which lap the mile-wide sunlit beach,
whereon Atlantic rollers break and
carry sturdy, lissom surfers on their crests
to slide gracefully to a sandy halt.

He stands, straight, slim, alone –
his eyes and face shaded by a denim cap,
gazing out to sea, to the others,
his twenty-odd years supported by two sticks –
and one leg.
The waves form far out and build,
rolling in relentlessly,
their very tips curled back into a light froth
by the strong shoreward wind.
Golden holiday youth,
bare and bronze,
battle and ride the waves,
now overturned, now skilfully running for the shore,
concentrated on physical endeavour,
without a dark thought, without a glance.
And there he stands, his one jeaned leg cooling in the sea.

The evening is warm, golden, joyous, active.
Each busies himself with his patch of sand,

255

his beachwear, his bat and ball,
his board and waves.

No one speaks to the young man.

Did some dread disease take off his leg -
Or was it some careless car or bike -
And are his parents broken-hearted -
And his girlfriend disinterested now?
Or is he maybe a casualty of the

troubled land of Ireland,
reject of that undeclared war and
unwanted army of the occupying power?

We shall never know.
For I, like the rest,
making the best of each new wave,
and striving to remain contained and strong
within my own private disaster,
did not dare to. speak to him.

Peggy Kessel

'ER THAT NATTLE

t'Thrang day o'er an' er that nattle: Gubbins,
Fleakt i' bed, tews chauvin' for ter sattle 'er –
B'r owt aw does, fer mi livin' or luvin', 's
Slur'd when hoo snurls, "Tha shaps like a tackler."

Jone O' Broonlea

Thrang, busy; nattle, bad tempered; Gubbins, soft self; fleakt i' bed,
lying naked in bed; tews, works hard; chauvin', ("rubbing together", eu-
phemism) making love;
snurls "turns nose up".

ACADEMIC BORED
AGITPOEM NO. 17. -

They fortified the Board.
We attacked
with an item for the agenda.

They cried, "Unconstitutional!" and set up a
working party to make suggestions on the forming
of a committee to make proposals on drawing
up of an agenda for a meeting which was to
discuss the setting-up of a working party
to report back on the forming of a committee (with an agenda) ...

We lobbed in a motion,
but they repulsed us crying,
"Loyalty", "Order", "Noblesse Oblige" and "Responsibility".

We tried three amendments
but they didn't fit the proper channels
in which the Board had entrenched itself.
They offered that "steps" and "measures" would be taken
- and even flew a kite!

We threw in a point of information:
they put up a smoke-screen of confidentiality.
It was no use
- in the end, we had to use dynamite.
Bob Dixon

MOVING ON

Mr. Polowski and Mrs. Polowski stepped from the platform of the number twenty one bus at the temporary bus stop-by the road widening works.

"This isn't the stop', the conductor yelled.

"What does he say?" All these years, and still so little English penetrated her. Her hand clutched his arm.

"That it's not the stop"

Not only was the road being widened but the beginnings of a new road rubbled in from behind pressing through the soles of their shoes. Mr. Polowski looked first one way, then the other. The traffic came thick and fast. He looked down at the white painted signs on the ground but they told him nothing.

"Quick now," he said. "Half way we can get, to the island."

Through the thin material of his coat he felt the sharp pressure of her seemingly fleshless fingertips. There had been a period in time when that pressure was ugly to him. When, a young man, he had awoken sharply from a dream feeling her fingers clutching him in a whirlpool of war and glassy-eyed faces, only to find she slept, coma-like, beside him.

He turned to look with satisfaction at the sea of traffic he had brought them through but already his wife's anxious eyes traversed three lanes to the other side.

"Now! Quick!"

She looked after a hooting car in pained surprise. "These motorists never do like to see a pedestrian going about his business."

"This afternoon we'll go to the cinema," he said. "What do you say to that?"

She smiled, and the pressure of her fingertips lightened. "And tonight we'll have stroganoff for dinner." She beamed and her fingers drummed a tune on his arm.

They reached the Ministry of Health and Social Security and a burly Irishman said, "Here's the Polak. What you tipping today, Polak?"

Mr. Polowski laughed. This was their standing joke though he had forgotten its beginnings and was uncertain why it was funny. He was not a betting man and preferred to see something tangible for his money. He liked to see his wife eat a jaffa orange and watch Putty put away a half a pound of liver.

Inside the building, Mrs. Polowski stood motionless,, unsmiling, her arms by her sides, fingers pressing tight through her black coat onto her lump legs. He smiled at her but it was no use. Surely she would know by now that it was advantageous to be attended to by the same lady each week.

"Polowski," he said to the girl at the desk.

She looked at him. She smiled. "Good afternoon."

"You remember I worked as a watchman."

"Yes that's right, do you have your note?"

He took the note from his pocket, small crumpled, and began to straighten it.

"Take this to the fifth floor. You know the procedure" He was glad when the cinema lightened and they could return home with the liver for Putty. He pointed out the card in the post office window advertising that Putty's kittens were free to a good home.

"And about time," she said. "Soon they will be too big to go!"

"Excuse me," said Mrs.. Brown stepping into their path, "But there's been a mattress in your back yard for four months now. Someone should report it to the Health Authorities.

"I know nothing of that" Mr. Polowski said.

"But it's in your back yard."

"It was there when I came. You want it, Mrs.?" He smiled. She could certainly have it, without payment. True their room was of the second floor but he was at present the tenant of longest standing and if anyone had jurisdiction over the mattress it was he. Of course, there was a possibility that the woman whose room looked directly onto the back yard could lay a claim to it.

"I certainly don't want it" said Mrs. Brown. "It's been there for four months and it's soaked through. It smells. Someone should report it to the Health Authorities.

He smiled. Perhaps she meant that the Health Authorities would use the mattress for a needy person.

"Come," his wife tugged. "Come away."

They walked away

"Someone should report your whole house. Layabouts. Cats. Stinking dustbins. Noisy prostitutes!" Yes she was right. The prostitute was noisy, but only on Saturdays. But the dustbin, the dustbin did not smell noticeably different from any other as far as he could tell.

He sat by the window. He liked to sit by the window playing with Putty's kittens. Putty ate the raw liver.

"Easy, Putty, easy. Don't make he glutton of yourself."

She crouched over the meat, growling as she picked up a large piece, snarling and looking from side to side. The door was ajar and the prostitute looked in.

"About time you stopped starving that cat."

"Half a pound of horse liver I'm giving to her." He smiled. "She thinks Tuesday's Christmas. I'm leaving today. No one else will feed her."

The kittens fought for her nipples.

"Go on, Tibby. Push in, Whitey." He stroked her head as she fed them and in turn she stroked Tibby's head with her quick rough tongue. "I've made you happy."

He heard his wife's slow tread from the kitchen to the bottom of the stairs, and then the plod of her footsteps on bare boards.

"Good Putty."

Putty turned and glared at him. He smiled gently and put a forefinger against Tibby's neck.

"Tibby, Tibby." His wife's footsteps sloped towards the door. She would not call upstairs. She was the most silent person he had known. She wore a blanket of silence day and night, even while speaking. He turned. She looked troubled. What could it be? Oh, that he had heard her coming up the stairs and along the landing and had not come.

"The stroganoff is ready."

She turned. He moved after her.

"Goodbye Putty."

In the kitchen he put a forefinger behind his wife's neck. "Tuesday is a happy day."

She did not smile. He brought a hand from behind his back and brandished a bottle of sweet white wine. She smiled, and they sat contented.

The prostitute put her head round the door.

"Someone at the door for you.

"Who?"

But she was gone.

"What is it? asked his wife.

"She said that there's someone at the door for us, for me."

"Who is it?"

"She didn't say."

"Don't go."

He pushed away his plate, scraped his chair back and stood.

"I wont be long"

"Don't go."

A child confronted him, a girl of ten or eleven with a pink face and a grey' neck.

"I'd like to have a kitten please." Not today. He couldn't let one go on such a happy day. It would spoil the day. It would be dangerous to take one away while Putty was feeding them.

"There are no kittens."

The girl looked puzzled. But she doesn't fool me Polowski thought, she doesn't look hurt, disappointed.

"No kittens."

"But you have a notice in the post office window."

He looked at her closely. She obviously possessed cunning, guile. It was clever of her to mention the presence of the notice, to casually refer to the post office. There was only one way to deal with this.

"There are no kittens."

"But I see you playing with them every day in your window."

Spying. But for a moment she looked hurt. Then she stared directly at him, challenging. He did not waver.

"There are no kittens. There are no kittens now."

The addition of that small word changed everything. For a moment she looked as though she would go.

"Did you drown them?" Questions, always questions while now the stroga-noff spoiled, the wine waited. "I must eat my dinner now. My wife is waiting." He waited. She did not move. Although reluctant to hurt her feelings, he closed the door and walked back along the boards to the big kitchen.

His wife sat anxious, eating slowly. "Who was it?"

"No one. A child."

"What sort of child?"

"A boy. Nine or eleven"

"What did he want?"

A kitten he wanted."

She looked pleased, relieved.

"But you know what they are," he said, "He wanted a special kitten. It had to be black and white with blue eyes."

"You should have taken him up to see them. If he was a normal boy he would have taken a liking to one of them. Perhaps two of them."

She was very intelligent at times, his wife. That was exactly true.

"No, no. It had to be of certain markings. A black cape and trousers, four white socks, a white bib and a black mask and hood. You know the ideas boys get into their heads.

"I wonder why he wanted such a cat." She ate more quickly now, now that she was reassured.

"Perhaps for a game" he said offhandedly

"Perhaps for a sinister game."

"Perhaps."

"Nice white wine," she said.

In a mood of tranquillity now she washed the dishes and amiable he wiped them, then they walked out over the boards to the rotting front door to walk along the lane and look in windows.

On Friday they dined on boiled potatoes and drank black coffee, then set off for the public library. At the bottom of the Terrace he caught a glimpse of Putty by the house wall of number three. The kittens pushed towards her nipples. She pushed them away. Mrs. Brown walked towards him.

"Is this your cat?"

"Yes," he said, smiling, proud.

"What are you going to do about it, and about these kittens? They're starving."

She was concerned, he thought. She liked cats. "You'd like to have them," he said.

"I have two cats of my own."

Yes, he had seen them. One was white, one was tabby. Suddenly it occurred to him that it was possible to share the responsibility.

"I think," he said, "That your cat is the father."

"My cat?"

"Yes."

"That's hardly likely. Both my cats have undergone operations and in any case are the wrong sex for that to begin with."

"I think the white one is the father."

"That's impossible. Just impossible."

His wife's fingers claimed his arm, pressuring and re-pressuring.

"Come. Come away."

"Someone ought to report this to the RSPCA," said Mrs. Brown.

At the corner by the chemist's shop stood the girl, grey-necked, grey-eyed, accusing.

"The kittens have come back.. Would you like to have one?"

"My mother won't let me."

His wife tugged at his arm. "Come away."

"Excuse me, but are those your cats?" It was a woman again, from a shop yard. "Because one of them is dead in the back street. I saw it licking the fever grate yesterday afternoon. It'll be poison or starvation. Either way it's causing germs and the children are touching it. It should be put in a dustbin. Or burnt."

"I don't know whose cat."

His wife tugged his arm. "The library." Her voice was urgent, her brow drawn.

"We have to go, Mrs" A light rain came, gently touching their faces. She smiled. It had rained when they met, a clear clean rain from the mountains and afterwards a rainbow.

For the afternoon he sat looking through Volume Five of the Encyclopedia Britannica and she gazed far out of the window to the green grass, the benches and the flowers, seeing old people sitting, and children playing.

"Do you see," he said as they walked back along the lane and passed the bicycle repair shop. "Do you see how the light is special and different at this time of the afternoon? Do you see the rays golden from the sun piercing through the clouds?"

She nodded. "Between afternoon and evening is a beautiful time."

From the lane he saw the woman who had reported to him that one of the kittens had licked the fever grate and died. She was talking with Mrs. Brown. They looked in his direction, waiting for him to reach them. He felt his wife grow tense beside him. Then he saw beside them the grey-necked girl.

"Excuse me," said Mrs. Brown.

"In a hurry, Mrs. ." he said.

Mrs. Brown stepped forward. Mr. and Mrs. Polowski stepped nimbly aside.

"Sorry. In a hurry."

They sat on the bed, each back pressed against the-wall, each pressed tight, each silent. The sunglow of evening gradually filtered out and the room was colourless in the dusk. She moved then, his wife, across the room and lifted a defeated cushion from a once upholstered chair. Stretching her hand inside she drew out one by one four single pound notes, put the cushion back and walked towards her husband. She took his hand and put the money in his palm, closing his fingers round it. He smiled but sadly and crossed the room to the wardrobe, and, stretching, took down the case.

Silent they came down the bare steps, silent to the door. On the bottom road the cobbles pressed through the soles of their shoes. There was a movement on the ground.

"Goodbye, Putty, Putty.".

"Come," said her fingers through .the thin sleeve of his coat. 'Come away."

Frances Mcneil

264

MASS PRODUCTION

We seen 'em all,
at the ball a fall,
aint it a strain,
good gulping mates,
everyone the same.
Tasting immortality
pint by pint,
the race and shove,
of hope and inanity.
Puff quickly.
Their schooldays,
Their army days,
Where they became,
pretend men.
A small experience,
biggest thing,
in a mediocre gift,
grown up, for once,
a pastiche of life,
seen on a petty plane.
Masculinity through
the barrel of a gun.
Perverse pleasure,
in the bullying,...
of the stereo-sergeant,
or some insane R.S.M.
Sten guns, bren guns,
armoured troop carriers.
A facade of boy scout,
irreversible experience.
The naive erecting
impenetrable barriers,
willingly tattooed, with
the stigmata of immutability.

Malcolm Wyatt

ROBERTS ARUNDEL

Who fears to speak of Roberts Arundel.
Who blushes at the name
When blacklegs mocked the pickets' fate
We bowed our heads in shame.
Though the pickets have gone there still lives on
The fame of me who tried,
With patience and persistence to conduct themselves
With pride.
Yet still there lingers a thought
Something must be rotten
When for a year and a half
These old men
Were by their leaders forgotten.

Paul Casey

A CONVERSATION

"So I'm telling you Barney, I don't want any Vicar, priest, Rabbi, Bush Baptist, or any of 'em parrotin' over me when I'm dead. When you're gone - you're gone.

There's nothing - nothing."

He banged the table with his fist. The pint glasses wobbled.

"You're finished. It's the end. And don't take me near a Church. One of the lads sayin' a few words will do me." His brown eyes glowed fiercely.

"An you are all witnesses to that. So I'm warning yer Barney, if you do - God help me, I'LL COME BACK AND HAUNT YER."

Jean Sutton

SONG OF THE EARTH

She, first observed
playing guitar cross-legged
lost in the subways, hands moving
like nail-bitten tarantula's
across the fret, eking sound.
We, speared by hard electric

shadows across cold concrete,
talking for no reason, our ragged
breath shifting the limp air only slightly.

Me, talking of flash-lights at 2 a.m.
disturbing a Skegness seafront wind-shelter.
Police clawing sleep from us,
hands seeking contraband like
inquisitive legal scorpions from
beyond the cones of light. And later,
with morning mist and cold sun
angling across an empty promenade
infested with last night's litter,
metallic sea breaking splinters of
sharp white ice across frozen shingle.
Ocean crouching alive with huge primal
energy - and we are untidy dwarfs breasting
air into early morning abandoned tea-rooms
where coffee smells stain the air,
and a muted radio voice beyond the
pinball machines promises to
melt the last vestiges of sour night.

She, disinterested eyes frail beyond
wire-rimmed glasses, is not pretty,
and her fingers move like
nailbitten tarantula's
across the fret,
eking sound.

Andrew Darlington

WHOSE ROAD TO SOCIALISM?

I cannot equate my road with Crossman's Road, or Healey's Road.
My road has no U-turns to suit economic myth or selfish interest
I, with my grass roots brothers stand bemused,
While others stand and wrangle over GANNEX Macs.

My road does not cater for the disillusionment of emerging youth
My road has seen that, years ago, at the Somme and Jarrow.
And yet, the more I see my leaders mouth their new ideals,
I see the gap grow wider, and for Jarrow, I can only see a Harrow.

267

My road did not cater for the ego of greedy men,
I did not think to see some comrade drunk with power,
Nor see their backers on their knees,
Begging for baubles from the gift box of Establishment.

So. comrade, where does our road lead?
It may be long my friends, but that does not matter
As long as our road leads straight and true and honest
And our ideals remain, as they were in the beginning.

And what of their road comrades?
Their road is cluttered with the debris of the
Browns, the careerists, the hypocrites.
Their road stagnates with the Woodrow Wyatts and
the coronets of labour peers
I'd sooner walk my road.

Because, my brothers they have,
in their betrayal already been defeated.
But we, thank God, still know the enemies of our beliefs.
Alas, but who needs enemies, with so called friends like these.

Ian Scott

ON GUARD

From the train
we watched the guard dogs,
all attention, straining
in our direction.

Myself I like animals.

God help anyone,
or anything,
that gets tangled
with them.

Bill Eburn

268

JUNE DAYS

Sunday

I know you will worry if you don't hear and imagine things worse than they are. So here's a straightforward blow-by-blow account of what has happened to us. And don't you dare believe any worse!

Here in St. Pancras we seem to be in the path of these "flying telegraph poles". But so far only three have landed within a couple of hundred yards. The rest have gone on to give hell elsewhere. You don't duck till you hear the engine cut out.

Today I was on late turn, so at midday I was cooking a meal for us both: Olive was on nights last week at her factory just down the road. I heard one of these little treasures coming so went out on to the balcony to have a look. There it was, 100 feet up, moving leisurely in our direction. I'd just told Olive it was going over when I saw its nose dip, though the engine was still running.

It's surprising how fast you can move when you must! I backed into the room, caught Olive by the arm, dragged her from the window and nipped down into a corner in a reverent position on my knees. It burst just after I'd dropped.

The blast blew the thick black curtains to! We were on our feet again before the house stopped rocking, Olive crying and shouting: "It's hit my factory!" I saw at once that it hadn't, from where the column of smoke went up. Snatched up hag and stumbled over a pile of plaster in the passage stripped off the ceiling, all the plaster off the ceiling of the porch and some of its beams down. It was already as dark as a London fog from the clouds of dust sweeping up Camden Road, and bits of wood and paper still falling. We rushed down the street through the fog and broken glass to where it had fallen 100 yards away on the other side of the road from her factory. We must have been there in less than 3 minutes and the rescue services were already at work.

Olive called at her Warden's post at the factory and then went into a house where a mate of hers lived, with the window frames all hanging out. I went to the doctor's house. In his garden a woman was sitting crying, her face blackened, a toddler on her knee. She was only slightly cut, but her skirt was soaked in blood, her injured mother having fallen against her. She was waiting while the doctor coped with the old woman and two others, who had been got out quickly for instant treatment. She wouldn't move until she had heard about her mother and until her father had come home from work. She herself was all right but very shaken and couldn't easily stop the tears. I took the kiddie on my knee. She didn't make a sound except when her mother cried out, and that she couldn't bear. The curly hair on her little head was full of glass and plaster but she was not hurt.

I told the mother to stop crying because it was upsetting the kiddie; and to Jennifer I said:

"You are a good girl! Why, you're a better girl than Mummy because she's crying and you aren't. Wouldn't your Daddy be proud of his brave girl?" Her mother fiercely dashed the tears out of her eyes and said: her Dad could see her now!

He wouldn't leave one of the bastards alive!"

Soon the grandmother came out, her arm bandaged, her face still covered with dried blood. While I was cuddling Jennifer at least five people came up to take them to safety and give them tea and a share of the dinner. It's a working class area, of course, and so you would expect it; but the warmth and neighbourliness was overwhelming. Finally I promised to wait for "Dad" to turn up and tell him they were safe and where they had gone.

While I was waiting I helped a man salvage some stuff from his hopelessly smashed rooms. He said he had just got dressed to go and visit his wife in hospital: she had had it in one of the two flying bombs here on Friday.

An old woman was being helped down the street. She had run out of church to come home to her family. As she reached this corner she had hysterics, throwing herself backwards and faintly screaming, saying she was dying and clutching her chest. We propped her up and told her sharply that unless she pulled herself together we would leave her and not help her find her family. She rallied at once..

Children were running to and fro crying -mostly the ten-year-old boys, I noticed. I stopped one and asked him if he knew where his Mum was, or had he got lost? He said, yes, yes, she was all right, but he didn't know what to do, didn't know what, didn't know ... He was just a bit frantic. I said: "I'll come with you and we'll go back to your Mum. However is she going to clean up the house if she hasn't got you there to help her?" He stopped crying, came with me to the end of the street. There he let out a shout and ran like a lamb to its ewe and jumped into a woman' s arms.

Another boy of 10 with a younger sister went by, both with tears pouring down their cheeks, the girl carrying a kitten, quarrelling savagely because they both wanted to carry it.

A bit further up the road, away from the incident, a woman was standing on her doorstep screaming at bystanders across the road: "Why do you stand there ruddy star-gazing? Why don't you help?"

270

Apart from these every one was very quiet and grim. The bomb had fallen in a little mews full of small workshops with dwellings over, wretchedly built. Four at least were knocked flat, but many more most be quite unsafe. Several people were killed asleep, having come home from sleeping in shelters at night. It was only a small "do"; I think the total casualties weren't more than 50. After a couple of hours I went home and Olive and I tried to clear up our own mess. By a strange fluke not a single window was broken and only one door was jammed. It was all this filthy plaster; arid of course everything was covered with this foul explosion dust; my hair is so thick with it I can't get a comb through. The downstairs people on the ground floor and basement had every window smashed but no plaster down.

I felt all right today - perhaps because there were things to do and one didn't feel so bitterly helpless. I'm writing this during "the cut" at work, and I still keep seeing faces and wondering how they are now - after seeing people so bare, one feels so close. The man and woman uninjured but homeless, walking down Camden Road to the Rest Centre, erect and proud-looking. A young woman suffering from shook, bent and shuffling like an old crone. A month old baby in a woman's arms, sleeping quite peacefully, wrapped in a shawl flecked with blood. A rough and ugly landlord, coming to see his house, bemoaning the damage, forgetting to ask if any of his tenants were hurt. A whole volume of life, and fine sturdy, angry people. The Jewish doctor, his own house uninhabitable, helping a woman along his passage and irritably kicking a fallen oil painting out of the way.

But I'll admit to one bad moment, when I was going past the incident to work three hours later. Just past the entry to the mews there is a disused garage and one of its shop windows has a display of artificial limbs. It was heavily blasted. All the glass went. And there lay some legs from the window, there on the pavement. I had to stop under the railway bridge there and take a deep breath and swallow it down.

Wednesday night

... Got it good and proper today. Am so relieved that Olive went off to the country Monday, her whole department being on holiday. For her factory got a direct hit - just across the road from Sunday's incident. And this house is a right mess, though just about habitable.

When it fell I was upset, because I knew the factory was working flat out except for her department. I went down the road at top speed. It seems a miracle that no one was killed outright though some were so badly injured that they won't live. Everyone had managed to get to the shelters because the roof spotters had given enough warning. They themselves had to jump for it off the roof; it was a direct hit.

Bit by bit, I found all Olive's friends, more or less O.K. Her special friend the cook -in the canteen in the basement under the adjoining building - had provided tea for all within ten minutes.. serene, blue-eyed, delicate, smiling and gentle, rather like a small deer! Soft voice and Cockney accent. Two hundred girls and fifty men assembled in the yard for roll-call; I didn't see more than ten in tears. They were perfectly steady and quite magnificent. I asked some back for tea and a rest, but with real warm and friendly thanks they all preferred to get back home sharp before the news got there. The little tobacconist, blasted three times in two weeks, next door put up a notice within ten. minutes: "No sightseers served here." I like that. Next to it the bootmakers has an odd little notice:

"Blasted boots repaired here." I went over to where an Irishman and his mate had been filling in the windows blown out of the artificial limbs display place. They saw the bomb coming straight at them, he said. At the very last moment it veered slightly and hit the factory across the road. "I was that petrified I never moved. I stood agarp, me hammer lifted." His wife and children went to Scotland two days ago. He said he was getting out of London after this, he hadn't felt afraid before. It wasn't quite his war, he seemed to feel!

He told me this because the landlords' agents agreed I should get the house made secure, and the Irishmen came and did it, and we restored ourselves with strong tea.

The inner doors of both flats with their six foot glass panels were blown out, and the main door wrenched right out of the frame. I couldn't go to work until it was made safe. For the house is empty. The downstairs people now live in the basements of the Criterion and only come home twice a week to feed the cats.

While my Irish pals were doing the work I swept up the glass - same old tinkle, tinkle as in 1940. I found a slight scratch on my forehead, when the woman next door told me it was bleeding. Probably when I ran out of the door I had shaken a glass splinter down on me.

Later this afternoon was fairly brisk, but only two of the things were duck-worthy. I'll write somehow each day, if only a line. Not to worry.

Angela Tuckett

SUMMIT

First, it was to be held at his - the man's place - the out-of-work man. But
Maureen's chief advisor objected:
is that a concession Kissinger would make at the start of negotiations?
He demanded new terms of reference which saw her, who paid the rent, as
hosting the Conference.
His Lawyer's speech was commended by all, and led to the first adjourn-
ment. Lambchops' pad was ruled out,
His being co-respondent to this thing; and as not to lose the impetus, they
decided to meet in the local Underground on a Sunday morning. It was
what you would call a triangle kept in shape by pressure of advice from
outside.
They were all poor people in a difficult. situation, whose choice of action
was limited. Suicide and other heroic solutions were out. Duelling was
from another tradition.
Why couldn't the three live somehow as one, or maybe two? But these
were civilized people - and fastidious. The brilliant Lawyer commended
Africa's traditional winner- take-all development policy: did we three lack
Africa's courage?
The West Indian thing was compromise-and-let-the-three-live sort of thing.
Whether this was a good thing (that thing again) objectively, was something they adjourned to think about. Lambchops said, to solve this one, was
to delve through the false bottom of West Indian ambivalence
to the bed-rock on which our great nation of the future
must be built. But Philpot thought it feeble of Lambchops to turn politician
just to win a woman
like Maureen. And so it went on. Advisors got bored,
changed jobs and families, left; but over the years
the triangle managed to keep something of its original shape; for it's a big
decision
when you come down to it, and poor people can't afford to be wrong all the
time.

Paul St Vincent

DOWN THE OLD KENT ROAD

I walks around the bleedin' place
An' faces thats I knows.
I sees the West 'ams shambles
Where no weeds will grow.
Bein' now a country boy
Ma 'art beats funny fings.
To see the park of pissy grass
Like sparrows wivout wings.
The pubs stand firm as ever
Yet the singin' is all gone

A buildin' tall an' stupid
At the site wheres I was born.
Me cockney blood gets colder:
Me brain finks funny foughts.
One shoulder gets the lower
At the school where I was taught.
Come Arfur, gets yer 'ome
To the cows and chicken pie
Befores yer spit upon yer shoes
Which tread on greener spires.
A puffer took me 'ome
From those ugly days.
But my dear old chap
I'll ever have cockney ways.

Arthur Francis

SONG OF MARXIST-LENINIST INTELLECTUAL

God bless the workers
the salt of the earth
the force of revolution
God bless the workers
and make them follow me

I'll learn to drink
beer with them
on Saturday nights
and then I'll teach them to think
coldly and rationally

274

I'll free them from their prejudice
about women and housework
and the role of theory
and I'll eliminate all traces
of bourgeois ideology
to make a new
revolutionary
socialist
proletarian
culture
(of course I was middle-class
once
then I read Capital
and now I am a Marxist-
Leninist professional revolutionary)

God bless the workers
who'll make the revolution
for me
God bless- but no
I haven't any confidence in
him
David Cobham

CONFUCIUS WAS CRUNCHING CARROTS

Confucius was crunching carrots when Chung Yu entered
And laughed. Confucius went on eating, saying:
The wise man doesn't fail to commend the carrot
A superior plant with twenty meanings, it's:

Honest - wears its heart on its overcoat
(Its rind shows all the promise of its centre),
Even-textured, gentle with the digestion
(and so a model for civilized discussion);

Prudent - supports itself, remaining stable
(Compare the bean, which relies entirely on poles),
Subtle - keeps its qualities under cover
(Compare the marrow, cheek-by-jowl with dog-dung);

Modest - doesn't flaunt its excellence
(All it shows to the world is its frivolous side),

275

Sage -like in its reply whenever addressed
(Usually cheerful and crisp, but now and then snaps);

Neither too hard nor too soft, a fine example
(Carved on public buildings) for kings and judges,
Neither too sour nor too sweet, and so a reminder
(Hung in bars and bedrooms) for lovers and poets;

Good for the health, especially for philanderers
(Improves your vigour, breath, and night-time vision),
Polite - in the way you should be towards women
(Present your posy first, your member second);

An easy-to-carry lesson in solid geometry
(Includes the paraboloid, hemisphere, and cone),
Ringed, with each ring representing eternity
(Defectively - which puts the idea in doubt).

It goes from thin to thick for ease of eating
(Knowing the hardest thing is to begin),
Keeps relationships few, is stiff among crowds
(Not like noodles or rice - over-familiar);

Resembles in section, when bitten, a human iris
(Wisely calm when watching its own destruction),

Keeps its juices decently well contained
(Not like oranges - uncontrolled and embarrassing);

Shows at one end the sage's rooted uncertainty
(About to establish a point, it tails away),
Acknowledges at the other Art supreme
(About to round things off, confects a flourish);

Prospers in soot, which symbolises Creation
(Dark and mess were prior to life and form),
Prospers also in wood-ash, signalling Hope
(Out of what's destroyed proceeds the new);

And these are the twenty attributes of the carrot.
To which Chung Yu, with a broad smile replied:
I shall carry your textbook, a carrot, in my sleeve,
Offer it you, and see if you eat your words.
Alex Barr

CREDO

I believe that days of war will come,
When birds will shrivel in the trees,
And these,
Our people then,
Our little children grown to men:
All dead, and stretched beneath the sun.
I do not dare, I do not dare,
To bend and touch the sea's blind glut of boiling sand
Or raise my live, five-fingered hand
To trace a fragile path in air,
Or stroke the barrel of a gun,
For I believe that days of war will come

To blaze the surface of this land.
That is why I do not dare
To strip a young girl's body, bare
Or bury my tongue in a woman's lips:
For cold class war must bring about
The anxious slumlands' stunned eclipse.

Break the parades! Shatter the patriotic shout!
The mesh of veins within the fern
Can make my stomach churn in fear
For I believe that days of war will come:
Still in its sleeve will the severed limb be blasted high
Spread tassels of blood to the rim of the sky.

I do not dare, nor dare foresee
The babies' match-boned bodies there
Where orderlies with sticks are poking
For the shreds of a scalp stuck fast to a tree,
Burned to a crisp and scarcely smoking,
Still with their blackened wisps of hair.

James MacVeigh

FOR A FINE COMRADE

I always like the thought of meeting new, young men,
although I'm married, and want to/ feel I ought to
see you only as a person
without sex.
I suppose as time goes by I become more skilled
at concealing my inner turbulence
as someone takes my fancy.
I savour awakening Desire furtively;
but more often than not, this subterfuge
confuses me, and I am left bewildered and inadequate.

I have not yet come to terms
with loving one man wholly and strongly,
and yet wanting others too;
loving others,
wanting you.
We have agreed we need development
and we have opened up our marriage
Though if he feels as shaken in the presence of my lover
as I in his,
then maybe we were wrong.

I was nervous and shook your limp hand
harder than you shook mine.
With your eyes you drew a line around my silhouette,
and I was honoured by it.

Your lanky framework lagged in ancient denim,
your gawky movements
cast me as a Lady,
made me feel a child.
I am younger, less experienced,
naive and I have suffered less;
but in this child, you move the Woman.
If there is to be no union,
and if there is to be no celebration,
then it needs to go on paper
so a thousand generations down the ages can be sure
Woman still wants Man.
Desire rules, O.K.

The strength of your image

generates energy in me,
moves me with internal combustion.
Piston Power.
Longing sways me as the boulder crumbles walls.
Visions of moving clenched fists -
or are they merely phallic symbols
of unrequited passion.

I am moved to bear your children
as were countless mothers moved before me.
Desire for our unison unites me with my Foremothers
and with all my Sisters past and present.
A fragment of the whole and yet exalted for a moment.

I would have liked to touch your hair and beard,
and maybe my fingers would have led
your lips to mine.
I wanted to feel the smoothness of your contours.
Your nakedness beneath that purple vest tormented me.
I would have left, my probing eyes were perceiving
reading perhaps too much into your drinking,
your limp and slouch.

Preternatural wailing from my ever present sisters -
was it a harmony or was it a warning?

I am young and strong.
I am a temporary vessel of life.
My womb is a door from the beginning to the future
At risk,
I would take you home and comfort you.

Wendy Whitfield

I AM A FRIGHTENING QUIETNESS

I am a frightening quietness.
That watches your absence with growing fear;
A silence that frightens us both;
I'd like to fill your sky with words
Like bright balloons;
Concepts and implications;
Bright empty balloons:
But I have only frightening quiet thoughts,

That weigh us down,
Don't they, love?

Les Barker

LIFE'S LIKE THAT

My dear friend Bob who knew I was "between jobs" arranged that he and. I started work the next day on a building site for the rather grandiose sum of £7.50 per day - a great job he promised, but what was the catch, I thought.

I turned up promptly at 8.0 a.m. but no Bob. He had sent along his kid brother instead because Bob reckoned brother Tim's need was greater than his own. The wind was freezing -sub zero or so it felt and from the north east, direct from Russia. No doubt benevolent Bob was still well and truly buried in his warm cosy bed.

A small Irish figure - the ganger man -soon organised us. The first lorry arrived and. our gang speedily unloaded thousands of tiles under the unremitting eye of the leprechaun ganger man. We sweated - which was surely an amazing feat considering the icicles hanging over our heads when suddenly he disappeared - the ganger. But as we relaxed I had a start. Surely I could perceive the leprechaun's eye peeping through the nearby hedge checking our progress. I was getting positively neurotic. My heart wasn't feeling so good either. I was convinced it was pumping erratically - surely I was made for the more genial administrative, managerial type of post. And here was I sweating blood for Sir Rupert McAlpine. "And now you know" said one of the gang, "why he was given a knighthood".

Another lorry loaded with hundredweight bags of plaster appeared. We threw it off quickly and having finished someone mentioned it was tea time. "No!" said the Irish gangerman, "five minutes to go - back to work." This man had a heart made of granite and his watch kept Irish time for sure.

Towards the end of the ten hour day -working under arc lamps and surrounded by night we barrowed loads of heavy hardcore and rubble up a steep ramp onto the hoist. I knew I had muscles now - every individual one ached so to look busy to the end I loaded the barrow with empty plaster bags and just managed to push them to the top of the ramp. Each minute was an hour as the clock slowly ticked towards knocking-off time.

Six o'clock and I had completed one whole day's work and earned the princely sum of £7.50. All I needed now were several weeks convalescence on the Costa Brava but preferably without a blonde - I wouldn't have the strength. And just wait till I see Bob. Perhaps I can do him a favour because I know where there is a terrific job going....mine.

Peter Relph

ISLAND

We are marooned today, little one.

Yesterday, washed by fevers,
We clung to our few feet of wall to wall Rock.

Now, limply, your rag doll and I
Gaze on giddy emptiness
Through drenched February windows
While you sleep.

There is no weather for distress signals.
We will alert no-one -
The world is weeping.
Only the distant, dark houses take us in.

They are as empty of people as we are.

My- body, shaken by a week of illness
Can hardly perform the small gestures
That maintain us both.
Your smile on waking - eyes green and alight -
Makes the first small kindling.

Pat Sentinella

DOUBLE DEAL

I' t' double bed an' hapt wi t' wife -
B'r aw've a cubby-'oile i' my yed
Wheer aw slive to a double life,
Tother woman, an' th' unkert bed.

Jone O' Broonlea

hapt, under the covers; slive, creep off; unkert, strange.

281

BEAUTY AND THE BEAST

Have you seen such beauty as the child?
Some day it will. grow up and kill one
just as beautiful.
The hand that can caress sending
shudders of joy through us can
squeeze or thud the life from us.
That lovely brogue lilting loveliness
From a land green and old as time
That has endured ages of sad days
Has even now its quota of misery
evoking events
A people that kill each other and us,
To quiet the raging beast that would
be still and compose again as
O'Casey and as Synge.
Calm and doting fathers everywhere
And mothers too
Yet in the name of preservation of peace,
For good, for progress for Humanity
Destroy its members, even babies
and declare war on love
An atheist's prayer is that
We should love one another
And we shall not kill.

Frank Parker

"Power Structure". Taken from a wood carving. Sol Garson.

Composition by Beverley Robinson.

Taverniti's work on the streets of Venice.

Sol Garson at work.

ISSUE 13

cover size 210 x 148 mm (A5)

CONTENTS

VOICES APPEAL

Total acknowledged in "Voices 6", £164.23. Since then, the following donations have been received for which we express thanks.

Mr and Mrs Tartakower £4,
Bob Dixon £2,
Peggy Kessel £3,
GiorgioTaverniti £10,
Kathy and Paul Levine £8.40,
M M Wiles £2,
Mr G Doyle £1.40,
May Ainley £5,
Gillian Cronje £3,
Horace Green £1.40,
Anon £5,
a total of £45.20, which brings the grand total to date 31 January, 1977, to £209.43.

We would like to wind this fund up by April 1, so please make your donations early.

VOICES Editorial Committee

Some changes have taken place recently. Alan Arnison has had to withdraw (temporarily, we hope) because of illness. Rick Gwilt has come on as Joint Editor with Ben Ainley. Greg Wilkinson has joined the Board to develop the idea of Writers Workshops. Maurice Levine is responsible for approaches to bookshops. Sot Garson becomes Art Editor. Frank Parker remains Treasurer. Rose Friedman and Val Ohren remain on the Committee, as does John Cooper Clarke. We have had regretfully to accept the position that Les Barker does not feel able to function on the Committee.

Our thanks are due for financial help from the North-West Arts Association.

YOU

You are glass.
Clear, bright, sharp-edged,
you shine, cut, pierce to the core.

Sometimes a prism,
you refract the light around you.
Ice-like you can even melt.
Or crack.

Occasionally you are shattered.
I know,
because your splinters are still in me.
Pat Arrowsmith.

THE TYNESIDE POETS

Tyneside Poets is a group of men and women residing in the North-Fast, who believe that poetry should not be an ivory tower activity, but should go out to the people. Since January 1973 we have given readings at various festivals, in pubs, car-parks, town centres and at folk groups. Members have been invited to Sweden, Germany and Iceland.

Tyneside Poets hold regular meetings, give readings, issue small press publications and stage occasional exhibitions on specific themes. We have appeared on radio and TV, and have presented readings at the Newcastle Festival.

We have had visiting poets from the USSR and Germany. We have set up exhibitions of Soviet poetry, and German poetry. Poets have come, at our invitation, to Newcastle such as: Maia Borisova, Michael Dudin, Violetta Palchinskyte and Joseph Nineshvilli from USSR; and Oswald Andrea and others from Germany.

Our small publications have included translations from many languages done by our members. In POETRY NORTH-EAST we seek to bring the work of our members to the notice of a wider public. We have had our poems translated into German and Russian and published abroad. We have had articles about our group in magazines in the Soviet Union, Sweden, and Germany.

Tyneside poets aim to encourage poets and writers; they also strive to develop better understanding between peoples.

Alan C Brown 10 November 1976

MAUD WATSON, FLORIST

bred in a market arch
a struggle
in a city's armpit

that flower
in your time-rough hands
a beautiful girl in a slum alley

all that kindness in your face

and you're right

the times are not what they were
this England's not what it was

flowers shrink in that crumbling vase
dusk creeps in on a cart

and Maud the sun is choking

Maud this island's sinking

and all that swollen sea is

the silent majority

waving

Keith Armstrong.

THE OCCUPATION

Eric sat at the kitchen table, chin in palm, and gazed vacantly across into the yard of the house which backed onto his. On the garden wall of the other house, someone had daubed a legend:

UNITED RULES-OK

He thought of the team about which he had at times cared so passionately and for which, last Saturday, he had fought. Now, on Monday morning, as the fact of his redundancy began to sink in, United seemed irrelevant. Besides, he hadn't really been fighting for them on Saturday. No, I was fighting for ... ah, I'm fucked if I know why I was fighting. I was in a mood, had been since they told us, a week before the event, that they were closing the factory. Then, at the match, I remember looking around the grounds at all the people who had jobs, looking up at where the directors sat puffing their cigars, dressed in their thick overcoats, and suddenly I got mad and felt ashamed all at once, like it was my fault that I had no job to go to.

When the game started, though, the shame disappeared as we cheered the side on. There were about twenty of us together, almost all from the same street, and it seemed like we could beat the world, the way we felt. I even forgot about me job-until the ball landed in the back of United's net, that is, and then I don't really know what happened. The fighting started down the front. The shame came back. The side was losing. A middle-aged feller next to me pushed me and called me a hooligan because I was with the crowd that was fighting, so I kicked his shins and belted him one. It was like he was saying it was my fault, when I hadn't done a thing. Then the fight spread and me mates told me afterwards that I had been doing most of it. They said it like they was proud of me, like it made them feel good to be my mate, but it was nothing to be proud of, not really. No, I wasn't fighting for United and I wasn't even really fighting against the people who got in the way of my fist either, because I remember now that every now and again I kept looking up at where the directors were, thinking you cunts, you're no better than the sum who closed down our factory and put us on the street.

Yeah, before the match, it had seemed like we could've beat the world, but then, when the fight was on, the law came and we were finished. Somehow, I managed to squeeze through the crowd and escape. That was the first time I'd been involved in anything like that and I hope it'll be the last. But that bloke shouldn't have called me a hooligan.

He pushed aside his cereal-bowl and scratched his uncombed head, wondering what to do with himself for the day. Then he heard someone at the side gate and realised that the front door-bell had been ringing. Big Dave's head appeared at the kitchen window.

Big Dave wasn't so much big as fat. He was eighteen, a year older than Eric, and he tried to appear worldly and adult, but Eric had long ago discovered that this was just a means of hiding his lack of self-confidence. He liked him anyway. When he opened the back door, Dave was standing there, squinting at him as he drew the last lungful of smoke from his roll-up, which he held pinched between thumb and forefinger.

"Where the fuck you been, then? I been ringing the bell for ten minutes now."

"Sorry mate, I was miles away. Come on in."

"You goin' down to the meeting outside the factory ?"

"Christ, I forgot all about that !"

Dave shrugged. "Can't see it doin' much good, anyway. Here, roll yourself a fag."

Eric rolled a cigarette and lit it, the first lungful of smoke making his stomach turn as a result of his cold breakfast.

"Where's the old lady, then ?"

"She's on mornings this week."

Dave had rolled a cigarette which looked like a piece of stiff white bootlace. He held it up to look at it and grimaced.

"They'll be layin' off people there soon, as well. Stands to reason, dunnit? We supply Preston's with parts and if we're closed down they can't get parts- 'less they get 'em from the factory up North, and that'll mean more expense, so they'll probably get rid of a few anyway."

"I hope you're wrong, Dave. Christ knows what we'd do with just me old man working. He pisses most of his wages up against the wall as it is." He bit his lip. "What's wrong with this fucking country all of a sudden ?"

Dave started a bonfire at the end of his cigarette. When the blaze had died down, he drew in a mouthful of smoke and expelled it through his nose. "I'm surprised at you, Eric," he said, narrowing his eyes prior to taking another puff. "After all, you don't have to look too far, do you ?" His stubby forefinger tapped four times on the table. "Too-many-black-bastards. I thought you had that all weighed up, the way you were taking the piss out of old Clement Atlee Armstrong the other day."

293

"Only because everyone else was, and then it was only over his name, nothing else."

Dave rolled his eyes. "Jesus Christ ! Whaddayou wanna stick up for him for-he's as thick as shit !"

"Well, my old son, he can't be all that thick, can he, 'cause he's got three A levels-three !"

"He'd still be takin' a white man's job even if he had seventy-three fucking A levels."

"Well, I wouldn't be too sure about that if I was you. I heard Donnelly talking about this business of blacks taking jobs from whites and it just don't work out that way."

Dave pursed his lips and folded his hands on the table. "Okay, what way does it work out, then ?"

"I can't remember, but you can ask Donnelly yourself at the meeting if you really wanna know."

"I wouldn't ask that cunt the time of day, the murdering Irish bastard." Eric threw up his eyebrows and pushed his chair back. "Well, I'm off to the meeting. Coming ?"

"Suppose there's trouble ? I passed a lot of law cars on the way here."

"Oh, I don't reckon they're anything to do with us, Dave -they must be on their way to arrest Donnelly for murder."

"Piss off."

The high street seemed somehow different this Monday morning, the shops drabber, the housewives and pensioners who were now, at nine-thirty, coming out of their husbandless, childless houses more ill-tempered, their faces pinched with a hundred small concerns and worries and probably by one or two big ones as well. The rubbish from Saturday's market still lingered, stuck to the street and the pavement by intermittent October rain. An old man was washing down the steps of the Ode on as Eric and Dave arrived at the bus stop; Eric glanced at the stills of Kirk Douglas dressed as Spartacus.

"Not a bad film, that," said Dave. "Went to see it last night. You seen it?"

"Only on telly."

As they stood in the bus-queue, Dave looked at Eric from the corner of his eye. "Of course, this meeting's gonna be a waste of time. You fancy nippin' down the employment to see if anything's goin' ?"

Eric grunted. "That would be a waste of time."

The industrial estate was five minutes' walk from the bus stop at the other end. There was a funny feeling in the air. Looking up at the razor-blade factory and the bakery as they passed, they could see men standing at the windows, looking out.

"Whaddayou think's up with them ?"

Eric pressed his lips together. "Dunno. They're looking down towards our factory."

Dave snorted. "It's not 'our' factory any more."

"It never fucking well was."

Dave looked at Eric, made to say something, then reconsidered and remained silent.

They were late. By the time they reached the factory gate, the two hundred men and women were listening to Donnelly as he wound up his speech. The Irishman was not big but, as he stood at the head of the meeting, his finger jabbing the air and his head thrown back so that his voice carried as far as possible, he looked as big as he needed to look. With a glance at the six or seven policemen who stood on one side, Eric and Dave joined on at the back and strained forward to hear what was being said.

"So that's their plan, brothers and sisters: first they put us on the street and then, in a week or two, Preston's will close through lack of parts, or at least that's what the workers at Preston's will be told. But the fact is that both operations will be carried on in Spain-they are being carried on in Spain as we stand here. In Spain, brothers and sisters, where the fact that the prisons are full of trade unionists will mean bigger profits than ever before, even bigger dividends for the shareholders than they got last year." Donnelly paused, placed his hands on his hips and looked around at the meeting. "So should we accept the fact that the business which we've built up over the past twenty years has been transferred to fascist Spain ?"

He listened to the chorus of noes and raised his eyebrows in mock surprise. Despite the seriousness of the situation, everyone could see that he was about to playfully chide them for past errors. "Ohhh, so now we all see what a tirrible thing fascism is, do we ? From the measly little collection we took for the boys in Spain a couple of Fridays ago, I wasn't thinking for a minute that we were all such dedicated anti-fascists. But now it's hit us in the belly, eh ?" He smiled. "Well, we're learning the hard way, but even that's better than not learning at all. And I'll tell you another thing: don't be too surprised if when this has all died down I get arrested and deported under the Anti-Terrorism Act-not for being a terrorist, but for being a

295

bloody good trade unionist. When you stand by and let a law like that get passed, you don't always stop to think that it might be used against yourself one day, but that's the kind of society we're living in, brothers and sisters."

Some among the audience thought that he had wandered too far. "Yeah, but what are we gonna do now ?" cried one worker.

Donnelly stretched up on his toes and looked beyond the crowd to where a blue Mercedes had drawn up, a police-sergeant bent to one of the rear windows. "Well, first of all we're going to let the governor in. We mustn't stop him from working just because he stopped us, now, must we ? Move aside and let the silver-haired old gentleman through. Of course I'm serious, brother-move aside and let the bastard through now."

In some confusion, the meeting obeyed and divided itself into two. The Mercedes crawled through and stopped at the gate, where the chauffeur alighted with a bunch of keys. While he was unlocking the gate, Donnelly swept off his hat, clasped it to his heart and approached the rear window of the car. "They're not at all bad lads, sorr," he said, laying the brogue on thick and heavy, "It's only natural that they should want to let off a bit of steam. Now pardon me presumption, sorr, but if your good lady has any scraps that she can spare ... well, it's the little ones, you see, sorr - they'll not be having much to eat since you're no longer able to give us work and look after us."

The managing director opened his mouth, licked his lips, frowned and told the returned chauffeur to drive through the gate.

Donnelly straightened up and called out: "And now, brothers and sisters, we're going to occupy the factory. Come on."

The men reached the office area before the Mercedes and so the managing director found the way barred. He waited around for ten minutes and then drove away once more, stopping outside the gate to converse with the sergeant. Donnelly, meanwhile, had sent a man over the back wall to the house of the night-watchman. The man returned forty-five minutes later with a full set of keys and by 11.15 the factory was occupied in the fullest sense.

A meeting of the shop stewards was called and this lasted until noon. The occupation, far from having been as spontaneous as it had appeared, had been planned over the weekend by the shop stewards and a handful of the most trusted workers. Now they ironed out the finer points, drawing up watch-rotas, arranging for bedding and food to be shipped in and for those workers who had not turned up for the meeting to be informed. Someone was sent across to Preston's to advise the shop stewards there of the occupation and of the future which lay in store for them.

As Donnelly left the meeting, one of the senior shop stewards walked with him across the yard. "I don't think you did us much good, Bob, talking that way to Jamieson."

Donnelly snorted contemptuously. "Get away with you ! He's so thick he couldn't make out whether I was taking the piss or not. Hey, young Eric!"

He left the shop steward and walked over to where Eric and Dave were standing. Eric looked up and, as if sensing that what Donnelly wanted to say to him was confidential, patted Dave's arm and moved away.

Donnelly placed a hand on Eric's shoulder. "My spies tell me that you were in some trouble at the ground on Saturday."

Eric dropped his eyes, not knowing how to meet the man's gaze.

"Well, at least you're ashamed of it-that's a good sign. But why did you have to get mixed up in a thing like that ?"

Eric swallowed. "It's hard to put into words. It didn't have much to do with the match, really. All kinds of feelings were mixed up in me. One minute I was glad, happy to be with me mates, then I was ashamed, 'cause all I was was a yob who'd just lost his job and didn't know any better."

The Irishman smiled down at him. "You know better, son-you know it and I know it and that's all that counts. Never mind what anyone else thinks, least of all bastards like Jamieson."

They walked across the yard together. Donnelly put his hands in his pockets, took in a large sniff of air and looked about him, as if visualising how things might be if, instead of a defensive action, this occupation were of a more permanent nature.

"You see, Eric," he said, "you'll find that every class system on earth, once it's outlived its usefulness and is dying, will give rise to violence and to what they call a 'breakdown in law and order.' That's because the system can't satisfy the simple demands of the people any more and because something tells them that the law is only a means of keeping them down anyway. But that doesn't mean that this violence is a good thing, because nine times out of ten it's just workers fighting workers. Then again, sometimes the violence is within the law, like it was in Rome, where they made slave fight slave. They're happy-the slave-owners, the barons or the capitalists-as long as worker fights worker, and that's what you were doing on Saturday. What people like us have got to do is turn workers' thoughts on creating a system where everyone can have a job, a house, enough to eat and enough to do with his spare-time, building up his mind as well as his body." He paused and grinned. "But you're not ready for that yet."

297

Eric felt better, no longer ashamed, because Donnelly understood. That was the trouble: not enough people understood.

"What d'you think's going to happen here ?"

The Irishman scratched his head. "Oh, the police will come along and try to get us out. If for some reason they don't succeed, then we'll try and get the government to support us. But even if we get that far, it won't be far enough."

"How d'you mean

Donnelly stopped, turned to Eric and smiled. "You go away and see if you can answer that one for yourself, then, when all this is settled one way or the other, we'll talk it over

Eric had been given a tiny piece of understanding and was beginning to realise that an experience was not half as frightening if it was understood. As he returned to Dave, he noticed Clem walking away.

Dave shrugged sheepishly when he saw the look on Eric's face. "Yeah, well, he ain't all that bad," he said. "You were right about them A levels, anyway. He was just telling me what the law might try to do to us-conspiracy to trespass and things like that."

Eric remembered what Donnelly had said about Rome. "Talking about Clem, did you say that you saw Spartacus last night ? Well, don't you re-member that bit where Kirk Douglas was forced to fight that black slave, and the black slave, instead of killing Kirk Douglas when he had the chance, attacked the poofs who were making them fight ?"

"Yeah, that was good, that bit." Eric had been hoping for more.

"Well, don't you see: he was a slave, the same way Kirk Douglas was; Clem is a worker, the same way we are. Why should we fight Clem when what we should be doing is taking on the bosses, us and Clem together !"

Dave frowned and nodded slowly. "That makes sense, I suppose, but how we gonna do that ?"

Eric thought desperately for a few seconds and then shrugged. "I don't know, but I reckon the time's come to find out."

In the early afternoon, word came that the police were ten minutes from the factory. Eric's stomach tightened for a moment, but then he drew on his new understanding and the fear passed. The thought uppermost in his mind was then what a pity it would be if the police succeeded in turfing them out, because in a few days people would have forgotten that the occupation had ever taken place. He went to the stores for a pot of paint and, when he returned, began to write on the wall: THIS FACTORY OCCUPIED BY THE WORKERS and then the date. A group gathered around him and so when he had finished he handed over the pot and brush to someone else.

The police were just entering the industrial estate. The workers, the men and the women, became tense. Hands fluttered nervously. Nails were bitten. Donnelly went into conference with the shop stewards and even his confidence seemed to be running out. Then the men on the gate began to shout, jump up and down and wave their arms wildly. So this was it. The end of the occupation was in sight.

Or was it ? There came a roaring sound, low at first but growing all the time. Men broke off their worried conversations and moved nearer the gate to see what was happening. Donnelly looked at his shop stewards and grinned victoriously. He knew what was happening. When the head of the column appeared, the workers at the gate began to cheer. The entire workforce of Preston's-750 workers-was marching to the factory to seal off the entrance from the police.

Eric threw up his arms and laughed. His laughter became infectious and Dave, Clem and others joined in. Eric caught sight of his mother among the marchers, which meant that she must have stopped on after her finishing-time. Relations at home were a bit strained at the best of times, but now he felt closer to his mother than he had ever felt before, and proud, filled up with pride.

As they ran to the gate, Eric noticed a sign which someone had painted:

THE WORKERS' RULE-OK

He smiled but knew inside that it was not strictly true. In the crowd at the gate, the feeling that washed over him was similar to the one he had experienced at the start of the match on Saturday, although the feeling now was far finer, stronger and more elevating than anything he had known before. Yes, together we can beat anyone and one day we will.

One day ... It was the biggest thing that had ever happened to him and yet even now he was asking himself just how big it really was. We're strong enough to beat the law today, but what about tomorrow ? What about all the other coppers and all the soldiers and all the judges and all the other bosses ?

He remembered the question he had asked Donnelly and the answer was there, at the back of his mind. Yes, when all this was over, he'd have a long talk with Donnelly.

Ken Fuller

AN EXPLANATION AND AN APOLOGY

In Voices 6 we printed a poem called "Alan". On the contents page it was attributed to Sam Watts. Under the poem itself, we had simply written "Watts". The poem was printed without an explanation of the circumstances under which it was written. The writer was Bridie Watts, the mother of Alan Watts, who was an active leading member of the Young Communist League in Liverpool, and an EC member. Alan was stabbed to death by a man who was drunk at the time. The family Sam (the father) Paul (the brother) Bridie (the mother) were shaken to the core by the tragic event. Bridie's verses are more a cry of anguish than a poem, but we believe it deserves to be printed. Here it is then with this explanation and with my apology for the way it was treated in the last issue.

Ben Ainley.

ALAN

No moon-no sun-no stars
No morning-no evening-no light
No trees-no flowers-no spring
No birds-no song-no rainbow
No seas-no sky-no streams
No smiles-no joy-no laughter
No music-no warmth-no love
No tenderness-no beauty-no feeling
No tomorrow-No Alan

Bridie Watts

BLEACHED GRASS

The colour in my mind is of bleached grass. "Some say the world will end in fire..." -gun-fire from Soweto to Derry this summer of '76.

Meanwhile, I am lulled in an August seclusion of rural peace, solaced by the image of a small child in pink frock and curls; a child taking her first shaky steps, holding only my breath, as she treads, tentative, on dry ground. This is the long, hot, summer of eternal childhood-the sunlit smile in sunlit fields-the snapshot which my mother has treasured for decades being identical to the one in my mind's eye today. We are accustomed to this continual regeneration-as accustomed as we are to water springing from the earth.

Still the gun-fire cracks across my brain, stridencies which also hold my breath, and the colour in my mind is of bleached grass. Perhaps it is my eyes that are too dry.

Pat Sentinella.

SAVAGES

(For the dispossessed people of Diego Garcia)

Those who
While the waters of the forest
Drop
Pare and trim and mill
A branch of mahogany
To a point

Or those who
With a casual cross
On a memorandum
Sweep away
Acres of men and women

Who sees the wood?
Who sees the trees?

John Salway

FROM HAIFA TO DIE IN LEBANON
Published in Arab Palestine "Resistance" No. 2
February 1976 by Palestine Liberation Army.

Images covered with dust; people!
My father pushing me in a cart
From Haifa ... to Die in Lebanon.
I was holding an open pomegranate
And a young sparrow!
I remember the sparrow
Picking at the ruby seeds
Sharing my bread-crusts
In Lebanon
Tossed about
Later: A target between two guns

I woke and stole a last look at the sun
Still here in my dead pupils
Take it ! !
I woke and died
Holding my child,
Dreaming:
I saw again fathers pushing carts
Then the burning red Flowers,
And a grey wave chasing me
Zionism closed my eyes
But you ... open them
But you:
Tear the hearts from the lifeless bodies
Take them back

Giorgio Taverniti

THE STRIPPER

They were the last to leave. Lingering slowly up the slope to the car-park. Mellowed by the night's drinking, reluctant to leave behind, the brightness and laughter. They were still laughing and joking, tossing comments across to one another, sharing a bond in the enjoyment of another evening together. They were content, like fully happy cats, who looked no further than the next saucer of milk.

Only Claire was quiet ... she gazed up at the sky, and the dark troubled clouds, that promised rain. Her attention was divided between her friends, and her own thoughts, and she made little contribution to the conversation. One couple shouted goodnight, and with arms entwined, walked away to their car.

There was ribald commentary on their early departure from the group. One of the men, clenched his fist, patted his upper arm with his left hand, and made a punching movement in the air.

"Wheigho! had a promise Jack ?"

Everybody laughed, including the couple in question.

"It's nowt to do with you John", shouted Jack good humouredly.

They climbed into the car. Jack sounded the horn, waved, and drove off down the slope, followed by shouts, and cat-calls.

They gazed after the disappearing car.

"She's certainly a character, isn't she ?"

"Aye. Marvellous for her age, and good fun."

"Good bloke Jack, too, he's sound, dead sound."

The men stood there, smiles on their faces, hands in pockets. Everything was good on a Saturday night. They looked forward to it all week. On Saturday nights, Monday morning was buried.

"What about that stripper last week Dave ? She was a real artist, that one." Claire came down to earth.

She was part of the group again, listening intently, and Dave was careful to avoid her eye.

"Did Dave tell you, Claire?" He didn't wait for an answer, but carried straight on. "A real genuine artist, and just listen"

He nudged Claire, unnecessarily, for her attention.

303

"... can you just see it, this stripper pranced up to Pete, pushed her bust right at him, and bear in mind she was topless, and then she said -'Take me knickers off.'"

He roared with laughter, his eyes dancing at the picture conjured in his mind. Claire laughed too. Dave chuckled, and shook his head from side to side. He was incensed with merriment at the reminder of Pete, and the stripper. He felt it safe to laugh, because Claire had laughed too.

Still smiling, he caught her eye, she stared straight through him.

"That was the benefit concert, wasn't it ?"

She directed her question at John, every time she looked at Dave, she opened her eyes wide and stared coolly at him, before flicking her glance back to John.

"Yeah, it was a great night, we didn't know there was a stripper on though." John's girl friend Liz had joined the group in time to hear the last words.

"I'll bet you didn't" she said.

Claire was careful not to let them guess that she was not in tune with their own jolly mood. Only by her eyes, did she convey the message to Dave.

She felt anger, not so much at their night out, but at their obvious enjoyment over it, with their small boy enthusiasm, and great shouts of laughter, as they remembered more details to relate.

"Do you know what riles me though ? If us women went to see a male stripper you wouldn't like it would you ?"

"Ah well, that's different, isn't it. I mean, it seems more crude somehow." This reasoning came from another of the male majority of the group.

"Why is it ?" Liz joined Claire, in her questioning.

"Well it just does that's all. Men have always gone to see a stripper."

"There, you see" said Claire. "Women's Lib kicks up about things like that not that I want to see a male stripper, but if I did I shouldn't be made to feel odd about it."

"Mmmm, true, true but it's still different."

John laughed, and patted Claire's shoulder.

"I'll agree there", said Dave. "It's like you always say Claire, one rule for men, another for women - it applies there." He slung his arm around her. She stretched her lips in a fair imitation of a smile.

His male ego, thought her silence signified defeat.

304

"Come on all you happy people" said Liz. "It looks like rain". John held his palm up.

"Here it comes."

The rain fell in large scattered drops, and before they reached the cars, a relentless sheet of rain, stung their lightly clad bodies. Their calls of good night to one another were brief and hurried. In the car Claire was careful not to mention the strip show and Dave made no mention of it either, no explanation of why he hadn't told her about it.

I'm not bothered about it, she told herself, but he might have mentioned it. Why didn't he ? If he'd told me about the stripper, I wouldn't have minded. A dark horse if ever there was one, and he had the nerve to say she was as deep as the ocean ... It was his stock phrase when he found her out in a white lie, or an omission of confidence.

There was no knowing men, that was for sure, and they talked about women. It was an effort to keep silent about it, a test of will power, but she managed and was quite pleased with herself. Yet she knew that at some future date she would have her say. She could sense his relief, and was slightly amused.

It had been a hot tiring day, and Claire thought longingly of the hot bath she had promised herself. She made the beds quickly, not bothering much about shaking the pillows up.

She was tired after her long day, serving in the shop, and wanted nothing more than to laze in the bath, reading and smoking.

Just then Dave entered their bedroom. He made a grab for her as she passed him, and she dropped her cigarettes.

"Ouch" she gasped, and pulled herself away from his fierce embrace.

"You were different downstairs, What's up, don't you feel like it ?"

"Yes, but I was just going for a bath."

"Never mind the bloody bath."

Movements and voices reminded them they were not alone in the house.

"The traffic around here is too congested" said Claire.

"Well come on then. Let's go into the bathroom."

From the lower regions of the house, someone shouted for Dave. He cursed. "I'll be up in a minute" he said to Claire.

305

"OK", she picked her cigarettes up off the floor, grabbed her magazine, and went into the bathroom, leaving the door unlocked.

She stripped down to her briefs, and stretched her aching body. Mmm, that felt good, She turned the bathtaps on, and threw in some bubble-bath, swishing the water, till it looked like pink candy-floss. She caught sight of herself in the mirror. The steam wouldn't do her hair any good, and they were going out later. She put some rollers in quickly, and wound a pink, chiffon scarf, mammy-fashion round her head. She reached for a bottle off the shelf. It was after-shave lotion. Footsteps pounded up the stairs. Ah well after-shave was as good as perfume. She splashed it liberally over her neck, and down her arms, and replaced it quickly back onto the shelf, seconds before Dave entered the bathroom. He stood looking at her. His eyes glistened. He locked the door without taking his eyes off her. The sound he made, could never be found in a dictionary. It was an ejaculation of appreciation, and expectation and sounded like 'Ffwar'

"Do I put you off?" asked Claire, referring to the rollers in her hair.

"God ! No. Come here quick."

She swayed towards him, pressed her breasts against his chest, and twined her arms around his neck.

She gazed deeply into his eyes, then lowered her lashes. She stifled a laugh.

"Take me knickers off then" she breathed huskily.

He pushed her roughly away from him.

The movement was so unexpected, she almost lost balance.

"You've put me off now" he said, and slammed the door as he left the bathroom. "And leave my bloody aftershave alone" he shouted from the other side of the door. She gazed at the door through which he had made his hasty exist.

Well ! There was no knowing men.

She was still smiling to herself, as she settled herself in the bath, lit a cigarette and reached for her magazine.

Jean Sutton.

AFTER YOU

"What will happen to us?"
she said. "That's what worries me

306

"We shall die" said I.
"Doesn't it bother you" she said
"not to know who will be the first to go ?"
"I had rather hoped" said I
diplomatically
"it would be me"
"That's what I mean" said she
"You men. Self first,
self second and self again.

Bill Eburn

RUSH HOUR

"Why do you feign sleep
as soon as I appear
looking for a seat
that isn't there ?"

"Madam-
(I kiss your hand)
I simply cannot bear
to see a lady stand."

Bill Eburn

ABSENT FRIENDS

"So many gone' said my Dad
"I'm afraid to look in the glass."
"For fear of what you'll see there ?"
"No son. For fear I shan't be there."
Bill Eburn.

MANGANESE NODULES AND YOU

Take me back to the land of the manganese nodules,
To Chorlton-cum-Lately in your soft cobalt twilight;
Half-past-my-lovely, iridescence-of-rainbows,
Shine on this whiteness of my phosphorus midnight;
My life needs your colours:
Take me back to the land of the manganese nodules
And share with me all of your magical wealth.

Cowrie Shells, Jingly-bells, seahorses minglingamonga
Cornucopia of giving to you: my life's treat:
If I were the Phosphate Commissioner of Tonga
I'd lay Queen Salote's Phosphate before your small feet:
My life needs your taking:
Take me back to the land of the manganese nodules
And share with me all of your magical wealth.

In Chorlton-cum-Sideways every Saturday evening
The rest of the world makes libations down dark entries:
But I stays where I is and give gifts of my thoughtness
That try to slip by your self's forbidding-cold sentries;
My life needs your listening:
Take me back to the land of the manganese nodules
And share with me all of your magical wealth.

Take me down by the shoreline of Chorlton-cum-Uppance,
Interweave with the laurel that grows down Hardy Lane;
Receive all that I give, from a world to a tuppence
Interweave with all that I am, whether life or rain;
My life needs your being:
Take me back to the land of the manganese nodules
And share with me all of your magical wealth.

Please sing me your sweet song that revolves round my earole,
Does two laps of my ear lobes and twice round my mind;
Please let your lips touch me with a song and with touching
Sing your sweet manganese song, sing my life, sing, sweet kind:
My life needs your kindness:
Take me back to the land of the manganese nodules
And share with me all of your magical wealth.
Les Barker

COMMENT ON A SCORNER OF MECHANISATION

It's easy to see this scholar thinks and feels,
changes his linen, takes his decent meals,
without perception of the household wheels.

She who provides the comfort for him leans
joyously on the comfort of machines,
like us, who worked at washtubs in our teens.

Those poets who rest in neolithic themes

have less in common with man's stone age dreams
than the tractorman by whom the tilled earth teems;

than the twisting girls in the noisy dance halls,
the swaggering youths by the factory walls,
whose hands make plenty, whose future calls;

calls to take charge of the toiling machines
that they make and work as Plenty's means.

Frances Moore

A SILENT MAN DISGUISED AS A COMRADE

A silent man disguised as a comrade.

We think we have a choice on the question of marriage
but for my class
the choice is narrowed merely to a choice between one man and
another
and even that is sometimes 'de rigueur'.
On the appointed hour we took our vows
never to regret but often to wonder what they meant
What had I meant?
Like all the rest we bump and grind along
each in our private cells behind a private door.
Never certain if it's only us who have problems,
never certain if the fault is ours
and had we made the wrong choice ?
Never realising we had no choice anyway.
Four years cloud the memory and was it always like this?
Did we always lie side by side
just watching the trees outside the window
and feeling desolate,
lonely?
In each other's pockets all the time
and yet we lock our minds away,
apart.
Occasionally we send long distance messages
Washed up, marooned on the island of marriage.

Bewildered, battling to constrain the circumstances
by the strength of my reason

and not succeeding,
I was picked off by a cruising shark
a spider asked me into his parlour.
Crushed by some enigmatic event
an emotional spastic
collecting women in his web
watching them struggle, tangle,
give in to his effortless superiority.
His malignant speculations pay off, and one by one
we fall into his bed
with the cold weight of coins in an empty safety box.

I deluded myself.
I thought I'd found an answer and opened up our marriage.
I was warmed by the glow of new communication,
by the conception of a network of non-exclusive lovers.
Free love. My love is available;
one owner only; slightly soiled though in good working order.
However, you seemed only in it for the parts.
You only wanted some spares
to patch up your own rusty framework.
Soon, that's all you'll be.
A rusty junk-heap of everyone else's left-overs.

If I believe it surely someone else does.
Why did you only want my icing?
Did you hope you were stealing my most precious possession?
Or someone else's?

My love is not finite, nor an absolute.
You looked through my letter box and thought you'd stayed the
weekend
You were barely on my threshold.
I was ready there to welcome you
You moved me, and I had faith, comrade.
Your mind and heart are not fresh, comrade.
You are not being honest with yourself.
You speculate in emotions
and call yourself a communist.

Your silence betrayed me.
I was at peace in it.
I liked your eggs and bacon,
it was nice to have my bath run,

but I'd get that at a hotel, wouldn't I ?
You were irritated by my reality
and the impermanency of sexual tension.
You were impatient with my pain
in a hurry to despatch me.
Quite relieved to strip away my confidence.
I could feel myself shrinking, my outlines reducing;
I felt a small child again.
not the woman that you'd made me.

When I had nightmares
you diagnosed a disturbed mind.
I sat all night with half a shandy
whilst you sat in silence,
and then said you didn't know me.
You didn't want to.
I said I felt unwelcome
and you kindly made me drunk.
Well fortunately I don't suffer from hangovers,
and that includes you.

However, I learnt a lot.
You said my art must be a contribution:
well here it is.
You said you only got to know people after you'd been to bed
with them.
That rules out a hell of a lot of people.
And you only know their bodies,
and even then it's not your eyes and mind,
it's just a hand, a thigh.
And once you've had one in the dark
we must all be pretty much the same.
Didn't you realise my body is only where the real me lives ?
I learnt to take the initiative myself
although I might have chosen better.
But comrade, you moved me.
It was a hard way to teach me my strengths
and your weaknesses.
I have weighed them up
but my love is not a sacrifice at your altar.
I'm not a martyr
nor a christian.
We might not have much choice
but you, a comrade, should know the way,

and I'm not running a charity.

You thought you had me in your orbit,
but I'm the centre of my own circle, comrade.
I'd planned a bit of nuclear fission
and a new red element
but something went wrong.

I rang the bells and threw open the doors
my light shone out,
but you chose not to enter.
Well, the loss is all your comrade.

Wendy Whitfield.

PHILPOT IN THE CITY

He's something in the CITY

an ENTREPRENEUR-and aims to start
a UNION of all the COMMUNICATIONS

men. He will include CLERK
and COMPUTER-OPERATOR, SECRETARY

and SYSTEMS ANALYST; OFFICE MANAGER
and CO-ORDINATOR; PROMOTER

and NEGOTIATOR and of course, his own
profession of LINK-MAN collecting

the tube-tickets. For extra CAPITAL,
he enters in a book names and addresses

of all the wonderful women
travelling without a ticket.

Paul St Vincent

LAMBCHOPS GOES INTO TRAINING

Chateauneuf du Pape; German/Hungarian/Yugoslavian
Riesling; Cotes du Rhone/du Provence; Cyprus

Sherry-that's not the half of what he's giving
up for the Contest. He must also say NO to his

better-half of a dream Sociologist, NO
to self-abuse to the SUN and MIRROR sin-page.

But Crusades have never been won by compromise.
He must nail the lie once and for all-of fecklessness,
lack of application, racial special
pleading. The early-morning job through

the park, six weeks on the building-site
and regular arm-wrestling have done wonders

for the body. But the mind, Lambchops, needs
muscling up. His strongest rival is a woman

using Psychology to unnerve him. She is out,
they say, learning to piss at the roadside without

wetting her shoes. It's been tried before,
darling, it won't wash, Lambchops will learn

to play chess, to count in Yiddish, to recognise
Mozart. He will be complete for the contest:

body of Muhammad Ali, mind of a great Cynic
and Chinese all over-with the world's computers

date-matching him. Training over, he relaxes
with a Shakespearean Sonnet, and stays awake

pondering the strangeness of things. Why for instance
do they need to use knives tomorrow for the darts match?

Paul St Vincent

NATURAL RHYTHM

It was on my return journey
That I began to realise who he was
Looking at him as though
For the first time
Striding forth to conquer some world or other.

I let him pass
Then called after him
"Why so fast ?"
He turned his head
To give me a tolerant smile
Before answering.

"It is our urgency
which helps to bring
The shape towards completion
Surely you are aware of this by now ?"
"How well did you spend your day ?"
But before I could frame my answer
He had passed out of sight.

Rose Friedman.

POWER TRIO

A Statesman
once a revolutionary became a politician matures
retires

A Politician
once a revolutionary aspires
retires.

A Revolutionary
never retires.

Vincent P Richardson

THE HUNT FOR THE BISMARCK

What's the buzz?
The Hood's gone down.
The Hood's gone down?
The Hood's gone down.
What's the buzz?
The Hood's gone down
That's the buzz
The Hood's gone down.

Twelve hundred pairs of eyes and ears,
Incredulous
Let's have it clear.
The buzz is that the Hood's gone down.
The Hood's gone down?
The Hood's gone down.
The buzz is that the Hood's gone down
That's the buzz
The Hood's gone down.

What's the buzz ?
The Hood's gone down.
What sank her ?
Tin fish ? Junkers?
The buzz is that the Hood's gone down.
A.R. End of message.

The Bismarck's out,
The Bismarck's out,
That's the buzz
The Bismarck's out.
The buzz is that the Bismarck's out
And we are looking for her.

What sank the Hood?
The Bismarck did.
The Bismarck did?
The Bismarck did.
What sank the Hood?
The Bismarck did
And we are looking for her.

The fog as thick as peasoup fell,

315

Concealing all around us
The skipper will address the crew
And so end all the rumours.

The Hood is gone
The Bismarck's out
A fleet is searching for her
The Ramillies has joined the hunt
Revenge will take her convoy

Twelve hundred men went down with Hood,
Two thousand went with Bismarck,
Where is the sense
Or what the good
That sends men seeking others blood
Is there a thing called brotherhood ?
I wonder

Bert Ward.

IN PRAISE OF LEARNING
*Bertolt Brecht (From the play "The Mother", based on the novel
by Maxim Gorki)*

Learn the simplest things.
For those whose day has come
It is never too late.
Learn your ABC. It's not enough, but
Learn it. Don't let it get you down.
Make a start. You must know everything.
You must take over the leadership.

Learn, man in the asylum.
Learn, man in prison.
Learn, woman in the kitchen.
Learn, sixty-year-old.
You must take over the leadership.
Find yourself a school, you who are homeless.
Get some knowledge round you, you who are freezing.
You who are hungry, grab yourself a book: it is a weapon.
You must take over the leadership.

Don't be afraid to ask, Comrade.

316

Don't let them talk you round,
Take a look for yourself.
What you don't know yourself
You don't know.
Check the bill,
You must pay it.
Put your finger on every item.
Ask: how did that get there?
You must take over the leadership.

(Translated by Rick Gwilt).

IRY

(This story is dedicated to comrades in UCATT, especially John Madden, who taught me a lot about being funny, and Bert Smith, who taught me a lot about being serious.)

Iry moved onto the top floor of the Bull Ring a few months after I did, just as winter-was closing in. It was a dull, wet Saturday and I'd been out selling the paper on my own block. It was one of those days when a lot of people hadn't bothered to get up, but those that had were more likely to buy a Star rather than splash their way to the shop. Later, the rain had eased off and I was out on the walkway, looking down over the parapet. In the adventure playground the kids were climbing railway-sleeper mountains and swinging their way across mud-puddle rivers.

In the corner of my eye I could see a figure approaching, hugging close to the wall. I turned to see an old man with very black skin and very white hair. He was very tall and walked as if he were trying to hide the fact. Under a faded grey suit, which fitted him the way a flag fits a flagpole, he wore a blue-green shirt open on the neck, so that the white tufts of hair could be seen sprouting up from his chest. On his face he wore a sheepish half-smile like a permanent apology. I never once saw him wear anything different, except for the one day when something happened that really cracked him up.

I showed Iry how to work the electric meter-told him it cost a lot but he'd get some of it back at the end of the year, providing the meter hadn't been robbed in the meantime, which was what usually happened. It reminded me of the night I broke Julie's meter open with a hacksaw-because it hadn't been emptied and too many people knew she was moving out. We took the whole box down to NORWEB next morning wrapped in a headscarf. After the meter, I explained to Iry about the central heating, and he kept nodding. I asked him if he understood and he nodded.

317

I didn't see much of Iry for a while. With a fifty-foot drop for a back yard and a latrine for dogs at the front, people on the Crescents didn't usually see much of their neighbours. It was getting on for Christmas when someone called and told me that Iry had been starving and freezing himself to death in there, paying £5.80 a week rent and still only getting £1.50 off the SS for his old room down the Moss. Some kids had found him sitting up in bed silent and shivering when they broke in to rob the meter. They'd gone ahead and robbed the meter anyway, because old habits die hard, but when they'd told someone's main, saying the door was already broken open and they'd just walked in to check up. It turned out Iry was only forty-seven-he just looked old.

Iry had come straight from his village in Jamaica to the boat at Kingston to the train at Southampton to another train at London to Manchester. It was the only journey he'd ever made in his life, and he'd been lost ever since. When he sat down to the dinner I'd cooked up, he didn't eat fast or hungrily, just steadily got himself outside it so I began wondering if he had hollow legs. I asked him if it was right that the woman from Social Services was getting him sorted out with the SS and he nodded. I told him that was better than if I tried to help-I always ended up losing my rag with those people. He nodded again.

I didn't see much of Iry for another few months. I saw him once shuffling down to the 'Junction', but I had a Union meeting to go to, so I didn't join him for a drink. It was the year Grocer Heath hit us with a three-day week and Wimpey's hit us with a transfer to Rochdale. Most of us couldn't take to rambling over the moors at seven every morning, and one by one we jacked up. I got a start with Hamer's in Salford, building a new telephone exchange.

It was all right while we were on digging the foundations, but as soon as I was doing a lot of work with a drill, cutting out columns that had been poured wrong, I started getting a head full of concrete dust and pretty bad ear-nose-and-throat trouble. I was surprised I'd managed to last so long-not so much on account of such natural causes as 'the dust', but because of the arrival of a gangerman called Ollie. We'd been labourers together when I was doing it for Taylor Woodrow's two years before. Anyway Ollie took one long hard look at me, then came out with that immortal line: "Haven't I seen you somewhere before ?" A day or two later, George was moaning as usual about the job, and I was ignoring him as usual. Then Ollie stops shovelling concrete and says to George, "There s the man to talk to. He's real strong for the Union. He'll sort your problems out for you." Now I had to hand it to Ollie for moving fast-he didn't want any trouble where he was gangerman and he'd chosen just the right man to put the bubble in, right under my nose. You could practically see the steam rising from George's ears, like he'd got the message and was already thinking about the shortest way to the office. George had been with the company fifteen years and was the nearest thing to a firm's man you'd find outside of Madame Tussaud's. Archie, the joiner, was another gold-watch candidate, and it was obvious the agent had given him the nudge.

"Hey, I hear somebody say you are a Union man?"

"Well, you can't believe everything you hear, Archie."

So I was just concentrating on keeping my head down for a while and not getting provoked, especially after Rod got the bullet first week we were there for asking questions about the bonus a bit too loudly.

It was in April it all happened. I remember that because I was in hospital on April 1. Well, there were telephone tables installed on fire escapes, backs getting scrubbed with yard brushes, sets of gnashers turning up in cups of tea and enemas being administered to folks with sinus trouble. And rumours being spread that I was trying to take my mind off the operation coming up. A couple of days of agony after I came back thrashing and moaning and minus tonsils, then I got around talking to the really old blokes. Two old Jewish blokes I remember especially. Mr Caradon was the one the nurses liked soft and appealing with rabbit's eyes. But I reckoned Mr Locker had a bit more life in him. Ugly old feller with short-sighted frog's eyes, too proud for most of them. Eighty-three and dying of cancer. So I was told on the quiet, as he wasn't supposed to know. But he knew all right, he just wasn't letting on. He'd decided he wanted to be alive till he was dead.

When I got back home, there was still no money from the SS and I was just about broke. So I signed myself off the sick and phoned the firm to say I'd be in on Monday. Then I phoned the SS, who swore blind they were going to put a giro in the post right away. Well, Saturday went and Monday came and still no giro. So it's off to work and see the agent, who's terribly sorry but there's no chance of a sub first day back. He seems a bit over-confident, like he's got everything set up since I've been away. Most of the lads seem less alive than usual, but may be that's just the way it seems to me. I'll have to get working on them again quietly.

Dinner-time comes and I'm off to the SS. In out of the daylight and the lunchtime rush on Ancoats Street. Into the dingy waiting room, where nobody moves, except for kids who fidget and scuff because they've not been taught how to behave yet. There's at least thirty-seven people, lined up in rows with glazed expressions, like it's the queue for Belsen. Hard chairs specially designed to break every bone in your arse if you don't learn to go numb. I see Iry there on the front row, and he smiles his half-smile and nods to me. I realise he fits in here, looks just like the rest of them. And something's boiling up inside me-like I'm not in the mood for queuing up here losing an afternoon's wages and may be my job. Only it goes deeper than that.

People turn to look as I go straight through the sliding door without any invitation from the loudspeaker. Then there's me and this clerk having this conversation not quite with each other; I've been waiting three weeks and I'm sick and tired of waiting; he's sorry to the young lady that this young man is behaving so unreasonably and preventing him from attending to her case; I'm saying don't fall for that love they're just trying to get us at each other's throats, and he's apologising to her for the annoyance and the delay. So that does it. Two steps back, up onto the counter, and straight over the grille. I felt like this once, after Id jumped the fence at the Scoreboard End and just before I started running across the pitch towards the Stretford End. The clerk calls through to the main office but I'm already through there to save him the trouble. No, I don't want to go through into the other office and wait for the manager. I don't want to go anywhere you can lock me in. You realise you're being very selfish and annoying all the other people waiting. I don't care. I've been waiting three weeks and I'm not leaving here till I've seen the manager you think you can just go on messing people around and they're just going to sit on their arses and take it well I want my money.

Just as I'm going out through the hall with everything settled amicably, who should pass me going in but a bloke in a blue uniform and a tall hat who probably just happened to be dropping in for a chat. So I take off down Lever Street like a lemming that's late for the last train to Blackpool.

When I got home from work that night I went straight to Iry's door. When he opens up something strange happens to his face. It cracks open like a whale just seen a big wave. Lights up like a pinball machine, balls rolling and dials whirring everywhere, never been played for years because there were no coins to fit.

"Hey Iry, have the law been round this afternoon ?"

"No man, they don't come round. Hee-hee, you was funny. We all have a larf. We can hear you through the walls and everybody larf."

"They weren't annoyed then ?"

"No man, they not annoyed. They larfing together like they not larfed in years. I been larfing all afternoon'

We talked for a while longer, leaning over the parapet. I noted that the sun was larfing too. It was turning into a fine April evening. Down in the adventure playground, the kids were crossing fuel-ash oceans and climbing scaffold-tube canyons.

Things soon came to a head at Hamer's. The following Monday we returned from a wet weekend to find he wanted us to work down a ten-foot trench with no shoring. It looked about as safe as Ronan Point. Everybody was muttering and agreeing it was dangerous, but no one would refuse to go down it. Come tea-break I walked over to the Precinct and phoned the Factories Inspector. He was there in the time it took me to walk back. He strolled right around the site before he just happened to notice the trench. The agent was listening and looking embarrassed, and the lads were watching and nodding and agreeing that it was about time and it had to happen sooner or later, and the inspector was telling the agent to claw all the earth back from the top of the trench with the digger. Everybody must have known it was me who phoned, but nobody said anything about it. I was annoyed with myself because it wasn't the way I wanted to do things. I suppose I did it mainly because I wasn't too struck on being crushed to death, but it was partly just exasperation too. Little things from the past week that had been building up, like the channel I was told to pick out so I got covered in muddy water, when I could have done it a cleaner way. And then it turned out it wasn't a spring causing the water at all-it was a leaking sewer from our own site toilet.

On the Monday afternoon we were down the trench filling the muck skip. George was at the top acting as banksman because the crane-driver couldn't see us down there. And George kept guiding the skip down to where I could almost reach to unhook it but not quite. And something started to boil again. I started shouting and swearing at George, using words I didn't know I knew. Then George offered to knock my block off and I began to sober up. I suppose it was partly a built-in sense that you don't get into a fight on the job, and partly that I didn't fancy the idea of fighting George (there was no glory in it if I won and a bloody nose if I lost). But mainly, I suddenly realised I'd lost my rag with the wrong bloke at the wrong time. When you start fighting amongst yourselves, it's time to jack up-which is what I did.

Being angry's a bit like laughter-you've got to learn to control it, because it can work two ways. I was working for Laing's once when we refused to leave the cabin after tea-break. The contracts manager came in and interrupted the meeting, said he didn't care how long he waited, it was his cabin and he wasn't moving. So I said how when I was a little lad I used to play football with a kid who would always take the ball home when he was losing, because it was his ball. Well for a moment I had two hundred blokes right there, faces lit up and throats barking. Even the agent was laughing.

Trouble was, when the laughter stopped, we lost out on the being serious, and all the anger fizzled out in a couple of days.

I don't really know if there's a science of being angry or being funny, except that when you see faces lit up, you think may be it's possible for people to be alive till they're dead. It's a bit like a lighthouse-it doesn't show you much, just keeps you in with an idea where you're aiming at.

Rick Gwilt

January 1977

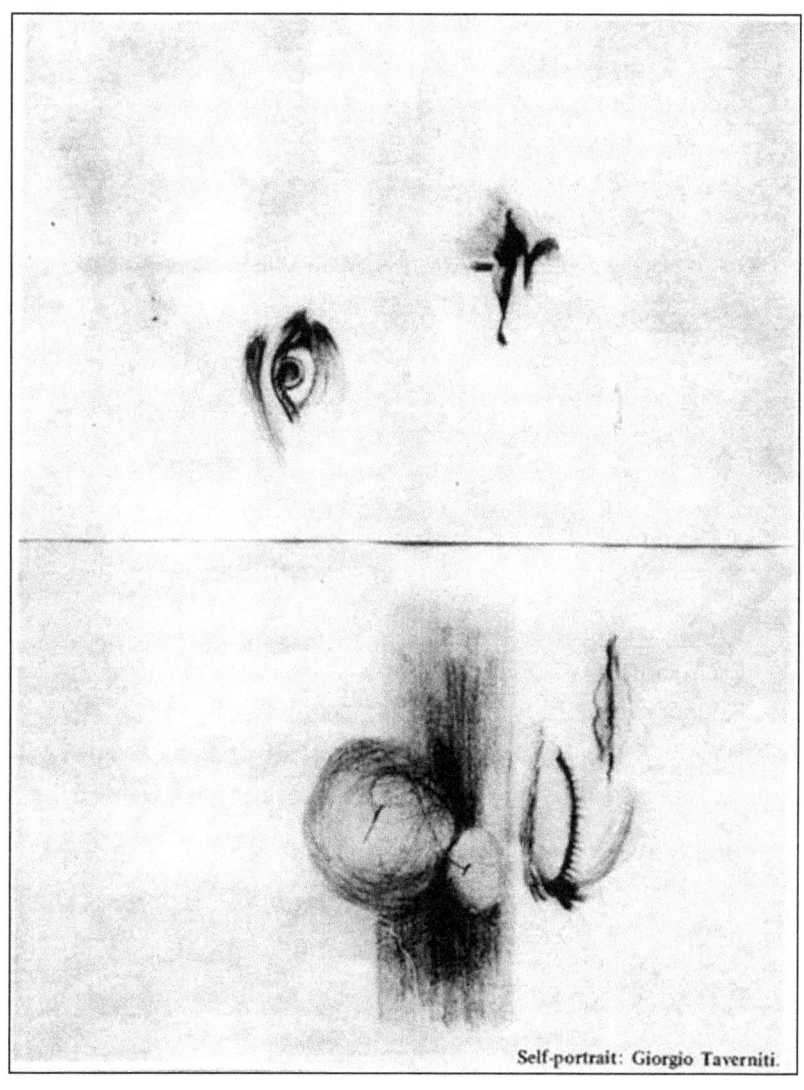

Self-portrait: Giorgio Taverniti.

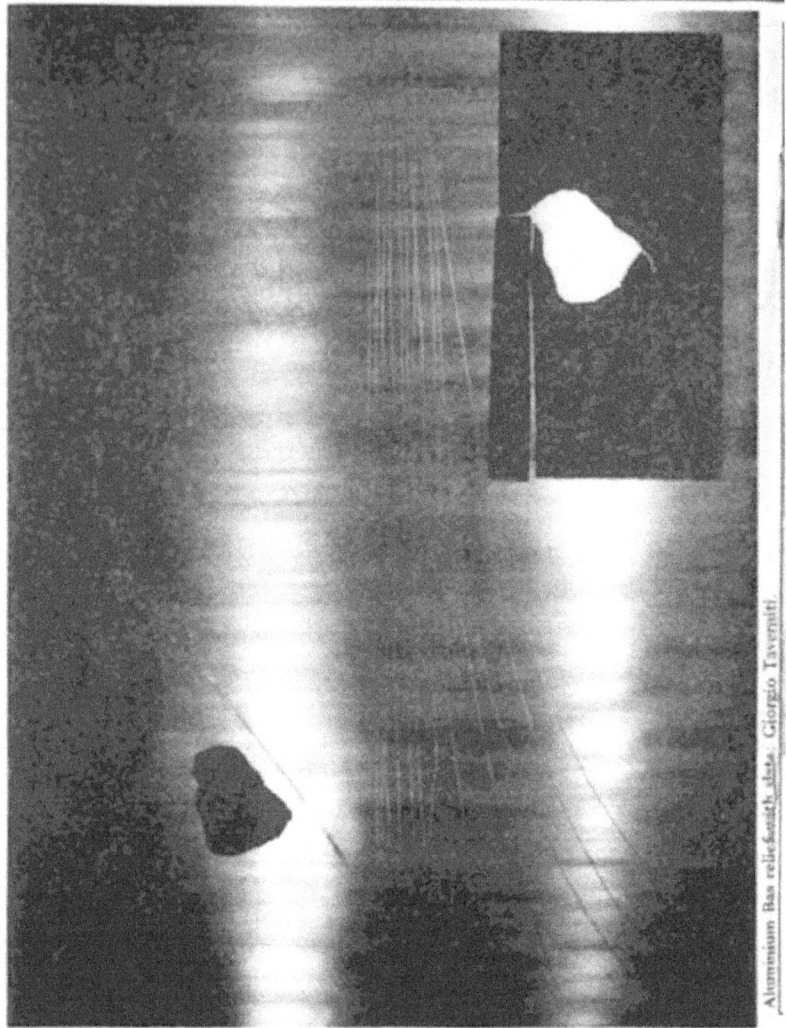

Aluminium Bas relief.smith plate. Giorgio Taverniti

Head of Newman: Sol Garson.

sol garson

invites

You to his first Major Exhibition
Sculptures & Paintings

**Tues. March 8th to Sat. March 12th.
28 Hathersage Road Manchester 13
(progress bookshop)**

2.00 p.m. to 7.00 p.m. admission free

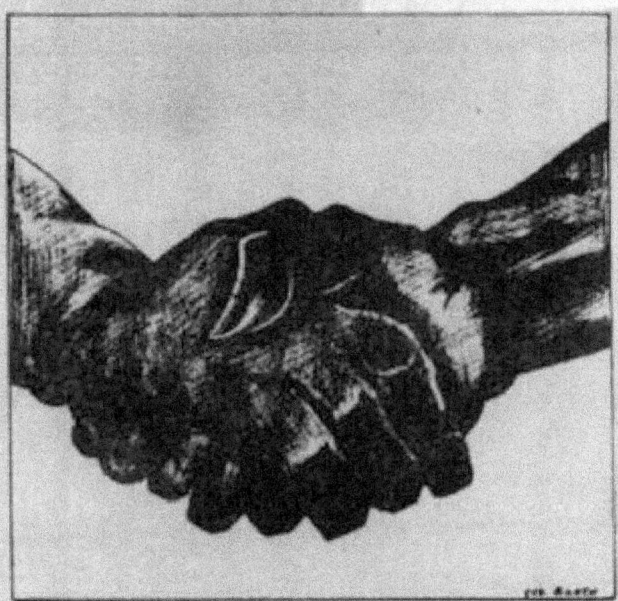

CONTRIBUTOR INDEX

Ainley, Ben *1901-1977*
Retired teacher. 50 years active in CP, Teachers' Union and Peace Movement. Present hobby book reviewing for various journals. (1972)

Voices a financial appeal (12)
Review of VP Richardson's Poems (11)
Editorial (11)

Anonymous
To Dame Margot Fonteyn (8)

Armstrong, Keith
Bourgeoisie (8)
Derelict (9)
Remember (9)
The Day the Tory Lights Went Out (10)
This (11)
Maud Watson, Florist (13)

Arnison, A
Listen to Me   (7)

Arrowsmith, Pat
After an Ultimatum (9)
Self View (10)
You (13)

Baker, Ray
Funny Weather (11)

Barker. Les
Noah's Ark (8)
In Memorium (9)
If (10)
Frightening Quietness (12)
Manganese Nodules And You (13)

Baker, Isobel
On Seeing a Film of Stalingrad   (7)
Thoughts on Death and Dying (7)
Written in Great Happiness (7)
The Cold War (8)

After Hearing a Radio Programme on the German Sailors' Revolt in 1918
at Kiel and Wilhelmshaven (10)
Portugal 1974 (12)

Balchin, Michael
A Week in the Life of Ivan Ivanovich (7)
Encounter at London Bridge (9)

Barr, Alex
Confucius Was Eating Carrots (12)

Brecht, Berthold
The Solution (11)
In Praise of Learning (13)

Brown, Alan C
The Tyneside Poets (13)

Butler, M.D.
Productivity Deal (11)

Casey, Paul
Roberts Arundel (12)

Clay, Ken
Nietzsche's Birthday (9)

Cobham, David
Song of a Marxist-Leninist Intellectual (12)

Cooper-Clark, John
No, We Don't Like to be Seaside the Seaside (8)
The Lions of Longleat (9)
National Dried & All Bran (9)
For a Nameless Joe (12)

Crispin
Time has no Beginning (7)

Darlington, Andrew
Freeway Flier (7)
Song of the Earth (12)

Dearle, Marjorie
Simon – (11)

Dixon, Bob *b1931*
Born in Spennymoor, Co. Durham. Got quite high up educational ladder but has almost found his way back to earth again. Now an English lecturer in a teachers' training college.

Agitproletpoem (7)
Academic Bored (12)
Agitpoem No. 22 for BBC Careless Silence Costs Lives (11)

Doyle, M
1976 (11)

Eburn, Bill
Boy messenger, postman, civil servant. POW in far East. A late developer - member of Derek Stanford's poetry class at the City Lit. London. Trade Unionist. Optimist - still hopes to be around when the gates of folly fall. Now retired.

Mixture as Before   (7)
O My Brothers (7)
The Left were always Right   (7)
Mutual Aid   (7)
Highgate Cemetery (8)
Deterrent (8)
The Loner (9)
Change of Countenance (9)
Poet at Work (10)
Success Story (10)
The Irreconcilable. (10)
In Defence of T.S. Eliot (10)
Adam & Eve & Pinch-Me (11)
On Guard (12)
Rush Hour (13)
After You   (13)
Absent Friends (13)

Ferns, M
Captain Ned   (7)
Poor Albert (9)

Ford, Connie M
Splintering (8)
Meditation in a Folk Club (9)
The Road to Baracoa (10)

Francis, Arthur
Down the Old Kent Road (12)

Friedman, Rose
I describe myself as a first generation Jew, my father having come to Eng-
land from Imperialist Russia. I was born in the heart of the Cheetham Hill
district and spent my earlier formative years in the Cheetham Hill and
Strangeways, Manchester area. My values are geared to Marxist princi-
ples. I was a founder member of the now defunct "Kersal Jewish Discus-
sion Circle". I have written about 40 poems, but I now find that my style of
presentation differs greatly from my earlier work-although the moral con-
tents remains the same.

Epitaph For Maggie (8)
Practitioner in Emancipation (11)
Talking Points (12)
Natural Rhythm (13)

Fuller, Ken
End of the Line (7)
The Fugitive (8)
The Occupation (13)

Gibson, Christine
War (8)

Gordon, Alec
Money on the Brain (12)

Gwilt, Rick
Building labourer. Various jobs - docker, warehouseman, groundsman,
fruit picker, dishwasher, translator, fork lift truck driver. Very widely trav-
elled - Havana, Acapulco, New Orleas, Montreal, Stockholm, Berlin, Jeru-
salem, Baghdad, Tehran, New Delhi etc.
"26. Communist. Former Manchester building trade unionist. Still member
T&GWU. Now at Lancaster University studying Working-Class and So-
cialist Writing under David Craig. Writes/translates/directs plays. Fluent
in French/German/Spanish. Captain of university athletics team, runs for
Stretford AC, interested in history of sport." -Joint Editor of Voices (76)

Tribute to a Union Man (8)
Iry (13)

Hamblett, John
Hello You Walrus Faced Bastard (9)

Handley, Martyn
Prophecy of Revolution (8)
Quebrada (10)
The Good Christian (12)

Harcup, T
Love Poem (7)
No Ball Games Allowed (11)

Hargreaves, C
To Peace (8)
Further Comments on In Defence of TS Eliot (11)

Hartley, Ray
Double Meaning (8)

Hazelton, Fran
The Headache (10)
A State of Affairs (11)
Real People (12)

Herdman, Brian
November Poems (8)

Horne, A.M. *b1944*
Married 2 children Sara and Jonathan. Fitter and shop steward AEU. Vickers -shipbuilding Barrow. Secretary Barrow branch CP. Delegate to TU council. Enjoys struggling to bring up a family, struggling for socialism and struggling with a pint. (1973)

The Journey (7)

Hosey, John
John William Hosey -Sean (9)

Hughes, D *b (1949*
Married (1)daughter. French. Came to England as student from Paris Sorbonne. Has taught in Morocco, France and now England (1973)

Exile (7)

Idris, Yusuf
The Bearer of Chairs (7)

Jamieson, A
R.N.A.D.Beith (7)

Johnson, Anne
Heritage (11)

Jones, K.L.
Building Site (7)
Love Song (7)

Kay, J
Hearts of Stone (11)

Kessel, David
Song of Soho (7)
For Desmond Trotter (10)

Kessel, Peggy
Crantock Beach (12)

King, Robert
Saturday's Savings (9)
Dic (10)

Leff, Vera
Pollution (8)
Strange Graffiti (9)

Leslie, Vivien *b1948*
Family moved from Devonshire to Scotland 1962. Trained as Display Art-
ist but after several poorly paid jobs, took employment in an electronics
factory. Currently at home with a one year old son. Finds time for a bit of
writing and reading and intends to complete education (1973)
-Galloway, Scotland who was working in an electronics factory in Edin-
burgh when she first wrote for VOICES a few years ago, is now bringing
up a family out in the country. "I grow lots of vegetables and fruit, sew and
bake without feeling I'm betraying my sex, and I try to keep writing's
(1977)

Try on a Hypothesis   (7)
The Chapel (8)
Euthanasia (8)
Biscuits (9)
Old Albert (10)
The Parting (10)

Lester, Paul
The Place where Suitcases Happen to Explode   (7)

MacFarlane, J
Waiting for the Train (7)

McGee, F
The Two Johns (11)

McNiel, Frances
Moving On (12)

MacVeigh, C.J.
Birdsong (7)
Manifesto (9)
Credo (12)

Mitchell, Roger
Start (8)
Someone's Worn this Thing Before (10)

Monaghan, PJ
Thrush at Long Kesh (7)

Moore, Francis *b1913*
Married 3 children, 5 grandchildren. Teacher active in NUT and Communist Party. No time to write but has to, and is kept up to it by the response of the non-literary audiences to which she manages to read sometimes. (1972)

Declaration (7)
Approach to Work (7)
Suspense (7)
Woman's Question (9)
A Sheffield Woman looks at Hugh McDiarmid (10)
Floor Show (11)
On a Lowry Picture (12)

Comment on a Scorner of Mechanisation (13)

Moore, Robert
It passed on by (9)

O Broonlea, Jone
Pace t'Egg (7)
Double Deal (12)
Er That Nattle (12)
Rainbow (10)
Durch den Kamin (10)

Oxford, Gillian
Fire and Brimstone (8)

Parker, Frank *b1926*
Married 2 daughters, 2 grandsons. Mechanical fitter. Shop steward
AUEW. Left school 1940. Ambition to have all my plays produced, and
also an opera. (1973)

The Man who moved Mountains (10)
Psyche (11)
Beauty & the Beast (12)

Pentelow, Mike
Friday Night is Music Night (9)

Pooley, Jean
The Magic Medicine (9)
A Matter of Temperature (10)
Tomorrow' Notebook (10)

Reed, Ian E *b1944*
Unskilled worker -unemployed. Booted out of the army -for obvious
reasons. Communist - main interests: literature, mainly poetry, music and
world affairs. Writing poetry for ten years.

Man (7)
Thunder (7)
Old Bill. (8)
Why Carry Bricks? (8)
Santiago Sunshine (9)
Loneliness (10)

Relph, Peter
Xmas Day (7)
Life's Like That (12)

Richardson, V.P.
Subsistance Level (7)
Lost Leader   (7)
The Great Wind (8)
The Credibility Gap (12)
Power Trio   (13)

St. Vincent, Paul
Racial Prejudice Day (10)
A Slow Developer (11)
Summit (12)
Lambchops in Training   (13)
Philpot in the City   (13)

Salway, John
Salt of the Earth   (7)
Soldiers (8)
Savages (13

Scot, Ian
Whose Road to Socialism? (12)

Sentinella. Pat
Warning to the Poet   (7)
Fairy Tale Charter (7
For My Daughter (8)
Island (12)
Bleached Grass (13)

Seyd, Fred
Villanelle (12)

Sims, Raymond
The Challenge (8)
Sutton, Jean *b1934*
Married 5 children. Employed in works canteen. Would prefer to stay at home and write short stories and poetry. Regrets wasted schooldays at secondary modern school. Hates racial prejudice (1973)

Grey Day (11)

337

A Conversation (12)
The Stripper (13)

Tatford, David
America (7)

Taverniti, Georgio
From "Palestine Resistance" April 76 (12)
From Haifa to Die in Lebanon (12)

Tuckett, Angela *b1906*
Married 3 step-children and 5 step-grandchildren. Became first woman solicitor in the west of England. Assistant Editor of the Labour Monthly many years, currently writing the official histories of the Blacksmiths' Union and the Shipwrights Society. Chairman of the County Womens Hockey association. NUT life member. Politically active? Of course. (1972)

June Days (12)

Ward, Bert
The Hunt for the Bismark (13)

Watts, Bridie
Alan (12)
An Explanation and Apology Alan (13)

Whitfield, A.R.
Poem (9)

Whitfield, Wendy
For a Fine Comrade (12)
A Silent Man Disguised as a Comrade   (13

Wyatt, Malcolm
Mass Production (12)

www.ingramcontent.com/pod-product-compliance
Lightning Source LLC
Chambersburg PA
CBHW060943030726

47503CB00003B/712